REDEMPTION

While studying for a degree in IT, Will Jordan worked a number of part time jobs, one of which was as an extra in television and feature films. Cast as a World War Two soldier, he was put through military bootcamp and taught to handle and fire weapons in preparation for the role. The experience piqued his interest in military history, and encouraged him to learn more about conflicts past and present. Having always enjoyed writing, he used this research as the basis for his first thriller, supplementing it with visits to weapon ranges in America and Eastern Europe to gain first-hand knowledge of modern weaponry. He lives in Fife with his wife and son, and is currently writing the second novel in the Ryan Drake series.

REDEMPTION
WILL JORDAN

arrow books

First published in Great Britain in 2012 by
Arrow
Random House, 20 Vauxhall Bridge Road,
London SW1V 2SA

www.randomhouse.co.uk

Addresses for companies within The Random House Group Limited can be
found at: www.randomhouse.co.uk

The Random House Group Limited Reg. No. 954009

A CIP catalogue record for this book
is available from the British Library

ISBN 9780099574460

The Random House Group Limited supports The Forest Stewardship
Council (FSC®), the leading international forest certification organisation.
Our books carrying the FSC label are printed on FSC® certified paper. FSC
is the only forest certification scheme endorsed by the leading environmental
organisations, including Greenpeace. Our paper procurement policy can be
found at www.randomhouse.co.uk/environment

Typeset in Palatino 12.25/15 pt by
Palimpsest Book Production Limited, Falkirk, Stirlingshire

Printed and bound by CPI Group (UK) Ltd, Croydon, CR0 4YY

For Bill; a father and a friend.

Prologue

Iraq, 13 May 2007

This is how it ends.

Lying there with one hand loosely pressed against the bullet wound in his stomach, he was alone. His strength was exhausted, his reserves gone, his blood staining the dusty ground. A trail of it led a short distance away, mute testimony to the desperate, feeble crawl he had managed before his vision swam and he collapsed.

He could go no further. There was nothing left to do but lie here and wait for the end.

A faint breeze sighed past him, stirring the warm evening air and depositing tiny particles of wind-blown sand across his arms and chest. How long would it take to cover his body when he died? Would he ever be found?

Staring at the vast azure sky stretching out into infinity above him, he found his eyes drawn to the contrail of some high-flying aircraft, straight as an arrow. Around him, the sun's last light reflected off the desert dunes, setting them ablaze with colour.

It was a good place to die.

Men like him were destined never to see old age, or

to die peacefully in their sleep surrounded by family. They had chosen a different life, and there would be no reward for them.

You know your problem, Ryan? You're a good man.

Had she been right?

Could he look back on his life honestly and say he'd been a good man? He had made mistakes, done things he wished he could undo, and yet his final act had been one of trust and compassion.

That was the reason he was lying here, bleeding to death. That was his final reward.

A low, rhythmic thumping was drowning out the sigh of the wind. The pounding of his heartbeat in his ears, slowly fading as his lifeblood flowed out between his fingers. He might have slowed the bleeding, but he couldn't stop it. Nothing could.

He was dying.

You know your problem, Ryan? You're a good man.

However he had lived, he knew in that moment that he would die as a good man. And that had to count for something.

A faint smiled touched his face as the thudding grew louder. He closed his eyes, surrendering to the growing darkness that filled the world around him.

Part One

Liberation

Confront them with annihilation, and they will then survive; plunge them into a deadly situation, and they will then live. When people fall into danger, they are then able to strive for victory.

Sun Tzu's *The Art of War*

Chapter 1

Seven days earlier, Mosul, Iraq

'Come on! Get out of the way!' Nassar Alawi growled, honking his horn in frustration.

His efforts did nothing to hurry along the rusty, dilapidated white saloon in front of him, its rattling exhaust spewing grey exhaust fumes as the driver revved the engine. Like Alawi, he was trying in vain to fight through the narrow streets and thronging crowds.

They were approaching one of the many open-air markets that dotted the city, and traffic was always heavy there. Ancient stone buildings festooned with satellite dishes and drying laundry leaned precariously inward as if they might collapse at any moment.

Alawi leaned back in his seat and ran his forearm across his brow. He was hot and uncomfortable, his open shirt already damp with sweat. The van's air conditioner hadn't worked in years, and rolling down the windows meant allowing in the relentless wind-blown sand, the fumes of other cars struggling to run on cheap gasoline, the reek of animal shit and countless other unsavoury odours.

He was a builder and electrician by trade; a source of great pride for both him and his family most of his adult life. A skilled job, a trade to be proud of. Now there was even greater demand for his services, both in Mosul and many of the surrounding towns. Everything that had been bombed and destroyed in the chaos of the invasion had to be painstakingly rebuilt.

A man like him could make a fortune in just a few years. Enough to provide for his wife and for his two young sons until they became men and followed in his footsteps, enough to live in comfort, enough to escape the grinding poverty that his peers endured.

If only he could get where he needed to be!

He honked his horn again, and at last a gap began to open up. The beaten-up white saloon started to trundle forwards, exhaust rattling. He stepped on the accelerator as well, eager to keep their momentum going.

Relieved to be on the move again, he reached for the packet of cigarettes lying on the passenger seat, tapped one out and held it to his lips as he fished his lighter out of his pocket.

Maybe today wouldn't be so bad after all, he thought as he clicked the lighter.

The sudden flash of light up ahead was so unexpected that he didn't even have time to react to it. The cigarette fell from his mouth as the white car in front disappeared, consumed along with everything else by an expanding wall of orange flame that rushed forward to meet him.

Central Intelligence Agency Field Ops Centre, Baghdad, Iraq

'This had better be good,' operations chief Steven Kaminsky grumbled as he strode from his office, doing his best to ignore the painful twinge in the small of his back. A compressed disc from a high-school football injury, the pain came and went, though in recent years it seemed to be coming more frequently and with greater intensity.

All things considered, today was a bad day, and judging by the urgent summons that had just come through to his desk, it wasn't likely to get better.

With computer terminals crammed into virtually every available one of its 5,000 square feet of floor space, the Pit, as it was known, was reminiscent of NASA's mission control centre. The comparison was an appropriate one, because in many ways it served a similar function. The computers in this room allowed their operators to control a fleet of twenty unmanned Predator drones deployed throughout the country.

The place was bustling with activity, and judging by the concerned looks and urgent tones, the news was not good.

'Somebody talk to me!'

He was joined within moments by Pete Faulkner, the floor officer, and the man responsible for the day-to-day running of the twenty control suites in the Pit. Faulkner was only in his forties, but with his overhanging beer gut, perpetually furrowed brow and thinning grey hair, he looked at least ten years older. He was always tired, always out of breath, always sweating.

'We've got a problem,' he said, wasting no time on preliminaries.

Kaminsky made a face. 'So I heard. What's going on?'

Faulkner gestured over to terminal 6, where most of the anxious-looking technicians were gathered. The flat-screen monitors that should have been transmitting feeds from the Predator's on-board cameras and instrumentation were blank, as though there was nothing going on.

'Three minutes ago we lost contact with one of our drones over Mosul,' he explained as they strode over. 'Data feeds, telemetry, the works.'

Kaminsky frowned. 'Has it been shot down?'

Faulkner shook his head. 'It was orbiting at ten thousand feet. The only thing that could shoot it down from that altitude is a surface-to-air missile, and we had no threat warnings before we lost contact.'

'Equipment failure?'

'It's possible,' Faulkner admitted. 'But unlikely. Unless it was a catastrophic engine failure, we'd have seen some sign before we lost the feeds. Make a hole here, gentlemen!'

The junior technicians clustered around the terminal parted like the Red Sea, giving them a clear path to a young man working over one of the few remaining monitors still up and running.

Terminal 6 and its associated drone were his responsibility. He knew he had done nothing wrong, but if something happened to the multi-million-dollar aircraft, the blame would fall on his head first.

'Anything, Hastings?' Kaminsky asked.

Hastings shook his head without looking up from the screen. 'I can't find anything wrong, sir. Engines, instrumentation, on board computers . . . everything was good right up until we lost contact. It's like it just . . . vanished.'

'So if it's still in the air, it's flying without direct control.' Kaminsky glanced at Faulkner. 'Contact air traffic control. Find out if it's still airborne.'

Shit, I hope it's not over a populated area, he thought. The drone might have been an unmanned aircraft, but it was still an aircraft with engines and on-board reserves of fuel, not to mention any munitions it might have been carrying. Plenty of things to go boom if it crashed in the middle of a town.

'If it loses incoming control, it'll revert to its automated flight programme,' Faulkner assured him.

8

That wasn't much comfort.

'Maybe it's a problem at our end?' Kaminsky suggested.

'The other drones are fine. If it was a problem with our uplink, we'd have lost control of everything.'

Kaminsky opened his mouth to reply, but before he could say anything, the monitors around him suddenly flickered back into life as the data feeds resumed, telemetry readings once again reporting the status of an aircraft hundreds of miles away.

Faulkner glanced at the technician. 'What did you do?'

'Nothing, sir. It just came back all of a sudden.'

Cursing under his breath, Kaminsky reached into his pocket and put on a pair of reading glasses, leaning closer to the screens to take a look for himself. Now in his early fifties, he needed glasses more than he cared to admit.

'Get me a full system diagnostic, now,' he ordered, his eyes darting across the various screens. Altitude, heading, airspeed, engine temperature, fuel pressure . . . All of it looked fine.

Such was his concern for the technical status of the aircraft, he almost didn't notice the feed coming in from the downward-looking nose cameras. Designed for battlefield observation and intelligence gathering, the high-resolution digital cameras could zoom in close enough to pick out individual facial features from 10,000 feet.

Now, however, they were focused on an urban area of some kind. Characteristic of the ancient cities that dotted Iraq, it was a maze of narrow streets, walled courtyards and old sandstone buildings.

It was a scene of utter chaos.

One of the buildings had taken a direct hit, blasting out an entire wall and collapsing part of the roof. Smoke and flames billowed from the ruined structure, rescue crews and fire fighters trying to fight their way through the destruction and search for survivors. And everywhere, scattered on the streets around the building, lay the motionless forms of the dead.

'Sir.'

Tearing his eyes away, Kaminsky looked at Hastings. The young man was pale, a faint sheen of sweat on his forehead. He looked as if he was about to be sick.

'What is it?'

Hastings swallowed hard. 'All three Hellfire missiles have been deployed.'

Shock and disbelief were reflected in the eyes of every person in the room. Nobody uttered a word.

With slow, deliberate care, Kaminsky removed his reading glasses and turned to his subordinate. 'Pete, better call Langley right now.'

Chapter 2

Washington DC, 7 May 2007

It was a damp, cool Sunday morning in the capital, with a low fog lingering over the muddy waters of the Potomac. Summer days in Maryland were hot and humid, but the mornings often started out chill and misty.

A lone jogger shuffled along beneath the dripping leaves, following a muddy track that wound through Anacostia Park. To a casual observer he would have seemed perfectly unremarkable: mid-thirties, medium build, standing an inch or so above 6 foot. His short dark hair was damp with sweat, his face downturned, his eyes on the ground ahead.

Just another anonymous bureaucrat, just another DC office worker trying to stave off the beer gut and high blood pressure. The sort of man one might pass in the street and forget within moments.

But for those who cared to look beyond the obvious, a different picture emerged. Though tired, he moved with sure, confident strides, maintaining a steady ground-covering pace that would be familiar to soldiers the world over.

And those eyes, which seemed loosely fixed on the muddy ground ahead, would often flick left and right, quickly taking in his surroundings, maintaining constant awareness of his situation.

Those who knew what to look for would see he was no office worker.

Trying to ignore the burning in his lungs and the ache in his legs, Ryan Drake glanced at his watch, noting the time and comparing it with the familiar landmarks around him. He'd jogged this route so many times that he knew exactly where he should be at any given time, and he wasn't there today.

He was falling behind.

'Shit,' he said under his breath, pushing his body to even greater efforts to try to make up for lost time. He didn't care about the fatigue that clawed at him, didn't care about the thumping of his heart or the burning in his muscles. None of that mattered. He plodded on with single-minded determination.

He'd read somewhere that running was supposed to release endorphins and other feel-good chemicals in the brain. That had yet to happen for him, though. Maybe his brain wasn't wired that way.

In any case, the usual result of his morning forays was that he came home exhausted, sweaty and often soaked by a sudden rain shower. The damp climate in DC almost made his childhood home in England seem tropical by comparison.

Leaving the quiet parkland behind, his route took him straight down Maryland Avenue towards the towering dome of the US Capitol building. Almost all of the roads in DC converged on this one structure, like the spokes of a gigantic wheel. As long as you could see it, it was almost impossible to get lost in the city.

At 5.30 on a Sunday morning there wasn't much traffic on the streets; just delivery trucks out making the rounds and a few poor souls heading to work in some office or government ministry. Most were bleary eyed and clutching cups of coffee as though their lives depended on it.

He sympathised.

Skirting the Capitol building, Drake headed west through Henry Park towards the Washington Monument.

Lit from below by floodlights, the vast marble obelisk stood stark and white against the dim backdrop of the early-morning sky. For a lot of people, this structure was a symbol of America itself, an indomitable monument to democracy and all that other good stuff. For him it meant he was almost finished his run.

Everyone was a winner, then.

Beyond lay the Lincoln Memorial building at the end of the Reflecting Pool, backed right up against the Potomac. That was his finish line.

Summoning his flagging reserves of energy, he pushed himself in one final effort down the length of the Reflecting Pool.

Almost doubled over, he ascended the fifty-eight steps to the base of the memorial. Fifty-eight steps, each one sending a stab of pain through his tired and aching muscles, and drawing deep from his meagre reserves of strength.

At last he staggered to the top, winded and exhausted, clutching one of the stone columns for support.

He felt like shit, plain and simple. His muscles ached, his lungs burned and his head pounded with a vicious headache. Still no sign of those elusive endorphins either, he thought with a wry smile. But the smile soon faded when he checked his watch – a minute slower than yesterday.

Ten years ago, back when he'd been a young soldier

in the Special Air Service, he'd done runs like this just to warm up. Now he was killing himself trying to make it through.

He closed his eyes for a moment as the blood roared in his ears and a wave of nausea hit him like a brick wall. But this was no injury or fatigue brought about by exercise. It was a hangover.

It was a good couple of minutes before the nausea abated and he felt composed enough to stand up straight. Taking a deep breath, he pushed himself off the pillar and descended the steps once more, heading north-west to the Roosevelt Bridge, and crossing over from Maryland into Virginia.

Stopping off at a coffee shop along the way, he ordered a bottle of water, a white coffee with no sugar and a bacon-and-cheese bagel. Hardly the breakfast of champions, but what the hell – nobody was here to lecture him.

He downed the water in one gulp, and was just exiting the shop with his bagel in hand when he felt his cellphone vibrating in his pocket. Frowning, he fished it out and checked the caller ID: *Dan Franklin (Work)*.

Shit.

Once a friend from his former life in the military, Franklin was now a combination employer, manager and occasional financial lifeline. As reluctant as Drake was to admit it, Franklin was the reason he had a job and a roof over his head.

He was calling from his desk at Langley, which Drake took to be a bad sign. If your boss called at 6.00 on a Sunday morning, it was unlikely that it was to invite you over for tea and biscuits. Especially if that boss worked for the Central Intelligence Agency.

There was shit brewing. He could feel it in his bones.

14

He hit the receive button, already bracing himself for bad news.

'Dan . . .' he began.

'Ryan, where are you right now?' Franklin asked, wasting no time in greetings.

'Good morning to you, too,' Drake replied with unveiled sarcasm. He was starting to wish he'd left the phone at home.

'I'm serious. We need to talk.'

Drake frowned. 'About what, exactly?'

'Not over the phone. We need you to come in.'

'Come on, mate. It's a Sunday,' Drake reminded him. 'And it's my first day off in three weeks.'

Jesus, he'd only just finished with the debriefings and reports and testimonies and all the other bullshit from his last operation. If this was to go over some mismatching statement or lost document, he was ready to tell Franklin where to ram it.

'Excuse me while I break out the violin,' Franklin replied without sympathy.

'Very funny.' Drake took a bite of his bagel as he walked, covering his other ear to muffle the sound of traffic on the main drag nearby. 'Is it a debriefing issue?'

'I wish. No, this is something new. It's important. There are some big pay cheques overseeing this, if you catch my drift.'

Yeah? I bet none of them come my way, Drake thought with a momentary flash of resentment. Considering the kind of work he did, the payments were unsatisfactory to say the least.

'This could be a big opportunity, Ryan.'

'For who?' Drake couldn't help asking.

Franklin said nothing for a few moments. 'Look, I was asked to recommend someone for a job. I told them you

15

were one of our best case officers. Don't be an asshole and prove me wrong.'

'You're so good to me, Dan.'

'What are friends for?' Franklin asked with a brief flash of humour. 'Look, come in and hear what we have to say. I want your professional opinion on this one. If you're interested, we'll take it from there. If you think it can't be done . . . well, we'll cross that bridge if we come to it.'

Drake sighed. He hadn't planned anything for today, which in itself was a welcome novelty. For the first time in a long time, he had no work to do, no reports to file, no briefings to attend or plans to review. He could afford to relax.

He had a feeling he could kiss goodbye to that idea.

'No promises,' he grunted.

16

Chapter 3

Central Intelligence Agency Headquarters, Langley, Virginia

Approaching the conference room where Franklin was lurking, Drake glanced down at the dark grey business suit he'd thrown on, resisting the urge to pat down a crease on the left sleeve. After taking a cab home, he had showered and quickly donned his suit before jumping in his car and battling through the morning traffic to get here. He hadn't even had time to shave.

Sunday it might have been, but dress-down days were an urban myth at Langley. Business suits, freshly ironed shirts, ties and gleaming shoes were the order of the day here. Everyone looked as though they belonged in an office-wear catalogue, and somehow it made him feel as though he never quite measured up.

He was an outsider here, and always, just beneath the surface, he felt it. A Brit working for the CIA – rare enough, and not altogether welcomed by some. He also had no real background in the intelligence game.

He was a soldier, not a spook. At least, he had been once. Now he occupied a curious middle ground where those hard-won skills were still put to the test, just by different employers.

He hesitated outside the door. Who the hell was going to be in there with Franklin? What were they going to ask of him? What could be so serious that they needed him in this early on a Sunday?

He was far from at his best today. His mind was still fogged by a combination of fatigue and hangover.

Well, too late to back out now. Just get it over with. Steeling himself, he reached for the handle and opened the door.

The conference room was designed to accommodate at least ten people in considerable comfort, with a long wooden-topped table running down the centre, its surface polished to a mirrored shine. Flat-screen televisions were mounted on the walls at each end, no doubt used for teleconferencing and presentations.

The decor was the height of corporate luxury: pristine carpets, wood-panelled walls, expensive leather-backed chairs, the works. Even the coffee set was made of silver instead of the cheap plastic Thermos units Drake was accustomed to.

The entire wall opposite consisted of tinted one-way windows that allowed for impressive views over the surrounding woodland and the Potomac river beyond. The sky was lightening now as the sun crept higher, slowly burning through the early-morning fog. It was shaping up to be another hot, humid day, but one would never know it in there. The air conditioners kept the room at a steady 18 degrees Celsius no matter what the weather.

Despite its size, the room was occupied by only two men, both of whom were sitting at the table with several files and folders laid out in front of them.

The first and younger of the two was Dan Franklin.

Thirty-eight years old, Franklin had served much of his career in the US Marine Corps. He came from a distinguished military family and bore all the baggage that went with it; a graduate of West Point, top 10 per cent of his class, the whole spit-and-polish routine.

He'd served in an elite Special Operations group hunting bad guys in Afghanistan, and had looked set to have a long and distinguished career until a roadside bomb took out the Humvee he was riding in, leaving him with lumps of the device and the vehicle embedded in his legs and spine.

After a difficult rehabilitation, he'd transitioned into the Military Intelligence Corps for a brief time before the CIA headhunted him. That wasn't the kind of offer you refused, and so for the past five years he had been working out of Langley.

Desk work might have been more suited to his physical abilities these days, but Franklin was still lean and fit despite the injuries that had ended his military career. His dark blond hair was always cut short, his suits were always well pressed, and he carried himself with the confidence typical of his military heritage. His grey-blue eyes sparkled with quick intelligence as he nodded in greeting.

The second man was older, probably in his mid-fifties. His greying hair was receding a little at the sides, and there were lines around his mouth and eyes. He was still in good shape though judging by his trim waist and broad shoulders, with no sign of the middle-aged spread that such men often struggled against. His face had the ruggedly handsome look of a movie star, and the slender reading glasses he was wearing suited him perfectly.

There was something oddly familiar about him too, but Drake couldn't place it. Still, one look was enough to confirm that he was one of the 'big pay cheques' that Franklin had alluded to. His suit looked as if it cost more than Drake's monthly wage, and he had the imposing bearing of a man used to giving orders and having them obeyed. This guy moved in circles that Drake would never be a part of.

Both men rose to greet him as he entered, Franklin moving a little slower than his companion but trying to hide it. Several spinal operations had failed to undo the damage done by that roadside bomb. Sitting in one position for more than fifteen minutes resulted in painful muscle spasms, so he was often found pacing the room during long meetings.

'Ryan. Good of you to join us.' He gestured to the man beside him. 'I'd like to introduce you to Marcus Cain, director of Special Activities Division.'

Drake's heartbeat shifted up a gear in that moment. Now he knew why this guy seemed familiar.

Marcus Cain was one of the big players within the CIA's complex power structure. As head of Special Activities Division, he was responsible for sanctioning black operations all across the globe. Basically, just about anything the US Government needed done, but could never admit to.

Cain smiled as he rounded the table to shake hands. 'Sorry to haul you in here at such short notice, Ryan. From what I hear, you were taking some long-overdue R and R?'

His grip was strong, his smile easy and confident. He was like a movie star pressing flesh with eager fans.

Franklin gave him a hard look, as if to forestall any objections he might have been mad enough to voice. For some reason, Drake felt foolish about his earlier complaints on the phone. Had Cain been listening in?

'It's no trouble, sir,' he lied.

Cain's amused smile suggested he wasn't fooled for a moment. Still, he said nothing further on the matter.

'Well, I appreciate your getting here so fast.' He gestured to a vacant chair. 'Please, take a seat. Coffee?'

'No, thank you.'

As Drake sat down, Cain returned to his own seat and poured himself a cup. 'Dan here tells me you're very good at what you do,' he remarked conversationally, taking a sip of his coffee. 'In fact, I'm led to believe you're one of the best case officers on the payroll. Would that be a fair assessment?'

Drake was leader of a Special Investigation Team, a small but prolific sub-unit of Special Activities Division formed to investigate, track down and, if possible, bring home missing CIA operatives.

The CIA employed thousands of operatives – they were never, ever referred to as agents – all across the globe, doing everything from intelligence gathering to espionage, kidnappings, political interventions, assassinations and undercover work.

Inevitably, some of these operatives would 'go dark' and stop reporting in, either because their true identity had been uncovered, they had been killed or injured in the course of their mission, or on rarer occasions, because they had turned against their former employers.

Whatever the reason for their disappearance, it was vital to know what exactly had happened to them. If they had been captured or uncovered, had they talked? If they were being held hostage, was it possible to recover them? If they had turned rogue, what were the chances of apprehending them before they did any serious damage?

Answering those questions was the task of a Special Investigation Team. Colloquially known as Shepherds, their job was to piece together whatever clues were available on missing operatives, find them and, if possible, bring them back into the fold.

The CIA could call upon six permanent Shepherd teams. Or rather, six permanent case officers, of whom Drake was one. Each was the core around which the rest of the team was built.

Again he felt his heart beat a little faster. Cain was putting him on the spot, seeing how he would react. 'I'd say you're better placed to make that assessment than I am, sir.'

Cain smiled. 'Typical Brit, always underplaying things. Well, you should consider yourself lucky that your reputation precedes you.'

Opening a folder on the conference table in front of him, he leafed through the pages with the mild interest of a man studying a novel he has already read. It took Drake a moment or two to realise it was his own personnel dossier.

'Let's see . . . You joined the Parachute Regiment in ninety-seven before moving on to the SAS two years later. You did two tours in Afghanistan, the second with Fourteenth Special Operations Group as part of Operation Hydra,' he noted with a flicker of interest.

Drake felt himself tense up. There were only a handful of people in the world who even knew about Operation Hydra, and it seemed Cain was one of them. With director-level security clearance, it was only natural that he would have been briefed on it, but still his casual revelation caught Drake off guard. Just hearing the name spoken out loud was enough to elicit a chill of recognition.

'You received two citations for bravery and a promotion to sergeant before you left,' Cain went on. 'You've been with the Agency four years now, and you have the highest success rate of any case officer in the past ten years. I'd call that a pretty decent record, Ryan.'

Drake said nothing. There was more to his military record than Cain had mentioned, but the man had tactfully left it unsaid. It seemed he was out to mount a charm offensive instead

'Which is just as well, because we need someone with your talents.' Cain set his dossier aside and slid a single photograph across the table to Drake. 'Take a look.'

Turning the photo around, he leaned in closer to study it. Drake's eyes opened wide when he saw the face staring back at him.

It was a woman. She was Caucasian, with a pale complexion and blue eyes. Her hair was light blonde, cut short and styled in a simple side parting that left a strand falling across her face. She wore no make-up.

She didn't need it.

She was beautiful; strikingly beautiful in fact. Her mouth was full and rounded, her cheekbones high, her nose narrow and finely chiselled. Her straight, clean jawline tapered down to a firm, well-defined chin. The shape, symmetry and arrangement of her features combined in elegant harmony to create a face that was almost captivating in its perfection.

Her age was difficult to tell, but there was something about her face that had lost the softer curves of youth and assumed the more definite lines of maturity.

But what he noticed most of all were her eyes. Icy blue and vividly intense, they held his gaze and wouldn't let go. Even in a photograph they seemed to stare right through him. Never in his life had he seen eyes like those.

'This is the most recent picture we have,' Cain explained. 'It was taken about six years ago.'

'Who is she?' Drake asked, still staring at the picture.

'Her true identity is highly classified, even for someone

with your clearance. What I *can* tell you is that she's a former paramilitary operative, working under the code name *Maras*. She worked black ops from the mid-eighties onward, then four years ago she went rogue and disappeared. In short, she's a relic of the bad old days. But unfortunately, we need her.'

Drake frowned. That wasn't exactly a detailed biography. 'Why?'

'Times change,' Cain said with a dismissive shrug. 'Even relics can have their uses. We need you to find her and bring her in for debriefing. Now, the good news is that we know where she is. But that's also the bad news.'

With that, he reached into his folder and slid another picture Drake's way.

It was an overhead, probably taken from a surveillance satellite. The image quality wasn't great, but it was sufficient to depict some kind of fortified facility surrounded by snow-covered wasteland. The building was a simple, uncompromising square enclosed by a high perimeter wall, with defensive towers at each corner and a large open space in the centre.

It looked like a castle or fortress, and a formidable one at that.

'Say hello to Khatyrgan Prison.'

'I've never heard of it,' Drake admitted.

Cain cocked an eyebrow. 'Then you should consider yourself lucky. Most people who end up there don't come back to tell any stories. It was built to house some of Russia's most dangerous criminals – murderers, crime lords, terrorists, enemies of the state . . . You name it, there's probably some guy there doing time for it.'

That stopped him in his tracks. 'Russia?'

Cain nodded. 'Siberia, to be exact. The Sakha Republic.

It's at least a hundred miles from anything resembling civilisation.'

Drake was starting to get an uneasy feeling. Cain was suggesting they try to stage some kind of jailbreak in a sovereign country with the world's largest stockpile of nuclear weapons.

He looked up. 'You're serious about this, aren't you?'

Cain's gaze didn't waver for a second. 'I'm afraid so.'

'Can't we cut a deal with the Russians?'

By this, he meant bribery. A few million dollars went a long way in Russia these days, and it wasn't as if the CIA was short of cash.

Cain shook his head. 'Not an option. She's too valuable to them. And if we open negotiations, we'll lose our window. Besides, we're working to a tight schedule. Our only viable option in this case is direct intervention. It has to be done quickly, quietly and, most important of all, anonymously. The Russians get one sniff that the Agency was behind this, and we're all in the shit.'

It also meant that if the Shepherd team involved was caught or captured, they could expect no outside support.

Now Drake was starting to understand why they wanted him on board. He was British, with no immediate connection to the CIA. He was an ideal choice for a job like this.

Drake leaned back in his chair, taking several moments to digest everything he'd heard. He felt as if he'd just landed in some cheap spy novel.

'So let me get this right,' he said at last. 'You want me to take a team deep into Russian sovereign territory, infiltrate a high-security prison, find and recover a prisoner whose name I don't even know, then somehow escape with her and make it back to US soil without anyone finding out who was behind it?'

'That's about the size of it,' Cain confirmed. 'And time's ticking, Ryan. We have three days. If we don't have her back on US soil by then, it's over.'

Three days to plan and execute what might well be the most difficult and dangerous operation of his entire career.

'That's . . . quite an ambitious timetable.'

To his surprise, Cain laughed. 'I'm not the Pope, son. You can speak freely here. In fact, that's exactly why we brought you in. I want an honest, no-bullshit assessment from you. Can it be done?'

Drake said nothing. The problem with honest answers was that once given, they were impossible to retract. He'd been on his share of operations that were slapped together at the last minute, and they rarely left him with pleasant memories. And this was one job where there could be no margin for error.

He glanced down at the photograph of the prison again, hesitating a moment before delivering his answer. 'It's possible.'

Cain's eyes lit up. 'So you'll do it?'

'I didn't say that, sir,' Drake amended. 'I said it's possible in theory. But theories have a tendency to fall apart when you're halfway around the world on a covert mission into hostile territory. And if this goes wrong, none of us will make it back alive.'

'Risk is part of the job,' Cain reminded him. 'If you can't handle that, it wouldn't be hard to find someone who can.'

The change that had come over the older man was startling. Without altering his posture or moving a muscle, his entire bearing had changed. He wasn't the smiling, affable movie star who had welcomed Drake into the room a few minutes earlier. Now he was cold, ruthless, businesslike. He was a king on this particular chessboard, and he had no time for pawns like Drake unless they proved their worth.

'With all due respect, I think it would, sir,' Drake replied, his tone calm and even. If Cain wanted to play hardball with him, then so be it. 'None of the other Shepherd team leaders will take this job on. They don't have the training or the background for it. You picked me because I helped run snatch-and-grab operations in Afghanistan. You could go outsource and use a special forces unit – say Delta or Task Force 88 – but then you'd have the problem of deniability if they were caught, and operational security if they weren't. Whatever history this "*Maras*" has with the Agency, I'm guessing you want to keep it in-house, quiet and deniable. So that leaves you with me.

'You asked for a no-bullshit assessment of the situation,' Drake went on. 'Well, mine is that this entire operation is a house of cards just waiting to fall over. And anyone unlucky enough to get caught up in it is either going to get killed or captured, which in this case is just as bad.' He sighed and glanced away for a moment. 'I'm not afraid to put my life at risk, but what I can't and won't do is drag a Shepherd team in without good reason.'

Cain said nothing for the next few seconds, just sat there regarding Drake with a thoughtful expression. Drake for his own part tried to meet the older man's inquisitive gaze without flinching, and resisted the growing urge to swallow.

'Ryan, I asked you to speak plainly, so I'll extend you the same courtesy,' he said at last. 'I told you that I read your dossier long before you walked in here. I know what happened to you out there, the business you got caught up in. I know you got yourself a court martial and a discharge from the military.'

Drake could feel his jaw tightening.

Always it came back to that. A dishonourable discharge – an embarrassment, a fiasco. It was like a black mark on his life, a penance following him everywhere he went. It would be there on every job application he ever made.

The only people willing to take him on had been the CIA, and then only because Franklin had fought his corner with such tenacity that his own career had been put on the line. He would never forget that, just as Franklin would never forget what Drake had once done for him.

Cain smiled a little, enjoying his discomfort. 'What if I was to tell you I could change all that?'

Once again he felt his heartbeat quicken. 'How?'

Cain shrugged, as if it was a matter of no consequence. 'We all have favours we can call in, and I have more than most. I can have the Judge Advocate reopen your case, get your conviction overturned, your record expunged. It'll be a blank slate. You can make a fresh start, either with the Agency or somewhere else if you want.'

Drake said nothing. His mind was racing. Could he really do such a thing?

Of course he could. Cain moved in circles Drake would never be part of. He could exert influence at the highest levels, strike deals, bribe or intimidate just about anyone. His power within the Agency and beyond was immense.

Cain was offering him a chance that would never come again. A chance to clear his name. A chance at redemption.

How could he refuse that?

'I have your word on this?' he asked quietly.

Cain smiled. It was the smile of a chess player who knows he has won the game, long before his opponent does. 'You come through for me, I'll come through for you. You have my word on that.'

Drake said nothing.

'I wish I could give you more time to think things over, but we have to move fast on this one. This is your chance, Ryan. Maybe your only chance. For your sake, I suggest you take it.'

Drake looked down at the surface of the polished table, saying nothing.

This was his chance. His only chance.

The choice was made before common sense had time to assert itself.

'I'd need free rein on support and logistics,' he said quietly. 'And absolutely all the intelligence we have on this prison.'

'You'll have it.'

'And my choice of team specialists,' he added.

'Done.'

Once more Drake glanced down at the photograph of Maras. Her piercing blue eyes stared back at him, as if to bore straight into his soul. What they would see there, he didn't care to imagine.

I hope you're worth it, he thought.

'All right,' he said without looking up. 'I'm in.'

Chapter 4

Cell No. 62, Khatyrgan Prison, Siberia

Forty-one, forty-two, forty-three . . .

Breathing hard, beads of sweat dripping from her brow, Prisoner 62 forced her aching arms to work, pushing her body up from the freezing concrete floor before slowly lowering it back down again. Over and over she performed the same exercise without rest or respite.

Forty-four, forty-five . . .

She'd had a name once. *Maras*; a code name given by a man who once cared about her. And before that, another name given by parents who once protected her. Both were gone now. There were no names in Khatyrgan. Here she was Prisoner 62, and that was all.

Wispy tendrils of steam rose from her warm skin, her body heat radiating out into the tiny unheated cell. She kept quiet as she worked, limiting her breathing to short gasps, knowing that any excessive noise might draw the guards to her cell. Guards with fists and boots and rifle butts.

Forty-six, forty-seven, forty-eight . . .

Always they came in force, too many to fight off alone in that cramped cell where she couldn't move properly. If they were angry or vindictive or just felt like having fun, they would beat her until she was close to blacking out, when she almost begged for the darkness to swallow her for ever. In those situations there was nothing she could do except curl into a ball and wait for it to end.

It had been worse when she first arrived here, before they learned the kind of grudging, reluctant respect they had for her now. In those first few months they had tried to beat her down, tried to subjugate and break her, but she didn't react like the other prisoners. She didn't cower in fear, she didn't meekly submit.

She fought back.

All too often they had come away with gashes and bruises of their own. And more than one unfortunate guard had to be carried out by his comrades, moaning and bleeding. She could fight like a wild animal if the need was upon her, lashing out with a ferocity that surprised even her jailers, and refusing to stay down until she was physically unable to stand.

Eventually, despite the ferocious beatings they exacted in revenge, they had grown tired of nursing their own injuries and suffering the indignity of being hurt by a woman, and they had relented in their assault. It was just as well, because by that point she was almost at the end of her rope.

Those had been some of the darkest days of her life, and she had seen many of those.

Forty-nine, fifty.

With one final push, she got her knees under her and rose up from the floor, clenching and unclenching her fists to get some circulation going again. She had wrapped her hands in rags to keep them from freezing, but still the cold seeped through. The cold was everywhere in Khatyrgan.

It was her true enemy. Not the guards or the other prisoners, but the remorseless, relentless cold.

It was why she exercised with such dogged determination each day, why it was the first thing she did when she woke each morning and the last thing she did before falling asleep at night. The body heat it generated kept the cold at bay, at least for a while.

In any case, there wasn't much else to do here. She was kept in solitary confinement twenty-four hours a day, carefully set aside from the rest of the inmate population. She knew there was an exercise yard in the prison, but she had never seen it since the day of her arrival. She hadn't seen sunlight since then either – there was no window in her cell.

How long had that been? Two years? Three?

She didn't know. She had lost count.

Better not to know.

This cell was her world now. 6 feet long by 8 feet wide and 8 feet high – 384 cubic feet. One toilet. One sink. One worn-out mattress laid on the floor. No window. Bare brick walls (she had counted the number of bricks in each wall). A single dim bulb in the ceiling that dictated her night and day.

The only change came when she was let out for twenty minutes each week to use the shower room. Always under armed guard, of course.

The possibility of escape was non-existent. She knew, because she had spent every day for months brooding on the problem, to no avail. She couldn't get out of her cell. The door was locked by a simple deadbolt on the other side, with a hatch set at eye level for observation or passing in food. The guards always came for her in groups of at least three, forcing her to stand back while they opened the door.

The other inmates might have opportunities, brief moments when they weren't being watched so strictly, but not her. Whenever she wasn't locked in the cell, she had weapons trained on her. It was hopeless.

More than once she had pondered the prospect of killing herself. It wouldn't have been hard. She knew how.

The simplest and most convenient way to die would be to make a run for it when they took her to the shower, allowing them to gun her down. Of course, there was always the chance that she wouldn't be killed outright, but would instead lie maimed and bleeding. Gunshot wounds could take hours or even days to claim their victim, and she had little desire to go out like that.

There were other options, though. The food, such as it was, was served on steel trays. Cheap, thin and flimsy things, battered and dented by years of use. A bit of bending and working would allow her to snap one in half, providing a rough edge she could use to slit her wrists. It would be hours before the guards made their rounds; plenty of time for her to bleed out.

Or she could tear up the thin blanket for her bed and knot the strips into a crude rope, winding it around the light fixture overhead to make a noose. Of course, she'd also have to tie her wrists behind her back before throwing herself off the edge of the bed. No matter how strong her resolve, the moment that noose tightened around her neck, she knew she would fight it.

And yet, she'd never done any of those things. Something had always stopped her. Perhaps it was sheer stubborn refusal to give in, as if she was somehow making a point by staying alive.

Or perhaps the will to survive was too strong in her. She had spent so much of her life fighting to hold on to the life she had, it was too deeply ingrained in her nature to give it up now.

So she waited.

She waited. For what, she didn't know.

Nobody was coming for her.

Nobody would help her.

Nobody cared about her.

She had accepted all of these facts long ago.

She was starting to feel the cold now that she'd stopped moving. Taking a deep breath, Prisoner 62 knelt down on the floor to start her next fifty.

Chapter 5

Drake took a deep pull of his coffee while staring pensively at the photograph of Maras pinned to the whiteboard in front of him. For some reason he kept finding his gaze drawn to that picture.

'She's something, isn't she?' Franklin remarked, spotting the object of his preoccupation.

That she was. But there was more to it than mere physical attractiveness. It was what was behind that face which intrigued him most; what secrets lay behind those piercing, icy blue eyes. What had she done to end up in a place like Khatyrgan?

'Who is she, Dan?' he asked now that they were alone. 'Why is Cain willing to go through all this to get her?'

Cain himself had long since left, sensing that his interference would be more of a hindrance than a help at this stage. In any case, his work was done – Drake was on board, and that was all he cared about.

Although he made a point of learning as much as possible about a missing operative as part of his job, he rarely concerned himself with them on a personal level. There was always a line he didn't cross, a gulf of professional detachment that separated him from the person he was required either to rescue or to hunt as the situation dictated.

But not this time.

Franklin shook his head. 'Sorry, buddy. Stuff like that is above your pay grade – and mine,' he added with an unhappy look. 'All I was told was that she was important, and we were to use any and all resources to bring her in. I chose you.'

'I'm honoured.' Drake took another gulp of coffee and rubbed his eyes. His mind still felt sluggish, and the headache from earlier hadn't left him.

His friend frowned. 'You feeling all right?'

'I'm fine.'

'You don't look fine,' the older man persisted. 'Late night?'

'Early morning,' Drake evaded, unwilling to say more.

Franklin exhaled slowly. 'Listen, I'm sorry for putting you on the spot like that. I didn't know Cain was going to give you such a hard time.'

Drake flashed a wry smile. 'You're a shit liar, Dan. You always were.'

'And you're a shit cook. What are you gonna do?' He grinned. 'Look, for what it's worth, I was trying to do you a favour. I thought it might be a chance to put all that shit behind you, make a fresh start.'

Drake sighed and nodded. Whatever else, Franklin was being honest about that. 'Well, I appreciate the thought.'

He took another drink of coffee and turned his attention back to the vast array of documents spread out across the conference table in front of them. 'Right then, let's plan our jailbreak.'

Cain had made good on his promise to provide them with all the intelligence available on Khatyrgan, literally dumping two packing boxes' worth of it in their laps. Everything from construction orders to design blueprints, personnel transfers, logistics arrangements and maintenance requests – it was all there. The National Security Agency was even working to tap into the prison's outgoing communications.

According to the files they'd been able to sort through, Khatyrgan had been founded as a penal colony under Stalin's regime in the 1930s, mostly using slave labour. Ironically enough, the construction crews who survived the brutal working conditions would go on to become the first batch of prisoners. Drake had to admire the Russian pragmatism, forcing men to literally build their own prisons.

In any case, its isolated location in the midst of a frozen wilderness made escape impractical as well as impossible, and Khatyrgan soon became a warehouse for some of the most dangerous enemies of the Soviet Union.

Thousands found their way there over the next sixty years, often without trial or parole. Most ended their days behind those grim walls, never to be seen or heard from again. Its current inmate population was just shy of three hundred.

And in all its seventy years of continuous occupation, there was not a single record of any prisoner successfully escaping from Khatyrgan.

Now Drake had three days to change that.

'This place is a beast,' Franklin decided, reviewing the blueprints with a critical eye. 'No wonder nobody ever escaped.'

The strength of Khatyrgan lay in its simplicity. The entire facility was just a big square, built with typical Soviet functionality in mind. The south side housed the guard barracks, mess hall, armoury, security centre, administrative areas, power generation and vital utilities.

It was also where the one and only gate was located. One way in, one way out.

Tunnelling would have been an exercise in futility. The ground beneath the prison was permafrost; permanently frozen soil with the consistency of poured concrete.

There were no windows, no ventilation ducts, no maintenance corridors or obscure passageways. Each of the cell blocks was secured at both ends by heavy reinforced doors that were impossible to breach with anything less than high explosives.

The east and west sides of the square housed the general population, while the north block contained the solitary confinement cells. This was where the most dangerous prisoners were kept, and where Maras was likely to be found.

In the centre of the facility lay the exercise yard – a wide open space that contained nothing useful to them. It was big enough to land a chopper in, if the pilot was feeling daring, but doing so would leave them covered from elevated positions on all sides.

Escape from within was impossible.

'It was designed to keep people in, not to keep them out,' Drake remarked, deep in thought. 'All their security measures are focused inward. There has to be a way we can use that.'

'Maybe, but you still have the problem of making entry. The only way in or out is through this main gate here,' Franklin said, indicating the gate on the blueprints.

After passing through a covered archway in the outer wall, one would find themselves in a smaller inner courtyard, presumably where supplies could be unloaded or prisoners disembarked. That courtyard and archway could easily be turned into a kill zone by a couple of guards with AK-47s.

'Plus you've got these watchtowers at each corner of the building.' He indicated the four buttress-like fortifications that ringed the prison. 'Each of them has a clear field of fire over the yard and the open ground beyond the prison.'

Again, simplicity was the key. The exercise yard was just one big open space, and there was nothing beyond the prison walls but hundreds of yards of icy ground, devoid of cover of any kind. Anyone spotted trying to cross that ground would have nothing to do but die.

Drake sighed and shook his head. They couldn't fight their way in, they couldn't scale the walls, and they couldn't get out without neutralising the guard towers.

A ground assault was a no-go.

'We could try a HALO jump,' he said at last.

HALO stood for High Altitude Low Opening, referring to the practice of jumping from an aircraft at extremely high altitude, free falling for the next couple of miles before pulling one's chute with just a few thousand feet to spare. The obvious advantage was that it rendered their approach almost undetectable, since the aircraft would be too high to spot visually and the assault team would be nothing more than a group of black-clad figures falling silently through the night sky.

It wasn't for the faint-hearted though, and the idea of parachuting straight into a prison filled with armed guards didn't fill him with joy. If one of the team got snagged on some obstruction or landed in the prison yard, it was dying time. Plus, if they overshot their target area, there would be no way to correct it.

Franklin was quick to see the problem as well. He might have been an administrator rather than an operative these days, but he still thought like a soldier. 'That's a pretty tight window to hit if you're free falling in.'

'It's the only way I can think of to get us inside. The last thing they'd expect would be an assault from the air.'

Franklin wasn't convinced. 'Ryan, use your common sense here. A HALO jump would mean flying an aircraft directly over the prison. The Russians might be a little suspicious if an unscheduled flight suddenly passes through their airspace.'

Drake said nothing, instead turning his restless gaze back to the map laid out on the conference table. Khatyrgan Prison lay in the extreme north of the Sakha Republic. Surrounded by Arctic tundra and with the nearest town lying 97 miles due south, it was without doubt one of the remotest places he'd ever encountered.

But something else about the location had piqued his interest. It was less than 40 miles from the East Siberian Sea.

'So we do a High Opening jump instead.'

HAHO, or High Altitude High Opening was, as its name suggested, the opposite of a HALO jump. Instead of free falling, they would pop their chutes a few seconds after leaving the aircraft. Exiting at 30,000 feet, and with a little luck and skill, the team could cover 40 miles or more before touching down.

'We come in from the north-east in some kind of long-range transport – maybe an MC-130 – and across the East Siberian Sea,' he said, indicating the route on the map. 'Then we start our jump just as the plane approaches the coast. As soon as we're out, the pilot turns away like he's realised he's approaching Russian airspace, and that's us on our way.'

Franklin stared at the map for several seconds, weighing up the reality of what Drake was suggesting. 'That's a good forty miles,' he said, dubious. 'You'd be at the limit of your range.'

'If you've got anything better, I'm all ears.' When

Franklin said nothing, Drake glanced at the prison blueprints again, imagining the scenario unfolding in his mind's eye. 'So assuming we make it that far, we aim to come down on the prison roof. It's flat according to the blueprints, so we shouldn't have any problems landing. We take out any guards or electronic surveillance up there and post a sniper to cover us. The rest of the team then makes entry through one of the tower stairwells, and Bob's your mother's brother. We're in.'

It sounded simple enough, but then most things did when gathered around a planning table with a cup of coffee. An awful lot of things could go wrong, yet he could think of no better way to get inside.

Franklin looked down at the blueprints again. 'You'll need someone who speaks Russian. If you want to find Maras quickly, you might have to start questioning her fellow prisoners.'

Which meant choosing a specialist, Drake knew.

Apart from the permanent case officer, most Shepherd teams were drawn from a pool of about fifty specialists who could be brought in when needed, then cut loose again. Most came from military backgrounds, trained in everything from assault to explosives, sniping, counterterrorism, electronic warfare, interrogation, computer hacking, safe cracking and any other skill that a covert operation could conceivably require.

The exact size and composition of a Shepherd team varied depending on the job, and it was up to the case officer to decide which of these specialists he needed at any given time. Teams could be as large as ten or as small as two – it depended on the job and the skills required, and to some extent, the officer heading it up.

However, it did sometimes result in disputes when

41

one specialist was needed by two or more case officers at the same time. Drake had seen such debates become quite heated at times, forcing Franklin to step in and mediate between bickering team leaders.

'Borowski speaks Russian like a native,' Drake suggested.

Franklin considered it only for a moment before dismissing the notion. 'He's also over the hill, and fifty pounds overweight.'

Andre Borowski was a Polish-born intelligence analyst who had been working with the Shepherd teams on and off for years. He'd been a field operative himself once upon a time, but at fifty-two years old, his active career was all but over. He was out of shape and out of the loop.

'So who, then?'

Franklin was silent for several seconds, weighing up his limited options.

'We need Dietrich,' he decided.

Drake shook his head. 'No. No way.'

'Come on, he's perfect. He speaks Russian, he's parachute trained and he works well under pressure.'

'He's also an arsehole,' Drake felt moved to point out.

Franklin was right about his skills. Jonas Dietrich was an excellent translator and an experienced field operative. He didn't just know the Russian language, he knew the Russian people. He'd spent years studying them and working against them during the Cold War. He knew how they thought, how they acted, and best of all, he knew how facilities like Khatyrgan operated. He had even taken part in similar operations twenty years earlier.

On paper he was the perfect man for the job. But he was also a man who Drake would happily have given his right arm never to work with again.

'Can you think of anyone better?' Franklin challenged.

Drake frowned, his mind churning over with thoughts of anyone else who might be suitable. He was drawing a blank.

Shit.

'Fine. Make the call,' he said, at last bowing to the inevitable.

The older man threw up his hands. 'Hell, no. This is your operation, buddy. You want him, you call him.'

If looks could kill, Franklin would have been lying stone dead at that moment.

Chapter 6

The phone rang for so long that Drake was beginning to think he'd missed Dietrich altogether. Then, at last, someone picked up and a familiar voice snapped a less than friendly greeting.

'What?'

Clearly the man had lost none of his charm.

Jonas Dietrich had been in the covert operations game most of his adult life, starting out in the mid-eighties working with the BND, the West German intelligence service, mostly in espionage and counter-intelligence – catching enemy operatives and interrogating them. During his time, he'd built up an extensive knowledge of the Soviet military and intelligence machine, as well as a formidable understanding of 'coercive interrogation' techniques, better known as torture.

After the fall of the Berlin Wall, he moved to the United States and offered his services to the Agency. Being fluent in Russian, English, German and Polish, not to mention highly trained in paramilitary work, he soon found his services in high demand, eventually becoming a Shepherd team leader himself.

But such professional success only served to bolster his already inflated ego, and he soon developed a reputation as a loose cannon who acted on his own initiative and often employed excessive force. Opinion was split between those who admired him and those who despised him, but everything changed when he and Drake worked together on a job in Estonia.

Drake had been new to the Shepherd teams at the time; just a specialist fresh out of the military. He'd been shocked by Dietrich's cavalier attitude towards mission planning, and his complete disregard for any advice or opinions presented to him. The final straw came when Dietrich, acting on his own initiative during a house assault, tripped an alarm and blew the entire operation. In the resulting firefight, two of his team were caught in the open and almost killed by enemy fire.

Drake, realising the man was as much a danger to his own people as their adversaries, had threatened to resign unless something was done about him. An internal inquiry soon followed, ending Dietrich's career as a team leader and demoting him to the role of specialist. It was a shitty thing to do, but he'd seen no other option.

And yet, here he was, pleading for his services.

'Jonas, it's Ryan.'

Straight away the line went dead. No wonder. Dietrich knew what Drake had done, and there was no love lost between the two men.

'How did it go?' Franklin asked.

'Better than I expected,' he replied, redialling.

Again it rang for a good ten seconds before Dietrich at last picked up.

'Don't hang up. This isn't a social call,' Drake cut in before the other man could speak. 'We've got a job for you.'

'I'm not interested.'

'It's important. We need a Russian translator.'

'Goodbye, Ryan.'

'They're offering double the normal rate,' Drake cut in.

Silence greeted him for several seconds. 'Who is?'

'Franklin. He's already signed off on it.' He gave his friend a meaningful look. Franklin had done no such thing, but he knew that money was about the only carrot he could wave Dietrich's way. Anyway, Cain was writing the cheques, and he'd already made it clear that Drake had a blank one at his disposal.

'Put him on,' Dietrich demanded.

Drake pressed the conference call button and replaced the receiver in its cradle. 'You're on speaker with him.'

Franklin leaned in a little closer. 'Hello, Jonas. It's good to speak—'

'I want triple,' Dietrich interrupted.

To his credit, Franklin stayed calm in the face of such an outrageous demand. 'Well . . . we can talk about that when you come in.'

'There won't be any talking about it, Dan. The only talking you need to do is "yes".'

Franklin glanced up at Drake. 'You're cutting a pretty hard deal.'

'These are hard times, Dan. Besides, we both know Ryan wouldn't have called me if he could find anyone else. So the job you have in mind must either be so difficult that you need my help, or so dangerous that nobody else is willing to take it on. Either way, it looks like you need me. So, triple the normal fee, or I'm hanging up right now.'

Drake saw Franklin swear under his breath. 'Fine. Triple. But we need you to come in straight away,' he added, as if it were some crushing final remark.

Both men could almost imagine Dietrich's amused smirk. 'Good talking to you again, Dan. Oh, and Ryan?'

'Yeah?'

'Say please.'

Drake frowned at the speaker phone in the centre of the table. 'What?'

'I want you to ask me nicely to come in,' Dietrich repeated slowly. 'Courtesy doesn't cost a thing, and I think you owe me some.'

Drake glanced up at Franklin, who merely shook his head.

'All right.' He clenched his teeth, having to force the words out. 'If it's not too much trouble, could you please come in?'

Dietrich chuckled down the phone. 'See? That wasn't so hard.' He let that hang in the air for a few moments. 'I'm on my way. Looking forward to working with you again, Ryan.'

With that, the line went dead.

'I don't fucking believe that guy,' Franklin said, turning the phone off.

Drake unclenched his fists and took a deep breath to calm himself. 'Like I said, it went better than I thought.'

'Well, we got him. At least that's something,' Franklin decided, putting an optimistic spin on things. 'While we're making calls, you might as well notify the rest of your team. I assume you've got some names in mind?'

Drake nodded, dragging his thoughts away from Dietrich to concentrate on the job in hand. The way he saw it, he needed three other specialists for this job.

He wanted a general assault and demolitions expert who could handle themselves in a firefight, plus destroy any physical barriers they might encounter; a decent sniper to provide observation and top cover for the team; and an electronics specialist to defeat any security measures on site.

The first role was the easiest to fill.

'I want Mason in on this. If I have to put up with Dietrich, I need someone else I can rely on.'

An ex-member of the Combat Applications Group, better known as Delta Force, Cole Mason had opted to leave the military at the age of thirty-five rather than take a promotion away from the front line. His speciality had been demolitions, and there was still a possibility they would have to put his skills to the test on this job, but mainly Drake wanted him on board as back-up. If anything happened to him, he knew Cole could take over and lead the team without difficulty.

'And Frost as our electronic specialist,' he added. 'We'll need her to take out their security system.'

Khatyrgan struck him as a low-tech sort of place, but even simple video cameras could compromise the team. Someone had to be on hand to eliminate them, and he could think of no one better than Keira Frost.

5 foot 2 inches tall and weighing no more than 100 pounds, Frost wasn't the kind of person one would immediately associate with clandestine operations into maximum security Russian prisons, but appearances could be deceiving. She was ex-US Army, working for their Signals Intelligence division before transferring to the Defence Intelligence Agency. Technically she still worked for them as an outside contractor, but more and more she was transitioning into the Shepherd teams.

She was fully combat trained and, as Drake knew from experience, not afraid to get stuck in despite her diminutive size. He'd once watched her literally throw herself at an armed man twice her size and many times her strength during an operation in Kosovo. He'd almost felt sorry for the guy, seeing the brutal and fiercely aggressive way she wrestled him down.

He didn't know what kind of experience she had at

high-altitude parachuting, but if necessary she could tandem jump with another team member. Either way, he wanted her on board.

Franklin had been nodding agreement thus far, obviously having anticipated his choices. 'Anyone else?'

Drake thought about it for a few moments. 'Keegan,' he decided at last. 'He's a bit of an old bastard, but he's the best sniper I can think of.'

Unlike most of their specialists who came from military backgrounds, John Keegan was a former FBI agent, serving in their SWAT teams as a sharpshooter for nearly ten years before leaving in search of better things.

He'd since drifted into CIA fieldwork, operating mostly on independent ops. One didn't have to read his file to surmise that most of this work involved assassinations, but that seemed to sit just fine with him. As far as he was concerned, it was up to God to sort them out – he was just the delivery boy.

At forty-seven years old he was pushing it a bit in terms of age, but he was fully certified for airborne operations, and his marksmanship was better than Drake and Franklin combined.

And that was it. Four specialists, plus himself. Not a large force for such a daunting operation, but between them they could draw on quite a range of skills and experience. And if the shit hit the fan, they were capable of causing a great deal of trouble.

He just hoped they didn't have to.

Franklin nodded. Now they had a rough plan of attack, and a list of the men and women needed to carry it out. Things were coming together.

'All right. Let's make some calls.'

Chapter 7

Prisoner 62 could hear footsteps in the hallway. Three sets, coming her way. Two were lighter and closer together. The third was slower, heavy and ponderous.

She felt her muscles tense up. It was *him*.

She didn't know his real name, didn't know any of the guards' names for that matter. There were no names in Khatyrgan. Instead she had come to know them by their physical characteristics. There was Bad Breath, Beer Gut and Lazy Eye to name but a few. Hardly the elite amongst the Russian penal system, otherwise they wouldn't have been stuck in this shithole at the end of the world.

The remoteness of the prison meant they couldn't go home at the end of their shift, couldn't relax and let off steam by drinking and fucking the way most men did. They were forced to live here, enduring the bad food and claustrophobic living conditions just like everyone else. They were as much prisoners of Khatyrgan as the people they guarded, and that situation was reflected in their outlook.

Most of the guards were moody and aggressive to varying degrees, sometimes taking out their frustrations on the inmates. It was nothing personal really – they were just bored and pissed off, and even she understood that on some level. She didn't like it, but she understood.

But the man she feared and hated most, she simply referred to as Bastard.

He was well named.

For him, random acts of violence weren't enough. He took some kind of macabre pleasure in seeing others suffer, and appeared to devote a great deal of time to dreaming up new ways of indulging his passion.

Stress positions, starvation, sensory deprivation – he had done all of those things and more, but they were really just variations on other people's ideas. Every so often, Bastard liked to get creative.

For example, he had once taken a dozen prisoners out into the snow-covered exercise yard in the middle of winter, forced them to remove their boots and socks, and left a single pair in the centre of the open space. For the next hour, he had watched from one of the towers as the desperate men fought each other like animals over that pair of boots.

She hadn't seen it herself, since she was never allowed out of her cell, but she had overheard the guards talking about it. They seemed to hate and fear him almost as much as she did.

Almost, but not quite.

She had become something of a fixation for him. He lusted after her while at the same time hating and despising her; she had seen that look enough times in the eyes of others to recognise it in him. Whereas the other guards had learned a certain respect, her resistance only fired his desire to break her. He had taken her many times when she was cuffed or held down and unable to defend herself, deriving immense pleasure from her impotent rage.

She suspected he was part of the reason the beatings had stopped, and her daily rations had improved beyond the starvation level she'd endured before. In his own perverted way, Bastard was trying to look after her so he could break her all by himself.

She sat up just as the bolt was drawn back with a harsh rasp and her cell door thrown open. Standing there were two of the regular guards – Lazy Eye and Rash.

Now in his fifties, she guessed Lazy Eye had suffered a mild stroke at some point, based on the way his left eyelid drooped and the difficulty he had pronouncing certain words. It hadn't slowed him down much, though – he was still more than happy to employ his fists and boots if he felt like it, letting them do the talking for him.

Rash was a comparatively young man in his thirties, and appeared almost timid and docile compared to his peers. He could perhaps have been considered handsome if it wasn't for the eczema that constantly plagued him. The skin around his neck was always red raw where he'd shaved and the collar of his uniform chafed, while his hands and forearms were often covered in scabs and welts.

Behind them both, towering like a statue, stood Bastard.

Standing 6 foot 6 inches and weighing at least 300 pounds, he was a massive, dominating physical presence. His uniform struggled to contain his huge barrel chest, wide stooped shoulders, thick bull-like neck and protruding gut.

His facial features were blunt and crude, everything somehow bigger and more pronounced than it needed to be. He must have been at least forty-five, but years of harsh winters, heavy smoking and cheap alcohol had aged him prematurely. The flesh of his face sagged, his skin was sallow and marred by wrinkles and small scars. His wide mouth curved back into a sneer as he eyed her up.

'Come on,' he said in Russian, beckoning her out of the cell. 'Shower.'

The one – and perhaps only – thing the guards took seriously about their duty in Khatyrgan was enforcing personal hygiene. Disease was always a problem, as were lice and other parasites, and given that the guards were often in close physical proximity to the prisoners, particularly while administering beatings, it was preferable to keep such things in check. Those prisoners who refused to wash were beaten and subjected to ten minutes of freezing water courtesy of the nearest fire hose.

Keeping a wary eye on Bastard, she lifted her chin a little and rose up from her mattress. Rash and Lazy Eye gave her plenty of room as she emerged from the cell, keeping their weapons to hand in case she tried anything.

Out of habit she glanced at their side arms, drawing on the vast well of knowledge she possessed on modern weaponry. Makarov PMs; semi-automatic, blow-back-action pistols. Eight-round magazines, firing 9mm full metal jacket projectiles. Effective range, up to 50 metres.

They weren't elegant weapons, but they were simple, cheap and durable. Just as well, because she doubted the idiots here could handle anything more complex.

Was there a possibility of escape that way? Countless times she had pondered it calmly, with clinical detachment as she followed the familiar route to the shower rooms. Even as broken down as she was, she could certainly take out one man with her bare hands, perhaps even use his weapon to kill a second, but the third would shoot her dead before she could draw down on him. They always came for her in threes.

Bastard led the way, tracing the familiar route past the other solitary confinement cells. She had never made any effort to communicate with her fellow prisoners, but she was sometimes curious about who else inhabited this shithole with her. Were they good people or bad? Did they deserve to be here? Did anyone?

Bastard unlocked the security door at the end of the block. It was a huge thing that probably weighed more than he did; the kind of door normally found on bunkers and pillboxes. Beyond the door they passed the cell control station for East Block. Another guard was manning the station, and gave her a leering stare as she passed.

Passing through a second heavy door, they took a sharp turn right, heading down the main concourse that housed the general population. Sleeping three or four to a cell, these were the prisoners considered a little less dangerous, or who required less severe punishment than herself.

It took about five seconds for the first inmate to notice her, then the shouting and abuse started. It seemed they spent a great deal of time thinking about what they would do to her if they were ever alone together, because she heard a new insult every time.

She almost smiled, thinking about what would actually happen if they tried it. Still, at least she encouraged their creativity.

Bastard took his time, letting everyone have a good look at her. She kept her eyes forward, showing no reaction to the disgusting epithets that were hurled her way, and carried on walking.

Almost there.

The shower room was a vast expanse of cracked tiles, mould, rusted pipework and dripping taps. The entire room could accommodate fifty prisoners at a time, but today she had the place to herself. She was always made to shower alone. She did everything alone.

'Strip,' Bastard ordered. His commands were always sharp and simple, because he was never sure how much Russian she understood. None of them did – she hadn't uttered a word since arriving in Khatyrgan.

With deliberate care, she pulled off her boots, trousers and sweat-stained shirt, finally removing the thin T-shirt beneath.

Her clothes lying in a pile by her feet, she stood unashamedly naked before him.

He took his time looking her over. He always did it, just because he could. She didn't flinch or make any effort to cover herself – there was no point, and she didn't want to give him the satisfaction.

At long last he pointed to the row of showers on the left side of the room. 'Go. You have five minutes.'

She masked a look of surprise. He was being unusually lenient. She had expected some kind of prank by now, but so far things had passed without incident. That made her nervous, but she could see nothing obviously out of place.

Hesitating a moment, she approached the row he'd indicated, the cold wet tiles sending chills up her legs. Sometimes the water was lukewarm enough to be considered almost comfortable, other times it was freezing as if it had come straight from the prison's cold water tanks. She'd always suspected the guards could somehow control the temperature of the flow.

Bracing herself for a jet of cold water, she selected a tap at random and reached out to switch it on.

Bang!

Something leapt out from the tap with an audible crack, striking her with such force that she was thrown backward against the tiled wall opposite. She hit hard, slumping to the floor, her ears ringing and with bright blobs of light flashing before her eyes. She couldn't move. Her entire body was paralysed, muscles locked tight as waves of pain flowed through her.

Vaguely, through the fog in her mind, she became aware of laughter. Blinking and struggling to focus, she managed to look over at Bastard and the two other guards, snorting and laughing with amusement.

'Did you see her go?' she heard Lazy Eye say in Russian. 'She came right off the ground!'

Bastard was beaming with pride at his accomplishment. 'See? I told you it would work.'

Now she understood. Somehow he'd wired the metal water tap into the room's electrical system, turning it into a giant cattle prod. As soon as she touched it, the resulting discharge had thrown her clear across the room.

Only Rash seemed to show any concern. 'I think she's really hurt,' he warned. 'Look at her. What if she dies?'

No doubt he was more worried than anything else about the repercussions for himself if a prisoner died on his watch. Even here, questions would be asked.

Striding forward, Bastard knelt down beside her and sat there on his haunches for a few moments, grinning as she tried feebly to move her arm. 'Had a little accident, did we?'

Her eyes blazed with anger. She wanted to reach out, to tear the bloated, sagging flesh from his face with her bare hands, to gouge his eyes from their sockets, but her body wasn't listening to the commands her brain was sending it.

'She's fine,' he decided. Rising up, he drew back his boot and slammed the steel toecap into her exposed abdomen. Unable to protect herself, she could do nothing but groan as a fresh wave of agony tore through her.

'See? Nothing wrong at all.'

The blow was repeated a second time with even greater force. This time she did move, but only to double up and be violently sick across the tiled floor. All of her food for the day, gone in a single moment.

Satisfied, Bastard took a step back, watching with a kind of amused curiosity as she groped and flailed for his boot. Was she trying to attack him? To plead for mercy?

She lay naked before him, helpless and vulnerable. Only her eyes still burned with defiance and rage. He could feel himself becoming aroused just looking at her.

He loved it when he saw that look of helpless rage in her eyes, when her mask of self-control slipped aside and he saw her for who she really was.

He looked at his two companions. 'Wait outside.'

The two men glanced at each other, but neither uttered a word of protest. The sound of their footsteps on the tiled floor receded. She heard the rasp as Bastard unzipped his trousers.

She was helpless, unable to protect herself, unable to resist as he grabbed her shoulder and rolled her onto her stomach. She could barely feel the chill of the tiles on her naked skin, but she did feel the first gut-wrenching penetration as he thrust inside her.

She closed her eyes and tried to separate her mind from what was happening, wanting nothing more than for it to be over.

Chapter 8

Of the four specialists that Drake had requested, Keegan was the first to arrive. Living in the small town of Brookeville just a few miles north of DC, he was within easy reach of CIA headquarters.

A short, wiry man with a wrinkled, deeply tanned face, dishevelled blond hair, pale blue eyes and a bushy moustache, he always looked as though he'd just dragged himself out of bed. He was the sort of guy who could make a thousand-dollar suit look bad, so it was just as well he wasn't a follower of fashion.

Ignoring the dress code at Langley, today's ensemble consisted of a worn brown leather jacket, a crumpled white shirt, faded Levi jeans and a pair of scuffed hiking boots. Pretty much the same thing he'd worn the last time Drake had seen him.

'Ryan. How the hell are ya, buddy?' he asked with his distinctive South Carolina drawl, cracking a toothy grin as they shook hands. He might have been built like a rake, but there was a robust strength in his wiry old muscles that belied his size.

'Keeping busy, mate.'

'Well, good. I guess you've got a real shit bird lined up, huh?'

Drake couldn't help but smile. Keegan was closer to the truth than he knew. 'You'll find out soon enough.'

Mason arrived next, having made the 30-mile drive from his home in Baltimore in under an hour. Unlike Keegan, he was a big man, tall and broad shouldered, with a lean, angular face, olive-coloured skin and dark eyes that missed nothing.

He always kept his hair shaved to the bone, typical of his military background, but Drake suspected he was getting thin on top and just didn't want to admit to it. In any case, he had dressed for the occasion, wearing a grey business suit that looked as if it had come straight off the peg.

'Jesus, Ryan, you look like shit today,' he remarked without preamble.

'Better than looking like shit every day,' Drake returned with a wry smile.

The older man grinned. 'I wouldn't know.'

Frost was next. She'd been about 100 miles south in Richmond when the call came in, though she arrived only a few minutes behind Mason. God only knew how many speed limits she'd broken on the way here, but Drake wasn't surprised. Speed limits had never meant much to her.

She was carrying her leather biker's jacket over her arm as she approached.

'This had better be good, Ryan,' she warned, tossing it over the back of the nearest chair. She reached up and brushed a lock of dark hair out of her eye. Frost had a temper like no one he'd ever met, especially in the morning.

'Interrupted your beauty sleep, did we?' Keegan quipped as he poured himself a coffee.

Frost gave him the finger.

'Grab a coffee and a chair,' Drake suggested. 'We'll get started in a minute.'

As it turned out, it was another ten minutes before Dietrich finally showed up, sauntering into the conference room as if he didn't have a care in the world. He only lived 10 miles away, yet it had taken him longer than any of the others to get here.

Drake was taken aback by the change in him. The Dietrich he'd known had been a muscular, intimidating man with piercing blue eyes and rugged good looks. He'd always worn expensive clothes, top-of-the-range watches, kept himself groomed to the point of vanity.

In contrast, the man before him was lean and spare, the veins in his exposed arms standing out hard against his skin. His dark hair was longer and dishevelled, greying a little at the sides, and he'd grown a goatee beard. But even that couldn't hide the hollowness in his face.

He was wearing a grey polo shirt and jeans – a far cry from the Gucci suits that used to be his apparel of choice.

But for all that, his eyes still gleamed with quick intelligence, and he moved with the confident, unhurried walk of a man firmly in control of the situation.

'Nice of you to join us, Jonas,' Drake remarked with a pointed glance at his watch.

'Good to be here, Ryan.' Taking in Drake's appearance, he frowned. 'You're looking tired these days.' He leaned in closer and added, 'Not as easy as you thought being a team leader, is it?'

Drake met his gaze evenly. 'Well, that's not something you have to worry about now.'

Dietrich's smile contained no warmth as he locked eyes with Drake. Then, without saying anything he helped himself to a chair and tilted it back, making sure he was quite comfortable before looking expectantly at Drake. 'Well, aren't you going to get us started?'

Chapter 9

Naked and half frozen, she was dragged into her cell and dumped on the floor without a word. Her mind barely registered the flash of pain as her head hit the concrete, but she did feel the cold begin to seep through her skin. Her clothes were tossed in a moment later, landing on the stained mattress.

Bastard had seen to it that she was dragged naked through the general population block, still dazed and struggling to regain control of her muscles after the massive electric shock she'd received. The other inmates had loved that one, yelling and banging on the cell bars. They had even hurled a few new insults her way, though she barely heeded them.

Still chortling with amusement at the earlier spectacle, Lazy Eye backed out of the cell and slammed the door shut behind him.

She was alone.

She coughed and spat, leaving a trail of bloody phlegm on the floor. She must have bitten her tongue when they'd shocked her. She could taste copper in her mouth, but the pain didn't register.

Pain was something she had become so accustomed to, it was almost the norm for her now.

For nearly a full minute, she didn't move a muscle, just lay there watching her breath misting in the cool air.

She almost didn't want to move. She felt as if she had been beaten from the inside out.

It had been some time since Bastard had had her, and he'd done his best to make up for lost time. Twice he had raped her in that cold shower room. Twice she had had to endure the weight of his massive, heaving bulk on top of her, feeling his hot breath in her ear as he grunted and thrust away. She couldn't decide which was worse; the hard, fast and brutal first time, or his slower and more thorough second attempt.

She should have felt anger at what had happened. She should have felt revulsion and hatred and disgust and grief and a dozen other emotions that normal women would have felt.

No such feelings stirred within her now. The only anger she felt was towards herself and her body – her soft and vulnerable body that could be so easily hurt. Had she been born a man, she could have endured places like Khatyrgan with ease.

She could have endured many things in her life.

She was tired. Tired of this place, tired of waiting for the next round of pain and humiliation, tired of being cold and eating the same shit food every day.

She had thought herself strong once, able to endure anything, able to fight her way out of any situation. Years ago she had been a soldier, a warrior, a killer who struck without remorse, without fear, without conscience or regret, and who none could stand against. She had once stood on the brink of greatness, commanding power and respect that most could only dream of.

Yes, she had been strong then, and arrogant.

And wrong.

Now, lying there naked and shivering, with her insides

aching and burning, she understood just how wrong she had been.

Yes, she had been wrong, and she was paying the price for that every single day of her life. Every day in this 6-foot-by-8-foot world, she lost a little more of that strength. Every day another piece of her died, until at last there wasn't all that much left to call her own.

If she was to just lie there, the cold would eventually take her. It was such an easy thought, such an easy escape.

She would fall asleep, and that would be it.

Maybe it was better that way.

Suddenly, unbidden, her mind echoed with a voice that was not her own, speaking words that had once been recited to her long ago, words which had been drilled into the very core of her being, words which had sustained her many times when her hope had faded.

I will endure when all others fail. I will stand when all others retreat. Weakness will not be in my heart. Fear will not be in my creed. I will show no mercy. I will never hesitate. I will never surrender.

Her eyes snapped open, focused now with a clarity that her torture and rape had all but extinguished. A fire of defiance, of hatred and rage flared up inside her, driving away the weariness and the thoughts of surrender and despair.

I won't die here. I won't. They can kill me if they want, but I won't lay down and die for them. I won't give them that pleasure.

Get up. Get up now.

Slowly, painfully, she managed to get her arms beneath her and pushed herself up from the floor as she had done so many times. The effort left her trembling and gasping for breath, but she was up.

Forcing her rigid, frozen muscles to work, she reached out and grasped her clothes in a white-knuckle grip, dragging them across the floor towards her.

I will never surrender.

Chapter 10

'Good morning, everyone,' Drake began. 'I'm sorry we had to call you in at such short notice, but we have an urgent situation and very little time to bring you up to speed. Here's an overview of what we have so far . . .'

He had spent the past two hours collating their objectives, the fledgling assault plan, the vast array of intelligence documents retrieved by Cain, and his own thoughts and recommendations into what he hoped was a logical and concise briefing dossier.

It was still rough, strewn with typos and dangerously vague in places, but it was the best he could do in the time available. Any gaps would have to be filled with verbal questions and answers as they went.

For the next twenty minutes, he outlined in broad terms what had happened thus far, what their objectives were, how they were to be carried out, as well as everything he'd been able to learn about Khatyrgan Prison.

'So to summarise, our goal is to find an operative answering to the name *Maras*, secure her and get her back to US soil as quickly as possible. The entire operation has to be carried out with total deniability. Questions?'

Frost wasn't shy about voicing hers. 'Is this for real? I mean, launching a covert op against Russia? Parachuting into a maximum security prison?'

'It's very real,' Drake confirmed. 'Next question.'

Dietrich was next. 'Who exactly is this woman?'

Drake glanced to his right. Cain, along with Franklin, was sitting in on the briefing. Officially they were present to review Drake's plan and give it the green light, but he suspected Cain was simply there to keep a handle on what was being discussed.

'Her identity is classified,' Cain answered.

'You're asking us to risk our lives for her. I think we deserve to know.'

Cain gave him a look that would have made most men squirm in their seats. 'You're not in a position to make that call. If that's not acceptable, you're free to leave any time, Mr Dietrich.'

At this, Dietrich simmered down a little. Even he knew when to back off.

Drake cleared his throat, carrying on with the briefing. He was quite happy to watch Cain tear him a new one all day, but they were short of time already. 'Needless to say, if any of us are caught or captured, the Agency will deny all knowledge of our existence.'

'Surprise me,' Keegan remarked with dry humour.

'I'm serious,' Drake cut in. 'Before we go any further, I want everyone to be clear about what they're getting into. If anyone wants to back out, this is the time. Nobody will think less of you.'

He looked at each of them in turn, giving them all a chance to voice their thoughts. Frost looked uneasy but determined. Keegan was smiling, as if amused by the whole thing. Mason was his usual composed and implacable self, while Dietrich's face betrayed no emotion at all.

None of them said a word.

Drake nodded, satisfied. 'All right. Now, let's move on to the plan of assault.'

In his briefing dossier, he'd outlined five major challenges that needed to be overcome if the operation was to succeed:

1. Getting to the target area.
2. Making entry to the prison.
3. Neutralising the guards and security measures.
4. Finding and extracting Maras.
5. Getting out of the target area.

'Phase One, getting there,' he began. 'Because of the time constraints and the nature of the target, we can't approach by land. Our only option is insertion by air.'

'We have an MC-130 transport standing by,' Cain chimed in. 'Our jumping-off point will be Elmendorf Air Force Base in Alaska.'

Drake moved over to the map he had pinned to the wall behind him. 'The plan is for our transport to fly as close to Russian airspace as possible, right along the coast here. We then exit and parachute towards Khatyrgan Prison,' he explained, indicating the rough drop zone on the map, and the proposed descent route.

He then switched his attention to the prison blueprints. 'Phase Two, making entry. Our aim will be to land on or adjacent to the south-west defensive tower,' he said, indicating the tower on the plans. 'We'll take out any sentries that are on station, and neutralise any security measures nearby. Keegan, your call sign for this op is Delta. Your objective will be to set up a sniping position in this tower and cover the remaining three towers, plus the exercise yard.'

Keegan raised an eyebrow. 'Jesus. Talk about multi-tasking, Ryan.'

Frost grinned. 'Should have brought more women on the team.'

The veteran sniper gave her a withering look. 'You could do the job if you weren't smaller than the rifle.'

Frost tipped her coffee to him in mock salute but said nothing.

'Phase Three is to neutralise the prison's security and communication systems. Once Keegan is set up, we'll split into two teams. Keira and Cole, you're Alpha One and Two, respectively. You'll head to the prison's security station in the south block,' Drake said, indicating a room on the second floor of the prison which they believed served as the nerve centre for the prison's security cameras. 'Keira, your objective will be to secure the station and destroy or disable any electronic security measures on site, and take out their communications.'

The young woman smiled. 'Tell me what you want destroyed and I'll make it happen.'

This was the part of the job she enjoyed. Computer hacking and data-trunk bypasses had their place, but sometimes a good crowbar was just as effective. And easier.

'Good. Cole, you're on cover duty.'

Mason nodded. 'No problem.'

'Right, Phase Four – finding Maras. As soon as the security system is down, myself and Dietrich will split off as Bravo One and Two. We'll make our way along the roof to the north-west tower. That's our closest access point to the solitary confinement cells, where we're reliably informed she's being held.'

Cain nodded. 'She's not the kind of prisoner you'd want in the general population, unless you had a pretty decent infirmary.'

'How cooperative is she likely to be?' Dietrich asked.

Cain folded his hands and leaned forward. 'It's hard to say. She was a rogue agent, so she's unlikely to have much love for the Agency. There's also no telling what effect prison has had on her. Whatever the case, you should still consider her extremely dangerous.'

Dietrich looked dubious. 'She's only one woman.'

Frost gave him a hostile glare but said nothing.

'One woman who could easily kill every person in this room, son,' Cain warned him, his expression deadly serious. 'Believe me, I've seen what she's capable of. The second you underestimate her, you're as good as dead. Don't turn your back on her for an instant, and don't give her an opportunity to arm herself. Are we clear?'

Dietrich regarded the older man in silence for several seconds.

'Are we clear?' Cain repeated.

'Yes, we're clear,' he said at last.

'Good. You're not to make any attempt to communicate with her either,' he added. 'She might say or do things to make you drop your guard. *Don't* let yourself get taken in. Don't believe anything she says.'

The others exchanged curious glances but said nothing.

Drake cleared his throat to resume the briefing. 'According to the blueprints there are thirty-two cells in this block. Aside from searching them one at a time, our best chance will be to interrogate one of the prisoners and see if they know where she is. That'll be your job, Jonas.'

Dietrich nodded. He had expected as much.

'What kind of forces can we expect on site?' Mason asked.

Drake leafed through his dossier. 'According to their old personnel listings, there are a dozen guards, one warden and assistant warden, and about ten other support staff in various roles – technicians, cooks and so on.'

Mason raised an eyebrow. 'That's all? For a maximum security prison with nearly three hundred inmates?'

'Cutbacks. Russia isn't exactly rolling in money these days.'

'There's no need for them,' Dietrich added, indicating the map again. 'Khatyrgan is a hundred miles from anywhere, and well north of the Arctic Circle. Even if a prisoner made it out, they'd have nowhere to go.'

The prison itself was a fortress, but the real enemy was the icy wilderness beyond the walls. Without a vehicle, any escapee was as good as dead. The futility of their situation was probably enough to keep most of the inmates in line.

'Based on similar facilities in East Germany, I'd expect no more than two or three guards on duty overnight,' Dietrich went on. 'One patrolling the cell blocks, one in the security centre and one as backup. They'll all be tired and bored. They won't be expecting trouble.'

Drake nodded. 'Which brings me along to Phase Five – extraction. Once we've secured Maras, both teams will rendezvous with Keegan at the south-west tower. We'll rappel down the outer wall and exfil.'

'How do we get out of the country?' Mason asked.

'We'll have a Chinook transport chopper on standby,' Cain explained. 'Once you're out of the prison, it'll land nearby and pick you up. It's been modified for long-range operations so it should have enough range to get you home.'

Mason leaned back in his chair. 'Then it's back to Alaska in time for coffee and bagels, huh?'

'Here's hoping, anyway,' Drake said.

'The pilot won't be able to stay on station for long,' Cain reminded them. 'So I suggest you don't waste time.'

Drake raised an eyebrow, but said nothing on this. 'I suggest we use the time we have to cover as many contingencies as possible. I want to hear absolutely everything you think could go wrong, every concern, every worry you have. We plan this thing down to the last detail, because we don't get second chances in this job. We plan as a team, we go in as a team, and we come home as a team,' he added, giving Dietrich a significant look. He snatched up his cup of coffee and downed the remaining contents in one gulp. 'Let's get to work.'

Chapter 11

Drake was alone in his cramped office, surrounded by stacks of paperwork, folders, maps, photographs, notebooks and empty coffee cups. Light from the setting sun slanted in through his window blinds, casting thin strips of shadow on the opposite wall. It was a beautiful day outside, not that he was in a mood to appreciate it.

The entire afternoon and evening had been occupied with intense planning sessions, going over every aspect of the operation from beginning to end, trying to anticipate every potential problem and find ways to counter it.

What kind of defensive positions were sitting atop the watchtowers? Would there be a guard in each one, or none at all? If the stairwells leading down into the prison were locked, did they have the right tools to break in? Did the stairwell doors open inward or outward?

These were all questions that could mean the difference between success and failure – or more likely, life and death – when they were halfway around the world in a Russian prison. Drake had seen more than one operation almost end in disaster because of some minor hitch that nobody had anticipated.

Every member of the team had a chance to voice their concerns, and often did so in very vocal terms. But at last they'd hammered out an operational plan that everyone was more or less satisfied with; no mean feat considering how little time they'd had.

Now the planning was over, the real work began for Drake. As team leader, that meant reviewing every aspect of the op from beginning to end, processing equipment requests, and making sure everyone in the team was organised and ready to go.

His job wasn't unlike a parent watching over their brood of children before school, checking they had their lunches packed and clean clothes on. Except, instead of asking for crisps and cheese sandwiches, these kids were pestering him for assault rifles, blowtorches and hand grenades.

He looked up when a knock came at the door.

Frost let herself in. 'You asked to see me, Ryan?'

He nodded and gestured to an empty chair. 'I need a favour. Close the door, would you?'

The young woman did as he asked, then sat down. 'I'm listening.'

He leaned back in his chair, watching her thoughtfully for a few moments. 'What's your opinion of this operation?'

'It's a clusterfuck just waiting to happen,' she replied without hesitation.

Despite himself, he couldn't help but smile. Frost had never been one for sugar-coating things. 'Thanks for the insight.'

She shrugged. 'Just calling it as I see it. But I assume you didn't ask me in here for my opinions?'

Drake nodded and slid the file photo of Maras across the table. 'We're risking our lives to recover this woman, and we don't even know her name. We don't know a single thing about her, in fact. That's not acceptable.'

A slow smile spread across her face. 'Want me to do some snooping?'

Again he nodded. 'Can you do a facial recognition search?'

'No problem.'

He leaned forward, resting his elbows on the edge of the desk. 'Yeah, but can you do it quietly? If Cain gets wind of this, good things are not going to happen.'

In addition to her skills with electronic surveillance, Frost was a pretty decent hacker. Her problem was that she was a little too confident for his liking. He wanted to know more about Maras, but he didn't want Frost to end up in prison for her efforts.

'You don't trust him, do you?' she asked. 'Cain, I mean.'

'He's not giving us the full story, or any story at all for that matter,' he evaded. 'That makes me nervous.'

'You're not the only one.' The young woman grinned. 'But relax, he won't find out what I'm up to. I'm good at what I do.'

'And modest, too,' he observed.

'Modesty's for you Brits, along with warm beer and stiff upper lips,' she taunted. 'Look, I know a guy in the Office of Information Technology. He's pretty good. We'll make a few enquiries, see what we can come up with, and we'll cover our tracks real well.' She smiled sweetly. 'Promise.'

Drake grinned, returning to his computer. 'All right. Go to work.'

'I'm on it.' She rose from her seat, but seemed to think better of it. 'Oh, and Ryan?'

'Yeah?'

'Try to get some sleep, would you? You look like shit these days.'

'Sounds like good advice to me,' another voice remarked.

Drake and Frost both looked up to see Dietrich hanging by the door.

'Some people actually knock before coming in,' Drake pointed out with an angry look, wondering how much he'd overheard.

Dietrich shrugged nonchalantly 'Duly noted.'

'What do you want?'

'A word. In private,' he added with a dismissive look at Frost.

The young woman crossed her arms and returned his gaze with one of simmering hostility, making no move to leave.

'All right, Keira,' Drake prompted her. 'I'll pick up with you later. And remember what we talked about.'

'Yeah, I remember,' she replied, not taking her eyes off Dietrich.

'Better get to it,' he suggested. 'And let me know as soon as you have something.'

She seemed reluctant to leave, but at last nodded agreement. Giving Dietrich one last hostile look, she turned and strode out of the office, closing the door much harder than was necessary.

Dietrich smiled in amusement. 'Quite a little firecracker, isn't she?'

'She doesn't react well to certain kinds of people.'

This prompted a cocked eyebrow. 'Really? What kind?'

'Your kind,' Drake said. 'Look, I've got a lot to do. What do you want to talk about?'

The older man helped himself to the spare seat. 'You, actually.'

'What about me?'

'I want to know why you're here, Ryan. This operation has got fuck-up written all over it. Most people would have passed it up, but you took it on. You practically begged me to come on board despite our history. Why?'

Drake shrugged. 'Someone had to do it.'

'Bullshit.' The word was delivered with such conviction and finality that it reminded Drake of a judge passing sentence. 'They offered you something, didn't they? That's why you're so desperate to get this done. What was it? A promotion? Another step up the ladder?'

'I don't have time to listen to this—'

'Then make time,' Dietrich cut in. 'Because I'm not risking my life just so you can move into a bigger fucking office. You already killed my career on your way up. Are you trying to finish the job now?'

Drake had heard enough. 'If you weren't such an arrogant fuck-up, you'd still be a team leader,' he snapped. 'What? You think I did what I did just so I could take your job? Grow up. You almost got two people killed because you wanted all the glory for yourself. I wonder how many other lives you risked over the years.'

Far from rising to the bait, Dietrich merely sat there regarding him with a look of mild amusement. 'You know, when I first met you, you were just a shit-headed kid straight out of the military. And now look at you.' He gestured around the cluttered office. 'King of your own little hill. But if you think this is the start of something bigger and better, you're wrong. Men like Cain will tell you whatever you want to hear – anything to make you do what they want. And when they have no more use for you, they'll throw you away like a piece of trash.'

Drake clenched his jaw and looked away from the older man's probing gaze. 'Thanks for the moral lesson,' he said at last. 'Now piss off and let me get on with my work.'

Dietrich rose from his seat but didn't leave. Resting his hands on the desk, he leaned forward a little and locked eyes with Drake.

'Whatever they promised you, I hope it was worth it.'

Pushing himself away from the desk, he turned and marched out of the office.

Chapter 12

Breathing hard, Drake circled the heavy punchbag and laid into it with a flurry of lefts and rights. His T-shirt was soaked with sweat, his dark hair plastered to his head. The impacts jarred his arms, sending shock waves through bone and sinew, but still he kept on with grim determination.

Dietrich's words echoed in his ears.

But if you think this is the start of something bigger and better, you're wrong. Men like Cain will tell you whatever you want to hear – anything to make you do what they want.

He gritted his teeth as his fists slammed into the padded leather again and again. The heavy bag, patched and gaffer taped in places, lurched and swayed with the impacts.

And when they have no more use for you, they'll throw you away like a piece of trash.

His heart was pounding and his breath coming in gasps as he circled the bag, muscles burning and legs heavy. Still the anger burned inside him, unquenched by his punishing workout.

His knuckles ached from the punishment, blood seeping from the torn flesh to soak the tape and bandages around his hands, but he ignored it. He was like a man possessed, laying into the bag again and again.

Dietrich was an arsehole; an arrogant, bitter, jealous

bastard. But none of those things could change the fact that he was absolutely right about what he'd said.

With an exhausted sigh, he landed one final blow before leaning in against the bag, struggling to draw ragged, pained breaths.

His right hand ached, pulses of pain racing up millions of nerve endings to his brain. He'd broken it in a boxing match years earlier when he'd still entertained the idea of being a professional fighter, needing surgery to mend the shattered bones. The old injury still gave him problems from time to time.

All day he'd tried to find justification for his decision to accept Cain's offer. He'd tried to tell himself that if he hadn't taken on the job, someone else would have done it, if only because they'd been ordered. He'd almost convinced himself that they were doing a good thing by rescuing a woman from what was no doubt an appalling situation.

None of these excuses sat well with him, because that's all they were – excuses. They weren't the truth.

Whatever they promised you, I hope it was worth it.

'Yeah. Me too,' he said, pushing himself off the bag. He'd done enough for one night.

Their flight to Alaska was scheduled to leave Andrews Air Force Base tomorrow morning at 9 a.m. Once at their jumping-off point, they would have a few precious hours to check their gear, make any last-minute adjustments to their plan, and prepare themselves for what lay ahead.

Tomorrow was going to be a long day, for all of them. But as for tonight, they had nothing but time.

Leaving the heavy punchbag still swinging from the rafters of his garage, he shuffled through the utility room and into the kitchen, peeling off his protective hand wraps as he went.

His home was a two-bedroom, single-storey detached house in the suburbs west of central DC. The kind of house owned by mid-level government workers and young couples thinking about starting families but not quite ready to take the plunge yet. Not a bad place by any stretch. In fact, in the right hands it could have been pretty decent. Unfortunately Drake was most definitely not the right hands.

He'd been living here for the past three years, but the place still had that chaotic 'just moved in' feel. Many of his belongings were still in packing boxes in the spare bedroom, forgotten and destined never to be opened.

It was as if he somehow still thought of this situation as a temporary one, as if he might suddenly have to pack up and leave tomorrow. But it wasn't, and he didn't.

He knew none of his neighbours beyond the occasional nod of greeting. He'd wondered from time to time what they thought of the aloof Englishman who went away for weeks or even months at a time. He didn't suppose they held him in high regard, but that was fine by him. He was as much of an outsider here as he was in the Agency.

A takeaway pizza box was waiting for him on the kitchen counter; he'd stopped off to collect it on his way back from Langley. He wasn't all that hungry, but he knew he needed to eat something and couldn't be bothered cooking anything. There were a stack of similar boxes in the garage.

He flipped open the box and levered a thick slice free, long strings of melted cheese still clinging to it as he took the first bite.

His laptop was resting beside the pizza box, plugged into a charging point. He hit the power button, then sat at the breakfast bar and wolfed down his pizza while it booted up.

A quick trip to the fridge-freezer saw him return with a handful of ice wrapped in a kitchen towel. Holding the ice bag against his aching hand, he found his gaze drawn to the half-empty bottle of Talisker whisky sitting a few feet further down the breakfast bar.

It had been full last night.

His eyes rested on it for a few moments longer before the Windows chime drew his attention away.

Connecting to the Net, his first port of call was CNN. com and a quick skim of the day's news stories. Straight away his attention was drawn to the top news article: *Deadly blast kills twelve in Iraq.*

He clicked on the link, which took him to a video feed.

'We now have the number of confirmed deaths at twelve, with at least three missing and another twenty people injured by the blast,' the Iraq correspondent said, his expression as serious as his suntan. 'The Iraqi Coalition Government has yet to release a statement on the attack, but speculation is rising that a suicide bomber was responsible.'

The feed then switched to an overhead shot of a destroyed building, one entire side caved in by what looked like a high-explosive detonation. Smoke was still rising from the rubble while rescue workers and forensics teams poked around. The streets around it were heaped with debris, crushed cars and other wreckage.

'From the air, the scale of the destruction is plain to see,' the reporter's voice went on. 'This busy street in downtown Mosul was crowded with civilians when the explosion ripped through it, bringing down a nearby building and turning bricks and mortar into deadly projectiles. It's unclear at this stage what exactly caused the blast, leaving many to speculate that it may have been a suicide bomber. One thing is certain – another twelve people have been added to the steadily rising death toll in Iraq since the so-called "end of hostilities" . . .'

He'd seen enough. Closing the feed down, he spent a few more minutes skimming various other articles of lesser interest, then logged into Hotmail to check his personal emails.

Aside from the usual bill reminders, Viagra adverts and fake requests for him to confirm his banking details, there was only one email that held any meaning for him.

It was from his sister Jessica back in the UK. Just a personal correspondence, carrying no threat of rejection or disappointment, and yet somehow it was infinitely harder for him to face up to.

Jessica was everything he wasn't – sensible, organised, in a steady job, in control of her life, and happily married with two kids. She was totally at ease with what she did, with who she was and where she was going.

He envied her, because he knew deep down he'd never have any of the things she did. He wasn't destined for that kind of life.

The title told him everything he needed to know: *Have you seen my brother anywhere???*

Bracing himself for the worst, he clicked on the message:

Hello, big brother!

How's things? Not heard from you in ages! Hope everything going well out there and that you're happy.

Chloe keeps asking about her uncle and when he's coming to visit again. I'm not sure what to tell her, but I was hoping I could say you'll be back again before Christmas? It's her birthday next month, by the way. I'm sure I don't need to remind you of that, though!?!? :·)

Do get in touch again, Ry. I worry when I haven't heard

from you in over a month! And remember there's always a
spare room here for you (hint, hint!).
   All my love,
   Jess

Drake exhaled and rubbed the bridge of his nose. Jessica always made the effort with him, always tried to stay in touch, always sent little encouraging messages and took the time to speak to him on the phone. She didn't know much about what he really did for a living, and she was perceptive enough not to ask too many questions, but neither was she an idiot. She knew enough to be worried for him.

His fingers hovered over the keyboard, ready to start on a reply.

Nothing happened.

His mind went blank. How on earth could he explain that for the past month he'd been searching for an Agency operative who had vanished while investigating a Serbian arms-smuggling ring? How could he tell her that they had eventually found the man in several pieces, buried in a shallow grave in the woods east of Laznica? He didn't even want to think about it himself.

He had a cover story, of course. The Agency had seen to that. To anyone who cared to ask, Drake worked for a security firm, doing threat assessments for big corporations who operated overseas. His job could take him away for weeks or months at a time.

He didn't know how much of the story Jessica believed. If he was honest, he didn't want to know. He hated lying to her.

He hesitated for a moment longer.

It was always the same. Her emails were witty, expressive, caring and intimate. His replies, when he could bring himself to write them, were flat, bland and detached. It was as if he was writing to a stranger. He just didn't know what to say.

'Shit,' he growled, reaching for the bottle of whisky. He poured a generous glass, held it up for a moment and watched the changing patterns of light reflected in the amber-coloured liquid.

Hate yourself later, he thought, tipping it back and forcing himself to swallow the contents. He knew it was a bad idea, but that didn't stop him. It never had.

He was well into his third glass when the doorbell rang.

'What the hell . . . ?'

Shuffling through to the hallway, he unlatched the front door and pulled it open a crack.

Standing on his doorstep like the world's most delinquent-looking girl scout was Frost. She was wearing her leather jacket and clutching a helmet under her arm, her short dark hair sticking up in disarray. Her bike was parked on the sidewalk; some monstrosity of red plastic and carbon fibre that probably weighed less than she did.

'Keira . . .' he began, taken aback by her sudden appearance. 'What are you doing here?'

The young woman gave him a crooked half-smile. 'Some things are better not said over the phone, know what I mean?' She nodded over his shoulder. 'Are you going to invite me in, or leave me standing here in the friggin' cold?'

'Erm, yeah, of course.' He moved aside and let her pass, then closed the door behind her.

She glanced around the cluttered hallway, taking in the faded carpet and the stack of old newspapers and magazines that he'd been meaning to take away for recycling but hadn't gotten around to. 'Nice place you've got, by the way.'

Her sarcasm was obvious. 'I wasn't expecting visitors.'

'So I see. Anyway, relax. I didn't come here to be wined and dined,' she called over her shoulder as she strode through to the kitchen.

Dumping her helmet on the counter, she spied the pizza box straight away. Lifting the lid, she gave him a disapproving look. 'What? No pepperoni?'

'Can't stand the stuff,' he said.

'Is that a Brit thing?' She shrugged and pulled out a slice. 'Fuck it.'

Drake shook his head. 'Please, help yourself.'

'Hey, I've been busting my ass for you all night,' she retorted while in the middle of eating. 'The least you can do is spring me for dinner.'

His eyes lit up. 'On that subject, I hope you've brought more than just your charming attitude.'

'Afraid not,' she said, taking another mouthful. 'There's nothing on Maras anywhere. CIA, FBI, police, Interpol . . . all our searches turned up nothing. She's a ghost.'

Drake suppressed a sigh of frustration. It was a long shot, but it was disheartening all the same. 'Someone must know who she is.'

'Yeah – Cain,' she said.

He sighed and rested his hands on the counter. 'You did what you could. Thanks for trying, at least.'

'There's something else.' She laid her pizza slice down. 'Out of interest, I did a little research on the name Maras.'

Drake leaned closer, intrigued. 'I'm listening.'

'Well, my first round of searches turned up a property letting agency, and a diesel generator supplier from Pittsburgh. Hardly the kind of thing that would inspire a CIA code name, so I counted them out. Then, when I thought about her being in a Russian prison, I changed the search parameters . . .'

Drake picked up his glass of whisky and took a gulp. 'Just give me the short version,' he said as the potent alcohol settled in his stomach. 'What did you find?'

Frost eyed the drink with a raised eyebrow.

'I'm off the clock,' Drake reminded her irritably. 'Talk or walk.'

'Suit yourself,' she said, shrugging. 'If I've got my facts straight, Maras refers to a legend from Baltic paganism. It was all the rage a thousand years ago, but it's almost an extinct religion now. Anyway, according to them, Maras is a goddess of war.'

Drake frowned, feeling all the more uneasy about what they were about to do. And more important, about the woman they had been sent to rescue.

A goddess of war.

'Heavy shit, huh?' Frost prompted. 'I'm not sure what I should be more worried about – the prison, the parachute jump, or her.'

'I'd go for all three.' He flashed a weak smile. 'Good work, Keira. Thanks for doing this.'

'No problem.'

'Now go home and get yourself some rest,' he said. 'We've got a long day ahead of us.'

Again that curious half-smile. 'Every day with Dietrich is a long day.' Her eyes rested on the glass again, and the smile faded. 'Are you going to be all right?'

'Same as always,' he evaded.

'That bad, huh?'

The look in his eyes told her he wasn't amused.

'All right, all right! I'm going.' She hesitated a moment, eyeing the pizza. 'Mind if I take a snack?'

'Go, Keira. Before I get my gun,' he warned.

Helping herself to another slice, she grinned at him. 'You were never that good, Ryan.'

'You're right. I was better.'

He watched her go, but his smile soon faded when he heard the door close and the roar of her motorbike fade into the distance.

Instead, his gaze shifted left, drawn inexorably towards the bottle of whisky. For a long moment he just sat there staring at it, as if he could will it out of existence, silence the urge to pour another glass.

He couldn't.

Chapter 13

East Siberian Sea, twenty-four hours later

The weather was lousy as the MC-130 ploughed its way through strong winds and snow clouds. Chunks of dry frozen hail hammered off the fuselage like shotgun pellets, while the deck lurched and swayed like a ship in a storm. The external windows had been sealed over with metal covers to prevent any light escaping from within, and the aircraft was running without recognition lights. It was a useful precaution, but it only served to enhance the feeling of claustrophobia for the small group of passengers imprisoned within the massive airframe.

Drake grimaced as another jolt slammed his head against the fuselage. Such abuse wasn't doing his headache any favours. It had been with him since the moment he awoke this morning in DC, dry mouthed and bleary eyed, courtesy of half a dozen glasses of Talisker.

He took another gulp of strong, black, bitter coffee. It was dangerous to drink too much – the last thing he wanted was to be nervous and jittery when they got on site – but he needed it to stay alert. His mind felt fogged and slow, two factors that could easily get him killed tonight.

What the hell were you thinking? he thought, angry with himself for being so self-indulgent last night. He should have been getting as much rest as possible before the operation began. But he knew he couldn't have slept without it.

Get a fucking grip and pull yourself together. This is the most important night of your life. You're not going to make a mistake. You're not going to fail. You're not going to hesitate. You're not going to let your team down.

Taking another sip of coffee, he glanced at his comrades.

Keegan, relaxed and laconic as always, was occupied with checking the action and optics on his sniper rifle. He'd been issued with a Dragunov for this operation, a big heavy Russian weapon that fired a high-velocity 7.62 mm projectile. The veteran sniper wasn't thrilled by the choice of rifle, preferring lighter weapons that were easier to handle, but circumstances dictated otherwise. Anything American made was out of the question. All of the team's weapons and equipment had had the serial numbers removed, making them impossible to trace.

Drake almost smiled when he saw the necklace dangling from Keegan's neck. A simple black leather thong, it held a silver crucifix, a dice and a wedding ring, symbolising his three loves in life – religion, gambling and women.

He'd been married a bunch of times, but for some reason it never seemed to take. Three messy divorces hadn't diminished his enthusiasm, though. God only knew how he afforded the lawyer's fees.

Maybe that explained his second love in life.

Keegan was more superstitious than a gypsy, and wore the necklace on every operation he took part in, either around his neck or tucked into a pouch in his webbing. Nothing on earth would persuade him to leave it behind.

Frost on the other hand looked nervous and agitated, and Drake didn't blame her. Her experience of parachuting was, as they had discovered during the planning session yesterday, almost non-existent, forcing her to tandem jump with Mason. It was far from an ideal solution, and it would leave them vulnerable until the two were able to disengage from their harness, but it was the only way to get her on site.

She was sorting through her electrical kit for the tenth time. Weight restrictions meant she was very limited in what she could take, forcing her to make some difficult choices. The situation was further complicated by the fact that they knew little about the security system employed at Khatyrgan. Dietrich had provided a few educated guesses based on similar facilities he'd visited during his days with West German intelligence, but Drake was inclined to take what he said with a grain of salt.

The man himself was sitting away from the others, saying and doing nothing. If possible, he looked even worse than Drake felt. He was pale and haggard, as if he hadn't slept a wink. Was he sick? Drake had no idea, but it left him uneasy.

'I just spoke to the pilot,' Mason said, taking a seat next to Drake. 'He says we've got a storm front coming in from the north-west tonight. We should touch down before it hits, but it might make extraction difficult.'

Drake raised an eyebrow. Just what he needed – another problem to worry about. His gaze remained on Dietrich.

'We're gonna have trouble with that one,' Mason remarked in a low tone, following his line of sight.

Avoiding his friend's questioning gaze, Drake took another sip of coffee. 'I can handle him.'

'Yeah? But can you handle him and Maras at the same time?'

Drake said nothing for a few seconds. 'What do you suggest?'

'We don't need any loose cannons tonight. Not on a job like this.' Mason's expression was the kind one might wear in casual conversation, but his words were deadly serious. 'Wouldn't be unknown for him to have problems with his breathing gear, or maybe a badly packed chute that stops him from jumping . . .'

Drake looked at him. He understood what Mason was trying to do, but he wasn't prepared to cut Dietrich loose.

He shook his head. 'We need him. He's an arsehole, but we need him on this one.'

The older man shrugged. 'Fair enough. I'm glad he won't be watching *my* back, though.' He looked a little closer at Drake, noting the man's glazed eyes and drawn appearance. 'You all right, man? You look worse than him.'

Drake could feel himself tensing up. Was it that obvious?

Suddenly the aircraft's intercom buzzed, and the pilot's tinny voice echoed around the cabin. 'Attention, crew. We're at thirty minutes to drop zone. Thirty minutes.'

Downing the last of his coffee, Drake turned to his friend. 'Still in the fight, mate.'

Rising to his feet unsteadily on the pitching deck, he raised his voice to address the rest of the team. 'All right, final weapon and equipment checks! Gear up!'

Chapter 14

She lay on her back amongst the long grass, staring up into the endless blue sky overhead. No clouds marred its perfection or measured its vastness. It was a warm, still summer's evening, with just the faintest breeze rippling through the yellow stalks around her. The kind of evening that made her grateful simply to be alive.

Then, high above, she spotted the contrail of some aircraft tracing a line from north to south, straight as an arrow. It was hard and definite near the tip, seeming almost solid, but breaking up and dissipating as her eyes followed it northward.

Where was it going? She didn't know. But as she lay there staring upward, the sky seemed to carry on for ever. She felt so small she could almost lose herself in it.

She inhaled, tasting the scent of pine needles, grass, wild flowers, rich loamy earth and other growing things. She loved to lie out here on evenings like this, feeling a part of the world around her, having nowhere to go and nothing to do. She was at peace.

Her thoughts were disturbed by the rumble of a car engine crunching up the rocky road to the house.

Prisoner 62 blinked, opening her eyes a crack as a cell door slammed shut further down the block. Was it day or night? She didn't know. She never knew. Day and night had no meaning in a world where the sun was a half-forgotten memory.

She was cold. Her feet were blocks of ice. The blanket she'd been given wasn't long enough to cover her fully unless she drew her knees up to her stomach. She must have moved in her sleep.

She'd been dreaming again. It was a dream that came to her from time to time. A memory, an old memory of the distant, barely remembered time Before. Before she was alone. Before she had to fight just to live. Before the long list of bad things that had brought her here.

Dreams of Before always made her angry. Once they had left her with an aching, crushing feeling of loss and despair, but she had long since burned emotions like that away, cut them from her psyche as one might remove a gangrenous limb. It was a sacrifice necessary to keep the remainder of herself vital, to survive. Now the dreams just made her angry, because they reminded her of things she would never have again.

Family, love, protection, safety, compassion and tenderness . . . Those were luxuries she could never enjoy.

The cold persisted. Pushing herself up from the bed, she lay down on the floor and started a set of press-ups, ignoring the pain of her aching muscles. She had to get the blood and warmth flowing through her limbs again.

Sadness, regret, grief, fear . . . All of those things were weaknesses that she could no longer afford. If she was to survive in Khatyrgan, if she was to keep some part of herself whole and untouched, she had to remain strong.

Her life Before was gone now. Survival was all that

mattered. It was her goal, her objective, her one hope. It was no longer a means, but an end in itself.

Every day she survived was a victory. It was all she had now.

She endured.

She stood.

And she was utterly, agonisingly alone.

Chapter 15

'Three minutes to deployment! Three minutes!'

Drake felt his heartbeat quicken. This was it. Equipment and weapons had been given their final checks, all preparations had been made. The vast logistical effort that had started yesterday morning at Langley was now about to come to fruition halfway around the world, less than forty-eight hours later.

Drake was at the rear of the group. As the most experienced at airborne operations, he was serving as the group's jump master. His job was to observe each team member as they exited the aircraft and, if necessary, to assist them. The nightmare scenario would be if someone's harness became snagged on something.

If so, their only chance at survival would be for someone to cut them free. To this end, Drake was wearing a long-bladed combat knife strapped across his chest, its edge wickedly sharp.

It was a relic from his days with the SAS; a memento of his time there. The blade was a distinctive shape, thinner than the average knife, and longer. A deep groove had been cut into the hand guard. In close combat, that groove was designed to snag an opponent's blade and disarm them.

He hoped he wouldn't need it, either for combat or for assisting a comrade in trouble.

Keegan was in front of him, with Dietrich next and

Mason crouched down at the very edge of the exit ramp. He would be jumping tandem with Frost, so he was to be the first out.

He exhaled, hot and uncomfortable. The pressurised jumpsuit was heavy and cumbersome, weighing him down with thermal insulation, oxygen canisters, pressure gauges, altimeters, GPS navigation systems and primary and secondary parachutes. Combined with his personal weapon, spare ammunition, body armour and combat fatigues, he was carrying close to 80 pounds of excess weight. It was starting to tell.

He glanced down at the GPS unit, checking to make sure it was still tracking his position. Khatyrgan's latitude and longitude had been programmed in, leaving him with a series of waypoints leading all the way to his target. As long as he kept to them, they would reach the prison without difficulty.

He blinked as the aircraft's interior lights went out, replaced by dull red units that bathed the world around him in an unnerving crimson glow.

'Hook up,' he said, speaking into his suit-mounted intercom.

Reaching over, he attached his line to the anchor line cable running along the side of the compartment and gave it a couple of hard tugs to make sure it was solid. This was a fixed-line jump, meaning the parachutes would automatically deploy once they exited the aircraft. As long as they were hooked on properly, technology would do the rest.

Inspecting Keegan's line in front of him, he gave the man a slap on the shoulder to indicate he was good to go. Keegan repeated the process with Dietrich, who in turn checked Mason's line. It was a simple thing, but an important one.

With their final preparations made, Drake turned his eye to the indicator panel above the exit ramp. There were three lights – red, amber and green. The red one was already on, warning that deployment was imminent.

A moment later, the yellow light started blinking.

'Ramp coming down!' Drake warned. His heart was hammering away in his chest, and he could feel the adrenalin starting to kick in.

Even within his pressurised suit, he felt the sudden rush of air as the door slid down. The howling shriek of the wind filled his ears, the slipstream roaring by outside at 300 miles per hour. Within seconds, the ambient temperature inside the aircraft dropped to minus 40 degrees Celsius.

The world beyond the ramp was darkness, sheer and absolute. It felt as if they were about to leap into a void of nothingness.

'Get ready!' he called out, still watching the lights. The yellow light was burning steadily now to signify that the ramp was down.

They were only seconds away.

He closed his eyes for a second, sending a silent prayer to whatever deity might be inclined to listen at that moment. He thought of all the things that could go wrong, all the mistakes and problems that could spell doom for them all.

He thought about them, and then he banished them from his mind.

The green light came on.

'Go! Go! Go!'

He watched Mason take a couple of heavy, faltering steps toward the edge, cross his arms in front of him and then pitch forward. And just like that, he and Frost were gone.

Dietrich went next, hesitating for half a second before launching himself out into the darkness.

He saw Keegan stop just for a moment, cross himself, then take a run down the ramp and throw himself out like a long jumper.

Drake was alone. For one brief second, he was alone, staring out into infinite darkness. Somewhere far below lay an impregnable Russian prison, and within it, the woman who was their sole objective tonight.

A woman Cain was prepared to do anything to bring home. A woman for whom Drake was risking five lives in the most dangerous mission of his career. A woman who might well hold the key to his own redemption.

So much depended on one person. He just hoped she was worth it.

More than that, he hoped he was worthy of redemption.

Taking a breath, he strode forward, crossed his arms across his chest and stepped out.

Chapter 16

She lay awake on the hard lumpy mattress, watching her breath slowly misting in the cold air as she exhaled. She couldn't sleep.

She rested her hands behind her head and closed her eyes, trying to imagine the sun, trees, grass, warmth and light, the feel of wind on her skin, being able to run until her legs could no longer carry her.

It was an exercise she practised every once in a while, a means of escape, even if only within her own mind.

But not tonight.

She frowned, struggling to recall the familiar images; what it felt like to be outside, to stand beneath the sky with no walls around her, no ceiling above her, no hard and cold concrete floor beneath.

Nothing came to her. Every time she tried to picture it, she saw the same grey cell. Her world. The only world she knew now.

Have I forgotten?

For the first time in a long time, fear, sudden and uncontrolled, flooded her body. Her mind had been her last bastion, the one aspect of her life that she could still control.

But not now. Now she was a prisoner within as well as without. A cold, hard knot of dread and despair swelled up inside her, twisting and writhing in her guts like a snake.

You let it in, she thought with bitter recrimination. You let it get to you, and you lost the only thing that still mattered. You failed. This place has beaten you.

She squeezed her eyes shut, clutching the thin blanket in a white-knuckle grip as her muscles locked up. She screamed a silent, agonised, furious scream.

Suddenly the cell block reverberated with the harsh clang of a door being thrown open. Too heavy for a cell door. It was one of the bigger security doors that separated the solitary confinement cells from the rest of the building.

The one at the west end of her block had a rusted hinge that grated horribly when it was hauled open. It always made her cringe, knowing there were guards out there. Were they coming for her, or another one of the poor wretches in the adjacent cells?

She strained to listen to the sound of the footsteps, and frowned in confusion. There were three of them. She recognised the heavy tread of Bastard, but the other two weren't familiar. They were moving fast, coming her way.

Was this some new punishment that he had devised? Had he brought new friends along to help him? Did he ever stop?

Not again. Not again so soon. Please.

Her heart started beating faster as she pulled herself out of bed, already tensing her muscles, readying herself for what was coming.

She could hear voices, hushed and muffled. She couldn't make out the words. That only increased her unease. The daily grind of casual violence and abuse no longer bothered her, because it was predictable, and there was a certain security in that.

But deviations from the norm frightened her. She felt

100

out of control, about to be plunged into a new situation that she didn't understand.

What was going on?

They were coming for her. There was no doubt about it now. They were almost at the door. The footsteps were moving fast and urgent.

With her heart pounding, she rose to her feet, clenching her fists. Come on, then. Come on. Get it over with, you bastard. Have your fun and get it over with.

You won't take me so easily this time.

There was a rasp as the deadbolt was thrown back, then suddenly something slammed into the door with such force that it flew inward, old hinges creaking under the abuse.

She jumped, startled by the violent movement. And when her eyes took in the three figures standing there before her, she let out an involuntary gasp of shock.

Chapter 17

Twenty minutes earlier

Drake was floating in a void, a world without shape or dimension. There were no landmarks, no points of reference, nothing.

The parachute harness bit into his shoulders and crotch. Freezing wind whipped past his faceplate, the cold slowly seeping into his limbs despite the layers of thermal insulation between his body and the outside world.

He checked his altimeter: 6,500 feet.

The temperature was 22 degrees below freezing. It had been creeping up as they descended through the cloud layer, but it was still bitterly cold. Wind chill only compounded the problem.

His gaze swept to the GPS unit on his left wrist, though he was forced to wipe away a thin layer of ice to make out the image. They were just over 5 miles from their target, and slightly below their intended glide path. This was going to be close.

After they had exited the aircraft, there had been a few seconds of sickening, tumbling weightlessness before his parachute deployed, ripping him back with such violence that he felt as if he was about to be torn in half. There had been a few more moments of frantic effort as he fought to gain control and stabilise himself, then at last he was able to communicate with the rest of his team over the radio.

Forming up into a loose line known as a 'chalk', they had then begun their descent towards Khatyrgan, using satellite navigation and a fixed series of waypoints to measure their progress.

Covering ground was vital. They could do nothing to stop their descent; but they had to reach the prison before they ran out of altitude.

The first few minutes had seen them lose precious height as they struggled to orient themselves and fight with high-altitude crosswinds. By the time they were lined up and heading in the right direction, they were well below their intended flight line.

Only a sudden and unexpected northerly wind had aided their progress, increasing their speed and allowing them to claw back some precious ground. Now they were beginning their final approach, and there was still a chance they wouldn't even make the roof.

He checked his altimeter and GSP readings again: 5,400 feet, 4 miles to target.

His radio earpiece crackled into life. 'I think I see it.'

It was Keegan.

Squinting into the darkness ahead and below, Drake watched as the ragged strips of cloud gave way, revealing a dizzying panorama stretching out before him.

The terrain around Khatyrgan was formed in a series of undulating ridges and valleys running from north to south, as if some massive hand had been drawn across the landscape. Most of these ridges were no more than 100 feet high, their tops scoured down to the bare rock by devastating winter winds. Only in the most sheltered valleys did anything grow; gnarled pine and spruce, strong and resilient enough to eke out an existence in such a harsh environment.

It was an empty, wind-blown, desolate landscape, and one utterly devoid of people. Not a single light was visible from horizon to horizon, except for the uncompromising square of the prison complex lit up like a beacon in the darkness. It was impossible to miss.

'I see it too,' Drake confirmed, then checked his GPS: 3 miles. 'We're close. Stay tight.'

The imposing walls of the prison drifted closer, and so did the ground. They were travelling at close to 20 knots, but their speed was gradually slowing as they reached lower altitude. He could only pray that it was enough to get them over the wall.

He checked his readings again: 2 miles, 2,100 feet and descending fast.

Khatyrgan had looked an imposing, brutal structure even in the satellite photos, but seeing it with his own eyes, he was daunted. Grim concrete walls rose up from the frozen ground, devoid of windows or features of any kind. Squat watchtowers stood guard at each corner of the building, looking more like fortresses than guard posts, their tops enclosed by observation windows.

Beyond the grim walls he could see the exercise yard; a muddy, snow-streaked patch of earth illuminated by floodlights from several angles. No hope for anyone unlucky enough to land there.

'One mile to target,' he said, checking his readings again. 'Nine hundred feet.'

Christ, this was going to be close.

'Tango spotted,' Keegan reported, his voice flat calm. 'One tango. North-east tower.'

Drake's heart leapt. At least one of the watchtowers was manned. Peering towards it, he was able to make out the shape of a man within the enclosed observation post. He was still too far away to make out anything more detailed, but there was definitely someone up there.

'I see him. Do you have a shot?' he asked.

Keegan hesitated only a moment. 'Roger. I have the shot.'

Drake twisted around, trying to get a look at the veteran sniper, but Keegan was behind and above him, and his own parachute blocked his view.

In any case, he didn't need to see. He could almost imagine Keegan removing his rifle from its secure harness across his chest, checking the magazine and feed mechanism, bringing it up to bear, getting a good sight picture, correcting for wind and vertical momentum, and . . .

'Fire, fire, fire.'

Drake neither saw the flash nor heard the dull thud of the silenced shot. His eyes were focused on the watchtower.

A second or so later, the glass window in front of the guard shattered, and the wall behind him was painted with a sudden spray of blood. Killed instantly by the 7.62 millimetre projectile, he slumped down out of sight, never knowing what had hit him.

And that was it. As easy as pressing a button.

'Tango down,' Keegan reported, his voice as emotionless as a machine. However laid-back and relaxed he acted in daily life, when it came to his job there was no room for joking around. 'The other towers look clear.'

Drake had been so focused on the drama unfolding in the watchtower that he'd almost forgotten about their descent. The altimeter informed him they were at 200 feet, the dark walls of the prison looming up beneath him.

'This is it,' he said over the radio. 'Brace, brace, brace.'

There was nothing more he could do. Everyone was on their own now.

He watched as the north wall of the prison sailed beneath, leaving him with an unobstructed view of the brightly lit exercise yard. Rows of grim, barred windows looked out onto the yard, but he paid no heed.

The south block was coming up fast, but he was so low. Normally he would have pulled back to flare the parachute and slow his velocity, but in this case there was no choice but to keep going. If he slowed down now, he would slam into the unyielding wall with bone-breaking force.

He winced as the wall rushed at him, his feet just clearing the edge of the roof. It was beneath him now, rushing by at close to 20 miles per hour, hard and cold and uncompromising, littered with air vents and snow and accumulated ice.

He yanked back on his control lines. The canopy flared and the rooftop rushed up to meet him.

He landed hard, rolling instinctively to lessen the impact, only to slam into the metal frame of a heating outlet. The structure shuddered, and he stifled a groan as pain blossomed across his back and left shoulder.

It didn't matter. He could still move his limbs. Nothing was broken.

Robbed of its aerodynamic lift, his canopy collapsed in on itself, flopping down a few yards away. It was still a liability if an errant gust of wind caught it. The last thing he wanted was to survive the jump only to be pulled off the edge of the roof to his doom by his own chute.

Grabbing the limp lines and ignoring the pain of his bruised back and shoulder, he pulled the fallen parachute towards him, then unbuckled the harness and dropped it beside the vent. He couldn't see the others, but he wasn't really looking yet. His focus had to be on sorting himself out.

Freed from the parachute, he reached for the MP5 sub-machine gun strapped to his left leg and unzipped the harness holding it in place.

Compact, reliable and superbly designed, Drake had used them countless times over the years and never had cause for complaint.

He had it out within moments, and quickly pressed a magazine into the empty port, racking back the priming handle to chamber the first round.

He was still on internal oxygen. Disengaging the internal air supply, he pulled his clammy, restrictive face mask off and dropped it next to the other discarded gear. Straight away, freezing air and pellets of dry snow attacked his face, numbing his exposed skin.

He was wearing a balaclava beneath the oxygen mask, folded up so that it covered just his head. He wasted no time pulling it down to protect his face.

Kneeling down next to the vent, he did nothing for the next few seconds – just listened and waited, allowing his mind and body to tune into his new environment.

It was quiet. He could hear no alarms, no shouts or warnings, nothing. The only sounds were the pounding of his own heartbeat and the keening wail of the wind. Life in Khatyrgan went on as normal, whatever that was.

Hearing the crunch of footsteps on the roof, he glanced around as two dark figures ducked towards him, weapons out and ready. Like him, their faces were covered, but he recognised Mason and Frost straight away by their size and shape.

'That was interesting,' Mason remarked with a gleam in his eye as he knelt down beside Drake.

'We're in. That's good enough for me,' Drake said, then glanced at Frost. 'How are you feeling?'

Her response was simple but heartfelt. 'I'm never doing that again as long as I live.'

'Deal.' He smiled a little, then hit his radio transmitter. 'Keegan. Dietrich. Sit rep.'

Their radios were burst transmitter units cycling on a random frequency. To tune in, you needed the frequency key, which only Drake and his team knew. Without it, anyone listening in would hear nothing but the occasional static cough – certainly nothing that came close to human voices.

Dietrich replied straight away. 'We're in the south-west tower. Stop fucking around and get over here.'

Drake bit his tongue. Now wasn't the time for petty bickering. Gathering up his discarded gear, he glanced at Mason and Frost. 'We move. Three-metre spread. Go!'

He went first, with Frost behind and Mason bringing up the rear. Keeping low, he darted across the rooftop to the nearby watchtower, using whatever scant cover he could find.

The tower's observation deck was about 10 feet above roof level, accessed via a steel ladder fixed into the brickwork. The steel was corroded in many places, and some of the rungs looked dangerously weak, but nonetheless he made it to the top without incident.

Dietrich was waiting for him on the open parapet at the top. It was impossible to tell since they were both wearing balaclavas, but he could have sworn the man was grinning maliciously.

'Nice of you to join us,' he said, offering Drake a hand. He declined it.

'Where's Keegan?' he asked instead.

Dietrich tilted his head towards the observation room behind him.

'Help the others,' Drake instructed, following the parapet around until he found the single door leading inside. The padlock that had once kept it secure was lying on the floor beside it, snapped by a pair of bolt cutters.

The room within was a simple observation post, basic and unadorned, with a few plastic office chairs dotted around, a small desk in one corner with a telephone on it, and a stairwell in the centre that led to the lower levels. The stairwell was secured by a heavy steel door, no doubt locked from the other side. He had the feeling this place wasn't used much, which was hardly surprising. It was freezing cold and draughty, even with the door shut.

Keegan already had his sniper rifle set up and was sweeping from one tower to the other. He glanced around just for a moment as Drake entered before turning his attention back to the weapon.

'We're clear. No movement in any of the other towers.'

Drake nodded, dumping his parachute, harness and face mask in a heap off to one side. The other two men had already done likewise.

Mason and Frost ducked in through the door a moment later. Like him, they added their discarded gear to the growing pile. It had brought them here and sustained them during the hazardous descent, but now it was dead weight.

A thermite incendiary grenade tossed into the pile when the team pulled out would vaporise everything within several metres, eliminating any evidence of their presence.

Drake took a deep breath, trying to steady his wildly beating heart. As hard as it was to believe, they had landed and made entry without mishap.

Phase Two of their plan was complete. Now it was time for Phase Three – taking out the security system.

And time was of the essence. Mason's earlier warning about the storm front heading their way continued to play on his mind. The last thing he wanted was to rescue Maras only to find their transport was unable to retrieve them.

'Alpha Team, you're up,' Drake said, nodding towards the stairwell. 'Code names only from now on. Move!'

'On it,' Frost replied, withdrawing a small oxyacetylene cutting torch from her pack. They had no time to pick the lock, and using explosives to blow the door was out of the question.

The cutting torch was only a small portable unit, with enough fuel for about sixty seconds of flame. But with luck, that was all they would need.

Drake looked away, shielding his eyes from the blinding light as the torch went to work, rapidly heating the steel around the locking mechanism to combustible temperature. A secondary button on the cutting tool blasted the semi-molten metal with a high-pressure stream of pure oxygen, feeding it in a similar manner to a wood fire.

In under thirty seconds the lock mechanism was melted away, destroyed by the intense heat. They were in.

'Alpha, moving in!' Mason hauled back the door while Frost, gripping her MP5, pushed forward.

'Clear!' she hissed.

Within moments, the two members of Alpha Team had vanished, the sound of their footsteps fading as they descended.

Chapter 18

'That's it,' Frost said, indicating the steel door on their right as they rounded a curve in the staircase. Gripping the handle, she turned it just enough to check the mechanism, then glanced at her companion. 'It isn't locked.'

Mason raised his weapon and gave a single curt nod, indicating he was ready to move.

With a single deft movement, she turned the handle and pulled the door open. It swung inwards, just as the blueprints had said.

Mason was moving as soon as the door opened, and Frost was right behind him, trying to control her wildly beating heart. Her male comrade showed no emotion whatsoever.

They were in a wide corridor, supported by a series of concrete archways and lit by harsh fluorescent lights overhead. Typical of such prisons, the walls were painted half and half – lime green below, and white on top. At least, it had once been white. Years of cigarette smoke, damp and mould had turned them a horrible mottled yellow colour.

'Three doors down, on the left,' she whispered, replaying the route over and over in her mind. She had pored over the designs all day, and on the flight out here, committing every detail to memory.

She glanced up, spotting the telltale red glow of a

security camera mounted between two support arches about halfway along the corridor.

'Camera, one o'clock,' she said quietly.

'Got it.' Mason brought his weapon to bear and squeezed off a single silenced round without breaking stride. There was a thump, a crunch of disintegrating plastic, and the light went out. Frost barely heard the gentle ping as the spent shell casing bounced off the wall beside her.

They were almost at the door. They were committed now; they had to move fast. The guard manning the security room would soon notice that the hallway camera was out of action.

Two steps ahead, Mason gripped the door handle while Frost shouldered her sub-machine gun and withdrew what looked like a bulky plastic pistol from her webbing. It was an M26; a military version of the taser used by police forces worldwide.

Flicking off the trigger guard that served as a safety catch, Frost took a deep breath and gave the man a nod of acknowledgement.

This was it.

There was a click, and the door swung aside to reveal a low, dimly lit room beyond, filled with the soft glow of video monitors and the hum of machinery. Frost wasn't paying attention to that. Her eyes were focused on the guard sitting in front of the video screens, engrossed in a magazine.

Alerted by the sound of the door opening, he glanced up and swung around in his chair, no doubt expecting to see one of his comrades.

Without hesitation, Frost levelled the taser at his chest and pulled the trigger.

There was a loud hiss as the two electrodes leapt from

their housing on a jet of compressed air, their thin conducting wires trailing back into the device itself.

The guard's brows drew together in a frown as the tiny metal prongs pierced his uniform and buried themselves in his skin. He opened his mouth to speak, but his sentence was abruptly cut off as the taser discharged thousands of volts into his body. Robbed of control, he jerked as if he was having a fit, flopping off the chair and landing hard on the floor.

The torment carried on for a few more seconds, during which he could manage nothing more than a gurgling, agonised moan. He was paralysed, physically and mentally; out of the fight before it even began.

'Secure him,' Frost instructed, replacing the taser in her webbing. As Mason went to work cuffing the incapacitated guard with plastic cable ties, the woman's sharp eyes scanned the room, her mind quickly analysing and processing what she saw.

It was a basic security set-up – six monitors, each cycling through the feeds coming from various closed-circuit security cameras dotted around the facility. A control board on the desk in front of her allowed the user to access specific cameras if necessary. She guessed each monitor had access to four or five cameras.

Some were suffering from pretty severe signal degradation, no doubt due to age and faulty wiring.

This room also served as the prison's communications centre. A big old-fashioned radio unit in one corner, no doubt tied into a high-gain antenna on the roof somewhere, provided the facility's only contact with the outside world. Disabling it was as easy as slicing through the power cables and pouring the remainder of the guard's cup of coffee into a vent in the side.

Data backup was handled by a pair of high-capacity

hard drives busily humming away in one corner, recording everything that came in from the various feeds. They were perhaps the only pieces of sophisticated technology she had seen so far.

Ten seconds later she had cut power to both units, removed them from the metal storage rack they were resting in, and was busy dismantling them to reach the disk drives within. As soon as she had access to the disks themselves, she would use the cutting torch to reduce them to so much molten slag.

Interrupting her work for a moment, she hit the radio pressel at her throat. 'Alpha to Bravo. You're clear to move. Good luck.'

Chapter 19

'Copy that. Bravo, en route.' Drake let out a breath and turned to Dietrich. 'Let's go.'

They were moving within moments, quickly descending the metal ladder to rooftop level once more and sprinting along the top of the western block to the north-west tower.

Once more they found a ladder leading up to the observation area. Clambering up and shouldering their weapons, they spotted the guard taken down by Keegan during the descent. His single shot had done its work with deadly efficiency, splattering a good portion of the man's brains over the floor and walls. Flakes of snow were drifting in through the shattered window, already coating the exposed surfaces with a fine dusting.

Ignoring the grisly sight, Drake went straight for the stairwell door. Much to his relief, the guard on duty in the watchtower hadn't bothered to lock it behind him when he came up here.

'We're in luck.'

Dietrich hit his radio pressel. 'Bravo to Alpha, we're going down. What's the guard situation in north block?'

'Wait one.' Silence for several seconds. 'No activity on the video feeds. There's a lot of black spots, though. Watch your backs.'

'Thanks for the advice,' Dietrich replied in a sour tone. 'Out.'

Grasping the door handle, Drake hauled it open, revealing a spiral staircase that wound its way down into the bowels of the prison. Rather than bare concrete, the walls had been painted a horrible lime green colour. There were splashes of it on the steps where the painters had been sloppy, and in other places the paint was peeling and cracked. Electric lights were fixed into the wall at regular intervals, burning harsh and bright.

'Delta, any movement?' Drake asked.

'Nothing,' Keegan replied. 'It's all quiet.'

'Copy that.' Shouldering his MP5, he glanced at Dietrich. 'Ready?'

He received a curt nod in response.

Drake went first, his feet echoing on the bare concrete steps as he descended. He was hot inside his thermal suit now as a combination of nervous energy and physical exertion took their toll. Tiny beads of sweat trickled down his back, and the fabric of his balaclava was warm and clammy against his face, but he resisted the urge to remove it. Masks had to stay on until they were well clear of the prison.

His senses were acutely heightened, taking in every detail of his surroundings. The slight weathering on the stone steps where countless sets of feet had passed over the years, the barely audible sigh of Dietrich's breathing, the rattle of the weapon as he moved, the growing ambient warmth as they approach the inhabited section of the prison.

One of the lights mounted in the wall was flickering and cutting out, plunging the stairwell into shadow every couple of seconds. Drake averted his gaze as they passed. The light hurt his eyes, exacerbating the headache that still dogged him.

The stairs were strewn with rubbish – cigarette butts,

torn pieces of paper, bits of chewing gum casually spat out, crushed Styrofoam coffee cups . . . It was a mess. It reminded him of the kind of dilapidated public areas found in shitty council estates back home.

'What a dump,' Dietrich remarked, apparently thinking the same thing.

'I'll leave them a memo.'

In the security centre, the cutting tool had done its work well. The two hard-drive units had been reduced to a pile of charred, smoking debris that nobody could ever possibly salvage.

The security guard had been rendered unconscious for the next several hours courtesy of a shot of Etorphine from Mason. Originally designed for knocking out African elephants, it had proved remarkably effective against humans, and the CIA had soon found a use for it.

'Anything?' Mason asked, having taken up position by the door to cover the corridor beyond.

With the room secure, Frost had settled herself in front of the security monitors in the hopes of aiding Drake and Dietrich. She couldn't see either man yet because there were no cameras in the stairwell, but there was good coverage of the cell block they were heading for.

Whoever had installed the security cameras here was either drunk or an idiot, she'd soon decided. There were blind spots all over the place, and cameras that were either out of action or defective to the point where their output was unrecognisable.

She shook her head. 'It's all quiet. No wonder this guy was bored,' she added, holding up the porn magazine the guard had been so engrossed in.

Mason cracked a smile. 'Anything good?'

'Only you could think of tits at a time like this.'

He shrugged. 'I'm all about the articles these days.'

Ignoring him, she turned her attention back to the screens, then froze when she saw the grainy image of a prison guard on one of the monitors.

They had reached the base of the stairwell. Beyond, according to the blueprints, lay the security station for the western cell block, with the master switches controlling the electric cell doors.

The solitary confinement cells were secured with old-fashioned steel doors and simple deadbolts, ensuring they could only be opened one at a time. But the two general population blocks followed the standard prison model of barred cells opened electrically via a remote access point. It was a necessary function to allow them to move large numbers of prisoners within a reasonable time frame, like during exercise breaks or shower visits.

It also ensured that any would-be escapees couldn't free their comrades. With heavy locked doors at each end of the block, any prisoner who somehow made it out of his cell would have nowhere to go.

Drake was just reaching for the door handle when his radio crackled.

'Bravo, you've got an incoming tango,' Frost warned, the urgency in her voice obvious despite the static.

Drake felt his heartbeat shift into high gear. 'Where?'

'Heading north through the general population block. He must be walking the perimeter. Where are you?'

'At the base of the tower, about to move.'

'Recommend you hold position until he passes by.'

'How long do we have?'

'Thirty seconds, maybe less,' she replied. 'It'll take him at least five minutes to do another circuit.'

Dietrich leaned in closer to speak to Drake. 'Perfect. We take him prisoner and use him to find Maras.'

'Twenty-five seconds.'

Drake was torn. It was quite a gamble to try to subdue an armed man without making any noise. But then again, there were thirty-two solitary confinement cells on this block, and searching all of them would waste precious time. Plus, the inhabitants were unlikely to react well to a pair of armed men in full assault gear.

'Twenty seconds.'

'Drake, don't be a fucking coward,' Dietrich hissed, staring intently at his comrade. 'This is our best chance.'

'Fifteen seconds. Bravo One, talk to me. What's going on?'

Drake chewed his lip, knowing he had only moments to make his decision. 'All right,' he conceded at last. 'We're going for it. Alpha One, let me know when he's outside the door.'

'Copy that. I hope you know what you're doing.'

Dietrich nodded, checking that the safety on his MP5 was disengaged and the under-barrel flashlight switched on. Drake gripped the door handle again, getting ready to throw it open.

'Ten seconds,' Frost said. 'He's unlocking the security door at the north end of the block.'

Sure enough, they could hear the clank of keys in a lock just outside their own door. According to the blue-prints, each cell block was secured at both ends with heavy steel doors, designed to contain prisoners in the event of a riot. Their cutting torches could do nothing against 2 inches of solid steel.

Drake glanced at his companion. 'Remember, no English.'

The older man gave him a look of pure disdain.

'Five seconds. Door open.'

Taking a deep breath, Drake gripped his weapon tighter with his free hand. The man on the other side wouldn't be expecting them. He would be bored and tired, and slow to react.

They had the drop on him. They could do this.

'Now.'

Unlatching the door, he pulled it open with a hard yank, feeling old rusty hinges grating and rasping.

Dietrich was first through, and Drake was right behind him, weapon up at his shoulder, eyes searching the dimly lit room for a target.

It wasn't hard to find one.

The guard in question was a beast of a man, easily weighing 300 pounds and standing at least 6 foot 4. His hands looked as if they could crush boulders, his neck was thick and bull-like, his face wide and fleshy. He was dressed in a fur hat, military boots and a thick, heavy winter overcoat that further enhanced his massive frame.

He froze at the sudden clang of the door being thrown open, and for a good second or so stared open-mouthed at the two weapons now trained on him, squinting into the twin flashlight beams shining right in his face.

By the time he finally thought to reach for the weapon at his hip, it was far too late.

'Don't fucking think about it!' Dietrich hissed in Russian. 'Down on your knees! Down now!'

He was being too aggressive, Drake knew. People don't react well to having guns waved in their faces at the best of times, and if their captor is screaming and ranting, the primitive, illogical part of their brain takes over.

That could spell disaster in a situation like this. They needed the man calm and compliant, not panicky and unpredictable. Especially when he weighed almost as much as both of them combined.

Still, this guy was no mild-mannered civilian. Overcoming his shock, the guard did a quick assessment of the situation and decided that resistance in this case would equal instant death. With some difficulty, he lowered his massive frame to the ground.

'Hands behind your head!' Dietrich ordered. 'Do it!'

What was with him? Drake wondered. Dietrich was a veteran of operations like this. Why was he suddenly acting like a rookie in his first firefight?

Again the giant complied, eyes flicking between the pair of flashlights. They were careful to keep the beams in his face and eyes. If he couldn't see them properly, he was less likely to make some foolish move.

While Drake kept him covered, Dietrich quickly removed the giant's side arm from the holster at his hip, ejected the magazine and tossed the weapon into a corner.

Reaching into his pocket, Dietrich unfolded a printed photograph of Maras and held it right up at the guard's face. Was his hand shaking?

'Where is this woman?' he demanded.

The giant's eyes opened wide in shock, his mouth gaping open to reveal a set of yellowy, nicotine-stained teeth.

'Where is she?' Dietrich repeated, brandishing the sub-machine gun for emphasis. 'Tell me or you die now!'

'In solitary confinement,' the giant replied at last, his voice sounding like boulders tumbling down a mountainside. He pointed to another door on the east side of the room like the one he'd just come through.

'Which cell?'

'Sixty-two.'

Dietrich folded the picture and replaced it in his pocket, then took a couple of steps back. 'Up! Get up!'

Slowly the giant rose to his feet again, keeping his hands behind his head while his dark eyes surveyed both men. Clearly he was weighing up his chances of taking one or both of them out.

'Take us there,' Dietrich ordered before he had any further thoughts. 'Now! Move!'

Chapter 20

'Come on, Ryan,' Frost whispered, her eyes glued to the monitors as the three men advanced quickly through the second security door and into the solitary confinement block. They were marching the giant of a guard between them, Dietrich keeping him covered while Drake swept the corridor ahead.

He appeared compliant, but what if he made a break for it? What if he managed to grab a weapon? What if she was forced to watch the two of them gunned down over a grainy closed-circuit security system?

She tried to push those thoughts aside. Drake and Dietrich were experienced operatives, well trained and competent. They could handle this. They could handle anything.

But as hard as she tried, the fear wouldn't abate.

'Come on. Hurry.'

The tension was unbearable. Every second they stayed here increased their chances of being compromised. A dozen armed guards could come walking down that corridor at any moment, and even with Cole watching her back, she felt jumpy and paranoid.

What if they were caught? What would happen to them? What would happen to her? She was a woman, after all. The possibility of capture, interrogation and even torture was something she had understood and accepted on an intellectual level, without pondering too deeply. She hadn't wanted it to impede her performance. But now, sitting here, it was impossible to avoid thinking about.

She wanted to leave right now. She wanted to get out of this shithole and be on a warm plane heading back to the States.

But they couldn't leave. Not until the job was done.

They had come all this way for Maras. They were putting their lives on the line for her. They couldn't leave until they found her.

'I hope you're worth the trouble, you bitch.'

Backing up against the wall outside Cell No. 62, Dietrich pointed to indicate they had found the right one. Like the others, it was barred by a reinforced steel door, scarred by rust in places, with a slot for observation or sliding in trays of food. The door was secured with a simple deadbolt.

Nothing fancy, nothing elaborate. No way out.

Drake's heart was beating wildly. They had found it! After all the planning and worrying, thousands of miles of flying and a nerve-shredding infiltration of a high-security prison, they had reached their goal at last. Yesterday Maras had just been a face on a photograph, now he was about to meet her in the flesh.

Gripping the MP5 with his right hand, he seized the deadbolt and drew it back, then raised his boot and delivered a single kick powerful enough to send the door flying inwards.

His weapon was up in an instant, flashlight beam playing across the cramped cell beyond. Sink, toilet, bare brick walls and concrete floor.

Then his eyes fastened on the woman standing in the midst of it all. His breath caught in his throat.

'Jesus Christ.'

* * *

Two floors below, and entirely unknown to Frost, a young prison guard was pacing the wide, badly lit hallway, struggling to hold in check his mounting irritation.

'Where the fuck is he?' he muttered, waiting impatiently for that big bastard Lopukhin to return from his patrol. It should have taken him no more than five minutes to walk the blocks.

The prisoners he could handle; it was the other guards who were his biggest enemy, especially Lopukhin. The man was a nightmare to work with, surly and aggressive, and as vicious as an Arctic wolf with anyone who crossed him. He had cringed when he found out he'd drawn the night shift with him.

Stubbing out his cigarette, he picked up his radio and hit the transmit button. 'Lopukhin. Where are you?'

His request was met with nothing but static.

He frowned, an edge of concern now overshadowing the irritation within him. 'Lopukhin. Where are you? Respond.'

They had found her all right, but the prisoner standing before him bore little resemblance to the vibrant, strikingly beautiful woman he'd seen in the picture.

Her blonde hair, cut short and neat in the photograph, was now a tangled and greasy mass falling on either side of her face. Her skin was deathly pale, sallow and streaked with dirt. She had lost weight as well, the impression enhanced by her oversized clothes, clearly intended for a man. Her standard prison-issue shirt and trousers were filthy and threadbare, covered in grime and stained with blood and God knew what else.

But it was her – of that he was sure. Her appearance might have changed, but her eyes hadn't. He would have recognised those eyes anywhere.

She was staring at him with those eyes at that very moment, her gaze filled with a strange mixture of surprise, curiosity, apprehension and wariness. And something else; something he couldn't consciously identify, but which made a far deeper impression. Somehow he felt like an animal being observed by a predator; a predator still undecided about whether or not to strike.

For a good second or two, neither one of them said a word or moved a muscle. The smell of stale sweat, blood, dampness and mould permeated the air inside the tiny cell. Jesus, what had she endured in this place? How long had she been here?

Dietrich broke the silence at last. 'Maras?'

Her eyes opened wider, all other emotions washed away by complete and utter shock. But she didn't speak.

'Is your name Maras?' Dietrich demanded in Russian. 'Identify yourself or we'll leave you here!'

'It is,' she finally said, croaking the words as if the mere act of speaking was alien to her.

'We're here to get you out.'

Her eyes narrowed with suspicion. 'Who sent you?'

'No time. We're leaving.' He gestured with his weapon for her to come out of the cell. 'Hurry! Move!'

Her gaze flicked from Dietrich to Drake, before finally resting on the guard they had taken prisoner.

And in that instant, a change came over her, as if someone had flicked a switch inside her mind. The surprise and wariness vanished, replaced by something altogether different – something primal, something brutal, something cold and hard and deadly.

Then, without warning, she sprang forward, seizing the long-bladed knife sheathed at Drake's thigh. The blade came free of its metal scabbard with a harsh rasp, gone before he could even make a move.

126

Then, in one smooth motion born from years of practice and experience, she swept the knife up into the Russian's exposed throat.

There was no stopping the wickedly sharp blade as it cleaved its way through the soft tissue, destroying his windpipe before carrying on upwards into his skull. The man could do nothing but let out a horrible gurgling groan, his hands scrabbling at the deadly blade as it sank deeper.

His legs gave way beneath him and he collapsed, a mountain of flesh no longer obeying the commands sent by his brain. She went down with him, savagely yanking the blade free, severing vital arteries and coating her face and arms in a fine spray of blood. Raising the weapon up again, she plunged it deep into his chest, then twisted it free with enraged strength before swinging again, her eyes wild with vengeance and murder.

'Shit!' Drake growled, amazed and appalled by the speed and ferocity of her sudden attack. She had taken the weapon before he even knew what had happened.

You fucking idiot! he thought, berating himself for letting his guard down. She could have killed you! Didn't Cain warn you about her?

'Crazy bitch!' Dietrich said, drawing a taser from his belt kit and flicking off the safety. Imprisonment here must have broken her, driven her over the edge into insanity.

Well, they would just have to stun her and carry her out. Not the ideal solution, but probably for the best. At least they could keep her under control. He didn't give a shit what condition they brought her back in, as long as she wasn't dead.

Maras cared nothing for what either man did.

She was in her own world now; a world of pure,

hateful, bloodthirsty rage. Every rational instinct in her body had been driven out. Again she plunged the blade in, feeling it slip between two ribs to strike deep into internal organs. She had done it many times before. She knew just the right angle to strike from to ensure the blade didn't foul.

Over and over, images of the torments and humiliations she had endured at this man's hands flashed through her mind like lightning bursts, whirling together into a maelstrom of unstoppable, uncontrollable fury.

Bastard's feeble struggles had subsided, his eyes blank and staring as she pulled the knife out and raised it up for another strike, blood dripping from the blade.

She couldn't stop herself. She couldn't control herself. She didn't want to.

Weakness will not be in my heart. Fear will not be in my creed. I will show no mercy.

But suddenly her arm jerked to a halt, her wrist was caught in an iron grip, preventing her from dealing another blow. Jerked out of her rage, she swung around to find herself staring down the barrel of a weapon.

Her mind did an instant threat assessment. An MP5, 9 mm sub-machine gun, excellent weapon for close-quarters action. Thirty-round magazine capacity, firing either full metal jacket or hollow-point projectiles. She guessed FMJs for greater penetrating power. Effective range, anything up to 200 metres. The safety was off, his finger on the trigger.

The other man nearby also had a weapon trained on her. She couldn't take out both of them. No chance.

'Let go of the knife,' Drake said in English, speaking slow and calm. 'Let go now.'

Hesitating for a moment, she released the blade and

allowed it to clatter to the ground. Her work was done. He was dead.

Adrenalin surged through her veins, investing her muscles with a strength she hadn't felt in years. She felt alive

For the first time in a long time, she felt alive.

Releasing her wrist, Drake took a step back, still covering her with the MP5. She was breathing hard, her face and clothes stained crimson with the dead man's blood, her lips drawn back in what almost seemed like a feral smile. Her eyes were pools of ice in that sea of blood, staring at him, watching him like a predator, boring right through him.

She was horrific, nightmarish. A demon, an evil spirit made real.

Maras. A goddess of war.

A radio unit crackled with static, and a muffled voice said something in Russian. It took Drake a moment to realise it was coming from the dead man's jacket.

Kneeling down and unzipping the blood-soaked garment, Dietrich retrieved the walkie-talkie he hadn't even realised was there. Once more it crackled into life, and a voice spoke in Russian, sounding more urgent this time.

'Shit!' he hissed.

Drake frowned. 'What is it?'

'It must be another guard on patrol. He's asking where this guy is.' He glared at Maras. 'You stupid bitch. You've compromised us!'

Drake swore under his breath. Of all the bad timing.

Dietrich had searched the man. Why hadn't he found the radio? Why hadn't he realised it was there?

He had little time to dwell on this issue. Other prisoners had been awoken by the commotion, and were starting to realise something was wrong. The grim order of their world had been disturbed, kindling the mad, wild hope of salvation. Shouts of confusion, fear and pleading desperation began to echo down the corridor, coming from a dozen places at once.

'We have what we need,' Drake decided, trying to ignore the growing cacophony around them. They hadn't come here for these people. Whether they deserved to be here or not, this was where they were staying.

He looked at the woman. 'You speak English, I assume?'

She nodded, saying nothing.

'Good. We can get you out, but only if you do exactly as we tell you. Understand?'

Another nod.

He raised his weapon, keeping it trained on her. 'All right. Move.'

As they hurried towards the stairwell that would take them back up to the roof, Drake hit his radio pressel. 'Bravo to Alpha. We have the target. We're extracting now. Meet us at the rendezvous, and tell the chopper to start his run.'

'Copy that, Bravo,' Frost replied. 'Alpha is en route.'

Chapter 21

Pushing herself away from the security station, Frost grabbed her weapon and flicked off the safety. Her last act before leaving was to take aim at the trunk cable carrying video feeds from the security cameras scattered throughout the facility. A couple of silenced rounds destroyed the main junction box, rendering all six monitors useless.

'Come on, Frost,' Mason hissed. 'Move!'

'All done,' she replied, turning to follow. Switching frequencies on her radio, she selected the channel that would connect her to Zulu, the transport chopper standing by a couple of miles distant. 'Zulu, this is Bravo Team. Begin your run. I say again, begin your run.'

'Copy that, Bravo,' the pilot's crackly voice replied a moment later. 'Zulu is inbound. ETA, five minutes.'

'Copy that. Five minutes.'

As Mason ducked out of the room, she was right behind him. She knew the route back up to the tower like the back of her hand. Turn right at the intersection, follow the main corridor along until . . .

They both froze as a figure emerged from the stairwell at the far end of the corridor. He was a young man, perhaps in his mid-twenties, with short dark hair and green eyes that stared at them in blank, uncomprehending shock.

Mason was first to react.

'Contact!' he warned, dropping to one knee and bringing his MP5 to bear.

At the same moment, the guard turned and ducked back into the stairwell, realising the futility of trying to take on two armed opponents in full body armour.

A short burst leapt from Mason's weapon, the suppressor eliminating all sound save for the clean metallic click as the working parts drew a fresh round into the breech.

It was a hasty shot against a moving target, but at least one of the rounds found its mark, impacting his torso with a dull wet thud. A cloud of blood painted the lime green wall behind him, before he shoved his way through the door and disappeared into the stairwell.

'Shit.' Mason hit his radio again. 'Alpha Two to all teams, we have contact. One tango still active.'

A moment later, an emergency klaxon started blaring throughout the building. The injured guard must have made it to an alarm point.

'What's going on, Alpha?' Keegan demanded, his voice low and urgent. 'I hear alarms down there.'

'We're compromised!' Mason snapped, hurrying for the stairs up to the observation level.

Frost was right behind him.

Drake's heart was beating overtime as the three of them hurried to the security door at the west end of the solitary confinement block. Blaring alarms mixed with the plaintive cries of the prisoners still locked in their cells. This situation was unravelling fast.

'Alpha team, get to the rendezvous,' he ordered. His radio microphone used the vibrations in his throat to transmit what he was saying, meaning he could speak and be heard clearly even in the chaos around him. 'Delta, you're weapons free. Get ready to cover us.'

'Copy that. Weapons free.'

Drake pointed to the security door up ahead and glanced at Dietrich. 'Get it open. Hurry.'

Dietrich had taken the key chain from the dead guard. Skidding to a halt in front of the imposing security door, he fumbled with the chain, vainly searching for the right one. He wasn't familiar with this place, didn't know the locks, and there were a lot of keys to choose from.

'Work faster,' Drake implored him, keeping one eye on the door at the far end of the block and one eye on Maras. The woman was standing a few paces away, saying nothing, her gaze flicking between both men and their weapons.

'Shit!' Dietrich growled, pulling a key out and trying another one. Panic-stricken haste was making his hands tremble, further hampering his efforts.

'Don't panic. Just focus and get it done,' Drake said, forcing calm into his voice. Screaming and shouting would only make things worse.

Suddenly the door at the far end of the block swung open on rusty hinges, revealing three guards in various states of undress. But all three were armed with AK-47 assault rifles – a devastating infantry weapon that had been the mainstay of the Russian military for the past fifty years. There was no such thing as non-lethal force in this place.

'Contact!' Drake yelled, sighting the nearest target and snapping off a burst at his centre mass. At this range, there was no chance of more accurate aiming, especially with an MP5. They were great weapons for close-quarters battle, but at anything over 50 metres their lack of stopping power became apparent.

His aim was true, and the man crumpled with blood painting his chest and abdomen. The other two immediately threw themselves down and started capping off wild, uncontrolled bursts in Drake's general direction. Their aim was all over the place, with 7.62 millimetre rounds howling off concrete walls and doors on both sides of the corridor.

One of them ricocheted off a fire extinguisher mounted about halfway along the block, hitting with sufficient force to burst the pressurised casing and send a cloud of carbon dioxide vapour spewing out.

'Maras, get down!' Drake ordered, fearful she might get caught in the crossfire.

He needn't have worried. Unlatching the cell door nearest her, she hauled it open to form a makeshift shield and ducked in behind it. The emaciated wretch within had backed up against the wall, cowering in the corner, eyes blank and staring from cavernous sockets.

Her move proved to be fortuitous, as several heavy-calibre slugs whanged off the steel door in the next few seconds, leaving visible dents in the metalwork.

Taking advantage of the momentary diversion, Drake pulled one of the thermite incendiary grenades from his webbing, yanked the pin out and hurled it down the corridor with all the force he could command.

A second or so later the device detonated with a bright flash, followed by a vicious orange glow as the thermite compound within burned at 2,500 degrees Celsius.

Such grenades were more useful for destroying equipment than as actual weapons. Nonetheless, the flash produced on ignition was bright enough to temporarily blind anyone looking straight at it, and the extreme temperatures and noxious fumes produced by the thermal reaction would block the hallway for a good minute or so.

For good measure, he emptied the remainder of his magazine in a long, sustained burst. He couldn't tell if he'd hit anything, but it might have been enough to keep their heads down.

Still, their reprieve wouldn't last long.

'I need that fucking door open now,' he warned, turning towards the older man and ejecting the spent magazine. The time for calm, measured responses was long gone. Dietrich was panicking and fumbling with what should have been a simple task.

'Shut up! Shut up!' Dietrich hissed, jamming another key into the lock. This time it turned, and there was a faint click as the lock disengaged.

No sooner had the door swung open than Dietrich grunted in surprise as something hit him from behind, spinning him around as he fell through the doorway. It took him a moment to work out what had happened, but when he saw the blood on the floor and realised it was his own, the truth dawned on him.

'I'm hit!' Dietrich called out, his voice trembling with shock.

Drake ignored his plea. He couldn't do anything for the man until they were under cover. Grabbing Maras by the arm, he shoved her through the doorway. This was all for nothing if she got killed by a stray round.

He went last, pulling the heavy door shut behind him with a resounding clang. No sooner had he done so than he heard a couple of dull metallic dings as AK rounds slammed into the reinforced frame.

Dietrich was on the ground, struggling to sit up. He had been hit twice by AK rounds, first in the centre of his back and then again in his left thigh. His armoured vest had stopped the first round, though the force of the impact would likely leave heavy bruising and possibly have cracked a couple of ribs. Still, it wasn't a serious injury.

It was the leg wound that worried him. Drake knelt down beside him to quickly examine it. It was a clean exit, the round passing through the soft tissue of his thigh. It had done a good deal of damage on the way out, but he didn't think it had shattered the bone or severed the femoral artery. If it had, he would have been dead within a matter of minutes.

'It's bad!' he said through gritted teeth. 'Shit!'

'Calm down, for fuck's sake,' Drake commanded him. 'It's a flesh wound. It hasn't broken the bone. Can you walk?'

Medical attention would have to wait for now. If they didn't get out of here, they were as good as dead.

'Leave him,' Maras said, staring down at the injured man without emotion. 'He won't make it.'

'Shut up!' Drake snapped, then turned his attention back to his comrade. 'Jonas, we need to go right now. We'll sort you out once we're clear of the prison, but you have to help us. Can you walk?'

He was breathing hard from a combination of pain and exertion, but he managed a nod. He looked at the door again. 'They'll be following us.'

Drake nodded, an idea already forming.

'I'll take care of it.' He pointed at Maras again. 'You. If you want to get through this alive, help him up the stairs. He'll show you the way.'

'He'll slow us down,' she warned. 'They'll catch up and kill us all.'

'Just get it done. Leave the rest up to me.'

Standing undecided for a moment, she at last resigned herself to the inevitable, hooked one hand beneath Dietrich's arm and pulled him to his feet. He let out a

136

cry of pain as the weight rested on his injured leg, but remained defiantly on his feet.

Struggling with his considerable weight, Maras looked at Drake. 'What about you?'

'Don't worry about me. Just get up there,' he implored her. 'Go now!'

As she pulled the injured man towards the stairs, leaving a trail of blood in their wake, Drake snatched up the keys dropped by Dietrich and made for the door leading to the western cell block.

Unlocking it, he hauled it open and turned to the controls for the cell doors. Essentially just a series of levers controlling the electric locks on each cell, there were a good forty or so laid out on a numbered control board. Starting from what he hoped was the south end of the block, he went to work, pulling each lever in turn.

It didn't take long for the results to become apparent. He could hear loud metallic clangs echoing down the massive enclosed space, followed by frantic and confused shouts as prisoners suddenly found themselves released.

He had opened at least twenty cells by the time he heard the click of keys in the door leading from the solitary confinement block. The two surviving guards must have fought their way past the burning remains of the incendiary grenade, and were now eager to find the man who had thrown it.

He'd done enough here. Abandoning his task, he turned and rushed through the stairwell door, pulling it closed behind him.

Chapter 22

'Ninety-nine bottles of beer on the wall, ninety-nine bottles of beer . . .'

Sitting motionless in his sniping position and oblivious to the chaos around him, Keegan was a picture of calm as he slowly moved the sniper rifle from tower to tower, his keen eyes scanning for a target while he hummed a tune under his breath. It helped to keep him relaxed, and he needed it tonight.

The shit had well and truly hit the fan now. The alert had gone out, klaxons and sirens filling the night air with their harsh wails. Moments earlier the sharp crackle of gunfire had echoed up through the cell blocks. Who was shooting who? He didn't know. Confusion was everywhere.

The weather conditions were deteriorating by the minute. He could feel the wind getting up and the temperature dropping as a storm front came in from the north-west. The snowflakes were also heavier and more numerous.

If they delayed much longer, they might not make it out at all.

His comrades could well be fighting for their lives a couple of floors below him, but that, like the weather, was out of his hands. The best – and indeed only – way to help them was to hold his position and stick to the plan. That was what they were counting on him to do.

Operations like this broke down when people started panicking and acting on their own initiative without communicating with the rest of their team. No way was that going to happen today.

Out of the corner of his eye he caught movement in the north-east tower, and swung the rifle around, increasing the magnification on his scope to get a better look. It was a guard, eyes wide with panic, clutching an AK assault rifle as he stared down into the exercise yard. No doubt he expected prisoners to come crashing from one of the cell blocks at any moment.

Keegan wondered if he'd been ordered up there or if he had just gone there to survey the situation. How organised were their enemies? Had they planned for this? Was it part of their training, or were they running around in confusion and panic?

Whatever the reason, Keegan's response was the same.

'Take one down, pass it around . . .' he mumbled, adjusting his aim to compensate for crosswind.

Perfect sight picture.

Allowing himself to relax, he squeezed the trigger. The rifle kicked back hard into his shoulder, and half a second later the top of the man's head exploded in a spray of blood and brain matter.

Good kill.

'Ninety-eight bottles of beer on the wall . . .'

He didn't enjoy killing, but he did feel a certain satisfaction that came from exercising the skills he had spent long years perfecting.

Above the blare of alarms, he could hear the clamour of footsteps in the stairwell behind him. 'Alpha Team, sit rep,' he spoke into his radio.

It was Frost who answered. 'Alpha's in the stairwell. Hold your fire.'

A moment later, Frost and Mason emerged into the observation area, breathless and sweating.

'Good to see you again,' Keegan said without taking his eyes away from the scope.

'Good to be here,' Mason replied, keying his radio. 'Alpha's at the rendezvous point. Bravo, what's your situation?'

Dietrich's reply was gasped out through laboured breaths. 'Bravo Two. We're on the . . . stairwell . . . heading up. Get ready to cover us!'

'Copy that. You okay?'

'I'm hit, but . . . still in the fight. Where's . . . the chopper?'

'It's inbound right now. We're—'

Mason's sentence was cut off as a burst of automatic weapons fire sliced into the observation area, shattering the windows around him. Freezing wind and dry flakes of snow whipped through the now open platform as all three of them hit the deck.

'Shit! We're taking fire.' Frost had one hand pressed against a cut above her left eye where an errant fragment of glass had gashed her.

'Keegan, you see the shooter?' Mason called out.

Waiting until the incoming fire slackened off, Keegan peered over the edge of the concrete parapet long enough to scan the other three towers. Another burst of fire was enough to make him duck back down, but it didn't matter. He'd seen what he had to.

'South-east tower,' he said calmly, reaching up to grab something resting on the table above him.

His hand came back clutching a small metal control unit with a long wire snaking out, that Mason recognised immediately as an M57 Firing Device. Commonly referred to as a Clacker, it served as the standard remote trigger for Claymore anti-personnel mines.

'Fire in the hole,' he announced, flicking off the safety catch and depressing the simple flat trigger.

A bright flash followed by a concussive boom signalled the destruction of the south-east watchtower, along with anyone unfortunate enough to be inside it.

Peering over the parapet once more, Keegan nodded in satisfaction. A trio of Claymore anti-personnel mines daisy-chained together inside the observation area had done their work well, blasting the structure apart from the inside and shredding anyone within the blast radius.

The injured man was a heavy burden as she fought her way up the spiral staircase, practically dragging him along with her. He was flagging badly, weak from shock, pain and blood loss. His armour and equipment was dead weight that they couldn't afford.

For that matter, so was he.

She was breathing hard from her exertions, and only now did she realise how weak she had become. Training and exercising daily, it had been easy to convince herself that she had maintained some semblance of her former fitness. But years of poor food, beatings and injuries, and no opportunities to move around had taken their toll.

She couldn't help him. She'd be lucky to help herself in this condition.

Missing a step, Dietrich stumbled and fell, letting out a cry of pain as he landed on his injured leg. He lost his grip on the sub-machine gun, which clattered down the steps behind them.

'Get up!' she yelled, anger and frustration welling up inside. This was taking too long. He was slowing them down. They could be out of here by now if it wasn't for this idiot.

141

He was done. Better that he died now before he got them all killed.

Letting go of him, she turned to reach for the fallen weapon.

The click of a hammer being drawn back stopped her, and she turned to look at the injured man again. He was covering her with a USP .45 automatic pistol.

'Don't fucking think about it,' he growled in Russian. He spoke the language well, but she detected a faint accent. German or Austrian, she thought. A proud people, an arrogant people. Twice they had tried to conquer this country, and twice they had failed.

She did a threat assessment. A USP .45-calibre pistol. Twelve-round magazine. Effective range, about 50 metres in the right hands. Massively powerful. A popular choice for Special Forces operatives.

But it was a heavy weapon, and its owner was already weak from blood loss. He was struggling just to hold it steady. Broken down and diminished as she was, she could still disarm him before he managed to get a shot off.

She tensed up, muscles readying themselves for the sudden movement that she would soon require.

Weakness will not be in my heart. Fear will not be in my creed. I will show no mercy. I will never hesitate.

Before she could act, she was interrupted by the sound of footsteps on the stairs below. She turned in time to see the other man charge round the corner.

'Get up, Dietrich,' he said, grabbing the injured man and hauling him to his feet once more. 'We're almost there, mate.'

He managed the weight easily, she noticed with a flash of anger. He was young, strong, healthy, well fed and well rested.

The sharp crack of weapons fire echoed from below,

mingled with confused shouts and agonised screams. A furious battle of some kind was raging, and she could guess the cause.

A riot was brewing. He had unleashed something beyond anyone's ability to control.

'What did you do?' Dietrich asked as they resumed the painful ascent, leaving spots of blood on the concrete steps.

'They've got bigger problems than us to deal with now.' Drake pointed upwards. 'Maras, up the stairs. Move!'

She needed no encouragement. Freed from her heavy burden, she charged up the stairs, heart pounding, lungs drawing in gasps of freezing air. After years of being confined to a 6-foot-by-8-foot cell, the mere act of running unfettered was almost alien to her. The stairs were a strange and unusual obstacle that she hadn't tackled in a lifetime.

Finally rounding the last turn, she rushed through the open door at the top of the stairs and out into a covered observation area overlooking the prison yard.

Then she stopped, staring around in awestruck amazement, oblivious even to the biting cold and the sting of dry snowflakes on her exposed skin.

For almost as long as she could remember, her entire world had consisted of her 6-by-8-foot cell, and the length of corridor she walked to get to the shower rooms. She hadn't seen the outside world since the day of her arrival. She hadn't breathed fresh air or felt the wind on her face. She hadn't looked up at a sky that wasn't lit by cheap electric lights and blocked by grey concrete.

This was the world she had once been part of, and it was consumed with chaos.

Alarms blared throughout the prison, the crackle of gunfire resounded from various points throughout the facility, mingled with shouts and panicked cries. One of the imposing watchtowers on the south side had been demolished as if by explosives, the observation deck a mass of shattered glass and smouldering debris.

More shouts from below directed her attention to the exercise yard, where a group of prisoners had broken through the main doors and were pouring out into the open space. Where they planned to go, she had no idea. She wondered if they were even thinking rationally, or if the crazed lust for freedom had overridden all common sense.

Either way, she didn't doubt that Khatyrgan was going to fall tonight. There were too many prisoners and too few guards to hold them back, and they had suffered much in their time here. Their rage and lust for revenge would know no bounds.

She just hoped they were able to get out before the riot consumed the entire prison.

Tearing her eyes away from the chaos in the yard, she watched as her two rescuers emerged from the stairwell, breathing hard and close to exhaustion, driven by sheer determination.

'How do we get out?' she demanded.

Drake jerked a hand towards the remaining undamaged tower on the south block. 'That way. Hurry.'

Chapter 23

'I see them!' Frost called out, pointing towards the northwest tower.

Bringing his weapon with its powerful optics to bear, Keegan caught sight of three figures darting across the rooftop towards them, the woman in front and Drake behind, supporting an injured and heavily limping Dietrich.

He watched Drake reach for the radio pressel at his throat. 'This is Bravo. We're almost there. Get the rappelling gear ready!'

'It's done,' Keegan replied. 'Move your ass, Bravo. This place is going down fast.'

'Copy that!'

At the same moment, Keegan detected a noise above the shriek of the wind and the crackle of gunfire. A low, rhythmic thudding. It was their chopper.

Glancing upward, he watched in awe as a massive shape loomed out of the darkness to the east, skimming low over the prison as its twin rotor blades beat the frigid air.

His radio crackled into life again as the huge aircraft roared overhead. 'This is Zulu. We're about to set down outside the prison, but the weather's deteriorating fast. We can't stay on station long or we'll never get airborne again. Recommend you hurry.'

'Copy that, Zulu,' Keegan replied. 'We're on our way.'

Outside, Mason was standing on the parapet staring down at the 100-foot drop yawning beneath him. Their rappelling rope was a lone white line tracing its way down the grim stone flanks. A lifeline. Their only means of escape.

Beside him, Frost was just finishing clipping her harness into place. 'Move it. Go!' he urged.

She shot him a sharp glare. 'Easy for you to say.'

Swallowing down a sudden feeling of vertigo, the woman stepped out over the edge and pushed off, using the friction hitch in her right hand to control her rate of descent. She went far faster than she would have liked, knowing that time was limited.

Again she pushed away from the vertical surface and released her grip on the friction hitch, before slowing herself as she swung back in towards the wall again.

As soon as she touched down, Mason went to work clipping himself on. Their climbing harnesses were already a part of their uniforms, fixed in place and secured before they even boarded the flight here.

As he stepped out over the edge, he shouted to the sniper still inside the observation area. 'Keegan, we're clear. Fall back now!'

'Be right behind you, buddy,' Keegan replied without taking his gaze away from the scope.

No sooner had he said this than he spotted movement in the tower that Drake and the others had just emerged from. He couldn't tell if it was a guard or an escaping prisoner, but he caught the distinctive frame of an AK clutched in the man's hand, followed by a sudden muzzle flare as he opened up on full automatic.

'Ah, shit! I'm hit!' Mason cried.

Quickly lining up his sights, Keegan loosed a single

shot in response, scoring a fatal hit to the man's centre mass.

Not even bothering to watch the man collapse in his death throes, he turned towards the parapet in time to see Mason topple backwards over the edge.

'Cole!'

In a heartbeat he had dropped his sniper rifle and sprinted to the edge of the parapet, staring down and expecting to see his comrade's lifeless corpse sprawled on the snow-covered ground far below.

Instead, he found Mason dangling from his descent harness about 10 feet below, clutching his shoulder. His right arm hung slack by his side.

'Jesus Christ. You okay, buddy?'

The younger man looked up at him. 'Took a . . . round in the shoulder,' he managed to say, his voice tight with pain.

It took all of two seconds for Keegan to weigh up their options.

Bringing him back up would be an exercise in futility, while going down to meet him was impossible; the line was only rigged for one person. Their best, and indeed only, option was to get him to the chopper where they could treat his injuries.

He could see the aircraft coming in to land about 100 metres beyond the prison wall, the downwash from its massive rotors kicking up a storm of snow and ice. Their salvation was tantalisingly close.

'Can you still descend?'

'I think so,' Mason replied.

Without warning, he released his friction hitch and pushed off from the wall to start his descent. Pain, shock and blood loss had dulled his reflexes, making him careless.

The descent was far too fast. Realising he'd gained too much momentum, he squeezed the hitch closed, over-compensating and jerking himself to a halt about halfway down the wall. The sudden change in velocity upset the line, swinging him inward.

His injured shoulder slammed into the unyielding surface, and he let out an involuntary scream of agony as broken bones grated against each other. Dazed and almost blacking out with pain, he was barely able to keep a grip on the hitch as he slid down the wall, limp as a rag doll.

Frost was waiting for him at the bottom, and quickly unlatched him from the rope before pulling him to safety. It hadn't been pretty, but he was down.

Bravo team reached the tower only moments later.

'Move your arse!' Drake yelled, forcibly shoving Dietrich up the metal ladder to the observation deck. The man was tiring fast, and was using most of his strength just to hold on. Drake knew how he felt.

Then suddenly Keegan appeared at the top, gripped his outstretched hand and hauled him up in a remark-able show of strength for such a small man.

'Come on, asshole. Get up here.'

Drake went up next, then turned and reached out to help Maras. She didn't grip his hand, determined to make it by herself.

'Jesus, you really stirred up a shit storm here,' Keegan remarked. He had discarded his rifle now, knowing it would be impossible to take the bulky weapon with him.

'Only thing I could think of to buy us some time,' Drake explained. 'What happened to Mason?'

The older man's craggy face twisted in a grimace. 'Took a round in the shoulder. He made it down, though.'

There was nothing more he could do for now. Drake nodded towards the descent rope. 'All right. Get yourself down there.'

The sniper nodded. 'You be right behind me, you hear?'

It took him only a few moments to clip himself in. Wasting no time, he jumped up on the parapet, balanced on the edge and vanished into the night, fearless as always.

With Keegan gone, Drake turned his attention to Maras. He had brought a spare climbing harness looped into his belt kit, which he unlatched and shoved at her. 'Put this on.'

According to Cain, she was fully trained at rappelling and should be able to handle the descent with ease. Experience was one thing, but he had his doubts about whether she could manage the physically demanding task. She was already tired from her exertions, and obviously not in a good place mentally judging by her reaction to the guard.

Still, she seemed to understand what to do, and quickly pulled the two loops of the harness up around her legs, then set about securing the waist straps.

As she worked, Drake dragged Dietrich over to the rope. 'Come on, mate. This is the fun part,' he said as he clipped the older man in.

'I can't . . .' Dietrich protested weakly.

'Bollocks you can't,' Drake snapped. 'The hitch only needs one hand, and you can brace yourself against the wall with your good leg. Now come on. Move, you lazy arsehole!'

Without waiting for him to reply, he grabbed the wounded man around the waist and hauled him up over the edge of the parapet.

Drake had no way of knowing whether he would make it, but there was nothing he could do about it anyway. There was no time to lower him by hand, and they certainly didn't have time to rig up a tandem harness. One way or another, Dietrich would have to get through this by himself.

Seeing the fear and worry in his comrade's eyes, he leaned in close and gripped his shoulder. 'Just get it done quickly, all right? We can fix you later, but first we have to get out of here.'

The older man looked at him for several moments, then finally nodded, rallying whatever reserves of strength remained and steeling himself for what was to come. Bracing himself against the wall with his good leg, he pushed off hard and released his grip on the hitch, gritting his teeth against the pain.

Last of all, Drake turned to Maras, standing with him at the edge of the parapet. 'Can you do this?'

She offered a strange lopsided grimace that might have been a smile. 'It has been a while for me.'

With that, she clambered up over the edge. Then she stopped and looked at him for a moment. She said nothing. He couldn't be sure, but he thought perhaps he saw a hint of gratitude in her eyes.

Then she pushed off from the wall, released her brake, and was gone.

It was done. Drake turned back towards the prison. It was a scene of absolute chaos. Prisoners were running riot, smoke rose from the windows of both major cell blocks, and the rattle of weapons fire resounded in the open exercise yard. If there were any guards still operating as a cohesive group, they were going to have a nightmare bringing this situation under control. He imagined that none of the prisoners were under any

150

illusions about their fate here – they would fight to the last man.

Keegan had had the presence of mind to leave a thermite grenade beside their pile of discarded equipment. Seizing it up, Drake returned to the parapet and clipped himself onto the descent rope, then pulled himself up over the edge. His bruised back and shoulder blazed with pain, but adrenalin was doing a good job of suppressing it.

Now ready, he pulled the pin from the cylindrical grenade and hurled it into the observation room, then pushed himself away from the edge and released his brake.

He had made it about halfway down the wall when a bright orange flash erupted above, lighting up the terrain around the prison like a signal flare. The grenade had done its work well.

One last push brought him down to ground level, and he touched down with a bump that sent a jolt up his legs. Still, he was on solid ground, and never had it felt so good.

Keegan was waiting for him. 'Let's go, buddy.'

Unclipping himself from the rope, Drake followed him as he sprinted away from the prison, heading for the chopper about 100 metres away. He could just make out the child-like shape of Frost as she helped a heavily limping Dietrich aboard.

The pilot was already increasing engine power by the time Drake and Keegan fought their way up the rear cargo ramp, snow and ice swirling around them.

Staggering aboard, Drake switched radio channels to speak to the pilot. 'That's it, Zulu. We're all in. You're clear to lift off.'

The pilot was in no mood to hang around. Engines

151

roaring and rotors hammering the air, the massive chopper lurched skyward, buffeted and blasted by vicious crosswinds as the storm bore down on them.

Staring out the rear of the aircraft, Drake was just able to glimpse the outline of the embattled prison receding into the darkness before the cargo ramp slammed shut.

Chapter 24

As soon as they were clear of the prison, the Chinook turned and headed north-east at full speed, following one of the low valleys that criss-crossed the region. To avoid any radar installations in the vicinity, their altitude barely exceeded 50 feet, though it meant they took a hammering from the storm bearing down on them. The deck swayed and lurched beneath them like a ship in a typhoon, and more than a few shouts and curses were heard from the cockpit.

Still, they were alive, airborne and heading for home.

Drake removed his sweaty, clammy balaclava, closed his eyes and exhaled, allowing his heartbeat to slow to something approaching normal.

It was all behind them now. All the planning, the preparation, the fear, the worry, the danger and the problems. Somehow, against all the odds, they had succeeded.

He should have felt elation and exhilaration, but no such emotion stirred in him at that moment. The only thing he felt was crushing fatigue. For two days and one night he had been keyed up and consumed with his work. Now that the pressure was off, exhaustion was catching up with him at last.

The woman they had risked everything for was sitting opposite, staring right ahead but seeing nothing. She was a pathetic sight; thin, bedraggled, bloodied and filthy, she looked as if she'd just been liberated from a concentration camp.

'Keegan, keep an eye on Maras, would you?'

She didn't seem like much of a threat, but he was taking no chances after the earlier incident with the guard.

The old sniper nodded. 'On it, buddy.'

Undoing his seat belt, Drake stood up and, negotiating the lurching deck with some difficulty, staggered over to join Dietrich.

The man was seated on one of the metal benches running the length of the cargo compartment, tending to his leg injury. He had cut away the fabric around the wound, and was busy applying a compress to slow the bleeding. Drake saw a syringe of morphine lying on the deck beside him.

He didn't think it was a good idea for the man to be tending his own wounds after self-medicating himself with morphine, but it seemed there wasn't much choice. Keegan was needed to cover Maras, while Frost was busy tending to Mason.

'How are you doing, Jonas?' he asked, his expression grave as he surveyed the wound. The bleeding didn't look too bad, and judging by the fact that the man still had use of the limb, he suspected the muscle damage was minimal.

Dietrich looked up at him. 'I've got a hole in my leg that wasn't there this morning,' he remarked acidly. 'So not very good.'

'You're still alive,' Drake pointed out.

'So are you.' He sounded almost disappointed.

Whatever gratitude he might have felt towards Drake for helping to get him to safety had long since

154

evaporated. It was business as usual as far as Dietrich was concerned.

'Fine. Let us know if you need anything,' Drake said, grateful to leave him behind as he made his way further forward to join Frost.

The woman had removed her heavy, cumbersome jumpsuit, webbing, descent harness and armoured vest, leaving her in a sweat-stained T-shirt and combat trousers. She had a bandage pressed against the cut on her forehead.

'Are you all right?' Drake asked.

She flashed a defiant grin. 'Not exactly a career-ending injury, but I won't be doing any modelling work for a while.'

'And Mason?' he asked, gesturing to the injured man lying unconscious on a medical stretcher set up on the deck, IV lines snaking into his arm.

Her smile faded. 'I've sedated him and stabilised him as best I can. He should pull through, but he's going to need surgery on that shoulder for sure. I can't tell how bad it is without an X-ray.'

Drake nodded. Of all the shitty, unlucky things to happen, getting hit by a stray round while preparing to evacuate had to be one of the worst. It was one of those freak occurrences that was just impossible to plan for.

Still, at least they had been able to get him out.

'Do me a favour and take a look at Maras,' he said, glancing at the woman they had gone through all this to rescue. 'She doesn't look good.'

She hadn't moved a muscle since he'd left her. Keegan was watching her, keeping a weapon to hand in case she tried anything.

Drake wondered if perhaps it had all been too much for her and she'd gone into shock, but there wasn't

155

much they could do about her mental state. Their orders were to bring her back alive.

'Why me?' Frost asked, clearly unhappy.

'Because you're a woman.'

Frost glanced down at her breasts in mock surprise. 'Oh, so that's what these are.'

Drake gave her a disapproving look. 'She'll feel less intimidated by you. Now piss off and get it done. I'll keep an eye on Mason.'

The young woman flashed a defiant smile, but turned to head aft.

'Oh, and Keira?'

She paused and glanced over her shoulder.

'Good job, yeah?'

She nodded, looking sober and serious for once, then carried on without saying anything.

A satellite phone had been set up just aft of the cockpit where their two pilots were still wrestling against the appalling weather. Drake was in no mood for a full debriefing, but he knew Cain and Franklin would be clamouring for an initial report. Better to get it over with.

His back and shoulder were throbbing. He didn't know how badly he'd hurt himself during the rough rooftop landing, and wasn't keen to investigate. Coffee and pain-killers would have to do for now.

Summoning up his flagging energy, he picked up the chunky phone unit and dialled the number he'd memorised.

It rang only once before it was answered.

'Franklin.'

'We've got her,' Drake reported, deciding not to beat about the bush.

'Thank Christ. What's your situation?'

'There was trouble during the extraction. Mason took

a round to the shoulder. He's stable, but he'll need medical attention when we land. Dietrich's also been hit, but he's still in the fight.'

'I'll have medics on standby at Elmendorf.' He paused for a moment. 'And . . . Maras?'

Drake chewed his lip. 'Physically she seems intact. As far as her mental state's concerned, your guess is as good as mine.'

He was no psychologist, but it didn't take one to realise she had problems. She'd been physically abused, locked in solitary confinement for God knew how long, deprived of any stimulation. Who knew how she would adapt to this sudden change?

That gave the older man pause for thought. 'I hear you. Just get her back. We'll take care of the rest later.'

Drake got the message. Her long-term psychological needs were none of his concern.

Just then, he heard the sound of smashing glass, and Frost's panicked cry. 'What the fu—!'

Dumping the phone, he turned in time to see Maras gripping the woman in front of her as a human shield, one arm around her neck. In her other hand, she held a broken glass bottle against her throat.

Keegan and Dietrich, reacting to the sudden disturbance, drew their side arms and levelled them at Maras.

'Let her go!' Keegan yelled. 'Let her go right now.'

Drake's stomach twisted.

Not now. Not after all this.

Shutting down the satellite phone, Drake staggered aft, struggling to keep his balance on the lurching deck.

'Nobody fire,' he ordered. Aside from killing both women, the shots would likely penetrate the aircraft's fuselage.

Maras had backed up to the rear of the fuselage, still

keeping Frost in front of her. Her vivid blue eyes moved constantly between the three men surrounding her.

'Tell them to lower their weapons,' Maras said, her gaze resting on Drake. 'Do it.'

'Ryan, what are we doing?' Keegan asked.

'Shoot her,' Frost hissed. 'Shoot the fucking bitch!'

'Shut up,' Maras warned, pressing the broken shard into her throat hard enough to draw blood. 'Drop the guns now or she dies.'

'You're wasting your time,' Keegan said, managing to keep calm despite the situation. 'Look around. You got nowhere to go.'

She remained unmoved by his reasoning.

'She's fucked,' Dietrich decided. 'She's lost it.'

Drake wasn't hearing them. His eyes were locked with the woman's, trying to understand what was going on behind them. He had seen the wild lust for blood as she stabbed that guard to death, but it wasn't there now.

Her look was fearful, anxious, uncertain. She was in an environment she didn't understand, being taken somewhere she didn't know, and she was afraid. She was like a cornered animal.

She had reacted to that fear the only way she knew how – by lashing out and trying to take control.

'Lower your weapons,' he said at last.

'What?' Frost gasped, eyes wide in disbelief.

Dietrich's gaze flicked to him just for a moment. 'Ryan, have you lost your mind?'

'Do it,' Drake snapped. 'We didn't go through all this to lose someone on the flight home. Lower your guns, and then we'll talk.'

'Ryan, please . . .' Frost said, staring right at him.

'It's all right, Keira,' Drake promised her, wishing he

felt as sure as he sounded. 'Nobody's going to do anything stupid. Lower your weapons.'

Hesitating, the two men glanced at each other. Then, as if by unspoken consent, they lowered the side arms.

'All right. It's done,' Drake said, keeping his voice low and calm. Shouting would only provoke her fear. 'We're not here to hurt you. We came to help you.'

She said nothing, but a little of the tension had left her muscles. She was in control of the situation, or at least she thought she was.

'Where are you taking me?' she demanded.

'We're going to Elmendorf Air Force Base in Alaska.'

'And what then?'

'I don't know,' he admitted. 'We were sent to bring you home, that's all. The rest is out of our hands.'

She seemed to believe him. 'Who sent you?'

'The Agency. We're a Shepherd team, part of Special Activities Division.'

That made an impact. He saw the shock in her eyes, the recognition, and something else that he couldn't quite identify. Was it sadness? Nostalgia? Longing?

She swallowed, the muscles in her throat moving up and down. 'What year is it?'

Drake hesitated a moment, taken aback by her question. Jesus, how long had she been in there? 'It's 2007.'

The woman let out a faint gasp, almost a sob, and the look in her eyes changed to one of utter, crushing grief. And just like that, she released her grip on Frost.

The younger woman wasted no time twisting out of reach, visibly shaking with a mixture of anger and fear at her sudden brush with death.

'The goddamn bitch is out of her mind!' she snarled, rubbing the cut at her throat. 'Someone taser her, or I'll do it myself!'

'No.' Drake moved forward, putting himself between Maras and Frost. He lowered his voice to speak to the younger woman. 'I know you want payback. But look at her.'

Maras, who only moments before had seemed so dangerous and formidable, appeared to have crumpled before their eyes. She had sunk onto the bench, shoulders slumped, eyes staring straight ahead but seeing nothing. Her expression was one of utter desolation.

'Give her a break, yeah?'

Frost glared at the older woman for several seconds, then seemed to see her as Drake did. Her expression softened a little, until finally she sighed and shook her head in resignation.

'Just keep her the hell away from me.' With that, she turned and strode forward, making for a seat as far away from Maras as possible.

Releasing his breath, Drake rubbed his eyes and glanced at Maras again. The woman wasn't seeing him. She was in her own world. In her filthy bloodstained clothes, matted hair falling around her face, she was a pathetic, broken figure.

He had to do something. Leaving Keegan to watch her, he made his way to the front of the aircraft where food and drink had been stowed. Unscrewing a bottle of mineral water, he emptied it onto a hand towel until it was sodden, then poured some hot chocolate from a Thermos into a plastic cup.

Thus armed, he returned to Maras and held the towel out to her. 'Here,' he said gently. 'Clean yourself up.'

Her face and hair were still covered with congealed blood, grime, dirt and all kinds of other shit, but she seemed oblivious to it.

She stared at the towel blankly for several seconds, as

if struggling to understand his meaning. Then at last she reached out and took it. Her first effort at cleaning her face was tentative, almost experimental. She kept her eye on Drake the whole time, as if he might suddenly spring at her if she lowered her guard, but gradually she relaxed.

By the time she was done, the towel was soaked red with blood. Her face was still stained crimson in places, but it was a marked improvement.

She looked down at the towel, as if unsure what to do with it, then finally dropped it on the deck by her feet.

Drake lowered himself onto the bench beside her and held out the cup of steaming liquid. 'Here, are you thirsty? It's some hot chocolate. It's good.'

She eyed him with suspicion for several seconds before accepting the cup.

Drake cocked an eyebrow. 'You're not going to try to kill me with it, are you?' he asked with a wry smile.

Her expression didn't change.

'Sorry. Bad humour.'

She sniffed the contents, then finally took a drink. The taste must have pleased her, because straight away she took a much deeper gulp, ignoring the fact that the liquid was close to boiling.

'We've got food too, if you're hungry,' he said, gesturing forward.

She kept drinking the chocolate, saying nothing.

'We'll get you proper medical attention and clean clothes when we land at Elmendorf. In the mean time we—'

'Why are you doing this?' she cut in. She spoke excellent English, but it was obviously not her first language. There was a faint trace of an accent. Russian or Eastern European, he couldn't tell.

Drake frowned. 'Doing what?'

161

She laid the empty cup on the deck at her feet. 'Treating me with respect. I almost killed one of your team. You should have tasered and handcuffed me by now.'

He looked at her for a long moment. 'Would you prefer that?'

'No,' she decided.

Fair enough. 'Look, I understand this must be very difficult for you—'

Her eyes lit up. 'You understand?'

He sighed and looked away for a moment. 'All right, that was a stupid thing to say. I *don't* understand. But I can guess life hasn't been kind to you recently. I can guess you're used to protecting yourself, and I'd like to think that's why you acted the way you did back there.'

She said nothing and her eyes gave away even less, but he took her silence as tacit acknowledgement of his suggestion.

'But you don't have to be afraid. Not any more. Whatever happened to you in that place, whatever you went through, it's over. As long as you're with us, no one will hurt you. I promise.'

At that moment, something changed in her. He saw a flicker in her eyes, a lowering of the defences. For the first time since he'd met her, she looked open and vulnerable.

She smiled. A faint, wistful smile, filled with sadness. 'It has been a long time since anyone said that to me.'

He leaned forward a little and extended his hand to touch hers. He didn't know why he did it, merely that it felt right.

'Believe it. We're here to help you.'

Instinctively she moved her hand back. Not much, but enough to put it beyond his reach.

He'd pushed too hard. He shouldn't have done that.

Deciding to give her some time alone, he rose up from the seat. Keegan was hovering nearby to keep an eye on her.

'Like I said, we're here to help. You don't have to trust us, just don't threaten any of my people. We'll try to make your trip back as comfortable as possible. If you need something, ask. Okay?'

He had no idea what the future held for this woman, but she would come to no harm while she was with him. That was one promise he was determined to make good on.

He was just turning to leave when she spoke up again.

'What is your name?'

He stopped and looked at her. 'Drake. Ryan Drake.'

The woman looked at him for a long moment. Then at last she gave a nod of acknowledgement. Her face remained impassive, but the raw emotion in her eyes was impossible to hide.

'Thank you, Drake.'

With that, she turned her gaze away, leaned forward and rested her head in her hands. Drake lingered close by a few moments longer, wondering if perhaps he should acknowledge her thanks, then decided against it.

She had said what she wanted to say, and it was enough.

Chapter 25

Standing with his head bowed and his hands braced against the tiled wall, Drake did nothing for some time, allowing the hot shower to sluice down on him. The heat helped to loosen the stiff, knotted muscles in his bruised shoulder and soothe the pain across his back.

He was exhausted. The journey from Russia to Alaska had taken six hours, during which Maras had to be guarded at all times and Mason had required constant monitoring, further adding to the stress on the already weary team.

The plan had originally called for a quick aircraft change at Elmendorf, followed by an extended flight back to Washington DC for debriefing. However, given that two of the team were injured, and Maras was, in Drake's opinion, badly in need of proper medical attention, he had taken the decision to disembark at the earliest opportunity.

Never in his life had he been so relieved to touch down. Landing beside an isolated hangar at the eastern edge of the base, they were immediately met by an Agency retrieval team who escorted Maras to a waiting vehicle.

That had been the last he had seen of her. There had been no words of farewell, no expressions of thanks or good luck. She had simply allowed them to take her away, marching right off the chopper with her eyes straight ahead. Only as she was helped into the waiting vehicle did she look at him for a moment, though he couldn't tell what was going on behind those cold blue eyes.

Drake doubted he would ever see her again. It was the nature of the job. He was there to bring lost operatives home. After that, it wasn't his problem.

In the aftermath of their arrival, the rest of the team had been almost forgotten about. Debriefings and reports would inevitably come later, but for now they had been given some time to shower, change and rest. It was a temporary reprieve only, but a welcome one.

In a few hours they would be on a flight back to Langley, and once Franklin and the others had finished picking the operation apart, that would be it. He could put the whole thing behind him, and it would be up to Cain to live up to his end of the deal. A whole new chapter of his life was about to open up.

He should have felt elated.

If only it were that easy.

Mason had been hustled away by the base medical teams. It was too early to know the extent of his injuries, but an operating theatre had already been prepared for him. Drake had been assured he would receive the best care possible. He just hoped it would be enough.

Mason was a grown man who had known the risks when he accepted the job, but that knowledge did nothing to assuage the guilt Drake now felt. Whether consciously accepted by both men or not, it was his job to keep the older man safe, to lead him into harm's way and bring him back unscathed. He had failed in that responsibility, and nothing could change that.

165

With a sigh, he reached up and turned off the shower tap. The steaming deluge turned into a tepid drip, though it was another thirty seconds or so before he straightened up, wincing with the movement.

Running a hand through his soaking hair, he pulled open the shower door and stepped out onto the tiled floor.

The glass of whisky was still resting on the edge of the sink, half empty. He'd smuggled a bottle on the flight out from Langley, knowing he would need it when the mission was over. His body might have been weary and bruised, but his mind was still wired.

Snatching up the glass, he downed the contents and padded through to the small accommodation room loaned to him by the Elmendorf Base staff. It was a simple affair, with dented plasterboard walls, a narrow steel-framed bed, a desk and chair, and a TV in one corner. Still, it was a whole lot better than a freezing prison cell, he thought with a shudder.

Unzipping his kitbag, he found a change of clothes inside, along with his cellphone. He stared at it for a long moment before finally picking it up and switching it on.

He had poured himself another glass before he found the courage to dial the once-familiar number.

The phone rang and rang with no response. Drake had no idea what time it was in that part of the world, but he guessed it was an unsociable hour.

He was on the verge of hanging up when at last a sleepy voice came on the line. 'Hello?'

'Jessica,' he began hesitantly, not sure what to say.

'Ryan!' She was awake in an instant. 'My God, you haven't phoned in months. Is everything all right?'

'Yeah. Yeah . . . it's . . . everything's fine here.' He

looked down at the glass of whisky in his hand, feeling suddenly guilty. 'What time is it there?'

'It's . . . four in the morning.'

'Oh, shit, I'm sorry . . .'

'You've been in Washington for years. Don't you know the time difference by now?'

Unable to help himself, he downed another gulp. 'I'm not in DC. I'm in Alaska.'

'Alaska? What on earth—'

'It's work,' he cut in. 'My real work, not that bullshit cover they dreamed up.'

'What do you mean?'

Drake sighed and glanced up at the ceiling, struggling to find a way to say what he'd yearned to say for so long. 'Jess, I . . . I haven't been honest with you. About a lot of things. There's so much I've kept from you, and I told myself it was for your own good. But it wasn't. It was for mine, because I was afraid of what you'd think if you knew what I really did. I was afraid what you'd think of me.'

He could hear movement at the other end. She was getting out of bed, he knew. Going somewhere she could talk privately. 'Ryan, look, whatever it is, whatever you've done, talk to me,' she said, her voice quieter now. 'I'm your sister and I'm here for you, no matter what. You know that.'

'Yeah.' His voice was low, roughened by the drink. 'I know.'

She had always been there for him, even if he hadn't deserved it.

'So talk to me,' she implored him. 'Whatever you have to say, I promise I'll listen.' She hesitated a moment, trying to adopt a lighter tone. 'It seems like you could use a good listener.'

She was right about that, of course. Drake had no idea how much the other Shepherd team members told their friends and loved ones, whether they confided in any of them or preferred to keep their work to themselves.

He had always chosen the latter, but it was a hard path to take, and getting harder all the time.

'You know me too well,' he conceded.

'You're not that hard to work out.' Her words were playful, but her tone wasn't. 'So tell me, what are you thinking?'

Even he couldn't help but smile a little. 'I'm coming home, Jess.'

It was a good second or two before she could muster a reply. 'Back to the UK, you mean?'

'Yeah. For a while, at least.' After last night's efforts, he figured Cain and the Agency owed him a couple of weeks' leave. Anyway, what he had to tell her was no conversation for an open phone line. 'If you'll have me, that is?'

'Of course!' There was no thought of keeping her voice down this time. 'You know you're always welcome here.'

He smiled, but hearing those words made his heart ache. Her voice reminded him of much earlier times. Happier times.

'I have to take care of a few things here first, but I'll be in touch soon. Hopefully at a more sociable hour,' he added, managing to inject a little humour into his voice. 'Then we'll talk, okay?'

She understood why he was hanging up. She knew him better than anyone. 'All right. Look after yourself out there, Ryan. I love you.'

'I love you too.'

Killing the phone, he looked down at his drink, took

a deep breath and swallowed it in one gulp. The liquid burned all the way down.

But that didn't stop him pouring another glass.

'She's suffering from dehydration and borderline malnutrition,' the doctor explained, speaking in a soft voice that belied his stocky frame and heavy jowls already darkened with stubble. The name tag on his coat identified him as Cooper.

'We haven't got her blood work back yet, but we know she's anaemic. Lack of exposure to sunlight will have caused vitamin D deficiencies as well. Bone density is normally a problem in cases like this, but judging from her lean muscle mass, she's been exercising during her confinement. She must have been remarkably fit when she was imprisoned.'

Franklin stretched, doing his best to ignore the painful spasm in the small of his back as he did so. The flight from Andrews Air Force Base to Alaska had been an ordeal, forcing him to sit in a cramped, uncomfortable seat for what felt like an eternity as his back slowly locked up.

But there had been no question of coming here. Cain would brook no delay when he found out the Shepherd team and the woman they had risked so much to recover had disembarked in Alaska. He had insisted on flying there straight away, even charting his own flight for the purpose.

The object of their attention was seated at a table fixed into the centre of the room, a plastic cup of orange juice lying untouched in front of her.

The first order of business had been to perform a full medical examination and health assessment. She had shown little sign of weakness, but one look at her was enough to confirm the years of abuse and neglect she had suffered. There was no telling what kind of impact her imprisonment had had on her health.

'There's also evidence of sexual assault, and sustained physical abuse over a long period,' Cooper went on. His tone had changed a little, becoming colder and more clinical. 'She was reluctant to let us examine her, which is understandable, so it's hard to know if there's any internal damage. Preliminary HIV screening has come back negative, but we can't rule out the possibility of other sexually transmitted infections.'

'What are we doing for her?' Cain asked.

He was staring at Maras, jaw clenched tight, his forehead knotted, deep worry lines plainly visible. For the first time since Franklin had met him, he looked his age and more.

But it was the look in his eyes that took Franklin by surprise. There was sadness there; deep wells of sadness and pain and grief.

'We've already started her on an aggressive course of antibiotics, plus vitamin supplements to combat her mineral deficiencies. We'll put her on a high-calorie, high-nutrition diet to help bring her body back to its normal BMI. You can't go too fast with cases like these – the body can't cope with a sudden change in food intake. You have to build them up gradually. She'll need additional therapy to deal with sunlight, since her skin hasn't been exposed to ultraviolet rays in years. More than anything, she needs time to rest and recover.'

'What about her mental state?' Franklin asked, turning his attention back to Maras. The woman was like a statue at the table. She hadn't moved a muscle throughout the whole conversation.

'You've got me, sir,' Cooper admitted. 'I can treat her

physical injuries, but long-term psychiatric care is another issue.' He exhaled slowly. 'Off the record, I'd say you'll be looking at severe post-traumatic stress disorder. There are likely to be other long-term issues like coping with open spaces, depression, trust and fear of authority. It depends on her psychological make-up. Patients who have survived experiences like this can take months or even years to adjust to normal life.'

'We don't have that long,' Cain said.

'Sir, I don't think you understand,' the doctor protested. 'This patient has been through—'

'She's been through worse,' Cain assured him before turning to Franklin. 'Dan, I want you to get in there and talk to her. We need to bring her up to speed.'

Franklin frowned. 'Me? Shouldn't you be the one to debrief her?'

Cain shook his head. Normally calm and composed, and possessing a natural authority that others deferred to almost by instinct, he now looked nervous and agitated.

'There's too much history there. We need her to focus on the present.'

'What if she asks about you?'

Cain looked away for a moment. 'Tell her I retired from the CIA two years ago. Health reasons. *You're* now the Divisional Director.'

Franklin hesitated. He didn't like the way this was heading. But on the other hand, he knew what was at stake as well as Cain did. If they failed, the repercussions could be devastating.

'Do you have a problem with that?' Cain challenged him.

Raising his chin, he reached up and straightened his tie. 'No. No problem.'

* * *

171

Following a two-hour surgery to pin his shattered shoulder back together, Mason had been wheeled out of theatre and into a private recovery room. Drake was able to track down the surgeon responsible for the operation: a thin, balding, dishevelled-looking man in his fifties.

'He came through pretty well,' the surgeon informed him. 'It's lucky he was in such good shape – that should bode well for his long-term chances. We patched him up as best we could, but it's likely he'll need further surgery, and he'll definitely need a long period of rehab.'

Drake glanced in through the little window in the door. Mason was propped up in his bed, shoulder heavily strapped and bandaged, staring out the window without seeing anything.

'Does he know?'

The doctor nodded. 'Yeah, I told him.'

'Can I speak to him?'

The old man chewed his lip. 'Five minutes.'

Mason didn't look around as Drake entered the room. 'I had a feeling you'd be dropping in, Ryan,' he said, his voice heavy with painkillers.

The view from the window looked like something out of a picture postcard, with vast tracts of evergreen forests stretching off towards the towering snow-capped peaks of the Chugach Mountains to the east.

To the west lay the shimmering blue expanse of Cook Inlet, with commercial ships ploughing their way up and down the channel to the nearby Port of Anchorage. Elmendorf Base backed almost straight onto the town. God only knew what the locals thought about the scream of military jets landing and taking off, but Drake supposed people here learned to endure all kinds of hardships.

He helped himself to a hard plastic chair and pulled it up next to the bed. 'How are you feeling?'

With some effort Mason turned to look at Drake. 'The doc tells me I won't be pitching any curve balls for a while.'

'Can I do anything for you? Anything you need?'

Mason's face twisted in a smile. 'Got a spare arm I could borrow?'

Drake couldn't help but smile a little too. 'You'll be all right, you bloody wimp. A few weeks of rehab and it'll be like nothing happened. And look at it this way – you'll have plenty of young nurses to harass.'

The older man laughed. 'This is an Air Force base, man. Most of the women here make *you* look attractive.'

'Shit, it must be bad, then,' Drake said. But his smile faded as he looked at Mason's ruined shoulder again. 'Look, Cole . . . I'm sorry about . . .'

Mason reached out with his good arm and gripped Drake's shoulder, staring hard at him. 'Ryan, the worst thing you can do is beat yourself up over things that weren't your fault. This was bad luck – nothing more, nothing less. You had nothing to do with it.'

Drake appreciated the sentiment. He just wished he could believe it. Mason wouldn't even have been in that prison if he hadn't accepted Cain's deal.

'I'll check up on you later,' he said quietly, rising from the chair.

He was almost at the door when Mason spoke up again. 'Ryan?'

'Yeah?'

'I hope she was worth it.'

173

Chapter 26

Only one door led in or out of the holding room, and it was locked from the other side, with two armed Military Police officers on standby.

Franklin felt a twinge of apprehension as the door buzzed and the electronic locks disengaged. If Cain was to be believed, the woman beyond that door could kill him as easily as tying her shoelaces.

'Remember, sir. Keep your distance from her at all times,' the burly Hispanic guard warned, moving aside to let him pass. 'Don't attempt to give her anything or touch her in any way. If there's any trouble, we'll be there within seconds.'

Franklin gave him a curt nod, resisting the urge to swallow. Too late to worry about it now, he thought as the door swung open.

The room itself was devoid of features – just bare brick walls, padded rubberised flooring and a small table in the centre, fixed into the floor. One wall was dominated by a mirror that was clearly more than just a mirror. Cain was on the other side of it, watching every move he made. The thought was not a reassuring one.

The lighting remained low, leaving her face half hidden by shadow. Her eyes were still sensitive to bright light and would take time to adjust.

Maras remained seated when he entered, didn't look

up, barely moved a muscle in fact. She was just sitting there, oblivious to what was happening. And yet, just by sitting there she seemed to exude an air of quiet, brooding menace. She was far from oblivious to what was going on.

He felt the hairs on the back of his neck prickle as he approached.

'Good afternoon,' he began.

No response.

'My name's Franklin. I'm here to handle your debriefing.' There was a seat opposite her at the table. Clearing his throat, he gestured to it. 'Mind if I sit down?'

Still she said nothing.

Taking her silence as acquiescence, he eased himself down, trying not to show any sign of discomfort or difficulty. His already knotted back muscles sent ripples of pain through his body.

'I understand you've been through a lot today. This must all be very difficult for you, so if there's anything you need during this process, just let me—'

'Anything I need?' she suddenly asked, lifting her gaze from the featureless table surface to focus on him.

'That's right.'

Her intense blue eyes hardened, and he noticed the muscles across her shoulders tightening. 'How about four years of my life back? Can you give me that, Franklin?'

He swallowed and glanced away for a moment, feeling as though she was drilling right into him with those eyes.

'What happened to you was . . . regrettable,' he said, knowing how feeble those words must have sounded. 'But it's over now. You can put it all behind you. We'll make sure you get all the help you need.'

He shifted position in his hard plastic chair, trying to find a comfortable way of sitting. The woman sat motionless, watching him as a predator might observe a weaker animal falling behind the herd.

'A lot has happened while you were away. We don't have much time, so let's get—'

'What do you do, Franklin?' she asked, interrupting him.

He frowned. 'Excuse me?'

The barest flicker of a smile lit her face. 'What do you do? For the Agency, I mean. That's who you work for, isn't it?'

'I'm . . . the director of Special Activities Division.' He had hesitated just an instant too long, and he knew it.

'A little young, aren't you? What are you – thirty-five, thirty-six?'

'Thirty-eight,' he corrected her. For some reason he felt like a teenager trying to buy liquor for the first time, nervous and self-conscious.

Again that strange, knowing smile. 'What happened to Marcus Cain?'

'He retired.'

'Why?'

'Health problems.'

'What kind of health problems?' she pressed, enjoying his discomfort. The questions were flowing out as fast as he could answer them. She was testing him, trying to make him sweat.

It was working.

'Heart attack; hardly surprising given his age and workload. The doctors warned him he'd be dead within a year if he didn't quit, so for once he actually listened. I spent a month working alongside him before he retired. He was a good man,' he said, giving her the full story he had rehearsed in his head. 'Now, if you're finished with Cain's life story, maybe we can move on to the issue at hand . . .'

'Why am I being kept in a holding cell?' she demanded.

He sighed in exasperation. 'For protection.'

'Yours or mine?' she asked, allowing the question to hang in the air. When he didn't answer, she looked down at her hands, slowly clenching and unclenching them. 'I could kill you right now, with my bare hands. You would be dead before the two MPs on the other side of the door could even buzz themselves in.'

Franklin stiffened. She wasn't even close to joking.

'Or maybe you're worried I would smash that observation window over there and find Cain watching you make a fool of yourself?'

'I told you. Cain's gone.'

She smiled again. 'You're lying to me, Franklin.'

'What makes you say that?'

'It is not difficult. The muscles in your throat and shoulders tighten just a little, you straighten your left index finger, and your rate of breathing increases,' she explained, like a doctor making a diagnosis. 'You're consciously aware of not glancing to your left like most people do, so instead you stare fixedly at something, a point of reference, like a cracked brick eight rows up in the wall directly behind me?' She looked at him a little closer. 'You're sweating. Is it warm in here?'

Franklin exhaled and leaned back in his chair. To protest further would be worse than pointless, it would be humiliating. He had failed spectacularly in his task. He could almost feel his stock plummeting in Cain's mind.

'Don't feel bad, Franklin,' she said, gentle and consoling now. 'You are probably an honest man in daily life,

177

maybe even an honourable one. Lying doesn't come naturally to you. You should be proud of that.'

His eyes narrowed, irritation flaring up within him. She was patronising him, treating him like someone to be pitied. A helpless cripple. 'You don't know anything about me.'

'Really?' That smile was still there. 'You have the look of a military man, Franklin. I should know – I have met more than a few in my time. The way you wear that expensive suit . . .' She shook her head. 'You would much rather be in uniform, which means you didn't join the Agency out of choice. You had trouble sitting down, and even though you try to hide it, I can see you're in pain.'

He clenched his fist, trying to hold in check his mounting anger. She was pressing his buttons, exposing his weakness without mercy.

'You're too young to have back problems, so I'd guess you were injured in the line of duty. Shrapnel, maybe? Spinal injuries? Tell me, does it make you feel less of a man, knowing you can't do the things you once did? Run, fight, make love to a woman . . .'

'That's enough!' he snapped. Before he could stop himself, he had slammed his fist down on the table with enough force to send the shock of the impact travelling up his arm.

She watched him with mild interest. She had broken him as easily as swatting a fly on her arm.

Maras leaned forward across the table, lowering her voice in a mock conspiratorial tone. 'He's watching us right now, isn't he? The man behind the curtain, as you say.'

Without waiting for an answer, she pushed away from the table and strode over to the mirror, pacing back and forth along its length as if gauging its strength. But even her icy blue eyes couldn't penetrate the reflective surface.

'Come out, come out, wherever you are, Marcus,' she said mockingly. 'I know you're in there.'

Franklin rose from his chair with difficulty. 'This is going nowhere . . .'

She ignored him. 'It's been a long time since we spoke face to face, Marcus. Don't you have anything to say to your "old friend"?'

But staring into the mirror, she couldn't see the man she was looking for. All she saw was herself, aged and depleted by her years in captivity. Broken down, robbed of her former power and strength.

Suddenly her face twisted in anger, cold fire burning in her eyes as she glared at the mirror.

'Come out, you coward!' she snarled, drawing back her fist and slamming it into the glass with such force that the impact reverberated around the room. 'Come out and look me in the eye!'

Half a second later the cell door flew open, and the two MPs rushed into the room with their weapons drawn. Maras whirled around to face them, fists clenched, body already aligned into a defensive posture. She was unarmed, weak, diminished, but she didn't care. She was still more dangerous with her bare hands than many fully armed soldiers.

'Wait!' Franklin cried, holding up a hand to stop the two men. She was no good to them dead.

Maras made no move to attack them, but neither did she back down. She was watching, and waiting.

'We went to a lot of trouble breaking you out of Khatyrgan,' Franklin said, struggling to keep his tone even. 'You owe us your life.'

'I owe *you* nothing, Franklin,' she spat. '*You* didn't break me out of prison. *You* didn't risk your life to bring me home. Get out and don't come back.'

Franklin had heard enough. She wasn't going to cooperate. Turning on his heel, he strode out of the room. He hadn't realised how hard his heart had been beating, or that he was perspiring.

'Goddamn it,' he said under his breath, loosening his tie as the door clanged shut behind him.

Cain was waiting for him when he returned to the observation room, a cup of coffee in hand. 'Well, that went pretty much how I expected.'

'What do you mean?'

'You're not a soldier – she doesn't respect you,' he explained, completely matter-of-fact. 'And you lied to her. That's a big no-no. She can read body language better than anyone I ever met, spot a liar as fast as our best interrogators.'

Franklin stared at him in disbelief. 'You knew all that? And you let me go through with it anyway?'

'I had to give her someone to vent her anger on, make her think she'd rumbled us.'

'I didn't much appreciate being insulted,' Franklin pointed out with more heat than he'd intended.

Cain shrugged and took a sip of coffee. 'It's a dirty game we play, Dan. Sometimes you have to take one for the team. Man up and grow a pair.'

Franklin glanced back into the observation room. Maras had returned to her chair as if nothing had happened, though the two guards remained by the door, hands on their weapons. She paid them not a glance.

'What happens now?'

'Let me show you something.' Turning to his laptop on the desk, he opened a video file and clicked the play button.

The image that appeared on the screen was a wide-angle shot of the interior of an aircraft. It took Franklin a moment to realise it was the Chinook that had brought Drake's team back from Russia. Cain must have installed hidden cameras throughout the aircraft, allowing him to see and hear everything that went on.

The image zoomed in on Maras, sitting on a bench at the rear of the aircraft. Drake was beside her.

'Like I said, we're here to help,' he said, his voice grainy against the ambient background noise, but perfectly recognisable. *'You don't have to trust us, just don't threaten any of my people. We'll try to make your trip back as comfortable as possible. If you need something, ask. Okay?'*

He was just turning to leave when she spoke up again.

'What is your name?'

'Drake. Ryan Drake.'

The woman was silent for several seconds, then Franklin saw a nod. Not much, but a genuine expression of thanks for respect. Something she had never come close to showing him.

'Thank you, Drake.'

Closing down the video, Cain turned to the younger man. 'We need to have a word with Mr Drake.'

Chapter 27

'Christ, I wish it would shut up out there,' Frost groaned, glaring up at the vaulted hangar roof 50 feet above as if it were her mortal enemy.

It was raining hard outside, massive droplets hammering off the tarmac runways and, more annoyingly, the building they were sheltering in. The noise was like being inside a washing machine filled with nuts and bolts.

With their operation concluded, the team had been ferried out to an isolated hangar on the east side of the base while they waited for their flight back to Washington. Their aircraft was currently refuelling for the long-haul journey, leaving them to do what any good soldiers do most often – sit around and wait.

Keegan, propped up against a stack of wooden cargo boxes, glanced up from the crossword he'd been working on. 'Hey, anyone know another word for irritant? Eight letters.'

'Asshole,' Frost offered.

'That's seven letters.'

'No, I was just calling you an asshole.' She shifted position, trying to find a comfortable way of lying on the three chairs she'd lined up to form a makeshift bed.

Like the others, she had changed back into civilian clothes now that they were no longer on deployment. Jeans, a black turtleneck sweater and a black overcoat were the order of the day now. This might have been summer, but it was still Alaska. The hangar was cold and draughty, the air heavy with the smell of fresh rain and salt.

Keegan ignored her. Inspiration had struck. 'Abrasive! That's it,' he said, filling in the entry. 'Goddamn if I don't have this finished by Thanksgiving.'

'Now you're getting ambitious,' Frost retorted.

At the back of the hangar was a small admin area with a couple of offices and some restrooms. Dietrich was in one of them at that moment, his left shirtsleeve rolled up and a piece of rubber tubing wrapped around his upper arm, causing the veins and arteries to stand out hard against the skin.

In his other hand he held a syringe, loaded with a murky brown liquid that he'd just rendered down using a spoon and a cigarette lighter. Diamorphine, also known as heroin.

It was ready to use.

His injured leg ached. When they'd touched down this morning, the base medics had taken him away, stitched him up and bandaged the wound properly. He'd been lucky – the round had only grazed him, causing little damage to the muscle beneath. He walked with a painful limp, but he was told he'd make a full recovery.

Lucky him.

His hand was shaking as he brought the syringe to his arm. It had been a good twenty-four hours since he'd last shot up, and the withdrawal effects were becoming more apparent with each passing hour.

Hesitating a moment, he looked at himself in the mirror above the sink, taking in his gaunt and haggard appearance, his pale clammy skin and dishevelled hair.

That's the reason you fucked up last night, part of him knew. You didn't search that guard properly or you would have found his radio. You almost got everyone killed when you couldn't find the right key. You were shot because you weren't thinking straight. You deserved to lose the entire leg.

You stupid bastard. You could have gotten everyone killed!

He looked down at the syringe again, seeing it as if in a new light. It wasn't the solution he so often believed it to be. It was the reason his life had gone to shit.

Last night had been a revelation, a sobering reminder of how much of a mess he'd made of himself, about the countless other missions that had come so close to failure.

Because of that innocuous little syringe.

He didn't even pause to think about what he did next. If he had, he might well have reconsidered. In a moment of sudden anger, he dropped it on the floor and stamped on it, crushing the delicate instrument beneath his boot, then looked back up at his pale, drawn reflection.

No more.

Never again.

Chapter 28

'Ryan, good to see you again.' Cain smiled in greeting as Drake entered the modest conference room that served as his makeshift office. He was in casual mode now, or as close as he came to it, having removed his suit jacket, rolled up his shirtsleeves and loosened his tie.

'First of all, I just want to say that you did a hell of a job—'

Drake cut him off with a raised hand.

'With all due respect, I don't need to be congratulated. I'm here because I was ordered to come. But if you want me to debrief Maras, I want to know who exactly she is and why we risked our lives to save her, and I want to know right now.'

Cain said nothing for several seconds. There was no angry retort, no exclamation of anger or censure like Drake expected. Cain just stood there looking at him, taking the measure of the man.

The silence grew oppressive in those few moments, and Drake's own surge of resentment and indignation paled in the face of such cool, controlled menace.

He felt colour rise to his face. The whisky he'd drunk earlier had made him surly and belligerent, yet now he perceived his actions for what they were. He was acting like a moody teenager faced with some unhappy chore, and shit like that didn't play too well with men like Cain.

Then, to his surprise, Cain smiled. 'Are you finished?'

Drake said nothing, and the older man was perceptive enough to take his silence for what it was. 'Good, because as it happens, I had a feeling you'd say something like that. Take a seat, Ryan,' he said, gesturing to an empty chair.

Drake did as he was asked, and Cain settled himself opposite, positioning himself behind the room's one and only desk. It was a cheap affair – metal frame with a wooden veneer top – but somehow his mere presence invested it with a sense of significance and authority.

The director of Special Activities Division studied Drake for several seconds. In other men, it might have seemed as if he was composing his thoughts, marshalling the information he wished to convey, but Drake knew better. Cain was the sort who always knew exactly what he wanted to say long before he said it.

He was keeping Drake waiting, because he could.

Then, at last, he started talking. 'Her real name is Anya – at least, that's what she answers to. You'll have guessed by now that she isn't a US citizen. She was born in Lithuania when it was still part of the Soviet Union, but she defected to our side when she was eighteen years old.'

Drake raised an eyebrow. 'Why?'

'It's a long story. Suffice to say, she wasn't happy with life behind the Iron Curtain, and knowing what I know, I don't blame her. She crossed over the Baltic to Sweden in eighty-three, and from there she made her way Stateside. She came to our attention about a year later,' Cain went on. 'She was young, resourceful, intelligent and eager to sign up. The military wasn't interested in her, so we put her to work.' He sighed, looking almost wistful. 'She exceeded our expectations in every way possible. Eventually she was even given her own para-military unit to command. No matter what we asked of her, she always came through. We ended up using her more and more.'

'So what happened?' Drake pressed.

'Same thing that happens to most people when they're pushed too hard, I guess.' Cain smiled, but it was more of a painful grimace. 'She snapped. Four years ago she went dark during a mission in Afghanistan, severed all contact with us. The last we heard, she was heading to Iraq. We tried to intercept her, but the Russian FSB found her first. You might say they had unfinished business.'

Drake could guess why. The FSB was the post-Communism incarnation of the old KGB – the ruthless and formidable Soviet intelligence agency that had terrorised the West for decades. He imagined they hadn't forgotten a woman like Anya, especially since she used to be one of their citizens.

'Anyway, however it happened, we'd lost her,' Cain concluded. 'Most of us thought she'd been executed. Hell of a way for someone like her to end up, but shit happens as they say – and it happens in this job more than most.' He raised an eyebrow, his eyes reflecting memories of countless other such stories. 'But as it turned out, we were wrong.'

Apparently so, Drake concluded. 'So why the sudden rush to bring her home?'

'This is where the waters get muddied.' The director sighed, reached into his shirt pocket and put his glasses on, then started tapping away at his laptop. 'You know what a Predator drone is, I assume?'

'Of course. It's an unmanned recon aircraft. We've got dozens of them flying over Iraq and Afghanistan.'

More than once he'd been on the receiving end of the vital intelligence provided by Predators. They were invaluable guardian angels circling overhead, all-seeing and all-knowing. They allowed troops on the ground to track enemy movements, spot ambushes, vector in air or artillery strikes, plan counter-attacks. He could scarcely imagine how many lives had been saved by the deceptively unassuming aircraft.

'Right. At least, we did.'

Drake looked at him curiously. 'What do you mean?'

'They're grounded. All of them. Our entire inventory.'

For an instant, Drake thought he was joking. Such a suggestion was so preposterous that it could only be made in jest. But one look at Cain's expression was enough to convince him otherwise.

'Why?'

'Three days ago we lost contact with one of our Predators in northern Iraq. Then, when it came back online, we saw this . . .' He turned the laptop around for Drake to see.

The image on the screen displayed a devastated urban street. One entire side of a big three-storey building had been demolished, rubble and twisted wreckage lying scattered across the surrounding streets.

The image was instantly familiar to Drake, though it took him a few moments to place it.

'I saw this. On CNN the other day,' he said. 'A Predator did this?'

Cain nodded grimly. 'All three of its Hellfire missiles deployed straight into a crowded city street. It's a goddamn nightmare.'

Drake wasn't about to argue. And yet, he wasn't seeing the connection between the two explanations Cain had just given. 'So how does Mar . . . Anya fit into this?'

Cain turned the laptop around to resume his work.

'Our working theory was that someone seized control of the drone remotely, found a way to bypass its encrypted firewall.' He paused for a moment, clicking the mouse a couple of times to access a new file. 'Then we received this.'

Once more he turned the laptop around, allowing Drake to see the video file that was starting up.

Staring out from the screen was a Caucasian man, perhaps in his late thirties or early forties. His skin was tanned, his hair dark and unruly, his jaw darkened by several days' growth of beard. Drake supposed he could have been called handsome in a rugged kind of way, though there was something about his eyes that wasn't quite right.

His left was pale blue-grey, focused and intense, while the right was a little off colour, and appeared oddly glazed and inexpressive. It took Drake a moment to realise it was a prosthetic.

The camera was focused in tight on his face, showing very little else except that he was standing against an olive green background.

'You know who I am.' He spoke with an American accent, his voice low pitched and gravelly. 'And by now you know what I can do. The explosion in Mosul was no accident, and believe me, it can happen again. I have the ability to take control of any Predator drone anywhere on earth, at any time. If you don't want this to happen again, you'll do exactly as I say.'

He exhaled slowly before going on. 'A former operative of yours is being held in Khatyrgan Prison in Russia. You knew her by the code name Maras. You will find her and bring her back to US soil, alive and unharmed within five days, after which you'll be given further instructions. This deadline is not negotiable, and I will not discuss terms with you. If you fail to comply with this demand, I will leak detailed information on how to hack the Predator's control program to every major terrorist group in the world. I will cripple your battlefield surveillance capability for years. Time's ticking, so I suggest you don't waste it.'

As the file came to a stop, Cain sighed and leaned back in his chair, appearing suddenly old and weary. 'Now maybe you'll understand our sense of urgency.'

Indeed he did. Drake never could have imagined there was so much at stake. 'Who is he?'

The older man rubbed his eyes. 'His name's Munro. Dominic Munro. Ex-Green Beret. He used to be one of our operatives, but he left the Agency seven years ago.'

'How does he know Anya?'

'She's the reason he left,' Cain explained. 'He was Anya's protégé, her star pupil I guess you'd say. They served together in Task Force Black.'

Drake frowned. He'd never heard of such a group.

'There are levels of secrecy even within the Agency, Drake,' Cain explained, noting his confused look. 'I can't go into all the details, but I can tell you that Task Force Black was a paramilitary unit formed back in the mid-eighties. They did a lot of clandestine work for us, and did it well. So well in fact that by the end of the nineties they had their own intelligence networks, their own logistical base, even their own funding. They were practically an organisation within an organisation, and Munro and Anya were running it all.'

Drake had no idea. He'd been a young shit-head in the Parachute Regiment while all this had been happening. 'So what happened?'

'They "fell out". I never did get the full story, but apparently Munro tried to have her assassinated.

Needless to say, he failed.' Cain adopted a pained expression. 'Anya tracked him down and took his right eye as punishment.'

That explained the prosthetic, at least, Drake thought.

'She was never the same after that. She handed Munro over to us, close to death, and made us promise to lock him away for ever. We threw him in a military prison for life. Then, about six months ago, he disappeared.'

Drake frowned. 'What do you mean?'

'He was being transported to Fort Leavenworth, but he never made it. They found the truck he was in – no sign of the guards or the driver, and no sign of Munro. Like I say, he just disappeared.'

Drake was stunned. 'And you didn't think that might be a problem?'

Cain fixed him with a hard glare. 'Of course we did. But Munro was trained at escape and evasion – trained by Anya, as it happens. If men like him don't want to be found, they won't be.'

'So he's doing all this for revenge?'

The older man shrugged. 'Who the hell knows what's going on in his head? But right now, he's got us by the balls, plain and simple. We've been forced to ground all Predator flights worldwide until we can resolve this, and you don't need me to tell you what a dangerous position that puts us in. Our troops in Iraq and Afghanistan are fighting virtually blind.'

'My God . . .' Drake breathed, stunned by what he was hearing. It didn't take a genius to see Cain's plan. 'So you need Anya's help to find him.'

Cain removed his glasses and stared at Drake across the desk. 'She trained him, taught him everything he knows. She's our best and only shot at stopping him.

But she's angry, paranoid, and probably scared. Frankly, I don't blame her, but someone has to talk her round.'

And so they'd come down to it. 'Why me?'

'I saw the video footage from the plane, Ryan.' When Drake's eyes lit up, he held up a hand to forestall any protests or explanations. 'It's a standard precaution on jobs like this. But I saw how she acted around you. She let you in, she let her guard drop, even if only for a moment. I think she might trust you, Ryan. And believe me, that's a rare thing.'

Once again Drake recalled the look in her eyes when he tried to reach out to her. She hadn't exactly bared her soul to him, but there had been something. A flicker of vulnerability, the tentative beginning of trust, of humanity in those cold blue eyes.

'I won't fuck her over,' he decided straight away. 'Whatever her history, she didn't deserve to end up in that place.'

'I agree,' Cain said. 'And nobody's going to fuck her over. We've got a Presidential pardon signed, sealed and delivered. If she helps bring Munro in, she can walk away. We'll keep tabs on her, of course, and she won't be allowed to leave the country at first, but in all other respects she'll be free.' He looked at Drake frankly for a long moment. 'As hard as this might be for you to believe, we're not monsters here. We look after our own, even if they go astray.'

He looked down and swallowed, as if struggling with himself. To Drake's surprise, there was genuine emotion in his voice when he spoke again. 'However she ended up, there was a time when Anya was very special. I considered her a friend, and I don't forget friends easily. I'll make sure she gets what she needs, but first she has to help us.' He looked up at Drake again. 'So what do you say, Ryan? I'm all out of options here. You're my last shot.'

Drake eyed him hard. If he was lying, he was doing a pretty good job.

But it was more than that. The image of Anya on that photograph, with her haunting blue eyes, remained burned into his mind.

The answer came almost before he realised it.

'I'll talk to her.'

Chapter 29

Anya sat alone in the holding cell with her hands on the table, savouring the quiet darkness and the novelty of being safe. She was in a clean, comfortable, heated room that contained no threats or dangers. If she wanted food or drink, she had only to ask and it would be brought to her.

She had showered – a long, hot, luxurious shower that she could have spent hours standing under – and changed into clean clothes. With her long blonde hair smelling of shampoo for the first time in years and her skin scrubbed clean, she was actually starting to feel human again.

Not long before, she had eaten her first hot meal in four years. Roast beef, potatoes, steamed vegetables, bread, butter, fruit and chocolate. Simple food, but more delicious than anything she could remember.

She shifted position a little, getting comfortable. She knew she was being watched constantly by video cameras and by people on the other side of the viewing mirror, but she didn't care. Let them watch.

For the first time in a long time, she didn't have to be on constant alert. She didn't have to worry about survival. No guards were going to come storming in. No ominous thumps, no slamming doors, no heavy footsteps announced another visit from Bastard.

She smiled inwardly, thinking about the violent, brutal

death she had inflicted on him. It was unprofessional to lose control like that, but she didn't really care. It had pleased her beyond measure to watch him die at her hands.

Her only regret was that she hadn't made it last longer, made him suffer more. She didn't normally take pleasure in needless cruelty, but for him she would have made an exception. Sadly there hadn't been time for it; it was more important to ensure he died.

The question now was what was going to happen to her. She wasn't afraid of what the future held – she had come too far, endured too much to feel fear now – but she was curious why Cain had gone to all this trouble after four long years of doing nothing.

Her thoughts were interrupted by the harsh buzz of the cell door. She looked up as the door swung open, and felt a moment of surprise as Drake walked into the room.

He had changed clothes since the last time she saw him, discarding the black paramilitary fatigues, webbing and body armour in favour of plain blue jeans, walking boots, a black T-shirt and a grey zipped jumper open at the neck. His dark brown hair was damp and dishevelled; he'd either showered recently or been outside in the rain.

Rain. She hadn't felt rain on her skin in four years.

For the first time, she really looked at him, seeing him not as a fellow soldier, a source of information or a potential threat, but as a man.

He was tall, she realised. Taller than herself, perhaps an inch or two above 6 foot, and well made. Not bulked up and barrel chested, but possessing instead an efficient, athletic physique that balanced both strength and agility.

It was obvious from the way he carried himself that he was a man accustomed to physical danger, to trusting his life in his own hands. He didn't strut or swagger, but there was an easy confidence in his manner that came from living an eventful and self-reliant life.

She should know.

His age wasn't easy to guess. He wasn't old and weathered, but neither was he young and boyish. His face was lean and tanned, the features hard and definite, with a certain intensity that only came with age and experience. His nose was straight and narrow, his jaw firm and determined, tapering down to a well-defined chin.

His eyes, vividly green she noticed, were focused on her, filled with an odd mixture of wariness, curiosity and most of all, surprise.

Surprise wasn't the word for it. Drake was astonished by the change that had come over the woman.

Gone were the grimy bloodstained clothes, the ingrained dirt and filth. Her skin, though still pale from years of darkness, was scrubbed clean and glowed with renewed vigour. Her long thick blonde hair, once greasy, matted and tangled, had been thoroughly washed and combed, and was tied back in a simple ponytail.

The plain white T-shirt she wore left her arms bare, exposing pale skin and lean sinewy muscle. Yet her gender was clearly evidenced by the curve of breasts beneath the T-shirt, the sensual fullness of her lips, the finely sculpted cheekbones and the clean, graceful line of her jaw. Despite everything she had endured, she remained a strikingly attractive woman.

He pushed these thoughts aside, feeling almost guilty for allowing them in. He was here to debrief her, not to gawk at her.

'Hello, Anya,' he said, taking a seat without asking permission.

It was her turn to look surprised, though her reaction

was quickly masked. 'It has been a long time since I heard that name.'

Drake shrugged. 'Cain was good enough to fill me in on the details.'

Anya's expression didn't change. Only her eyes betrayed her feelings, and Drake was perceptive enough to spot it.

She said nothing for the next several seconds, and neither did he, content to let the silence stretch out. He had watched a replay of Franklin's clumsy attempt to debrief her, and recognised a few of her tactics. She was a soldier, trained to find her enemy's weakness and exploit it. Poor Dan had been easy prey.

'What do you want, Drake?' she finally asked, a slight edge of irritation creeping into her voice.

'What do I want?' he repeated. 'What I *want* is to go home and do my best to forget this mess. But we don't always get what we want, do we? I came to give you a message.'

Reaching into his pocket, he pulled out a folded piece of paper and slid it across the table. Frowning, she unfolded it and read, her icy blue eyes quickly darting across the page.

'Let me save you the trouble. It's a signed Presidential pardon, granting you full immunity from prosecution, and a guarantee that you'll be freed when this is over. It's already been confirmed by the Attorney General. You can start a new life, buy a house and a dog . . . whatever you want.'

Her eyes were on him again in an instant. Were her hands trembling?

'There are conditions, I assume?'

He nodded. 'The Agency wants your help.'

'With what?'

Drake leaned back in his chair. This was the critical

moment. 'Does the name Dominic Munro mean anything to you?'

The flash of recognition in her eyes told him everything he needed to know. Still, she remained stubbornly silent for several seconds.

When it became obvious that Drake wasn't going to move on without an answer, she at last nodded. 'He was a student of mine. Our relationship ended badly.'

'So I heard,' Drake remarked. 'Apparently our friend Dominic likes to hold grudges. He escaped from prison, and three days ago he hijacked a Predator drone and used it to kill a lot of innocent civilians in Iraq. Now he's holding us to ransom unless we deliver you to him.'

One corner of her mouth lifted in a crooked smile. 'I see. You broke me out of prison only to hand me over to a terrorist? A Presidential pardon isn't much use if you are not alive to collect it.'

'They want your help in finding him, that's all. They don't expect you to hand yourself over,' Drake explained. 'You taught Munro everything he knows, according to Cain. You can out-think him.' He raised an eyebrow. 'Of course, if you're not up to it . . .'

The look in her eyes even gave him pause for thought, and it was a few moments before the look of anger and indignation abated. 'If you were in my position, would you agree to this?'

'I don't give a shit what you do. I'm just here to deliver the message,' he remarked bluntly. 'But for what it's worth, we risked our lives to break you out of that place. It would be a shame if that was all for nothing.'

He leaned back in his chair, watching her reactions and saying nothing further. As shitty a deal as it might have been, it wasn't as if she had other options. She just needed time to come to that realisation.

It didn't take long.

'If I do this, I have some conditions of my own,' Anya decided.

'Such as?'

The woman leaned forward, staring straight into his eyes. 'I want back in. I want to be part of the Agency again. I want my old unit re-formed, under my command. I want my full security clearance restored. I want my life back.'

'That's not going to happen.'

She shrugged and leaned back. 'Then I am not going anywhere.'

She was raising the stakes. He had little option but to call her bluff. 'Anya, twenty-four hours ago you were freezing your arse off in a Russian jail. Now you have a chance to start over. Do you really want to fuck that up by asking for something they can't give? That part of your life is over, but you can still make the most of what you have left. Isn't that enough?'

The woman remained silent. He had no idea what was going on behind that cold exterior and those icy blue eyes, but somehow he sensed his words had struck a chord.

Deciding to press his advantage, he pushed his chair back and stood up. 'Anyway, consider the message delivered. See you around.'

He was just approaching the door when she spoke again.

'Do you believe him?'

He stopped and turned around to look at her. She was leaning forward, staring right at him, her eyes wide, almost hopeful.

'Do you believe Cain will honour this agreement?'

There was no answer to give but the truth. 'I don't

know. But I believe he cares about you. And that he's sorry for what happened.'

She let out a faint sigh and leaned back in her chair. And for a brief moment, he caught that strange look of vulnerability and longing that he'd seen on the flight back from Russia.

'If I agree to your offer, what happens next?'

'You'll be flown back to Langley. Then we wait for further instructions from Munro.'

She nodded thoughtfully. 'Then I accept. But I want you to come with me.'

Drake blinked in surprise. 'You don't need me.'

'I don't need anyone,' she assured him. 'But I want you there.'

'Why?'

'Because you're the only one who hasn't lied to me.' She folded her arms, making it plain she wouldn't budge on this issue. 'That is my condition. If you agree to it, I will help you. If not . . . then as you say, see you around.'

Saying nothing, Drake turned and banged on the door three times. As it buzzed open, he gave Anya one last look before leaving the room.

Part Two
Deception

Regard your soldiers as your children, and they will follow you into the deepest valleys; look on them as your own beloved sons, and they will stand by you even unto death.

Sun Tzu's *The Art of War*

Chapter 30

Drake stretched and rubbed his eyes as the seat-belt light pinged, announcing that they had begun their descent towards Andrews Air Force Base in Washington. It had been a ten-hour flight from Anchorage, with a refuelling stop in Colorado to add to the fun.

He never slept well on aircraft. There was something about the warm, dry air and the cramped confines of the seats that set him on edge.

Beside him, Anya was wide awake, sitting with her eyes glued to the television screen in front of her. It was tuned to CNN.

The handcuffs around her wrists didn't seem to trouble her at all. Drake was left with the disconcerting impression that she could slip out of them any time she wished, and was merely going through the motions to humour him.

'Good morning,' she said without glancing over.

'Don't you ever sleep?'

He ran a hand through his hair, sticking up at all angles from his restless efforts at falling asleep. He didn't need a mirror to tell him he looked like shit. His eyes felt dry and gritty, his skin greasy and unpleasant.

She gave him a sharp look. 'I have been gone four years, Drake. I have a lot of catching up to do.'

His irritation vanished in a flash. Looking at her now, it was almost possible to forget what she'd been through.

'How are things looking so far?' he couldn't help asking.

'A mess,' she replied, visibly angry, as if she had entrusted the fate of the world to someone else in her absence, and they had dropped the ball. 'We are still stuck in Afghanistan.' She shook her head in disbelief. 'Twenty years ago I told them we would be back there one day, and here we are, fighting a war we can never win.'

'What makes you so sure?'

'The Mujahideen were the bravest soldiers I ever met. Not very disciplined, but completely without fear. You can't beat an enemy like that. The Red Army tried and failed. What chance do you think we have?'

Drake stared at her. The Afghan freedom fighters were legendary for the tenacious guerrilla war they had fought against the mighty Soviet army. Their humiliating withdrawal after ten years of fruitless conflict had signalled the beginning of the end for the Soviet Union.

'*You* fought with the Mujahideen? During the Russian occupation?'

'In another life.' She shrugged, dismissing the old memories as if they were of no consequence. 'Now . . . it is a different world.'

He was silent for a time, weighing up his next question. In the end, he couldn't help himself. 'Mind if I ask you something?'

She held up her manacled hands. 'It seems I'm in no position to refuse,' she remarked with a wry smile.

'Why did you turn rogue?'

The smile vanished as quickly as it had come. 'Is that what Cain told you?' His silence told her everything she needed to know, and she gave a resigned shrug. It was the weary, pained acceptance of an old injustice.

When she looked at him again, her gaze had

hardened. 'Let me ask *you* something, Ryan Drake. Do you believe in what you do? Do you think you serve a just cause?'

Her question caught him off guard, and it took him a few moments to summon up his answer. 'I suppose so.'

'I did. Once.' She sighed and leaned back in her seat, holding up her cuffs once more. 'And this was my reward.'

Their jet touched down at Andrews with the smooth, easy efficiency of a commercial airliner, taxiing to a halt inside one of the big hangars on the west side of the airfield. A couple of black Grand Cherokee 4x4s were waiting for them, along with four agents from the CIA's Office of Security – three men and one woman. Typical of the Agency, they were all dressed in dark business suits.

'Looks like the welcoming committee's here,' Drake observed.

Dietrich, Frost and Keegan went out ahead of him. They had accompanied him on the flight from Alaska, delaying their own return by a couple of hours. Drake suspected their decision had as much to do with the allure of travelling by executive jet as their sense of professional obligation, but he was grateful for their company all the same.

He glanced out the window and saw Keegan stretch and arch his back, then run a hand through his shaggy mane of blond hair. Nearby, Dietrich lit up a cigarette.

'Come on, let's get this over with,' he said, taking Anya's arm and helping her up. She shrugged out of his grip, determined to do it herself.

With Anya in front where he could keep an eye on her, they descended the stairs at the front of the aircraft to the concrete hangar floor. No sooner had they emerged from the plane than two of the security agents came forward to meet them – one of the men and the woman.

Approaching with sure, easy strides, the woman flashed her ID card. 'Good morning, sir. My name's Watts. I'm the officer in charge here.'

Drake shook hands, surprised by the strength of her grip. She was a good-looking woman. Smaller than Anya, with a neat, compact physique and short brown hair.

'Drake,' he replied. 'Good to meet you.'

'And you, sir. We're here to escort you to Langley.'

Drake glanced at the small group of agents. 'Only four operatives?'

'Believe me, there's not much we can't handle,' Watts assured him, her dark eyes flashing with a touch of professional pride as she steered them toward the Grand Cherokees. 'Anyway, Director Cain suggested we keep things low-key. Local PD have been notified, and we have an armed tactical team on standby. If anything happens, they can be on site within minutes. Plus, we have other security protocols.' She turned her attention to Anya. 'Can I see your left forearm, ma'am?'

She was being polite, but it wasn't a request.

Hesitating, Anya reluctantly held out her arms, cuffed together as they were. Watts rolled up the sleeve of her jumpsuit, while a second operative approached with what looked like a large hypodermic syringe.

'This may hurt a little,' Watts explained.

Pressing the device tight against her arm to form a seal, he pulled a trigger on the underside. There was a dull hiss, and for a moment the woman's face tightened in pain. A trickle of blood ran down her arm as the syringe was pulled away.

'What was that?' Drake asked.

'Satellite tracking device, implanted in the muscle

layer beneath the skin. Very hard to remove by force,' Watts explained. 'It transmits her location via secure satellite uplink to our monitoring station at Langley. With it, we can follow her anywhere on the face of the earth.'

Drake raised an eyebrow and glanced at Anya. She didn't look happy at being bugged in such an invasive way, but she said nothing. That seemed to be her standard tactic when dealing with authority.

'One more thing, sir. I'll take her handcuff keys,' Watts said, holding out her hand.

Drake frowned. 'She's my prisoner.'

The security agent gave an apologetic shrug. 'It's protocol, sir. I'm sorry. For the duration of the transfer, we're responsible for the prisoner.'

She was still holding out her hand. Realising she wouldn't take no for an answer, Drake gave her the keys. What harm could it do, anyway?

His thoughts were interrupted when his cellphone started ringing. He glanced at the number and frowned. It was Jessica.

His sister never called without warning, especially not on his work phone. It must be important.

'Secure her for transport. I need to take this call,' he said, then leaned a little closer and lowered his voice. 'Go easy on her.'

Watts nodded.

Turning away, Drake retreated a short distance and hit the receive button. 'I'm a little busy right now, Jess. Can I call you back?'

But his sister didn't reply. The voice that spoke was male, American, low pitched and gravelly. It was a voice that sounded ominously familiar.

'Don't talk. Just listen. If you ever want to see your

207

sister again, you'll listen very carefully to what I'm about to say.'

Those words froze him on the spot.

'There are three rules to this conversation. Rule One, if you don't cooperate fully, if you try to alert anyone, if you make any attempt to stall or lie to me, I will kill your sister in such a way that even you won't recognise her body. Rule Two, I'm going to give you a series of instructions in a few moments. If you fail to comply with them, see Rule One. Rule Three, you speak only when asked a direct question. Do you understand?'

The phone was shaking in his hand. 'Who are you?'

'Isn't it obvious?'

Drake exhaled, unable to suppress the shudder of fear that swept through him. Now he knew why the voice sounded familiar. It was Munro.

'You're bluffing,' he said, trying desperately to keep his voice under control.

'Am I?'

The line crackled for a few moments, and he heard muffled words in the background.

Then, just like that, another voice came on the line.

'Ryan?'

His heart leapt, the blood pounded in his ears, and a horrible tightening, sickening feeling twisted his guts.

It was her. No doubt about it. She was shaken, terrified, distraught, but her voice was unmistakable. It was his sister.

'Jess, where are you?'

'They told me to tell you they're listening in. Two men, they . . . took me when I was walking to my car last night.' Her voice was trembling. She was having to fight to stay in control. 'They're going to kill me if you don't do what they say . . .'

208

'Oh, Christ,' he said under his breath. 'Jess, listen to me. I'm going to fix this. I'm going to get you out of this. I promise . . .'

Suddenly there was a commotion on the other end, and Munro's voice came back on. 'You get the picture, Drake. Do what I tell you or bad things will happen to young Jessica. And believe me, they'll be real bad.'

Drake felt as if a knife had been driven into his stomach. 'You fucking—'

'Careful, Ryan! Let's not get off on the wrong foot here.'

It took a great effort of will to calm his voice. Shouting and screaming wasn't going to resolve this. Somehow, he had to stay calm and logical.

'What do you want?'

'You've been running plenty of errands for Cain lately. Well, now you can run one for me. You're transporting Anya back to Langley. I want you to break her free.'

This was insane. 'We were going to hand her over to you.'

'You actually believe Cain would give her up?' Munro chuckled with amusement. 'No, he'll use her to hunt me down. My old mentor, taught me everything I know, and all that bullshit . . . He's trying to make me play his game. The only way to beat him is to change the rules.'

Drake couldn't believe what he was hearing.

'Are you out of your fucking mind?' he hissed. Luckily for him, the roar of a departing jet masked his angry words from Watts and the others. 'She's in an armoured car, surrounded by agents with guns. It's impossible.'

'Just like it was impossible to get her out of prison?' Munro prompted. 'Come on, Ryan. You can do better than that. *Find a way*. If you don't . . . see Rules One and Two.'

It took every ounce of self-control in his body not to scream his next words at the top of his voice. 'If you hurt her, I swear to God—'

'I'm not a monster, Ryan, despite what you might have heard about me,' Munro cut in, a hard edge of anger in his voice. 'When the time comes, you have to act fast. I can help you, but only if you listen to me. Take out the agents in your car, secure Anya, and I'll give you further instructions.'

'How will I know when it's time?'

'I'll call you. As soon as your phone starts ringing, you have to act. If you try to warn anyone, your sister dies. If you fail and get caught, she dies. If I think you're not giving it your best, she dies. In fact, you're gonna have to work hard to keep her alive, so I suggest you don't fuck up. Good luck.'

The line went dead.

For several seconds, Drake didn't move. He just stood there in the cavernous hangar, rooted to the spot, his mind racing. Could he warn someone? But how?

The phone! Munro had called using Jessica's phone.

Tracking it would be a piece of piss for the Agency. Phones were like homing beacons for satellite tracking. If they could find it, they could send in assault teams . . .

But even if they did, Munro could easily execute her as a final act of revenge, or she could be killed in the crossfire. Or Munro might have destroyed her phone now that he'd made his point.

Confused and frightening thoughts whirled through his mind. He imagined Jessica being grabbed from behind by powerful men in black bomber jackets and bundled into the back of a waiting van. She wouldn't be able to fight them off. They'd be ready for anything.

Then he saw her being driven out to some cold,

deserted building, where they would have everything set up and ready for her arrival. Then they could go about their work without worrying about being disturbed . . .

'Ryan! Are you finished?' Dietrich called out from the second vehicle. 'We're leaving with or without you.'

Drake took a breath, clenched his jaw and flipped the phone closed.

'Yeah,' he replied, trying to mask his fear as he turned around. 'Yeah, I'm finished.'

Chapter 31

Something was wrong. Anya could tell the moment Drake slid into the back seat. The tension in his shoulders, the tight set of his jaw, the worry lines on his forehead, and most of all the haunted, almost desperate look in his eyes.

Her handcuffs were secured to a restraining point in the footwell, preventing her from moving far, but she leaned a little closer to him and spoke quietly. 'Is something wrong?'

He shook his head.

He was lying. Even if she hadn't been good at reading body language, she could tell he was lying.

'You look nervous.'

Anger flared in his eyes, but he quickly masked it. 'If I want your opinions, I'll ask for them.'

Anya leaned back in her seat as they rolled out of the hangar. Bright sunlight streamed in through the tinted windows, hurting her eyes, but she didn't care. It was worth any discomfort to see the sun again, to feel its warmth on her skin.

She had missed it desperately during her imprisonment, though she hadn't allowed herself to think about it too much. Like a diet of the mind, she only indulged that particular appetite on rare occasions, fearing she would drive herself to despair otherwise.

She ached to be outside, to feel the breeze in her hair and grass beneath her feet, to smell the scent of wild flowers, to lie on her back and stare up at the endless sky . . .

No. She pushed those thoughts away through great effort. Those were things she couldn't allow to intrude into her mind, weaknesses she couldn't expose. Not yet. Not when her freedom still hung in the balance.

Perhaps, when this was over, when she'd won true freedom for herself, perhaps then she could allow her guard to drop. Perhaps then she could open up that part of her mind that she had carefully shut away, studiously protected against the ravages of the world around her.

Her thoughts turned to their destination, and what would happen when they got there. It had been a long time since she had been to Langley. Even before her imprisonment she had disliked the place, avoiding it as much as possible.

It made her uneasy, as did most large buildings packed full of people. She hated the corporate suits, the clean pristine office environments, the computers and the constantly ringing phones. It was all noise, all chaos, all confusion.

At her insistence, she had received most of her orders and briefings in the field, moving from one operation to the next almost without pause.

There had even been a time, long ago, when Cain had ventured out into the field with her, briefing her in person on her objectives. They had both been younger then. Both adventurous, both optimistic about the future, both sharing a vision of what they were working to create.

A lot of things had changed.

Passing through the base's main security gate, they joined the Capital Beltway and headed west, making a wide loop around the city before heading north on Anacostia Freeway. It was a roundabout route, but she understood why. They were staying on the main drags where they could keep their speed up.

It wasn't long before they found themselves gliding past a world of leafy suburbs, comfortable detached houses and trendy coffee shops. Everywhere Anya looked she saw men in sunglasses and polo shirts, women in fashionable trouser suits chatting on their cellphones, big shiny SUVs and luxury sedans.

The whole place reeked of affluence and excess, of comfort and safety and air conditioning. It was so radically different from the world she had known for the past four years that for some time she just stared out her window, spellbound by the incongruity of it all.

Drake said nothing. He didn't seem verbose at the best of times, which pleased her immensely. She hated people who talked for the sake of it, particularly men. For her it betrayed a lack of confidence, as if they couldn't stand to share a silence and felt they had to fill it with pointless banter.

But in this case there was another reason. Whatever he'd heard on the phone earlier had left him deeply shaken.

She wasn't sure whether to feel worried or not. She didn't care about his personal happiness, but she wondered if his unease related to her in some way. Did he know something about what was to happen to her that was making him worried?

The dash-mounted radio beeped.

'Unit One. We have an RTA on the Anacostia Freeway, about three miles north of you. Recommend you take Frederick Douglas Bridge.'

'Roger that. Frederick Douglas,' the driver replied.

Anya didn't know his name, but it was the same man who had implanted her tracking device.

A big man, mid-forties, broad shouldered and muscular, probably ex-military judging by his appearance and body language. He had the relaxed, laconic air of a man who had been doing the same job for years and knew it inside and out. She suspected he was more used to intimidating people than fighting them, and probably wouldn't be hard to take down.

Clicking off the radio, he glanced at Watts and made a face. 'Same shit, different day.'

Turning off the freeway just as the traffic started to build, they headed north-west across Frederick Douglas Bridge, passing close to Washington Naval Yard with its solemn ranks of grey warships, before heading for central DC where they would connect with the Southwest Freeway.

'Been with the Agency long, Mr Drake?' the woman called Watts asked, twisting around in her seat and acting as if Anya didn't exist.

Watts was in her mid-thirties, neat and efficient looking, and pretty in a way that didn't draw too much attention. Anya caught the faint scent of her perfume. She couldn't remember the last time she had worn perfume.

Unlike the driver, this one didn't come from a military background. She was college educated, probably not to degree level, but still bright and motivated. She would have been through the Agency's marksmanship and advanced unarmed combat programmes – Anya had helped develop both, and knew their limitations.

By the looks of her, she trained a couple of times a week in the gym, supplemented by morning runs every few days. She didn't smoke, didn't drink to excess, probably didn't eat much junk food. But she trained to look good rather than because her job demanded it. There was a softness, a complacency about her that Anya found mildly irritating.

Of more interest was the weapon Watts carried in a shoulder holster on her ride side. The movement had caused her jacket to open a little, exposing the side arm. A Glock Model 22, chambered with .40 Smith & Wesson ammunition. Effective range, up to 50 metres. Standard issue for Agency security personnel.

Drake had spotted it too. Anya saw his eyes light up as they caught sight of the weapon, yet at the same time his look of tension and worry increased. What was he thinking?

'About the last four years,' he replied.

'We don't see many of our cousins from over the water working at Langley,' she remarked, her smile easy, almost playful. She was flirting with him, giving him an opportunity to talk about himself.

Accustomed as she was to reading tiny variations in posture and nuances of expression, Anya could see the almost imperceptible change in the woman's body language. She had become subtly more open, relaxed and friendly. She doubted Drake had noticed though. Aside from being a man and therefore oblivious to such subtleties, he had other things on his mind.

'Friends in high places,' Drake replied with a weak smile.

Mistaking his reticence for lack of interest, Watts turned back around, concentrating her attention on the satellite navigation unit mounted on the dash. She didn't have to do anything to it, Anya knew, but she needed a distraction to cover up the minor awkwardness he'd created.

They were almost at the freeway. Stopping at an inter-section, they waited for the lights to turn green before pulling away again.

Just 20 yards behind them in the second Grand Chorokee, Dietrich leaned back in his seat, taking a deep breath and trying to still his wildly beating heart. He was pale and perspiring, shivering despite the warm weather. His head pounded. His fists were clenched, trying to stop his hands from shaking.

He swallowed, but his throat was so dry it made no difference.

'Dietrich, you okay, man?' Keegan asked.

He blinked, returning to himself. 'What?'

'You look like shit. You all right?'

Anger welled up within him. Who was this arrogant little fuck to be telling him he looked like shit?

'Keegan, why don't you—'

His sentence was cut short by the jarring, shuddering impact as their Grand Cherokee slammed into the side of an articulated truck that had suddenly backed out onto the road. Dietrich grunted as he was thrown forward and jerked to a stop by his seat belt, jarring his neck in the process.

Such was his shock and surprise, it took him a few moments to collect his wits. Blinking several times, he shook his head and looked around.

He was surrounded by broken glass and equipment torn loose by the impact. Up front, a jet of steam blasted from the ruptured radiator, billowing out through holes in the buckled engine bay.

Their car had been totalled.

Suddenly there was a commotion of screeching brakes and honking horns behind them. Twisting around in her seat, Anya watched as a dump truck reversed out onto the main road from a side street, blocking the traffic behind them. Their backup car was nowhere to be seen.

A moment later the radio sparked up. 'This is Two. We're in an RTA. Some asshole just backed up onto the road!'

Shaking his head in anger, the driver reached for his radio. 'Copy that, Two. You okay?'

'No major injuries, but the car's fucked. Recommend you hold position until backup gets here.'

'Understood, Two. We'll wait at the next intersection.'

Already they were slowing down, getting ready to pull over.

Just then, Drake's phone started ringing. Anya could hear the soft vibration of it in his pocket. Instantly his muscles tensed up, his breathing started to come faster, his jaw clenched tight.

He was readying himself for something.

'Hey, Watts,' he called.

The woman twisted around in her seat again. As before, her jacket parted a little to reveal the Glock.

'What is it?'

He was going for it. Anya knew in that instant what he was planning. What she didn't understand was why he was doing it.

She could have called out a warning, could have put Watts on her guard in a heartbeat, yet she did nothing. She watched, and waited.

With a sudden, violent movement, Drake reached out, closed his fingers around the butt of the weapon and yanked it from its holster.

Watts was a trained security operative, used to responding to threats and reacting quickly to dangerous situations, but this was different. Drake was one of her own. He was an ally, a comrade. She had perceived no threat in him, and it took her half a second to realise what he was doing.

It was half a second too long.

'What the—?'

At the same moment, the driver started to turn, alerted by the noise.

'Don't move! Either of you!' Drake yelled, levelling the weapon at her forehead. His gaze snapped between the two of them, looking for any sign of resistance.

'Take out your phones and weapons. Do it now!'

Both operatives reached into their pockets, withdrawing their cellphones. The driver also produced a Glock similar to the one Drake was brandishing, holding the weapon loosely by the trigger guard.

'Throw them on the back seat.'

Again they complied with his order, moving slowly and carefully. Neither was going to provoke him in a situation like this, not when he had the drop on them. They knew better than that.

Watts glared at him. All trace of her former warmth was gone now. 'Drake, I don't know what you think you're doing, but—'

'Shut up!' Drake snarled before turning his attention to the driver. 'You – drive. Get us out of here. Turn left at the next intersection.'

Glancing at Watts, the driver sighed, threw the big vehicle into gear and pulled out onto the road. It wasn't hard to get out. Traffic was still backed up behind the dump truck, leaving the road almost empty.

Within seconds, they were off.

Drake's heart was pounding, his mouth dry, a trickle of sweat running down his back. In an instant, he had destroyed his entire career, turned himself into a wanted man, put his very life on the line.

The driver wasn't about to try anything stupid – not with a loaded weapon trained on the back of his head. Turning left at the intersection, he cruised along at a steady 30 miles per hour, keeping within the speed limit.

Anya said and did nothing. She was just sitting there, watching him with interest but not the slightest trace of alarm.

Drake allowed them to cover 100 yards or so, then selected an area in front of an empty retail unit. 'Pull over here.'

Again, he did as ordered without resisting.

'Keys. Give me the keys for her cuffs.'

Chewing her lip, Watts reached into her pocket and tossed him back the handcuff keys he'd parted with earlier.

'All right. Fuck off, both of you,' Drake instructed. 'Leave the engine running.'

'You've lost your mind,' Watts said, still trying to come to terms with what was happening. 'You're in central DC, for Christ's sake. You won't make it two miles.'

'Go!' Drake yelled, waving the pistol in her face.

She wasn't about to get killed over something like this. Opening her door, the woman slid out, slamming it shut. The driver did likewise.

Snatching up both cellphones and the spare weapon, Drake tossed them all into the passenger footwell, then clambered over the centre console and into the driver's seat. With a screech of skidding tyres, they were off, leaving the two security operatives in their wake.

In the rear-view mirror, Drake could see Watts running for the nearest passing civilian, no doubt looking for a cellphone. It wouldn't be long before the people at Langley figured out what had happened.

Chapter 32

'This is fucked up,' Frost decided, glancing around at the heavily congested road as cars struggled to fight their way past the accident scene. The blare of horns and the roar of engines was deafening.

Their own Grand Cherokee was a total loss. The impact had crumpled the engine bay, reducing it to so much scrap metal.

Dietrich rubbed his neck, still aching from the crash.

One of the agents poked his head out of the dump truck's cabin. Dietrich thought his name might have been Riley, though he couldn't be sure. He hadn't been paying attention when the man introduced himself. 'No sign of the driver, sir! He must have cleared out just after we hit him.'

Dietrich glanced at Keegan, standing a few feet away. The older man's sudden look of worry mirrored his own thoughts. This was no accident.

Jesus, why now?

He had to do something. He might have been reduced to the role of specialist – and an unpopular one at that – but he'd been a leader once, and part of him still remembered that. Limping forward, he reached into the cabin of their crashed vehicle and seized up the radio. 'Unit One, this is Two. What's your situation?'

His request was met by static.

'Unit One, respond.'

Frost picked up on his urgent tone straight away. 'What the fuck's going on?'

'You tell me.'

At that moment, their driver's cellphone started ringing. Frowning at the unfamiliar number, he answered it.

'Yeah? Watts, what the—?' The driver's face froze in shock. 'You're shitting me!'

Wasting no time, Dietrich snatched the phone from him. 'Watts. Report.'

'It's Drake!' The anger and shock in her voice plain to hear. 'He hijacked the vehicle and forced us out. He's got the prisoner.'

'Tell me this is a joke.'

'Does this sound like a goddamn joke? He pulled my own gun on me!' the woman hit back. 'Your man's been compromised.'

Dietrich looked away for a moment. This day was fast turning into a nightmare for all of them. 'Where are you right now?'

'Delaware Avenue.'

'Which direction did he go?'

'West.'

'Okay, sit tight. We'll get someone to pick you up.'

'Copy that.'

Shutting down the phone, Dietrich tossed it back to the young man he'd taken it from. 'Call this in right now. You've got a hijack situation on your hands. Suspect name is Ryan Drake, last seen heading west on Delaware Avenue in a stolen Grand Cherokee. Move!'

Drake's phone was ringing again. 'All right. I did what you asked. Now what?'

'Good work, Drake. Maybe you're more useful than you look,' Munro remarked. 'Where are you right now?'

Drake's eyes swept the road signs around them. 'Delaware Avenue, heading south-west.'

'Perfect. Turn right on Canal Street. You'll see an underground parking lot about a hundred yards further down. Go inside. Call me on this number when you get there.'

Closing down the phone, Drake glanced at the woman in the rear seat. She was watching him in silence.

'Here.' He threw the handcuff keys into her lap. 'Unlock yourself.'

'Jonas, say again,' Franklin ordered, holding one hand against his ear to drown out the din of half a dozen other people all talking over each other. Confused reports were filtering in from the Agency's Office of Security that Drake's convoy had been hit en route to Langley, but nobody seemed to know what exactly was going on.

The situation wasn't helped by his limited communications with their ground teams. He was still airborne, having taken a later flight back to DC so he could finish up his preliminary report. They had just started their descent towards Andrews and were a good thirty minutes from landing.

'It's Drake,' Dietrich growled into the phone. Judging by the blare of car horns in the background, he was struggling to hear as well. 'He hijacked the vehicle and took the prisoner hostage. He's on the run. I repeat, we *don't* have his location.'

At that moment, Franklin's blood turned to ice. It couldn't be. He'd known Ryan Drake for years. He owed his very life to him, in fact. Never had Drake given him cause to question his loyalty.

'You're absolutely certain of this?'

'Both agents in the car confirmed it – he pulled a gun on them and forced them out.' He paused a moment. 'And someone backed a dump truck into our car so we couldn't pursue him. This fucking thing was planned.'

For a second or two, Frankin said and did nothing. He couldn't believe the nightmare unfolding before his eyes. They had just lost the prisoner they had risked everything to secure, and one of their own men was responsible.

But not just any man. Ryan Drake – the man Franklin had personally vouched for, recommended, stuck his neck out for.

In some part of his mind, he knew that much of the blame for this debacle would fall on him unless he did something right now. Friend or not, Drake had to answer for his actions.

His grip on the phone tightened. 'Okay, Jonas. We're scrambling our field teams now. I'll have one of them pick you up.'

'Me?'

'We need every operative we can get our hands on right now. And the three of you know Drake as well as anyone. If this is a hostage situation, you might be able to talk him down.'

'Dan, I don't—'

'No arguments!' Franklin snapped. 'Just get it done.'

Closing down his phone, he raised his voice to address the other agents on the flight. 'All right everyone, listen up.'

Silence descended on the cabin.

'For reasons unknown, one of our operatives has hijacked the convoy and taken our prisoner hostage,' he began, his face grim as he relayed what he knew so far.

'Recovering them both is our highest priority. Notify Washington PD and scramble all available tactical teams. I want the prisoner's tracking module locked in. As soon as we nail her location, the assault teams move in. Remember, non-lethal force. I want both of them secured and brought in alive, and I want it done right the fuck now. We've got billions of dollars' worth of technology at our disposal, gentlemen. Use it.'

Chapter 33

The dimly lit underground car park was quiet as they pulled in, with most of the car owners already at work in the office block above. Drake's headlights illuminated rows of parked Chryslers, Fords, GMs and BMWs, all gleaming and showroom clean.

'Second row in, then five spaces down,' Munro instructed. 'Look for a silver Ford Taurus.'

It wasn't hard to find. Pulling up next to it, Drake killed the engine.

'The keys are under the driver's side front wheel arch,' Munro went on. 'They'll be scrambling their field teams, so I suggest you hurry. Leave your cellphone behind. There's another one in the car. I'll call you soon.'

Killing the phone, he turned to Anya, still sitting in the back seat. She had unlocked her cuffs, but had made no effort to escape or attack him. God knew why. If she'd been looking to make a run for it, she couldn't have had a more perfect opportunity.

'We're switching cars. Get out when I tell you.'

She nodded, intelligent enough to know that now was not the time to be asking questions.

Throwing open his own door and shoving the Glock down the front of his jeans, he hurried over to the parked Taurus, knelt down and felt beneath the wheel arch while trying to be unobtrusive about it. He couldn't see anyone else around, but that didn't mean he wasn't being watched.

He felt his fingers close around something taped to the inside of the arch, and pulled it off to reveal a key fob.

'Telford, do we have a location yet?' Franklin demanded, angrily pacing up and down the cabin while their plane passed through some low-altitude turbulence. His back was a mass of knotted muscle, waves of pain coursing through him.

'Working on it, sir,' the technician replied, looking as tense as he felt.

Franklin rounded on him. 'What's taking so goddamn long?'

'I'm trying, but we're getting a lot of interference, sir.'

'From what?'

The younger man gave him an apologetic look. 'Heavy concrete structures can muffle the signal. They could be underground.'

Franklin rubbed the bridge of his nose. 'Don't give me excuses, give me a location. Get on it.'

Wasting no time, Drake opened the back door, turned towards the Grand Cherokee and beckoned to Anya. The woman didn't need to be told twice, quickly crossing the gap and jumping into the back seat.

Drake sat down behind the wheel and glanced at the items laid out on the passenger seat beside him. There was a small first-aid kit – the kind carried by paramedics – and more ominously, a surgical scalpel sitting atop it.

A moment later, he heard the chime of a cellphone in the glove compartment, and opened it up to find a brand new BlackBerry inside, its screen illuminated by an incoming call.

He hit the receive button. 'What now?'

'They implanted Anya with a tracking device,' Munro informed him. 'Give her the scalpel and first-aid kit. She'll know what to do.'

Drake paled at the thought. 'You're fucking kidding me . . .'

'Time's running out, Ryan. I'd say you have three or four minutes before CIA tactical teams seal off the building. You want to wait it out?'

'Shit,' Drake said under his breath, grabbing the first-aid kit and the scalpel. He twisted around in his seat and held them out to the woman. 'We need to get that tracker out of you.'

Far from looking appalled or even apprehensive at what he was suggesting, she merely offered him a grim smile. 'I expected as much.'

Moving with the calm deliberation of a surgeon about to go into theatre, she unzipped her orange jump suit and pulled it off, leaving only her white T-shirt beneath.

Stretching out her left arm, palm facing upward, she gripped the scalpel and made an inch-long incision on the site of the hypodermic injection. There was an initial moment of taut resistance as her skin tried to stretch with the pressure being applied, then the razor-sharp blade sliced in. Straight away, blood began to well up. She made no sound as the blade bit into her flesh, but he could see the muscles in her jaw tightening as she went about her grim task.

With the incision made, she set the scalpel aside. Next she opened the first-aid kit with her free hand, unrolled a dressing that she was sure to need in a few moments, and selected a pair of surgical pliers.

Drake watched in morbid fascination as she pressed the pliers into the cut, pulling apart the skin to expose the muscle and tendons beneath. Breathing through gritted teeth, she moved the pliers a little deeper and changed the angle, then gripped something. She had it. She began to pull back, but lost her grip, forcing her to push the pliers back in again.

This time she got a better hold, and with a faint groan of pain yanked the tracking module out of her arm. Gripped between her pliers was a bloodied metallic device no bigger than a capsule of aspirin. Her hand was shaking just a little.

It took a moment or two for her to calm down and suppress the pain that was doubtless screaming through her brain. Winding down her window, she dropped the tracker outside and set about bandaging the wound.

'Jesus, don't you hurt?' Drake couldn't help asking.

She didn't look up, but he saw a blonde eyebrow raised. 'Unfortunately I do.'

'I've got her,' Telford exclaimed. 'She's in a parking lot on Canal Street, central DC. Part of a larger office complex. Must be an underground facility.'

Relief surged through him. 'Vector in all available tactical units, and have local PD standing by to support. Remember, non-lethal force.'

'Yes, sir.'

'Where's Dietrich and his team?'

'En route now, sir. Tac team Bravo picked them up on the way.'

'Good. Get me aerial coverage of that building – choppers, satellite recon . . . whatever. I want eyes in the sky. And contact the building manager, have him close off all entrances and exits! Nobody gets out of that fucking place until our tac teams get there.'

As the younger man went to work, Franklin fished

out his cellphone and dialled Drake's number. He wasn't holding out much hope, but there was still a chance he could talk his friend down, convince him to see sense before he got himself killed.

There was no response. The phone just rang out, unanswered.

'Jesus, Ryan. What the fuck are you doing?'

'All right, it's gone,' Drake said, glancing at Anya in his rear-view mirror. She hadn't uttered a word as she quickly bound the wound with the ease born from long experience, applying pressure to slow the bleeding.

'Good. Now, get the fuck out of DC and head south-west into Virginia,' Munro replied. 'There are clothes on the back seat and money in the glove box. I've done what I can, the rest is up to you. Go now.'

Starting the car up, Drake threw it into gear and drove off, leaving the stolen Grand Cherokee and the tracking module behind. Ascending the ramp to street level, he turned right and gave it some gas, merging with the busy traffic. Within moments, they were just another anonymous car amongst thousands.

Chapter 34

The CIA tactical team arrived on site with a screech of brakes and the smell of burned rubber, black-clad figures in body armour piling out of the two vans that had brought them there at top speed. In under a minute they had blockaded all entrances and exits, shut down the building's elevators and posted armed operatives on all stairwells.

The parking lot was locked down. Nobody could get in or out.

Clad in heavy body armour, armed with assault rifles and sub-machine guns, and with their faces obscured by balaclavas and combat glasses, they were a fearsome sight. Following in the wake of the armoured advance were Dietrich, Frost and Keegan, also sporting body armour over their civilian clothes.

'All units, move up,' Ramirez, the team leader, hissed into his radio. 'Go! Go! Watch the left flank. Get a man over by that annexe.'

'Perimeter secure.'

Franklin was watching the whole drama unfold via secure satellite link. His attention was focused on the direct feed from Ramirez's helmet-mounted camera as the team rushed past the ranks of parked vehicles, converging on the homing signal being emitted by Anya's tracking unit. Already he could see the distinctive bulky frame of the Grand Cherokee, gleaming black and menacing under the electric arc lights.

'Walker, cover left. Sorrentino, right,' Ramirez said, his voice tight with anticipation. 'You still got good track on the target?'

'Affirmative,' another voice replied over the Net. 'She hasn't moved.'

'DaForte, on me. Ready?'

'Roger.'

Franklin leaned a little closer to the screen. This was it.

Ramirez halted for a moment beside a parked Nissan Skyline, weapon at the ready. 'Go! Go! Go!'

In a blur of movement, the team surged forward. Suddenly there were dark figures everywhere, all yelling at the same time.

'Hands up!'

'Freeze!'

But there was no sight of either Drake or Anya. All Franklin could see was the parked government vehicle, the back door still hanging open.

'Clear!'

'Clear!'

'I got nothing!'

Franklin's forehead knotted with concern. 'What's happening? Someone talk to me.'

'There's no sign of them, sir,' Ramirez replied.

'They have to be close. Her tracker hasn't moved.'

'Dan, you'd better take a look at this.' It was Keegan.

Franklin watched as Ramirez strode over. The old sniper was kneeling beside a patch of dark blood on the bare concrete floor.

'What you got?' Ramirez demanded.

Pulling on a rubber glove, Keegan reached down and

fished something up off the ground. Franklin felt his stomach knot as the object swam into focus. It was the tracking module.

'Shit.'

Chapter 35

The closest highway was the 395, heading south-west. Fighting his way through heavy traffic to reach the on-ramp, Drake at last found an opening and stamped on the accelerator. A few minutes later, they were on the interstate and cruising along at a steady 65 miles per hour, leaving DC behind.

He had calmed down a little now that they were out of immediate danger, able to think more logically about their situation.

As soon as they found the tracker, the Agency would expand their search grid. His best hope was to put as much distance as possible between themselves and DC before that happened. After that, he had no idea.

Opening the glovebox again, he found a paper envelope stuffed with used bills of various denominations, perhaps 400 or 500 dollars' worth.

In the back seat, Anya had removed her orange coveralls and was busy pulling on a pair of jeans. It was no easy task in such cramped confines, but she worked quickly, lifting her midsection to pull them up over her hips. This done, she shrugged her arms into the leather jacket provided by Munro.

She caught his eye on her in the mirror.

'You knew this was going to happen,' he began.

'What makes you say that?'

'Don't play fucking games with me. You didn't do a thing when I pulled that gun. You didn't even look surprised.'

'I knew you were going to take the weapon,' she admitted. 'I saw it in your eyes, but I didn't know why you were doing it.'

'Why didn't you warn anyone?'

She looked at him honestly. 'Because I don't trust the Agency. I would rather take my chances with you. For now, at least.'

Running her fingers through her hair, she looked down at her left hand, tensing and relaxing the fingers as if to check that everything still worked. It did.

'Are you planning to kill me?' she asked, matter-of-factly, as if it were just a casual enquiry about his plans for the day.

'No.'

She didn't look as relieved as she should have. Then again, he suspected that killing her would be no easy task. He still had the Glock he'd taken from Watts, but she had the scalpel on the back seat – a fact he was now uncomfortably aware of.

'Who are you working for? Munro?'

'I'm not *working* for anyone,' he bit back. 'I was forced to do this.'

'By Munro.'

'Yes, by fucking Munro!'

She had enough sense not to push further. 'Where are we heading?'

'South.' He could say nothing beyond that, because he didn't know. His immediate priority was to put as much distance between them and DC as possible.

After that, it was up to Munro.

* * *

235

'We've done a floor-by-floor search of the entire building. No joy,' Ramirez reported. He had removed his mask and combat eye protectors to reveal a narrow, middle-aged face with olive skin and dark, faintly menacing eyes.

Dietrich rubbed the back of his neck, wincing at the twinge of pain that ran down his spine. Great – as if he didn't have enough physical ailments.

'If they came in here, they had to leave somehow. They must have switched vehicles.' He glanced up, spotting a wall-mounted security camera; one of several covering the parking lot. 'Get in touch with the building super-intendent. I want the footage from those security cameras right now.'

Ramirez nodded. 'On it.'

As the older man hurried off, Frost shook her head. 'I can't believe Drake would do something like this.'

Dietrich gave her a sharp look. 'Believe it. We need to find him before the stupid bastard gets himself killed.' He sighed and looked down. 'Go help Ramirez. They'll need a technician to pull the security footage.'

Her eyes flared. She didn't take too kindly to being ordered around by a man like Dietrich. Still, she understood the logic behind his order. It was what she would have done anyway. Hesitating a moment, she strode off to join the tactical team leader.

'Doesn't make any goddamn sense,' Keegan remarked. 'If he wanted to take her hostage, he could have hijacked the chopper on the way back from Russia.'

Dietrich regarded the older man with disdain. A brilliant sniper he might have been, but he knew nothing about covert extractions. 'And he would have had our Air Force after him on one side and the Russians on the other. No, this was the perfect place to lift her, when she was lightly guarded and we were expecting no trouble. The question is, what does he intend to do now?'

Drake's thoughts were interrupted by the buzz of his new cellphone.

'What now?'

'Good. You're still alive,' Munro remarked.

'You haven't answered my question. Where do I hand her over?'

'Who says I want you to hand her over?'

He frowned. 'Run that by me again?'

Munro allowed him to languish in silence for a few moments. 'Your new best friend was working on something before she was captured; something the Agency will go to great lengths to get their hands on. I want you to find what she was looking for, and deliver it to me.'

'That wasn't our deal,' Drake hissed.

'You're in no position to make deals,' Munro replied sharply. 'It's simple. You do what I say, or your sister dies. Is this in any way unclear?'

Drake didn't reply, just stared straight ahead, seeing nothing.

'I'm waiting, Drake,' Munro prompted.

'We're clear.' He had to force the words out through clenched teeth.

'Good. You have four days. I'll be keeping my eye on you, so I suggest you don't do anything stupid. Keep your cool, get the job done and you'll get your sister back unharmed. Good luck.'

With no further instructions, he hung up.

'Fuck!' Drake snarled, slamming his fist against the wheel.

'What did he say?' Anya asked.

He glared at her in the mirror. 'You were working on something before the FSB captured you. What was it?'

The woman stared at him for several seconds, saying nothing.

'Talk to me, for fuck's sake.'

Still she did not reply.

He thought about the weapon still shoved down the front of his jeans, but quickly discarded the possibility. Threatening her would be worse than futile. She didn't give a shit about being hurt, and there was no way he could cover her while driving.

'Look, he's got my sister, for Christ's sake,' he said, deciding his only choice was to be honest. 'Jessica. She's thirty-three years old. She has a husband and two kids, and he's threatening to execute her if I don't give him what he wants.'

He could feel his throat tightening as he spoke. 'You're the only one who can stop him. You might not give a shit about yourself, but she's innocent. If you don't help me, she's dead, Anya.'

The woman sat in silence, listening to his pleas without emotion. He was losing her, he realised. She was shutting down, putting up the barriers again.

'What are their names?' she asked.

The question caught him off guard. 'What?'

'Your sister's children. What are their names?'

'Chloe and Julia. Julia is three and Chloe turns five next month.'

Anya glanced out the window, as if weighing up the matter in her mind. 'I was in Iraq just before the invasion,' she finally said. 'Trying to make contact with a source in the Mukhabarat.'

Drake recognised the name well enough. Mukhabarat had been the Iraqi intelligence service under Hussein's regime.

'Why?'

'He claimed to have evidence that the Iraqi government had imported stocks of illegal weapons from a foreign supplier. Chemical, biological, even nuclear material. He was willing to hand over the evidence in exchange for money and a new life in the States. I was all set to meet with him on the Iraqi border when the FSB caught me.'

It didn't take a genius to understand the FSB's interest in her. Russia had been openly acknowledged as one of Iraq's biggest suppliers of military hardware for decades, up until the First Gulf War at least. After that, their assistance had become more covert but no less extensive.

'You think they were trying to cover their tracks.'

She shrugged. 'It seems logical.'

'So why does the Agency want it so badly?'

The woman gave him a withering look. 'You don't understand, Drake. Evidence like that would give the Agency huge leverage over the Russians.'

'Blackmail,' he breathed. 'So what the hell does Munro want with it?'

If he was merely after extortion, he already had a serious bargaining chip in the form of the Predator.

'I don't know. But he would not go to all this trouble for no reason.'

'No shit,' Drake observed darkly. He had a whole lot of questions and few answers. 'All right, whatever. First thing we have to do is make contact with your source. He's the key.'

Anya looked dubious. 'That won't be easy. He could

have gone into hiding after the invasion. He could even be dead . . .'

Drake's grip on the wheel tightened. If her source was dead, then so was his sister. 'Then we'd better get to work.'

Chapter 36

'We searched the entire complex top to bottom. There was no sign of them,' Dietrich reported. 'As you can see, the tracking module was forcibly removed. Drake also dumped the vehicle and his cellphone. We have no way of tracking him.'

Franklin rubbed his jaw, surveying the scene with dark eyes.

After landing at Andrews, he had made a hasty car journey out to the scene of Drake's last-known whereabouts to see the place for himself.

'So they switched vehicles before the tac team got here,' he surmised.

Dietrich nodded. 'That's our theory. But without knowing the make and model of the car they switched to, it's hard to say.'

Franklin glanced up, catching sight of the CCTV cameras covering the parking lot. 'What about surveillance footage?'

'Looks like he had that covered too,' Frost said. Reaching into her pocket, she held up a plastic evidence bag.

'I found this attached to the main trunk cable.'

Franklin leaned in closer, frowning. Inside the bag was a black plastic box about the size of a cigarette pack. One end of the plastic casing had been removed, revealing a tangle of wires and a battery unit.

'It's a microwave emitter,' she explained, sensing he had no idea what he was looking at. 'Powerful enough to disrupt any data feeds nearby. It kicked in a couple of hours ago. Every camera on this level recorded nothing but static.'

Franklin rolled his eyes. 'Why didn't the building manager report it?'

'We spoke to him already,' she explained. 'There are no permanent security staff on duty down here. The cameras are there to record, not to observe. Nobody was watching the feeds, so the problem wouldn't even have been recognised until someone tried to manually access them.'

'There's no way Drake could have made this happen by himself. If you break this down, there's only one conclusion,' Dietrich went on. 'He's working with Munro.'

Franklin looked down at the dried bloodstain. 'I can't believe Ryan would do something like this. I've known him for years.'

'Maybe so. But that doesn't change the facts,' Dietrich pointed out.

The younger man's face was grim when he looked up again. 'I want you to head up the search, Jonas. Find him and bring him in.'

Dietrich blinked.

'Don't look so surprised,' Franklin said, unimpressed by his feigned disbelief. 'You're a Shepherd team – this is what you do. More important, you're Drake's team. Between the three of you, you know him just about as well as anyone. You're our best shot at finding him right now.'

Dietrich had managed to assume a look of surprise and even reluctance, but inside he was jubilant. At last he was beginning to perceive the opportunity that lay before him.

This was his ticket back, his chance to reclaim what he'd lost. Despite injury and fatigue, he was still doing his job, and doing it well. That sort of thing got noticed.

Even better, Drake's betrayal had cast a shadow over his entire career: every decision he'd made, every operation he'd headed up, every case officer he'd cited to negligence. This was Dietrich's vindication, the proof that he had been wrongly persecuted.

If he played this one right, he could find himself back on top again. He could put all his past mistakes behind him, move on with his life.

And Drake . . . well, he would get what was coming to him. Dietrich would make sure of that.

'All right,' he agreed. 'We'll find him, Dan.'

Franklin nodded. 'Pull whatever resources you need. They're setting up a command centre at Langley tasked to this operation. Everything we have is at your disposal, so use it.' With that, he turned on his heel and strode back to the waiting vehicle. 'And for Christ sake, get some food down you. You look like shit!'

'Where are you going?' Dietrich asked as Franklin opened the door.

'Back to Langley. I have to explain to Director Cain that we managed to lose his prisoner.' He swallowed. 'I'm counting on you, Jonas. Don't let me down.'

'Asshole,' Frost remarked as Franklin's car roared up the ramp to street level. 'All he wants is to save his own ass.'

For once, Dietrich was inclined to agree with her.

'I don't care about his ass.' He turned his attention to Frost. 'We have to find the car they switched to.'

'How?' she asked, exasperated. 'I told you, all the

243

cameras in here were out of action. It's a waste of fucking time.'

His headache was still pounding. 'There have to be other cameras in nearby buildings,' he said, swallowing down a sudden feeling of nausea. 'Traffic cams, lobby security . . . whatever. Find one that was pointed at the exit ramp at the time of Drake's escape, trawl through the footage and see what vehicles went up it.'

Frost looked dubious. 'That's a long shot.'

'It's all we have for now. Just get it done.'

But she didn't move. She just stood there looking at him.

'Do we have a problem?' he demanded irritably. He felt as if he was about to throw up.

'I think we do,' she confirmed. 'You might have Franklin fooled with all that "reluctant hero" crap, but not me. You're loving this. You're just itching for a chance to put Drake down, aren't you?'

'I don't have time for this . . .' he said, moving to push past her.

She caught his arm as he went, her eyes burning into his. 'Then make time, Dietrich. Because I won't stand by while you hang Ryan out to dry.'

He shrugged out of her grasp and glared at her. 'Do your fucking job, Frost, or I'll find someone who will!'

Frost, almost a foot shorter than he, stood unmoved by his threat. Her chin jutted stubbornly, her eyes blazing. 'The hell you will.'

It'll look bad if you lose control so easily, his rational mind told him. Don't ruin everything now. Get her to cooperate.

With every ounce of self-control he possessed, he forced calm into his voice. 'Look, you might not like me—'

244

'I don't,' she assured him.

'But Franklin put me in charge of this operation, and that's the way it is,' he said firmly. 'Now, you can either fight me or you can work with me, but Drake stands a better chance if you take the second option. If you really want to help him, then help me find him.'

For several seconds she did nothing. She just stood there watching him, as if looking for some sign that he was lying.

'If you try to fuck him over, I'll kill you myself.'

Turning on her heel, she walked away.

Reaching into his pocket for a cigarette, Dietrich watched her go. It wasn't exactly a winning reconciliation, but he sensed that was the best he was likely to get from the hot-tempered young woman.

He didn't care. In truth, he didn't give a shit if she liked him or not, just as long as she did her job.

When he was a team leader once more, he'd make sure he never had to work with her again.

Chapter 37

Drake sighed and rubbed his eyes. He'd been pushing the car hard all afternoon, wanting to gain as much of a head start on the inevitable manhunt as possible. According to the odometer they had covered well over 250 miles and were now deep into Virginia.

But they couldn't keep this pace up for ever. A glance at the fuel gauge told him they needed to stop soon.

According to the road signs, they were approaching a small town called Jarratt. Spotting a gas station on the outskirts, he decided to go for it.

The woman perked up as their speed dropped.

'We need fuel,' he explained.

Pulling into the forecourt, he stopped beside the nearest pump and stepped out, making sure to take the keys with him. He didn't think Anya intended to run, but he was taking no chances. He also had the Glock shoved down the front of his jeans in case the shit really hit the fan.

The terrain around the gas station was mostly dense woods and occasional tracts of farmland. He had no idea what they grew here but there were small fields all over the place, outbuildings and other utility structures scattered around. It was a quiet place, a backwater seldom used except by locals.

There was always the problem of CCTV surveillance – almost every gas station in North America had cameras in case of robberies – but there wasn't much he could do about that. In any case, their pursuers didn't know what kind of car they were driving or even what direction they were heading, so there would be no way to narrow the search. Short of trawling through footage from every gas station within 300 miles of DC, their chances of finding their targets that way were negligible.

All things considered, he couldn't think of a better place to stop.

The main building was a 7-Eleven. There were no other cars parked at the pumps, and there seemed to be only two attendants on duty, both in their teens. One was manning the cash register, and the other was restocking a shelf with bags of Doritos. Neither looked very enthusiastic, which suited him just fine. They were less likely to remember him.

There was a click as the back door opened and Anya stepped out.

'Better stay in the car for now,' he warned.

'No,' was her dismissive reply. She seemed entranced with the mere notion of being outside, and he understood why. She hadn't felt the sun on her skin in four years.

He reached for the petrol pump. 'Fine. Just . . . don't cause any trouble.'

She said nothing as she walked to the edge of the forecourt, closed her eyes and tilted her head back, raising her face to the sun. It was a warm day, and humid with it. Moisture seemed to linger in the air all around them. Some might have found it uncomfortable, but for her it was absolute heaven.

Sunlight, warmth, a faint breeze sighing past her . . .

The mere idea of experiencing such things again would have seemed ridiculous a few days ago. But here she was. Even if her life still hung in the balance, even if she was being hunted by Cain and God knew who else, in that moment, she was free.

'Hey,' Drake called out.

The spell was broken. Opening her eyes, she turned to look at him. He had finished pumping the gas and was screwing the fuel cap in place.

'We won't be stopping for a while. Do you need to use the bathroom?'

She shook her head.

'Suit yourself. I have to pay for the fuel. Stay with the car.'

He ignored her hostile look and strode into the convenience store. Straight away he was in an air-conditioned world of car magazines, soft drinks of all shapes and sizes, potato chips, cakes, chocolate, engine oils, alloy-wheel cleaning kits and countless other items that he had no time to take in.

Making for the counter, he paused to grab a couple of bars of chocolate, some crisps, pre-packed sandwiches, two bottles of Mountain Dew and two mineral waters. He didn't know what Anya's food and drink preferences were, nor did he care. She didn't strike him as a fussy eater.

Dumping his load of provisions on the counter, Drake fished in his pocket for some money as the cashier scanned his items.

'Having a good day, sir?' he asked, going through the motions.

'Yeah. Good, thanks,' Drake replied in his usual north London twang. He couldn't imitate an American accent to save his life.

When the kid's eyes showed interest, he pasted on a fake grin. 'We're on vacation for a couple of weeks, heading down to New Orleans.'

Drake couldn't tell if that explanation satisfied the cashier's curiosity, or if he just didn't care. Either way, he went back to what he was doing, scanning and bagging each item with no sense of urgency.

Outside, Anya turned as a Ford pickup pulled in to the gas station, music blaring. It was a new model that she didn't recognise, big and square and intimidating, red bodywork gleaming in the afternoon sun.

There were two men up front, one wearing a loose checked shirt, the other in a black tank top. The one in the tank top was in his twenties, young and strong, while the checked-shirt man was older, mid-forties. Both were working men, broad shouldered and well built, used to heavy manual labour.

The driver had his eye on her the moment they entered the station, and she saw him say something to his companion in the passenger seat. She couldn't tell what, but their grins gave her some idea.

She turned her back on them, staring out across the grassy expanse beyond the forecourt to a belt of trees beyond. She had no wish to speak to such men. Where was Drake?

There was a click and a thump as a door opened, and she heard the scrape of work boots on the concrete. Another metallic click as a fuel pump was unhitched, then a low rhythmic hum as the gas started to flow.

Another thump as the second door opened. Both men were out of the truck now. Glancing down, she could see their reflection in the window of the Ford Taurus.

'I don't see how we're gonna finish on time. You know we gotta get that floor laid down by Friday, then get all the wiring done, then get the air-conditioning guy in,' the one in the checked shirt remarked, his voice strangely high pitched for such a big man.

The one in the tank top sighed. This was a debate that had been going on for a while now, by the sounds of things. 'Not our problem. We can't do a goddamn thing till the joists get delivered. They want to ride us for missing deadlines, they can just go ahead and bitch to the lumber company.'

'Yeah, like that'll happen.'

The passenger elbowed his companion and nodded in her direction.

'Hey, darlin',' the young man in the tank top said. 'How you doin'?'

She didn't reply. Her mind was racing, trying to think of a way to back out of this situation. She didn't want to draw attention to herself, didn't want these men to remember her, but she couldn't think of a way to get rid of them.

'Hey. I'm talking to you, blondie,' he called out, a little more insistent this time. He was trying to be genial and friendly, but she caught an edge of impatience in his voice.

She had to speak to him. If she ignored him, he would lose face in front of his friend and that would piss him off. She wasn't concerned for her own safety, but she didn't want to get into a fight. Not now.

She turned around to look at them both, doing a rapid threat assessment as she always did. The one in the tank top was the taller of the two, probably 6 foot 3 and about 210 pounds. His arms were heavy with thick corded muscle, his shoulders broad and square – the kind of build that came from more than just hauling timber around a construction site. Maybe he'd been a football player in high school.

The other man was a few inches shorter, more fleshy and with a visible beer gut that came from hard work and hard living. She guessed his weight at perhaps 230 pounds.

The one in the tank top smiled at her. She was playing his game now. 'We just wanted to be friendly, y'see. What's a beautiful woman like you doin' all alone out here?'

He was unusually confident for one so young. Still, with his strapping build and ruggedly handsome face, he was no doubt used to approaching women and having his advances reciprocated.

'I'm waiting for my husband,' she lied. 'He's paying for the gas.'

His brows rose straight away at the sound of her voice. She had learned English a long time ago and spoke it with confidence, but a trace of her former accent remained unless she made great effort to hide it.

'Not from around here, are ya?' he asked. 'Where you from? Russia?'

She didn't like the way this conversation was going, and she didn't know how to turn it around.

Where the hell was Drake? What was taking him so long?

The man in the tank top had finished pumping his gas. Replacing the pump in its cradle, he rounded the pickup to approach her. He was still smiling, but the look in his eyes had changed a little. She had seen that look in men's eyes before. She had seen it in Bastard plenty of times at Khatyrgan. It wasn't as strong or malicious in this man, but it was there all the same.

'I don't want any trouble,' she said. It took a great deal of self-control not to assume a defensive posture which she knew would further antagonise him.

'Trouble? You don't have to worry about no trouble from me!' he laughed. He was enjoying this, toying with her, making her feel threatened. 'What kind of trouble you think I'm gonna cause?'

251

She glanced away, hoping a show of submission and disinterest would help him get the message. Come on, you had your fun. Just walk away.

'What? You too good to talk to me or somethin'?' he asked. 'What's your problem?'

This was going too far. She had given him every opportunity, but even she was starting to lose patience now.

Turning her baleful glare on him, she spoke in a low, cold voice. 'Listen to me, because I won't say this again. I don't want to speak to you or your friend. I just want to be left alone. Walk away. Please.'

Even he seemed momentarily daunted by the look in her eyes and the cold menace in her voice, and she saw him fight the urge to take a step back.

With that, she turned her back on him and walked towards the parked Ford Taurus, reaching for the door handle. All the while, she was watching his reflection in the window.

It took less than a second to see that her warning hadn't had the desired effect. Now that her back was turned and he was freed from her vengeful glare, anger and indignation had taken over. She was a woman, and she had made him feel fear.

'You fucking whore,' he growled, jabbing an accusing finger at her.

Just for a moment, she felt a fleeting sense of disappointment that she had failed to defuse the situation.

Then something snapped.

Turning, she grabbed his outstretched hand, bent it backwards and twisted it at the wrist, feeling the taut resistance as tendons and ligaments stretched. In a heartbeat, she had him in a supinating wrist lock. He was no threat to her now. He never had been.

His first reaction was a grunt of surprise, followed by

a cry of pain as she applied more pressure to the over-taxed joint. Instinctively his body went with the rotating motion, trying to find relief, but she knew it was a futile move. She could keep twisting the wrist as far as she wanted.

'What did you call me?' she asked through clenched teeth, pushing harder. 'Please, say it again. *Say it.*'

'Jimmy! Aargh, get this bitch off me!' he screamed, dropping to his knees. 'Get her off!'

Realising at last what was happening, his companion rounded the pickup, reaching into his back pocket. Anya followed his every move. Now she had a second opponent to deal with.

She couldn't waste any more time on the first man. But that was fine – she knew exactly how to remove him from the fight.

With a sudden, violent motion, she twisted his hand as hard as she could. As strong as the bones of the human forearm are, they are poorly designed to cope with radio-ulnar rotation. There was a moment of resistance, then a faint pop as his radius and ulna bones fractured just behind the wrist.

His scream of pain was cut short by a sharp knee delivered to the bridge of his nose, shattering it. He went down, blood spraying from both nostrils. He was out of the fight.

Drake was just handing over his money when he heard shouts coming from the forecourt. Straight away he turned towards the source of the commotion, and felt his blood run cold.

Turning her attention to the second man, she strode forward to meet him just as he brought something out of

253

his back pocket. A knife. Not a dagger, but a tool – a box cutter. Normally she disliked taking on opponents armed with knives, but she felt less apprehension in this case. He could slash with it and perhaps cause damage if the blade met her face, but otherwise it was a poor weapon.

And it didn't take long to decide that its owner presented little threat.

She ducked one wild slash, then twisted aside as he came at her again. She felt the blade brush her upper arm, but the leather jacket seemed to absorb it. He was slow and clumsy, not used to fighting with any kind of technical skill.

Still, she wasn't going to wait for him to take another swipe. Balling up her fist, she drilled him in the face with a hard cross, stunning him, then delivered a second blow to his fleshy stomach that doubled him over. A hard kick to the groin stamped out whatever fight remained in him, yet for some reason she found herself unable to stop.

A sudden surge of anger and fury rose up within her like a tide, so sudden and powerful she couldn't contain it.

The sound of their footsteps on the tiled floor receded. She heard the rasp as Bastard unzipped his trousers.

She was helpless, unable to protect herself, unable to resist as he grabbed her shoulder and rolled her over onto her stomach. She could barely feel the chill of the tiles on her naked skin, but she did feel the first gut-wrenching penetration as he thrust inside her.

This man had tried to kill her. He would have cut her throat, slashed that blade across her eyes, plunged it into her chest.

Drawing back her fist again, she slammed it into his face, feeling the cartilage of his nose give way beneath the force of the blow. The box cutter fell from his hand, and she caught it on the way down.

Gripping him by his shirt, she shoved him backward against the chassis of the Ford pickup. The vehicle shuddered under the impact.

He was limp meat in her hold, dazed and frightened, blood dripping from his nose and burst lip. His eyes met hers and she saw wild, primal fear in them. It sent a shiver of excitement through her.

Weakness will not be in my heart. Fear will not be in my creed.

She raised the box cutter to slash the exposed throat. But as she did so, a pair of strong hands seized her by the shoulders and threw her backwards.

She whirled around to face the new threat, gripping the weapon tight and preparing to lash out with it. No one could stand against her.

I will show no mercy. I will never hesitate.

Then she froze. The man standing before her wasn't an enemy.

'Stop it. Right now,' Drake said, bristling with anger.

The weapon fell from her grip and the uncontrollable rage vanished in an instant. For several seconds she just stood there, breathing hard, almost perplexed by what had happened.

Beside her, the man in the shirt had slumped to the ground beside the truck, clutching his nose and moaning softly under his breath.

'Get in the car,' Drake ordered, his voice cold. The anger had dissipated. He was all business now. 'I said get in the car. *Now.*'

She could think of nothing to say. Exhaling slowly,

she turned, opened the passenger door of the Ford Taurus and calmly sat down.

Drake was in the driver's seat a few seconds later. Throwing the car into gear, he stamped on the accelerator and floored it out of the garage, leaving the two injured men in their wake.

Chapter 38

Franklin was not in a good mood as he strode past Cain's private secretary and onward to his inner sanctum. She made no move to stop him. Cain had made it clear that Franklin was not to be delayed or questioned.

The director's expansive office made his own feel like a cardboard cubicle. Everything in it was expensive and meticulously crafted, from the leather sofas to the antique mahogany coffee table, the eighteenth-century bookcase crammed with leather-bound volumes, and the huge ornate writing desk.

Behind it sat Cain himself, busily working away on his computer. He glanced up and stopped working as Franklin approached, though one look at his face made it plain he had little time for idle talk.

Cain might have projected an aura of genial good manners when it suited him, but at times like this the cold, ruthless machine beneath became all too apparent. Heads were going to roll for this, and Franklin had a horrible feeling that his would be one of them.

'What's the situation, Dan?' he asked without preamble.

Franklin grimaced inwardly, bracing himself for the shit storm that was about to erupt. 'Not good. Drake switched cars without any of the security cameras picking it up. He removed the prisoner's tracking device and escaped before the tactical teams got there. Now they're on the run.'

'So it would seem,' Cain remarked with barely concealed scorn. 'Explain to me how this happened. You vouched for this man, you recommended him.'

'I've known him personally for years,' Franklin countered. 'He's never once given me reason to doubt his loyalty.'

Cain sighed and leaned forward, resting his hands on the desk. 'Well, you'd better start making sense of this real quick, son, because this is a situation that needs to be un-fucked right now.' He glanced at his watch. 'Drake gave your boys the slip two hours and forty-seven minutes ago. That's two hours and forty-seven minutes during which our search area has been growing exponentially larger. What are we doing to find him?'

'We've put out an APB to all law enforcement agencies and border patrol units. Airports and customs units are all on alert—'

Cain waved his hand dismissively. 'Drake knows the system. If he's half as smart as he should be, he'll know how to avoid all that. And if he doesn't, Anya will,' he added. 'Inspire me, son. Give me some reason to justify your pay cheque.'

Franklin could feel a trickle of sweat run down his back. 'We've brought in Drake's own Shepherd team. They're the best in the world at what they do, and more importantly they know him. They know how he thinks, how he reacts. They can pre-empt him. Drake got this far because he caught us off guard – we won't make that mistake again.'

Cain held his gaze a moment longer before releasing him and leaning back in his chair. 'That's not bad,' he conceded. 'Let's just hope they have something to report back on soon.'

'I've got every confidence in them.'

Cain's eyes flashed. 'Good for you. Let me know the moment you find anything.'

He didn't say anything further, just went back to work. Franklin had been dismissed. Taking his cue, he turned and hurried out, already reaching for his cellphone.

'Goddamn it, Ryan,' he hissed as he dialled Dietrich's number.

Anya stared listlessly out the window as they hurtled along the interstate highway, trees and fields and small towns skimming past.

She hadn't said a word since they left the gas station, and neither had Drake. He was just sitting there staring straight ahead, clutching the wheel in a white-knuckle grip. His simmering anger was obvious even to someone who couldn't read body language. But to her, he might as well have been screaming and pounding his fist against the dashboard.

She was more than a little unnerved by her own actions earlier. Using force to defend herself was one thing, but she had gone far beyond that. If Drake hadn't been there, she knew she would have killed both men and not regretted it for a second.

With Bastard, it had been different. He had deserved death many times over, and she had been more than happy to give it to him. But those two men at the gas station weren't out to kill or torment her – they were just idiots filled with pride and bravado, and she had almost killed them both.

She felt the need to speak, to say something, to offer an explanation, but she didn't know the right words. She wasn't used to explaining herself or apologising for her actions.

'Drake, I—'

'Shut the fuck up!' he snarled. 'I don't want to fucking hear it, Anya. There's nothing you can say to me. Nothing!'

For a few seconds, she just stared at him, completely taken aback by his outburst. She hadn't seen him truly angry before and wasn't sure how to deal with it. It wasn't that he frightened or intimidated her, but for some reason it made her feel guilty.

'You are right to be angry . . .'

'Of course I'm right!' he raged, twisting around to glare at her. 'You've compromised us. You'll draw their search grid right here. Don't you get it? Christ, you've done nothing but fuck up my life from the moment I met you. I wish I'd never even heard of you. I wish you were still in that fucking prison where you belong!'

Her heart sank, and she felt a sudden pang of hurt and sadness at his words – a reaction made more unsettling because it was so unexpected.

'I . . . I'm sorry,' she said, groping for the words.

Drake didn't respond. There was no angry rebuke from him, no storm of insults or expressions of hatred. He was silent and brooding, his eyes on the road ahead.

His silence encouraged her to go on.

'I'm sorry you are caught up in this, Drake. You don't deserve it, and neither does your sister. And I'm sorry for what happened back there. I lost my temper. It was . . . unprofessional, and it won't happen again.'

She watched him intently, studying every movement of his face, the set of his shoulders, the strength of his grip on the wheel, the look in his eyes.

For a few moments, she genuinely didn't know how

her apology had been received. His expression didn't change, and she wondered if he just didn't care any more.

That made her feel even worse.

'Talk's cheap, Anya.'

'I don't make a promise unless I intend to keep it.'

Then, at last, he turned to look at her.

'I've got your word on that?' he asked, staring at her just as intensely as she'd been watching him.

'You do.'

He said nothing, as if torn about how to respond. 'This isn't going to work if we can't rely on each other.'

'I agree.'

'I don't trust you,' he said.

She sighed and looked out the window at the green countryside sliding past. 'I don't blame you. But if you are worried about me running away, don't be. Munro will find me no matter where I go, so I have little choice but to see this through.'

Drake stared at her a moment longer before turning his attention back to the road. 'If you try to fuck me over, I'll shoot you myself.'

It took a lot of effort to hide the smile that threatened. He forgave her. Despite his threat, she could see that some of the tension had left his shoulders. The look in his vivid green eyes had softened just a little.

'You can try.' It was the closest she had come to playful banter in a very long time.

He gave her a sidelong glance before his gaze flicked to her left arm. 'You're hurt.'

Frowning, she looked down to see a straight gash cut in the leather sleeve of her jacket. She hadn't even noticed. Pulling it off, she examined her arm.

The box cutter had sliced through the leather and nicked

the skin, leaving a long straight cut across her upper arm. The pain barely registered, in the same way that shaving cuts often go unheeded, but it was a sobering reminder of how close she had come to more serious injury.

The blade could have sliced right through muscle, tendons or nerves, putting her arm out of action for good. And it wasn't as if they could just drive to the nearest hospital.

Saying nothing, she reached for the first-aid kit on the back seat.

Ten years ago that blade never would have come near her. She'd become slow, sloppy, careless. Her time in prison had dulled her reflexes, eroded her skills.

Or maybe it's more than that, she thought to herself. Maybe you're just getting old. That was more frightening than any injury.

'So you *are* human after all,' Drake observed.

It was just as well his eyes were on the road, and he missed the look she gave him.

Chapter 39

Clutching the edge of the sink, Dietrich grimaced as his stomach constricted in another painful heave, its contents flying into the bowl. There was nothing he could do but ride it out and wait for it to be over.

When at last the sickness subsided, he was breathing hard, a thin line of mucus hanging from the corner of his mouth. He turned on the tap and did his best to clean himself up, splashing cold water on his face several times.

When he looked up at his reflection, he almost baulked at the sight that confronted him. Four years ago he had been a ruggedly handsome man, tall and muscular, with a piercing gaze and strong features. Now he looked like a walking corpse, his complexion pallid, his cheeks sunken, his eyes dulled.

Jesus Christ, what have you done to yourself?

He couldn't even remember when he'd first started shooting up, only that it had been a long time ago. When he worked in West Germany twenty years earlier, drugs had been ubiquitous. Everyone was high on something, and being young and reckless and invincible, it hadn't taken him long to jump on that particular bandwagon. Heroin, cocaine, LSD . . . he'd done it all.

Only when he'd moved to America in the mid-nineties and joined the Agency had he learned to curb his habit. It had been a new decade and a new employer; one who didn't take kindly to their operatives showing up on the downside of a weekend-long cocaine binge.

For a time, he'd learned to live on the straight and narrow. But life had a way of throwing him curve balls, and after a failed marriage followed by a messy divorce, he found himself using again. Heroin this time. The feeling of euphoria and invincibility the drug imparted reminded him of his carefree youth. It provided an occasional escape, an outlet for a million frustrations and regrets.

But far from an escape, his growing drug habit soon became a prison in its own right. Now he needed it just to get through the day.

The withdrawal was kicking in hard, and it was going to get worse before it got better. But he had to keep going. His career, and perhaps his life, depended on it. If they found out his secret now, at such a critical time, it was over for ever.

'Come on, you bastard,' he whispered in his native German. 'Pull yourself together.'

He could beat this. He had to.

He was limping back out to the parking lot when he heard his name called out, and glanced up to see Frost striding towards him with a laptop clutched under her arm.

Snatching up his cup of coffee, he downed the tepid contents. 'If you don't have good news, I don't want to hear it.'

'You'll want to hear this. I think we've got them.'

Opening the laptop, she set it down on the hood of a nearby police car. The unit had been sitting on standby and booted up immediately.

Selecting a video file, she hit play. Straight away a black-and-white image of the parking lot's entrance ramp appeared. It was a wide-angle shot, taken from a building further down the street.

'This was taken at 10.04 this morning, approximately five minutes after Drake hijacked the vehicle.'

Dietrich watched as a black Grand Cherokee turned off the main road and tore down the ramp into the darkened recesses of the building.

'So, we have him making entry,' he agreed. 'What next?'

Frost selected another video file. 'Skip forward four minutes and twenty seconds, and we have . . .'

And just like that, a silver saloon emerged from the parking lot. Hesitating a moment at the junction while the driver waited for a gap in the traffic, the vehicle turned right and took off down the street. It was travelling away from the camera, which was unfortunate, but it was a lead; the first they'd had since the hunt began.

'Looks like a Ford Taurus to me.'

'Correct. A 2003 model as best I can tell. It's the only vehicle that entered or exited the parking lot during our time frame,' Frost explained. 'The tactical teams arrived less than a minute later. It's got to be them. I hate to say it, but your hunch just might have paid off.'

Dietrich felt the first stirrings of excitement since this whole thing began. Still, he wasn't about to break open the champagne. A four-hour-old CCTV image was a small step, not a giant leap. 'Can we get a licence plate?'

She shook her head. 'Not from here. I sent the raw data files back to the image processing lab at Langley to see what they can do with them.'

He nodded, struggling to order the thoughts racing through his mind. Everything felt like an immense effort in his current condition. 'Notify all agencies of the vehicle make and model. And see if you can cross-reference with any traffic cams in the area. Maybe we can get a better shot.'

It was akin to searching for a needle in a haystack, but if anyone could do it, the woman in front of him was likely their best chance.

'Already on it.' She turned to leave, then thought better of it. 'By the way, you all right? You look like you're about to keel over.'

He made a dismissive gesture. 'Painkillers. They don't agree with me.'

She hesitated, as if poised to say something else. There was a dubious look in her eyes that he didn't like one bit.

'Will there be anything else, Frost?'

'No. Nothing.'

As she strode off, he glanced over at the tactical team leader. 'Ramirez! Pack everything up. We're pulling out.'

They had done what they could here. Forensics could finish up with the vehicle, but right now he wanted to be back at Langley.

Pulling into the motel forecourt, Drake killed the engine and switched the lights off. They had pushed on south for most of the afternoon, crossing the state line into North Carolina. Again they were spurred onward by the threat of police pursuit, and wanted to put as much distance between themselves and that gas station as possible.

The logical thing to do after leaving the gas station would have been to change direction, which was exactly why he had maintained the same heading. He hoped his pursuers weren't smart enough to predict this move, or stupid enough to assume he would just carry on his way as if nothing had happened.

266

He was just grateful that Anya hadn't killed either man. As it was, the incident might be treated as nothing more than aggravated assault, with limited police follow-up. He didn't imagine the men involved would be eager to advertise the fact that they'd been hammered by a woman half their size.

Either way, they had encountered no further incidents throughout the day. In fact, nothing much of anything had happened.

They needed a place to hold up and plan their next move, so here they were, parked outside a cheap motel on the outskirts of some backwater town called Shannon. It was a bland, single-storey affair that looked as if it had seen better days judging by the flaking paint and cracked windows. Still, the neon sign above the entrance advertised vacancies, and that was good enough for him.

'Stay in the car. I'll check us in.'

'Better if I do the talking,' she countered. 'Your accent will draw attention.'

He looked at her as if she were mad. 'And yours won't?'

She spoke impeccable English, but a trace of her native accent remained. She would stick out like a sore thumb, especially in this neck of the woods.

She managed a faint smile. 'Trust me.'

Sighing, he pulled his door open. It was a hot, damp, uncomfortable night, the humidity oppressive. Straight away he could feel it clinging to his skin. The chirp of crickets in the long grass on the other side of the parking lot mingled with the distant drone of traffic on the main highway.

Anya went first, walking with sure, easy strides towards the glass doors leading inside. With little choice but to trust her, he followed her lead.

The check-in desk was manned by an overweight woman in her fifties, wearing a floral patterned dress and a look of casual disinterest. A TV sat to one side, tuned to a local news channel. The air conditioners were cranked up to maximum, making the place feel like a refrigerator compared to the stifling heat outside.

She looked up as Anya approached the desk, pasting on what she probably thought was a professional smile. 'Good evening. How're y'all doin'?'

Keegan would have been right at home here, Drake reflected.

'We're just fine, thank you,' Anya replied, speaking in an accent that perfectly mirrored the woman's own. It was all Drake could do to stop his mouth hanging open. 'You got a room we can stay in for the night?'

'Sure thing. Just one night?'

It took a couple of minutes to sort them out with a room key, the process made even quicker when Anya paid in cash. This was the kind of place that didn't ask too many questions, and Anya was a perfect customer – polite, relaxed, cooperative and charming.

A 50-dollar security deposit? No problem.

Check-out at 10 a.m.? Sure thing.

What brings us here? I grew up in Atlanta. Just heading down there to visit with family for a few days, thought I'd show my boyfriend some of the scenery along the way.

The woman gave Drake an indulgent smile as she handed over the room key, by now completely at ease with Anya.

'You two enjoy your stay,' she said. 'Any problems, dial hash on your room phone.'

'Sure thing,' Anya replied, then stopped just as she was turning away. 'By the way, y'all got a place we can eat around here?'

'There's a steak house a couple hundred yards down the road,' the woman said, pointing. 'The food's pretty good.'

Anya flashed a dazzling smile. 'Much obliged. You have yourself a good night.'

Drake waited until they were outside and well beyond the woman's line of sight before voicing his thoughts. 'What the fuck?'

'What do you mean?' she asked, feigning ignorance.

'Where did you learn to speak like that?'

She shrugged. 'Movies, mostly. And just listening to people.' She had lapsed back into her normal accent as if removing a pair of uncomfortable shoes. 'It is not so hard once you get a feel for the rhythms and speech patterns. But I'm glad she didn't want to talk for long.'

Like a lot of motels, the rooms were laid out in a long block facing straight out onto the parking lot, with a wooden roof extending outward for protection against bad weather. Their room was at the far end of the block, which suited them fine.

Then, halfway across the parking lot, Anya stopped in her tracks.

'What's wrong?' Drake asked, scanning the shadows.

'Wait,' she replied, slowly turning her face up to the sky. 'Be quiet.'

A few moments passed and nothing happened.

Then, suddenly, something landed on his shoulder. He was about to speak when he felt a wet splash on his cheek, and another on his forehead. Turning aside, he ducked under the covered walkway as the heavens opened in a sudden deluge, massive droplets hammering on the roof and bouncing off the tarmac.

Anya didn't move. She just stood there in the middle of the parking lot with her eyes closed and her face turned upward, letting the rain soak her. Was she smiling?

'Anya! Come inside, you bloody fool!' he called, his voice almost drowned out by the rain's onslaught.

It was another thirty seconds or so before she opened her eyes and walked over to join him, soaked to the skin, her long hair hanging in wet, limp strands around her face.

'What was the point in that?' Drake asked as he unlocked their door. 'You're soaking.'

Again he saw that faint, wistful smile. 'Do you know how many nights I dreamed of feeling rain on my skin?'

That gave him pause for thought.

'You should move to England, then,' he suggested, trying to lighten the mood. 'You could live the dream every day.'

Their room was a cramped, spartan affair – a double bed opposite the door, a closet set into the wall to the right, a bathroom with shower to the left, and a small chest of drawers next to the door with a TV on top. The carpet was pale green and threadbare, the mattress thin, the chest of drawers battered, scored and ringed with coffee stains.

Still, it was a roof over their heads. Drake had slept in worse.

Grabbing a towel from the rail in the bathroom, he threw one to the woman. 'Here. Dry yourself off.'

Without waiting for a reply, he began hunting for a remote for the TV. Unable to find it, he concluded that it was a get-up-and-do-it-yourself job, and pressed the power button. It took a good five seconds for the old unit to warm up, displaying a slightly grainy picture.

He flicked up through the channels until he found a local news broadcast, wondering if there might be anything about them. The fight at the gas station certainly wouldn't make the news, but Cain could have leaked a story about them. Dangerous killers on the loose, or something similar.

But it seemed no such thing had happened. The focus of tonight's broadcast was some kind of protest against cuts in government subsidies for local farmers. That was the kind of news he could live without, he thought, turning the volume down.

'So what now, Drake?' Anya asked, perching on the edge of the bed. The old mattress springs creaked under her weight.

'Now you're going to tell me all about Munro, what happened between you two, and everything about your source in Iraq.' He ran his hands through his hair. 'Then I'll decide what the hell I'm going to do next.'

'What *we're* going to do,' she corrected him. 'I am not baggage to be dragged around. We work together or we don't work at all.'

Drake couldn't help but smile. 'All right. What *we're* going to do.'

'Better,' she agreed. 'But first, we eat.'

For a moment he actually thought she was joking.

'Out of everything we have to deal with, *that's* the most important thing you can think of?'

'Survival is our first priority. Anyway, I work better on a full stomach.' She looked at him. 'So, we are going to go to the restaurant she told us about, you are going to buy me dinner and then we will talk.'

Drake looked at her in dismay. 'Would you like to catch a movie too?'

Anya said nothing, but the look in her eyes made it obvious she wasn't going to take no for an answer.

'Fine, we'll eat.' He glanced at her sodden clothes. 'But

I'm not taking you anywhere looking like that. You're a mess.'

She picked at the wet hem of her shirt. 'I don't care how I look.'

'But other people do. They'll notice you, they'll remember you, and that's not what we want, is it?' He felt as though he was dealing with a petulant child. 'So . . . stay here, dry off, I'll bring dinner back and then we'll talk. Deal?'

She eyed him as if he were a car salesman trying to pitch a bad deal.

'Fine,' she conceded.

Chapter 40

The temporary command centre set up by Franklin was in reality just a general purpose conference room; one of many scattered throughout the Agency's vast headquarters building. Still, it had everything they needed to run an investigation like this – phones, fax machines, computers with high-speed network links and pots of coffee on standby.

There was also a group of six technicians and signals analysts whose job it was to collate the vast influx of field reports, briefings, situation updates and false sightings, and condense it down into a format that Dietrich and the others could get their heads around.

From this room they could marshal an awful lot of technology and human resources. The trouble was, Dietrich had no idea where to direct it.

'Tell me something, Keegan. If you were Ryan, what would you be doing right now?' he asked, forcing down a mouthful of cheese sandwich. He didn't feel hungry in the slightest, but he knew he had to eat something. At least the nausea had abated for now.

The older man thought about it for a moment. 'Praying,' he decided. 'He'd have to know the kind of resources we can throw at this one.'

Dietrich sighed wearily. 'He's been one step ahead of us so far. He must have a plan.'

'Hell if I know,' Keegan said, then took a slow, thoughtful sip of his coffee. 'Can't say I'd want to be in his shoes, travelling with that woman day and night.'

Dietrich was inclined to agree. He remembered the look in her eyes when they had faced off against each other in that dingy stairwell in Khatyrgan. She would have killed him in a heartbeat if she'd had the chance.

In his opinion, she was completely unhinged, either because of her ordeal in prison or as a culmination of years of fighting and killing. He couldn't imagine why anyone would be willing to risk their life for her.

'Sir, I think we've got something,' one of the technicians called out. He was a gangly young man with dark hair who Dietrich vaguely remembered as Sinclair.

Both men were by his terminal within moments. 'Talk to me,' Dietrich ordered without preamble.

Sinclair gestured to the laptop in front of him. 'We just got a report in from Virginia state police. Sorry it took so long, but we've had a lot of incoming sit reps to deal with . . .'

Dietrich waved his arm impatiently. 'I don't care about the details. Just tell me what you found.'

'We've got an aggravated assault report at a gas station near a town called Jarratt. The suspects were a female with blonde hair and a male matching Drake's description. Both of them left in a silver Ford Taurus.'

Dietrich's eyes opened wider. He couldn't believe it. Were they really that lucky?

'Where are the two victims?'

'Southern Virginia Medical Center, a few miles south of Jarratt.'

'We need to be there right now,' Dietrich decided, off and moving within moments, and doing his best to hide

274

his limp. 'Keegan, get your gear. We're heading to Emporia. And tell Franklin what we're doing.'

'Wait. Shouldn't you be the one to tell him?' Keegan protested.

'Yeah. But I don't want to talk to him,' he called over his shoulder.

Struggling to balance his load of shopping bags and takeaway cartons, Drake booted his motel room door twice, waited a couple of seconds then followed it with a single knock.

A few moments later, he heard a click as the lock disengaged, then the door swung back. Anya had showered in his absence. She smelled of soap and shampoo, and was wearing only a towel wrapped around her chest. Her hair was still damp and slicked back.

Faint wisps of steam billowed from the bathroom.

'You were gone a long time,' she remarked, moving aside.

Drake gave her an irritable look. 'Your new best friend can't judge distances for shit. Must be a woman thing.'

The steak house which was apparently a 'couple of hundred yards' away turned out to be more than a mile distant, situated right in the centre of town. It was obviously a favourite stopover for truckers and labourers, because everywhere he looked he'd seen guys the size of polar bears tucking into plates piled high with meat, gravy and mashed potatoes.

Still, one advantage of the location had been the twenty-four-hour convenience store opposite. While waiting for his order, he'd wandered over and stocked up on everything he could think of – toothpaste and brushes, deodorant, hair combs, a disposable razor, bottled water, chocolate and bagels for breakfast, and a couple of bottles of beer for tonight.

He'd also bought a jar of multivitamins, a pair of sunglasses and high-factor sunscreen for Anya. He'd noticed her screwing up her eyes when the sun was out. No wonder – she hadn't seen it in years.

He threw the carrier bag full of supplies on the bed, then laid down the takeaway food boxes more carefully. 'I didn't know what you wanted, so I kind of ordered a bit of everything.'

'It doesn't matter. Food is food.' She walked back into the bathroom to retrieve her clothes, unwound her towel and casually dropped it on the tiled floor at her feet.

Drake stopped, unable to keep from staring.

He had met plenty of people in life who kept themselves in good physical shape, either for professional reasons or for sheer vanity. But there were a few people, a very few, who he could only describe as looking *right* – people who weren't struggling against their weight or trying to shape their body into something it wasn't. People who looked the way they did because that was exactly what they were meant to be.

Anya was such a person. Lithe and strong and finely made, the contours and lines of her body were moulded and sculpted in elegant harmony, all combined together in a form that embodied both strength and uncompromising beauty.

She was tall for a woman, perhaps 5 foot 9. But there was no hint of the gangly awkwardness that often came with such height. She stood confident and unselfconscious, shoulders back, chin up.

Her physique was lean and muscular, partly because of the deprivations she had endured during her imprisonment. But more than that, she remained physically fit,

276

with taut, sinewy muscle visible beneath her skin as she moved. Her stomach was flat and hard, her arms and shoulders sculpted by years of physical activity.

Her body possessed the compact, efficient musculature of a gymnast or a dancer, combining both strength and agility. He had seen for himself the bursts of sudden, explosive speed she was capable of, and their devastating effects.

But for all her deadly strength, she remained unquestionably female. His eyes were drawn inexorably to the soft curve of her breasts, the nipples pink and erect in the cooling air. Her long and shapely legs gave way to firm, rounded buttocks, swelling a little at the hips before dipping in to a narrow waist.

Then something else caught his eye. A faint patchwork of scars criss-crossed the otherwise unmarred skin of her back. It was like a spider's web, countless strands all going in different directions.

They were old scars, long since healed and faded, yet they had obviously been inflicted with great pain. In fact, they looked almost like whip lashes . . .

She turned to look at him, and he glanced away uncomfortably, angry at himself for gawking at her. What was he – a fifteen-year-old trying to peer into the girls' locker room?

'You can look at me, Drake,' she said, amused by his reaction. 'I won't have you arrested.'

By the time he turned back, she had pulled on her jeans again and was buttoning up her shirt.

'Do I make you uncomfortable?' she asked, curious.

'Are you trying to?'

Her eyes flashed. 'You didn't answer my question.'

'And you didn't answer mine.' He held out the take-away box. 'Here. Your feast awaits.'

277

Dinner consisted of sirloin steak, barbecue ribs, fries, corn cobs, salad and more pots of coleslaw, mayonnaise, garlic butter and ketchup than he could keep track of. Just one of them looked as if it could feed a whole platoon. Drake was full before he even got halfway through his, though Anya showed no signs of slowing down. He couldn't blame her.

'Mind if I ask you something?'

'Of course.'

'Those scars on your back. Did you get them in Khatyrgan?'

For a moment she stiffened, and her eyes darkened as an old memory resurfaced.

'No,' she said, distracted. 'They are from a long time ago.'

'What happened?'

'When I was in Afghanistan the first time . . .' She glanced away, and he saw the muscles in her throat moving up and down as she swallowed. She shook her head, banishing the memory. 'It doesn't matter now. It's in the past.'

She wasn't going to say anything more. Deciding not to press the issue in case she clammed up altogether, he fished out one of the bottles of Corona and held it out to her.

'I don't drink,' she said. When he popped the lid and downed a mouthful, she added, 'You shouldn't either.'

'Duly noted.'

She eyed him critically. 'I could smell drink on you in that holding cell in Alaska. Your hands were trembling. Do you often drink like that?'

He shrugged, trying to appear nonchalant. 'Depends how bad my day's been. Today, I think I've earned one.'

She leaned forward a little. 'In my experience, men drink to forget things. Failures, regrets, mistakes . . . Tell me, what are you trying to forget, Drake?'

He laid his half-finished box aside, no longer hungry. 'I'm not here to swap life stories. Right now, I want to know about your source in the Iraqi government. Who was he?'

Again he saw that faint, enigmatic smile. She had scored a point, exposed a chink in his armour. That was enough for now.

'He would not tell me his name.'

He eyed her dubiously. 'All right. What division did he work in?'

'I don't know.'

He was starting to feel uneasy. 'So what *do* you know about him?'

'You don't understand, Drake,' she said. 'Men like him don't just give you their name and address. I made contact with him through a broker, and after that we communicated through anonymous email accounts.'

'Who was the broker?'

'An Israeli Mossad agent named Russo. I had worked with him before, and he had contacts all throughout the Iraqi government.' She shook her head. 'But I will not approach him again. He has close ties with the Agency. He may even be the reason I was captured four years ago.'

It was hard to fault her logic there. Frowning, he turned the situation over in his mind. 'Any chance your source is still checking his emails?'

A blonde eyebrow rose a little. 'There is only one way to find out.'

Reaching into his pocket, Drake handed her Munro's cellphone. It was the latest generation BlackBerry with full

279

Internet and email access. She eyed the device curiously, then looked up at him as if expecting an explanation.

It took a moment or two for Drake to understand her confusion. The world of technology had moved on since her imprisonment. 'You can access your email account from here,' he explained, taking it back and enabling the Internet connection.

She said nothing, though she didn't look happy. He suspected she wasn't pleased at having her ignorance exposed.

It took twenty seconds or so to bring up Hotmail. Using the tiny keyboard with some difficulty, Anya searched for her old email account. It didn't take long to discover that it had long since been deleted due to inactivity. With no other choice, she set up a new account under the name Jane Lynch and composed her first message in four years.

> Greetings from an old friend. It has been a long time since we last spoke, but I am prepared to honour our previous agreement if you will meet with me. Please respond as soon as possible.

Her brief missive complete, she addressed it to *Typhoon157@dnsnet.com*, prayed she had memorised the address correctly, and clicked send.

And just like that, it was done. She had played her last hand.

She tossed the phone back to Drake. 'There is nothing more we can do. Now we must wait.'

Chapter 41

'I don't know what the fuck happened,' Marshall Davis groaned, his normally deep voice rendered thin and nasal by the splints in his broken nose. 'One minute I was at the gas station minding my own business, the next . . . I was getting the shit knocked out of me.'

That didn't look like an easy task. Davis was a big man, tall and broad shouldered, with big square hands calloused from hard labour. According to his file he was a construction worker, twenty-eight years old, with a previous history of violent encounters, mostly bar-room brawls. A strong man in his prime, used to handling himself in a fight, now laid up in a hospital bed.

His face was a bruised and swollen mess, cut in places, with massive discolouration spreading out from his shattered nose. His right arm was in a plaster cast, the wrist snapped like a twig, while his ribs were heavily bandaged up.

'Can you describe the man who did this to you?' Dietrich asked. It was late, and they'd had to fight with the doctors to be allowed in, but he wouldn't take no for an answer. He'd spent a long and uncomfortable hour in an Air Force chopper just to get here tonight.

'Man? It wasn't no man who did this,' Davis corrected him. 'It was that crazy bitch he had with him.'

Dietrich could feel Frost's eyes on him. She'd had her

own encounter with Anya, and harboured no love for the woman. 'Tell us what happened,' she prompted.

Davis clenched his jaw for a moment, clearly uncomfortable. 'We'd just stopped to fill up and we saw her standing at the pump next to us.'

'What did she look like?'

'Tall, blonde hair. Good-looking, I guess. She spoke with a foreign accent, maybe Russian or something. I don't know.' He shook his head, as if such things were a mystery to him.

Dietrich wondered if the stupid bastard had ever been outside Virginia.

'Anyway, we tried to talk to her, real friendly like, and she just ignored us. Made me think maybe she had something to hide, so I tried to approach her, then she just snapped. Went crazy, broke my wrist and my nose. My buddy Hooper tried to help me out, and she did the same to him. Crazy bitch could have killed us both.'

That certainly sounded like the Anya he knew. The more he learned about her, the more he relished the thought of taking her down.

'And you didn't do anything to provoke her?' Keegan asked, dubious.

Davis glared at the older man. 'If making conversation is provoking someone, arrest me now.'

Dietrich was keen to keep the conversation on track. 'What happened after that? Do you remember?'

He shook his head. 'I couldn't see real good, but I remember shouting. The other guy came out and told her to get in the car. He had an accent too – English, I think. She must have listened to him though, 'cause a few seconds later they tore ass out of there. That was the last I saw of 'em.'

Dietrich nodded. He didn't think Davis had anything

else useful to say, and there was already more than enough to keep him occupied.

'We're done,' he said, standing up.

'Hey,' Davis called after him. 'You find that bitch, you let me know. I'll feel real good knowing she's behind bars.'

Dietrich said nothing as he left the room.

An officer from the Greensville County Sheriff's Office was waiting for them in the corridor outside. He was a tall man in his fifties, skinny as a rake, with thinning grey hair and a bushy moustache. The tag on his uniform said his name was Merritt.

'Y'all get what you needed from him?'

Dietrich nodded absently, still mulling over everything he'd heard.

'He was lying about one thing,' Keegan chimed in. 'He wasn't just trying to make conversation when she attacked him.'

Merritt gave a wry smile. 'Young Mr Davis in there likes to throw his weight around. We've had him in the county lock-up a few times for fighting – nothin' serious, just bar fights and suchlike. According to the gas station attendants, he was givin' the female suspect a hard time.'

'Asshole,' Frost grunted. She had no love for Anya, but men who preyed on women were beneath contempt as far as she was concerned.

Dietrich didn't care about the man's history. 'Did you manage to pull any surveillance footage?'

The old sheriff nodded. 'Got the whole thing on tape. Makes for some interesting viewing, let me tell you. I could use someone like her as a deputy. Anyway, they took off in a silver Ford Taurus, heading south.'

'What about the licence plate?' he pressed. 'Did you get it?'

'Of course. We put out an APB to all highway patrols.'

As far as Merritt was concerned, this was little more than a petty brawl. An All Points Bulletin was a standard response in cases like this, but all it really did was advise other cops to be on the lookout for a suspect or vehicle.

It was far from a guarantee of an arrest.

He turned to Keegan. 'Call this in with Franklin. Get that licence plate out to all agencies as soon as you can.'

'The fight happened hours ago,' Frost reminded him. 'They could be in Alabama by now.'

Dietrich glanced at his watch. It was just past midnight. 'They would have found a place to hole up for the night,' he decided. 'Somewhere that doesn't ask for ID. Can you bring up a list of motels in the area?'

'How big of an area?'

He did some quick calculations in his head. 'Say . . . two hundred miles. Concentrate your search to the south.'

'How do you know he carried on south?' Frost asked. 'Wouldn't it make more sense to change direction and throw us off?'

'Yeah, it would.' Keegan was starting to catch on. 'That's what we'd expect him to do. He'd know that.'

Dietrich turned his attention back to the sheriff. 'We need to start calling round those motels.'

Merritt gave him a hard look. 'Y'all gonna tell me what this is about?'

'It's a matter of national security,' Dietrich evaded, too weary for a more detailed response.

'So I heard. That shit doesn't wash too well with me, son. I'm too old, too tired and too ugly for that cloak-and-dagger bullshit.'

Dietrich swallowed down his irritation with some difficulty. 'We were promised full cooperation from your

Sheriff's Office,' he reminded the older man. 'Are we going to have a problem?'

Merritt glared back at him from beneath bushy grey brows. Despite his slender frame, there was a wiry toughness about the man that many would have found intimidating.

Dietrich was not one of those people and therefore met the man's hostile stare without hesitation.

'No,' he said, making little effort to hide his scorn. 'No problem at all.'

As he walked away, Dietrich closed his eyes and rubbed the bridge of his nose. His head was pounding and his leg throbbing.

'Fucking rednecks,' he mumbled in German.

Anya's mood was somewhere between elation and trepidation at the thought of making contact with Typhoon again. She had risked everything to find this man four years ago, and had paid a heavy price for it. She had no wish to repeat the experience.

Yet the secrets he held just might make it worth her trouble.

The moment Drake mentioned him, an idea had begun to form in her mind; an idea spurred on by her desperate desire to claw back what she had lost. It was the same reason she had abandoned her fruitless mission in Afghanistan to pursue Typhoon four years ago, the same reason she had risked her career and her very life on a desperate gamble.

Redemption.

Her standing within the Agency had suffered greatly after the debacle with Munro, and the conflict that had torn her unit apart. Indeed, she had grown so disgusted with the whole affair that she resigned her position and disbanded what remained of Task Force Black, spending almost a year in virtual isolation while brooding on her mistakes.

Only the September 11 attacks and the subsequent US-led invasion of Afghanistan had been enough to lure her out of her self-imposed exile. But even then, she'd known she would never regain the prominence she'd once held, would never stand as high as she had on the eve of Munro's treachery.

The chance to find proof of Iraqi weapons of mass destruction had seemed like just the boon she needed to rebuild her reputation, to redeem herself in Cain's eyes and prove she was still an asset to the Agency.

She had lost that chance once, yet here it was again.

It was part of the reason she had accompanied Drake this far. She could have escaped a dozen times already, taken him hostage or even killed him with ease. Instead she had chosen to stay with him, knowing he could lead her to Munro. He might even be useful in finding Typhoon.

If she delivered both Munro and Typhoon, perhaps, just perhaps, she could return to the Agency on her own terms. Perhaps she could serve again.

'Tell me about Munro,' Drake said.

Anya blinked. She was back in the cheap motel room again, and such dreams were, for the moment, far away. 'What do you want to know?'

'What really happened between you two?'

She flashed a grim smile. 'I thought Cain told you already.'

'I got his version. I was interested in hearing yours.' He took a sip of beer. 'How did you meet him?'

She sighed, thinking back to a time in her life when things had been very different. 'I recruited him,' she began.

'My unit was short on manpower, and Cain kept pressuring me to bring in new operatives. I was against it. I didn't want to bring in outsiders, but . . . Cain persuaded me. So I chose a few candidates, and one of the men I picked was Munro.'

Even now she could still picture Munro the first day she'd met him. He had been lined up alongside the half-dozen other candidates in a training hall in Camp Peary, Virginia, known within the Agency as the Farm.

Young, eager, and perhaps a little full of himself, he'd had an infectious grin and a natural charisma that others seemed to respond to.

'Most of the others fell away during selection, but not Munro. He took everything I could throw at him and kept going. I had never seen a more dedicated soldier.'

She had gone through the same gruelling selection process a decade earlier, had endured every attempt to break her and force her to quit, and emerged stronger for it.

Wary of showing favouritism, she'd gone even harder on him, determined to test his mettle. But still he wouldn't give in.

His perseverance had earned him the one thing that so few others had ever gained – her respect. She had sensed a kindred spirit in the young man called Dominic Munro, and knew then that she wanted him in her unit.

'He was a brilliant tactician, a gifted soldier, an excellent operative in every way. He understood people and how to bring out the best in them. I taught him everything I could, and he never let me down. He helped bring more men in, oversaw their training, made sure they were put in roles where they excelled. Within a few years, Task Force Black had become more than just a paramilitary unit. We had our own intelligence resources,

287

our own supply and logistics. And after a while, we even had our own funding.'

Drake frowned. 'So what went wrong?'

'I made two mistakes. I trusted Munro, and I trusted the Agency,' she admitted. 'By the end of the decade, Task Force Black had become so large and complex that it took all my time just to keep it running. I started to rely more and more on Munro to plan and carry out operations. I gave him free rein, and he used it.'

She swallowed, facing up to it at last.

'I suppose that was when it started. The newer crop of recruits were trained and led by Munro. They were loyal to him, and him alone. Some of them even began to question why I was still in command. As for the others, they began to think I had abandoned them, that I didn't care any more. If I hadn't been so distracted, I would have realised it was starting to come apart.

'I was back at Langley when Munro contacted me in the middle of an operation in Bosnia. He told me he needed to speak urgently, so I agreed to meet him in Sarajevo. That was when he tried to have me killed.' She shook her head, remembering the horrific ambush on her vehicle as she drove through the muddy pine forests near the Bosnian capital. 'My own men, the soldiers I had led into battle myself, and they tried to murder me. They almost succeeded.

'I couldn't believe he would do such a thing. Not Dominic. But there was no denying it. He had planned it for a long time, carefully placing men loyal to him in key positions all throughout the task force, ready to act the moment he gave the order. He was trying to stage a coup.' Even now she still felt the aching, gut-wrenching pain of his betrayal. 'He assumed I was dead, and he ordered anyone still loyal to me to be arrested or shot. But I survived, and I managed to track him down.'

With tears in her eyes, she looked down at the broken, bleeding man lying on the ground at her feet. Their fight had been short but brutal, with no quarter asked or given.

She had fought with a savagery that none could withstand, breaking bones, slashing flesh and tearing muscles without mercy.

Around them, the woods were quiet, a faint mist drifting between the ancient boles. The air smelled of pine needles and damp soil. It reminded her of another place; a place she had left behind in another life.

How many of her comrades were dying at this very moment? Men who had served with her since the beginning, now spread all across the world. How many were fighting for their very lives?

Everything she had worked so hard to build, everything she had sacrificed so much for was being torn apart. Because of this man.

'I trusted you, Dominic,' she said, her voice an agonised rasp as she watched his feeble attempts to rise. He was struggling to draw breath as broken ribs pressed against his lungs. 'I trusted you.'

Anger welled up inside her like a tide. Kicking him in the chest, she sent him sprawling on his back.

The knife was in her hands before she knew it, the blade eager and gleaming as she knelt atop him, pressing her knee into his throat.

'You took everything I had left,' she said through gritted teeth, ignoring his pathetic, desperate efforts to push her off. 'Look at me, Dominic! Look at me, and see what you've done.'

His ragged gasps for breath soon turned to agonised screams as she went to work with that keen blade, carving out one eye while the other stared at her, pleading for mercy.

She had none left in her.

'I let him live,' she said at last. 'Even then, I couldn't bring myself to kill him. But I wanted him to remember me, remember what he'd done.'

Drake had been watching her in silence as she related her grim tale. 'What happened to the rest of your unit?'

'Most of the newer recruits were loyal to Munro, or were made to believe I was the enemy. But those who had been with me since the start refused to join him. The two factions fought, and the entire task force almost tore itself apart in a single night. When it was over, only a handful of us survived. I left the Agency soon afterward.' She exhaled slowly. 'I was finished.'

She looked at Drake again. 'It was my fault, Drake. I made a mistake when I let him live, but I won't make the same mistake twice.'

They spoke little after that. Both were tired and occupied with their own thoughts, and it wasn't long before Drake's turned to sleep.

He had no idea how long it had been since he'd slept. His body clock was thoroughly ruined after crossing countless time zones, but he did know he was exhausted.

'You should get some sleep,' she remarked, as if sensing his thoughts.

'I don't need it.'

'Yes, you do. Lying is not one of your skills, Drake.'

He frowned, irritated that she seemed so sure about everything. She was right, of course, but he had no intention of going to sleep before her. He didn't trust her enough for that.

Standing up, he tossed a couple of pillows down on

the carpet by the door. With a little luck, the hard floor would keep him awake for a while.

'You can have the bed. Don't say I never give you anything.'

To his surprise, she shook her head. 'I prefer the floor.'

'You're kidding.'

'I have lived most of my life without a bed. I'm too old to start now.' She offered a faint smile. 'But I appreciate the gesture.'

Feeling guilty and self-conscious, Drake sat down on the hard, lumpy mattress and pulled the Glock out of his jeans. He'd kept the weapon with him throughout the day, chambered and ready to fire, partly in case they ran into trouble, and partly as a deterrent against Anya trying to escape.

Keeping a wary eye on her, he laid the weapon down gently on the bedside table. Anya watched him, and smiled in amusement at his suspicious glance.

'I don't intend to shoot you in your sleep.'

'How comforting,' he remarked, peeling off his T-shirt. He couldn't help the sharp intake of breath as the heavy bruising across his shoulder made its presence felt.

Anya saw it too, and stared a moment too long at the discoloured flesh. 'You're hurt.'

He flashed a weak smile. 'It happened when we parachuted into your prison. A close encounter of the air-vent kind.'

'I did not know.' She sounded almost touched by his admission.

He shrugged. 'It goes with the job. I've had worse.'

Saying nothing further, she settled herself on the floor near the bathroom. A single pillow was her only nod to comfort.

Lying back with his arms behind his head, Drake stared

up at a cobweb hanging from the light fixture overhead, drifting slowly back and forth on some unseen air current. The Artex ceiling, once white, was yellowed with age and cigarette smoke.

'Typical. Your first night of freedom, and it's in a place that makes my house look like the Savoy.'

Her voice was soft and quiet when she replied.

'Most nights in Khatyrgan, I would have killed every man in the prison to be where I am now. It is warm, I can move around, talk when I want. There is food and clean water. I can walk outside and breathe the night air. I can fall asleep without worrying about being raped when I wake up. It is good here.'

Drake sighed. 'How did you . . . do it?'

'Do what?'

'Survive. Stay sane.'

'The same way I have always survived – by shutting it out. Keeping a part of myself untouched no matter what happened.' He heard her faint exhalation of breath. 'They could do what they wanted to my body. I couldn't stop them, but my mind was my own. They could never control that.'

He doubted he could have endured what she had.

'I didn't mean it, you know,' he said at last.

She sat up to look at him. 'Mean what?'

'What I said earlier, about wishing you were still there. I didn't. Nobody deserves that place.'

She looked genuinely surprised. 'Not even me?'

'I don't know your history, but I know you're still here.' He raised himself up on one elbow to look at her. 'That has to count for something.'

Anya said nothing, though she held his gaze for several seconds, and he saw that same fleeting look of sadness and vulnerability he'd seen on the flight back from Russia.

292

When she laid her head down on the pillow again, he did likewise. For the next couple of minutes he heard nothing, just the faint hum of the air conditioner and the sound of his own breathing, until his mind at last surrendered to sleep.

Chapter 42

Drake watched as the windshield disintegrated in slow motion, thousands of tiny spiderweb cracks spreading outward from each point of impact. Miniature fragments blew outward in lazy arcs, drifting like snow in front of his eyes.

And beyond it, he caught a glimpse of blue dress, dark hair and wide, pleading eyes.

Drake awoke with a start, instinctively reaching for the weapon beside his bed. He wasn't thinking rationally, his mind still caught somewhere in the nightmarish world that had assailed him.

But instead of closing around the cold, rough grip of the Glock, his fingers found only the flat tabletop.

'Looking for something?'

His head snapped around. Anya was standing over by the door, light from the rising sun peeking through gaps in the blinds behind her. She held the Glock in a loose, easy grip.

Drake felt his throat tightening as he stared at the weapon. She could do anything she wanted. She could shoot him dead and he could do nothing to stop her.

She stared back at him, her eyes still shining faintly with that same predatory look he had seen in Khatyrgan, as if she could sense his fear and relished it.

Then, in the blink of an eye, her gaze softened. She

laid the weapon down on the TV stand, picked up a cup of coffee that was steaming beside it and approached him, holding it out like a peace offering. Her hair was hanging loose, a little tousled and dishevelled from sleep, but otherwise she looked rested and refreshed.

Lucky her.

He looked at her with a hint of suspicion, then finally took it and gulped down a mouthful. If she intended to kill him, he doubted poison would be her modus operandi.

'You don't sleep well, do you?' She picked up her own cup and took a drink. 'Bad dreams?'

'Bad memories,' Drake replied, avoiding her gaze.

She was perceptive enough not to press him on the matter. 'I checked the emails on your phone earlier. There was no reply from Typhoon.'

Drake raised an eyebrow. 'Becoming a real technophile, I see.'

She ignored his jibe. 'If he hasn't heard from me in four years, it is safe to say he won't check his mail every day. In any case, we should leave soon,' she decided. 'If Cain and the others haven't found out about what happened at the gas station, they will soon enough.'

He was in agreement. The question was, where should they go?

His priority yesterday had been mere survival, escaping the immediate search area. They might have accomplished this by the skin of their teeth, but from here their way forward was uncertain. Getting out of the country was going to be problematic to say the least.

'Well, we can forget about the airports,' he decided straight away. 'We have no passports and almost no money.'

Even if he'd had access to his passport, it would have

been red-flagged straight away by the Agency. Any attempt to use it would have resulted in immediate detainment and a one-way trip back to Langley. Not to mention the fact that Anya didn't even have one to begin with . . .

There was only one realistic solution that he could think of. 'We might have to try and slip over the border to Mexico. After that –' he threw up his hands – 'we either start busking for money, or we'd better polish up our bank-robbing skills.'

Anya however remained unfazed by the numerous problems standing in their path. 'I know a man who can help us.'

He cocked an eyebrow. 'Who, exactly?'

Again she gave him that knowing, enigmatic smile. 'Come on, get out of bed,' she said, avoiding the question. 'We don't have much time.'

After a hasty breakfast of pre-made bagels and instant coffee, they abandoned their room without bothering to check out. They had paid in advance anyway, so their departure was unlikely to draw undue attention.

And now here they were, with nothing but the rumble of their tyres on the road and the muted roar of the wind whipping by to break the silence.

Beside him, Anya looked as if she was having the time of her life. With her window down, seat wound back, feet up on the dashboard and eyes hidden behind her new sunglasses, she was a picture of laid-back calm.

'Enjoying yourself?' he couldn't help asking.

'It is more enjoyable than my average day.'

It was tough to argue with that.

'Tell me something about yourself, Drake,' she prompted.

'Why?'

'If we are going to be working together, it's only fair that we know something about each other. You seem to know a lot about me already, but I know very little about you.'

'That's the way I like it.'

'I don't.' She looked at him for a long moment. 'Of course, I could make a few guesses . . .'

'This should be good,' he remarked.

'You were in the military, probably Special Air Service judging by the parachute insertion and the tactics you used at Khatyrgan,' she began. 'Also, the knife on your webbing that night was standard SAS issue. The notch on the hand guard is designed to snag an opponent's blade in a knife fight.'

Drake was impressed, both by her knowledge of weaponry and the details she had noticed in the heat of the moment.

'You are divorced,' she went on. 'I see the mark where the ring was. It has faded, so it must have happened a few years ago. You are not in a relationship now.'

'And how would you know that?' he asked, irritated by the accuracy of her 'guesses'.

'There were no pictures in your wallet. I checked while you were asleep.' She smiled at his discomfort. 'And I saw the way you looked at me last night. You haven't slept with a woman for a while.'

He couldn't stop the colour rising to his face. He understood now why she'd undressed in front of him. She wanted to see how he would react.

'You been reading my Facebook page or something?' he shot back.

This at least put her off balance, if only for a moment. 'What is a Facebook?'

'Never mind,' he said. 'Anyway, if you've got all the answers, what do you need me for?'

'Because there are some things I can't work out. How did a man like you end up working for a man like Cain?'

He said nothing for a while, and neither did she, but he could feel her gaze boring into him.

'I don't work for Cain,' he said at last. 'I work for Dan Franklin.'

'The man with the bad back?'

Drake nodded. 'He and I served together in Afghanistan. We were part of a special task force sent in to capture Taliban bad guys. We became good friends, and when I left the regiment, he found a job for me with the Agency.'

'Why did you leave?'

'I'd rather not talk about it,' he answered tersely. There were a lot of things about his time with 14th Special Operations Group that he wasn't proud of, particularly the manner of his departure. He certainly wasn't going to share such things with a woman he barely knew.

To his surprise, she didn't push him. 'Well, it seems we both have things we'd rather not talk about.'

Feeling uncomfortable, Drake switched on the radio. It took a few moments to seek out whatever tinpot station was playing locally, but when it did, the strains of Bob Marley's 'Three Little Birds' filled the car.

'No, thanks,' Drake decided, reaching for the tuner.

'Wait,' Anya said.

He glanced over at her. She was sitting with her head resting against the seat, her hair whipped up by the breeze from the open window, her eyes closed. There was a look of such peace and serenity on her face that he couldn't bring himself to change the station over.

'Never had you pegged as a Bob Marley fan.'

'It was the first song I heard when I came to America,' she explained. 'I was being driven to Langley for the first time, and it was playing on the radio. The driver asked if I minded him listening to it.' She smiled a faint, wistful smile. 'I was shocked. Nobody had ever asked for my permission to do anything. Nobody had ever cared what I thought or what I wanted. It was the first time I really felt like I was . . . free. And it felt good.'

Drake said nothing. There was nothing he *could* say to that. The best thing he could do was shut up and let her enjoy the song.

Not for the first time, he found himself wondering about his strange, enigmatic passenger; who she really was, where she came from, and where she was going.

They made good progress throughout the day, stopping only once at a gas station in South Carolina to refuel and use the restrooms. Thankfully there were no idiot locals on hand this time, and they left without incident, Drake nursing a large cappuccino and his companion a bottle of Coke.

They ended up driving straight through Georgia without stopping, crossing the state line into Florida by mid-afternoon. As they continued southward, the terrain around them changed, with trees and fields giving way to palm trees and swampland. They were in a subtropical climate now, with high humidity, soaring temperatures and unpredictable weather.

At one point about an hour after crossing over from Georgia, the heavens opened with such ferocity that Drake could barely make out the road ahead. Even the wipers working overtime couldn't clear the monsoon-like deluge from the windscreen. Traffic on the highway slowed to a crawl as the onslaught continued.

Then, fifteen minutes later, the sun was beating down from an almost cloudless sky, leaving only the steaming tarmac as evidence of the intense downpour.

'Mind if I ask you something?' Drake began.

He was coming to understand that there was a right way and a wrong way to question his companion. She didn't like to talk about herself for long periods, didn't like answering too many questions all at once. If he pushed too hard, she would clam up and say nothing, simply choosing to ignore him.

Information had to be teased out of her, yielded up in small pieces. She had to be given time to accept it.

'No.'

'What's the deal with you and Cain?'

She stiffened up. 'What do you mean?'

'Come on. You know what I'm talking about. You're not just another operative to him, are you?'

She was silent for a long moment, and he wondered if perhaps she was going to give him the silent treatment again. 'He recruited me into the Agency, when I first came to America. He gave me a chance when no one else would, and over time we came to respect each other. For a while, I believed there was nothing we couldn't do together. I think even he believed it too . . . for a while.'

'You were friends?'

She glanced away, but he'd seen the look in her eyes. 'We were close,' she answered, refusing to elaborate.

'So what happened?'

'He was willing to compromise. I wasn't.'

She would say no more, and he knew better than to ask.

Chapter 43

An hour later, Drake pulled into the parking lot of a vast shopping mall and killed the engine. They were on the outskirts of Daytona, a popular tourist trap on the shores of the Atlantic, and a mecca for NASCAR fans the world over. But Drake wasn't here for racing.

They needed supplies. They had exhausted their food and drink some time ago; a fact that both of them were growing increasingly aware of. But more than that, they needed a change of clothes. Anya had a plan to secure money and passports for them both, but for it to work, she needed something a little more stylish than jeans and a ripped leather jacket.

In that regard, he couldn't think of a better place than the shopping mall before them. It was the size of a small town itself, filled with dozens of clothing outlets. If Anya couldn't find what she needed here, they were in trouble.

But as he got out, his stiff legs protesting, Anya remained in the car. She was staring at the huge building like a rabbit caught in the headlights.

He ducked his head back in. 'You coming or what?'

'Shouldn't we try somewhere smaller?' she suggested, looking uncomfortable and agitated. 'We passed shops on the way.'

'Not unless you want an "I love Spring Break" T-shirt and a beer hat,' he said with a wry grin. 'This place is big, it's busy and it's anonymous. In short, it's exactly what we need. So come on.'

Resigning herself to the inevitable, she stepped out of the car and followed him towards one of the building's many entrances, looking like a sullen teenager being dragged along by her father.

Passing through the automatic doors, Drake found himself in an air-conditioned world of organised chaos. The place was built on three levels, with escalators and lifts running between them, packed with people of all ages. Security guards zoomed around on Segways, flitting between groups of shoppers like sharks circling schools of fish.

Salesmen at temporary stalls enthusiastically touted everything from cellphones to novelty balloons to chocolates and beauty treatments. A big plastic flight simulator was shuddering and pitching back and forth, accompanied by delighted screams from within. Music was playing from a dozen different sources, all blending together with excited chatter, cellphone chimes and PA announcements into an indistinguishable white noise.

Checking the multi-level store directory, he found that the mall was laid out like a giant crucifix, and that they were standing at the end of the eastern wing. The nearest general purpose clothes outlet was about halfway down their wing, on the floor above.

'Right, off we go. Looks like J.C. Penney's about to relieve us of some cash,' he said, heading for the nearest escalator.

Anya followed behind, but she wasn't walking with her usual quiet confidence. The gap between them widened as her pace slowed, though Drake didn't notice amidst the chaos. Finally the woman stopped altogether and just stared around, eyes wide.

She was overwhelmed. As grim and tortuous as her imprisonment in Khatyrgan had been, she'd found a certain security in the monotony. A single 6-by-8-foot prison cell had grown to encompass her entire world. The lack of stimulus had sharpened her awareness of even minor changes, made her acutely aware of her surroundings.

But here there was so much going on that her brain couldn't cope. She had never liked crowded places at the best of times and had always detested shopping malls, and that feeling had grown stronger in recent years.

She felt panicked, breathless, trapped by the thronging press of humanity all around. Despite their vastly different ages, sizes, shapes and genders, all of them somehow blended together into an indistinguishable mass of people. But not her. She was different.

A teenage girl walked past. 5 foot 5, 130 pounds, dark hair, no obvious weapons. She eyed Anya with a mixture of curiosity and derision. She could sense something was wrong. She sensed someone who was different and she didn't like it.

A young man in a business suit and open collar passed by on her other side, chatting into a cellphone and almost bumping into her. She jumped back instinctively, having to fight hard not to put her arms up to protect herself. She did an automatic threat assessment.

Male, late twenties, blond hair, lean build, 5 foot 11, 160 pounds. He didn't move like a fighter. Was he armed? He could have a weapon in a pancake holster at his back.

The man gave her an irritable look and sidestepped her, but there were others behind. There were others everywhere.

She didn't belong here. She knew it. Did they know it too? Were they casting surreptitious glances her way, wondering who she was and what she was doing here? She had no idea. Normally she could read people easily, could sense if she was being watched, but here it was impossible.

She felt exposed, naked, vulnerable. She felt as if she was lying on the floor of that shower room again, unable to move, unable to protect herself . . .

No!

Survival instinct took over. She turned to flee, then hesitated, not knowing which way she had come. She was overwhelmed by the chaos around her. She couldn't see properly. She was tall for a woman, but there were men everywhere, many of them far taller than herself. Together they formed a wall of flesh and bone and bright clothing that she couldn't see over. She couldn't see the exit.

You have to get out!

Get out now!

Then, suddenly, a figure emerged from the blurred mass around her. Not some impatient shopper eager to push past or a gawking teenager, but a man who knew her, who recognised and understood her fear.

She felt Drake's hand on her arm and didn't resist as he steered her towards the exit.

'It's all right,' he said quietly as they walked. 'I'm here.'

For the first time in a long time, she felt as if she wanted to cry. She was frightened, confused and lost. More than that, she was angry. Angry at Drake for bringing her to this place, angry at him for helping her and making her feel as though she needed it, angry at the people around her who crowded in so close, angry at herself for being so weak and afraid.

'I need some air,' she whispered, not trusting herself to say more.

Drake felt like shit. He should have known better than to drag her into a place like that. The poor woman had been living in virtual isolation for four years – she should have been in therapy, not fighting through crowded shopping malls.

Most of the time she acted so implacable and confident, it was easy to forget what she had been through. But even she had her limits, and he'd just pushed her beyond them.

You fucking idiot. She could have lost it, could have killed someone.

She was sitting in the passenger seat, her head lowered and her eyes closed, stray tendrils of blonde hair whipped up by the breeze. She hadn't said a word since they'd left the mall and returned to the car.

Now they were heading south on a quiet coastal road, the hustle and bustle of the thronging town behind them. To their left, the shimmering waters of the Atlantic stretched off to the horizon, the endless rolling waves marred only by the occasional yacht or surfer.

'Anya, I'm . . . sorry,' he began. 'I should have realised—'

'Realised what?' she snapped, raising her head to glare at him. 'Realised that I'm weak and pathetic? That I can't even stand to walk through a damned shopping mall?' She blinked and looked away, tossing her head to move a loose lock of wind-blown hair out of her eyes.

'You're not weak. Believe me, you're not.'

'Then what am I, Drake?' she asked, her voice trembling. 'I can kill a man with my bare hands, go home and fall asleep without regrets. But walking down a

305

crowded street leaves me shaking like a frightened child. What does that make me?'

Without waiting for an answer, she glanced out the window again. 'Stop the car.'

'What?'

'I said stop the car, Drake!' she snapped.

Slowing, he found a convenient lay-by and pulled over. They were on a largely unpopulated stretch of road, with just the occasional beach-front condo to the north and south. The vast swathe of white sand before them was almost devoid of people.

Anya wasted no time. As soon as they came to a halt, she threw open her door and got out. She was off, striding toward the beach with fast, purposeful strides. She didn't look back.

'Where are you going?' Drake called after her.

She didn't reply.

Chapter 44

Vast, pristine white sand stretched from horizon to horizon, its perfection marred only by the occasional pier or breakwater. Anya could feel the sand between her toes – another novel sensation – as she strode down towards the waterfront.

A light breeze blew in off the ocean, warm and salty, pushing her hair back from her face. She closed her eyes and inhaled deep, just allowing the wind to blow past her.

She headed north, walking with no particular goal or objective. She wasn't trying to get anywhere, she just wanted to be alone with her thoughts.

But as she walked, her pace quickened almost of its own volition, as if her legs were working independent of her mind. Before she knew it, her aimless walk had turned into a steady jog, which in turn gave way to an all-out sprint.

She ran, feet pounding the sand, muscles bunching and releasing, lungs greedily sucking in gasps of air. She ran, not caring where she was going. The tension, the nervous energy, the adrenalin that had coursed through her veins in the shopping mall had at last found an outlet.

She ran until she could run no further.

When she at last staggered to a halt, breathless and exhausted, heart pounding, she had left Drake and the car far behind.

She was alone. For the first time since this all began, she was alone.

Lowering herself onto the sand, she leaned back and stared up at the sky. It was a beautiful, clear evening, the sun starting its descent towards the western horizon and lending the few high, wispy clouds a pinkish tinge.

It was quiet here. She couldn't hear cellphones or music or car engines or inane chatter or any of the countless other sounds she found irritating and even frightening.

All she could make out was the deep, vibrant roar of waves breaking against the shore, the sigh of her own breathing and the strong, steady beat of her heart. She was alone on an endless beach, staring up into the infinite sky.

How many nights did you lie awake dreaming of this? How many times did you force it away, telling yourself it would never happen? How many times did you want to cry with frustration in that tiny cell, holding it back, refusing to give in?

It was over now. Whatever else happened, she would never again go back to that place, or any like it. She would die first.

Weakness will not be in my heart. Fear will not be in my creed.

Fear. She had felt it today, stronger than she ever imagined.

In that shopping mall today, she had felt like the little girl she had been Before, the little girl she could barely remember as herself. She had felt frightened, panicked, lost and alone.

She had promised herself she would never feel like that again, would never permit weakness or fear into her mind. Her mask of self-control had been her armour.

It had protected her from the horrific things she had seen and done in her long life, it had allowed her to stay sane in an insane world.

But it was a heavy burden to carry, and she was tired.

How did it come to this?

I did everything that was asked of me. Everything. Is this my reward?

To stand when all others have fallen. Alone. Scared. Lost.

A soldier without a war. A patriot without a country. A life without meaning.

Giving in at last, she squeezed her eyes shut as tears flowed from them. She cried for everything she had lost, for everything she had done and all that had been done to her, for all the mistakes and the regrets, for all the sacrifices and pain.

She cried, and no one saw her.

She felt different when she at last returned to the car. Lighter, somehow. She had discarded something she'd been carrying with her for a long time, and it felt good.

Drake was waiting for her, sitting propped against the side of the car. Honouring her request, he had stayed behind, giving her the time she needed. She didn't even know how long she'd been gone, but the sun was closer to the horizon than it had been when she'd left.

She sat down beside him, both of them staring out across the glinting waves in silence. There were things she wanted to say, but she wasn't sure how to begin.

'How do you feel?' Drake asked, as if sensing her difficulty.

She thought about it for a few seconds. 'Better.'

'I'm sorry for putting you through that, Anya. It was stupid to go there.'

She shook her head. 'I wasn't angry at you.'

He said nothing. That was one thing she appreciated about him. He spoke when he had something to say, and he knew when to shut up and let the other person talk.

'I know I must be . . . difficult,' she said, groping for the right words. 'I know your life has been made harder because of me. But if it means anything, I'm grateful for the things you've done.' She sighed and looked down for a moment. 'It might sound stupid, but you are probably the closest thing I have left to a friend, Drake.'

He turned to look at her then, saw the same look in her eyes that he'd caught a glimpse of on the flight back from Russia.

He smiled gently. 'It doesn't sound stupid.'

They sat together in companionable silence as the waves rolled in off the sea and the occasional car droned past on the road. Neither spoke, because neither had anything to say.

And that was all right with them.

The mood was finally broken when Drake's phone chimed, notifying him of an incoming email. He passed the phone to her.

Anya's heart leapt. It was a message from Typhoon.

'He's still alive.'

Drake leaned in close as she opened the email. To his surprise, there was no message as such, just a hyperlink to a website.

'What do you think?' For some reason he found himself aware of the warmth from her skin, the closeness of their bodies, the faint tang of salt in her hair.

She glanced at him, then back at the screen. 'Only one way to find out.'

She clicked on the link, but to Drake's disappointment it returned a blank window with a *Page Not Found* error message. Whatever was on that website, it seemed they were unable to read it.

'Maybe it's not compatible with the phone.'

Anya shook her head. She was smiling. 'No. This is a little trick of his — a toot, to make sure I am who I say I am. This screen is the password.'

He frowned. 'I don't understand. There's nothing there.'

'Yes, there is, if you know where to look.' Manipulating the phone's fiddly tracker ball, she highlighted the *n* in *Found* and clicked on it.

Straight away the error message disappeared and they were transported to a new page. It looked like a dialogue box used in the old Internet chat rooms of ten years ago.

Clever man, Drake thought. Most people finding an error like that would have dismissed it as a broken link and navigated away. Only someone who knew where to look could find the way in.

An automated message appeared: `Connecting with host . . .`

'He will know we are online,' Anya explained. 'In my day it would have sent an email to his computer, but now I imagine it has messaged his cellphone.'

Sure enough, thirty seconds later the status changed: `Host is online.`

Typhoon, whoever he was, wasted no time on greetings.

`Host: PASSWORD.`

`Guest: EUPHRATES.`

For the next several seconds, nothing happened. Then, at last, Typhoon seemed to accept that she was who she claimed to be.

`Host: WHERE HAVE YOU BEEN???`

Face tight with concentration, Anya set to work on

her reply. This was a delicate task. If she said the wrong thing, she could lose him for good.

Guest: I WAS ARRESTED BEFORE OUR MEET. RUSSIANS - FSB. HAVE BEEN IN PRISON FOR FOUR YEARS.

Host: *HOW DID YOU GET OUT?*

Guest: CIA BROUGHT ME HOME. AM WORKING AGAIN.

Host: *WHAT DO YOU WANT?*

Guest: TO FINISH WHAT WE STARTED. CAN YOU HELP ME?

This was a critical moment. If she couldn't convince Typhoon to help them, it was over.

Host: *YOU LET ME DOWN.*

Guest: I HAVE NOT LIED TO YOU, AND I WILL NOT.

Host: *THE WORLD HAS CHANGED SINCE WE LAST SPOKE . . .*

Guest: BUT I HAVE NOT. NEITHER HAS MY OFFER. HELP ME, AND I WILL HELP YOU.

Host: *YOU WILL HONOUR OUR AGREEMENT IN FULL?*

Guest: YES.

Host: *HOW DO I KNOW I CAN TRUST YOU?*

Guest: YOU DO NOT. BUT I AM YOUR ONLY HOPE, AS YOU ARE MINE.

There was no reply for some time. Drake couldn't blame him for being hesitant. He'd be doing the same thing in Typhoon's position – pondering whether or not she was telling the truth, whether it was worth the risk.

Then, at last, it came.

Host: *IF YOU'RE STILL IN, THEN SO AM I. MEET ME IN IRAQ. I WILL GIVE YOU MORE INSTRUCTIONS WHEN YOU CROSS THE BORDER. FOR YOUR SAKE, I HOPE YOU KEEP YOUR WORD THIS TIME.*

Guest: FOR ALL OUR SAKES, I HOPE YOU KEEP YOURS. I AM LOOKING FORWARD TO MEETING YOU.

The dialogue box changed again: *Host   is   now*
offline.

Handing the phone to Drake, Anya leaned back, closed
her eyes and sighed with relief. 'He will meet us.'

Drake didn't quite share her sense of jubilation. 'Great.
Now all we need is enough money for a flight to the
Middle East, a couple of passports and a way to slip
over the Iraqi border undetected.'

Anya smiled at him. 'Come. We have work to do.'

Chapter 45

Jessica coughed, hot stifling air and dust irritating her throat. The heat in her tiny concrete cell was unbelievable; never in her life had she experienced anything like it. The very air seemed to radiate heat. There was no escape from it.

She wiped a forearm across her brow, slick with sweat. Her clothes, the same ones she'd been wearing when they snatched her, were stained and grimy. She'd been given nothing else to wear, and no opportunity to wash.

Over and over she replayed that terrifying moment when her safe, secure world had been torn apart. Walking to her car after staying late at work, she had heard footsteps on the concrete behind. She hadn't questioned it. She wasn't a woman prone to jumping at people just going about their business, or tensing if she passed a man while out walking alone.

Only when the pace quickened and the steps came closer did she suspect what was about to happen. With an eerie sense of detachment she had started to turn, her hand already reaching for the pepper spray she kept in her bag.

Too late. Gloved hands had clamped around her mouth, and an instant later she felt something sharp jabbed into her neck. There had been a dull hiss, and within moments it was as if she had been relieved of control of her body.

Drugged and barely conscious, she could do nothing

to protest as a grey van pulled up beside her and she was bundled into the back, a gag placed across her mouth and a hood over her head.

The next couple of hours existed in her memory only as a kaleidoscope of sounds, smells and sensations. She remembered the smell of diesel fuel and oil in the back of the truck, the lurching movement as it trundled over rough ground, the throaty roar of the engine.

She remembered being seized by strong hands and pulled out into chill wind and rain, being dragged over rough concrete with grass growing through in places. She recalled hearing the high-pitched whine of a jet engine, and smelling the sharp tang of aviation fuel. An airfield, then. An old one, seldom used.

Up a flight of steps, and into a cool, confined interior space. The smell of plastic and leather and air conditioning. The inside of an aircraft.

More movement. The bump and rumble of wheels on rough tarmac, then a final lurch and suddenly everything became smooth and quiet.

She couldn't say how long the flight lasted, but it was several hours at least, during which her senses gradually returned and she was able to think more clearly.

When at last the jet touched down and she was led down the steps once more, she'd known straight away she was in a desert country. The air was hot and dry, the wind carrying stinging pellets of sand, the hot sun burning her exposed skin.

Only when she was thrown into this dingy cell had her hood been removed and her hands unbound. She had been here ever since, wherever 'here' was.

Her mouth was parched, her stomach achingly empty. She hadn't eaten in at least a day, and hadn't been given a drop of water since this morning.

She wondered for a terrifying moment if her captors had simply left her here to die, if she was destined to watch her life slowly fade away in that miserable cell. She would die, and her family would never even know what had become of her . . .

No! You can't allow yourself to think like that. If they went to the trouble of bringing you here, they must want you for something. You're alive, and they intend to keep you that way, for now at least.

Her captors were nothing if not organised. She had been around enough military men in her life to recognise them when she saw them, and these were professionals.

Her thoughts were interrupted by a harsh rasp as a deadbolt was withdrawn. Scrambling away from the door, she watched as it swung open to reveal Him. She didn't know his name, but he seemed to be the leader around here. The big man with the glass eye.

His very presence was frightening, not because he was aggressive or violent, but because of the icy mask of self-control he wore. Deep down she knew that was far more dangerous.

He was holding a plastic bottle of mineral water, which he tossed on the floor beside her. When she hesitated, he smiled in amusement.

'Drink it. It's not poisoned,' he prompted. 'Or would you like me to take it away?'

Snatching the bottle up, she almost tore the lid off and gulped it down, relieved to finally slake her thirst.

'You'll want to take it slow,' he suggested. 'You might not get any more for a while.'

'How long?' she asked, almost afraid to speak to him.

'That depends how long your brother takes to bring me what I want. If he lets me down, you might be waiting a very long time. You know what it feels like to die of dehydration? Your head pounds, your vision fades, you're so tired you can't even stand up. You'll start to hallucinate. I wonder what you'll see?' he mused. 'Maybe your brother. Maybe your husband or your kids . . .'

'Why are you doing this to us?' Jessica asked, anger flaring up in her at the mention of her children. 'We've done nothing to you.'

His single remaining eye gleamed in the harsh light. 'You think I'm an evil man, right? Some fucking terrorist nut job out to kill innocent people?' He chuckled under his breath. 'If only you knew what brought me here, you'd be cheering me on right now.'

'Somehow I doubt that.'

Far from being angry, he grinned in amusement. 'Just like your brother. I'm sure he'd be real proud to see you overplaying your hand like this.'

'What would you know about Ryan?'

'I know he's not the saint you seem to think he is,' the big man informed her coldly. 'He never told you what he did out in Afghanistan, did he? Or why he left the military? Official secrets, and all that bullshit. Or maybe he was just too ashamed to admit the truth.' He glanced down at the half-empty bottle in her hands. 'Enjoy the water.'

Jessica shuddered as the door slammed shut.

Dietrich was in a bar across the street from Greensville County Sheriff's Office nursing a bottle of Heineken when Frost caught up with him.

'Agent Frost. To what do I owe this honour?' he asked, looking at her with bloodshot eyes. A half-finished cigarette lay smoking in the ashtray beside him.

The young woman glanced at the bottle with disapproval. 'You turned your phone off.'

He shrugged. 'I'm off the clock.'

He was sick of taking calls, listening to Franklin's demands for information he didn't have, chasing up false alarms and hoaxes. He needed some down time.

The headaches and nausea had gradually abated, for which he was eternally grateful. Still, several days of sickness, pain and discomfort, not to mention lack of sleep, had left him wasted and drained.

'What do you want, Frost?' he asked, an edge of irritation in his voice.

'To talk to you.' She took a vacant stool next to him and, when the bartender spotted her, ordered a bottle of Miller.

She said nothing further while she waited for her drink, as if enjoying the uncomfortable silence. When it arrived, she took a long, slow mouthful, still making no effort to converse with him.

'You don't like me much, do you?' he asked.

'Nope,' she agreed casually, setting her drink down.

'You think I'm an arrogant, egotistical piece of shit. And you wish it had been me who took that round in the shoulder.'

She nodded slowly, still looking down at her drink. 'That's about the size of it.'

Dietrich sighed. It was a shame Frost was such an irritating little bitch. In all other respects she was the kind of woman he would have found attractive – strong, fiery, passionate and without fear.

'You know something? You remind me of my ex-wife.'

Frost raised an eyebrow. 'I'm amazed any woman could stand you long enough to get married.'

He took another sip of Heineken. 'Well, if it makes you feel any better, it didn't last long.'

'It does.'

He couldn't help but smile. She really was a heartless bitch. 'What about you? Is there a Mr Frost chained to a radiator somewhere?'

'Why? You in the market for divorcee number two?' she taunted.

Dietrich didn't say anything.

'Nope,' she said at last, turning her attention back to her drink. 'Never been married, never will be. Not my style.'

'Smart girl.'

She surveyed him with a critical eye. 'You look sick.'

'The painkillers—' he began, the excuse rolling off his tongue.

Her knowing smile stopped him cold. 'Forget it. You really think I'm that stupid? We both know what's wrong with you, and it's got nothing to do with painkillers.' She leaned forward conspiratorially. 'How long has it been since you got high? A day? Two? You're really feeling it now, huh? The headaches, the nausea, the hand tremors . . . Withdrawal's a bitch, or so I heard.'

'I . . .' He trailed off. He could think of nothing to say.

His silence told her everything she needed to know. 'You're a fucking disgrace, Dietrich. And a liability. You could have got us all killed in that prison. If I'd known then what I know now, I would have killed your dumb ass myself,' she said, her voice low and menacing. 'As it is, the only reason you're still here is because your guesses seem to be panning out.'

That last remark caught him off guard. 'What do you mean?'

'We got a call in from a motel in Shannon; a little town in North Carolina. Two guests matching Drake and Anya's description stayed there last night. They left without checking out this morning.' She chuckled under

319

her breath. 'Looks like your hunch paid off. They're still heading south.'

Dietrich leaned back, his mind a whirl of confused thoughts.

'Like I said, I haven't told anyone what I know, because even if you're an asshole, you're still useful to us. But when this is over, you walk. Walk away, or I swear to God I'll ruin you.'

Draining the last of her beer, she pushed herself away from the bar. 'Thanks for the drink.'

With that, she turned and walked off, leaving him to pick up the tab.

Chapter 46

'You realise this would be an ideal place for the Agency to snatch us,' Drake remarked, glancing up and down the corridor.

Like most such buildings, Bayside Self Storage was a spartan affair, with concrete floors, brick walls and harsh fluorescent lighting overhead. Still, it was also clean and efficient, and obviously secure judging by the electronic locks that guarded each of the storage rooms. And most importantly, it was open twenty-four hours a day.

'Nobody knows about this place,' Anya said as she studied the numeric keypad in front of her. 'I made sure of that when I opened it.'

'You've been gone four years,' he reminded her. 'They might have auctioned your stuff off by now.'

'Unlikely. The lease was paid for thirty years in advance.' Hesitating a moment, she started punching in numbers. 'The only thing I need . . . is the access code.'

There was a beep, and the indicator light on the keypad turned green.

Anya smiled. 'Easy.'

Kneeling down, she gripped the roll-down door by the handle at its base and hauled it up. Steel rollers clanked and rattled as it retracted, revealing a small room beyond, perhaps 6 feet square. A single fluorescent light burned overhead, having switched on the moment she opened the door.

'Inside,' she said, holding the door up while he entered. As soon as he was in, she allowed it to fall back into place, suppressing a faint shudder at the harsh clang.

The room was small, claustrophobic, not much different from another small place she had spent a great deal of time. Drake could sense her unease and guessed the cause, though he decided not to mention it, instead concentrating on their surroundings.

The locker was an empty shell. No furniture, no shelves or recesses. In fact, it contained nothing apart from a single metal toolbox set beside the far wall. Kneeling in front of it, Anya gripped the lid and flipped it open.

'Shit,' Drake gasped. He knelt beside her, staring in awe at the box.

Inside lay bundles of money wrapped in plastic bags; used bills of various denominations that he couldn't begin to count. Beside the money was an automatic pistol that he recognised as a Colt M1911, complete with two spare magazines and an unopened box of cartridges, all dismantled to make it suitable for long-term storage.

Also included in the box were various documents and cards with Anya's picture on them: driver's licences, credit cards, business cards and most important, passports.

Anya picked up the two passports, one Finnish and the other American, and leafed through to ensure they were still in date.

'Good,' she decided, transferring the money into her jacket pockets.

'How much do you have there?' Drake couldn't help asking.

'Ten thousand dollars,' she answered casually. 'That's

what I keep in each of my funds. We call them security blankets.'

He eyed her cynically. 'You're trying to dazzle me with jargon now.'

She shrugged. 'I am only trying to educate you.'

'How many of these things do you have?'

She gave him that same enigmatic smile he'd come to know all too well. 'A woman is entitled to a few secrets.'

Finishing with the money, she tucked the passports and other documents into her jeans, leaving the weapon behind.

'We need to get to Miami International,' she said, closing the lid. 'With luck we can book a morning flight.'

'We still need clothes,' Drake pointed out. 'There's no way we're getting through an international airport dressed like this.'

Aside from the fact that their attire was looking decidedly worse for wear after two days of travelling, Cain would have alerted airport security to be on the lookout for two people matching their description. They needed to change their appearance.

'We can buy clothes on the way.'

'Great. You can't buy me a passport, though,' he felt moved to point out.

Her icy blue eyes flashed. 'Trust me.'

A few phone calls revealed that the first available flight was with Emirates, departing at 06.45 the next day and bound for Riyadh in Saudi Arabia. Using one of the credit cards from her contingency fund, Anya booked them two seats in business class, deciding to use her Finnish passport to get into the country. They were to be representatives of an architect's firm, travelling to Riyadh to serve as consultants for a construction project.

With this in mind, they had stopped off at the Emporio Armani store en route to the airport, paying ridiculous prices for clothes to make them suitably businesslike. Drake had been reluctant to let her go inside, remembering her earlier reaction to the shopping mall at Daytona, but she was insistent. And to his surprise, she coped well with the experience.

Laden with their bags of designer clothes, they booked a room for the night at the Embassy Suites, about a mile from the main terminal. With thick, pristine carpets, expensive furnishings and a luxury king-sized bed, it was everything Drake would have expected from a top-rate hotel. There was even a bottle of complimentary champagne on ice.

However, Drake had other things on his mind than living it up on his companion's dollar. Leaving Anya to change in the room, he had quickly donned his own suit and excused himself, making his way downstairs.

The hotel bar was about half full at that time of night. Typical of an expensive hotel near an international airport, most of the patrons were businessmen in their forties and fifties, blowing off steam after a long day of air travel.

The place was dimly illuminated with spot lighting, and there was enough ambient noise and general activity for Drake to slip in unnoticed. He took a corner booth out of habit, both to scope out the other drinkers without attracting attention, and to prevent anyone watching him without his knowledge.

There wasn't much subtlety to what he was planning. Essentially his goal was to find someone who looked broadly like him, follow him outside and mug him, steal his room card and use it to get access to his passport. Of course, there was always the problem of what to do with the unfortunate businessman afterwards, but he'd discovered there was more than enough room in the trunk of the Taurus to hide an unconscious man. They wouldn't be needing the car now anyway.

He had spotted one man amongst a group of drinkers who he considered to be a passable likeness of himself. Fortyish, dark hair, tall and in good shape. He was also knocking back the beers like there was no tomorrow, which was fine with Drake. He would be easier to subdue.

Preoccupied as he was with his potential target, he didn't notice the attractive blonde approaching until she sidled into the booth beside him.

'I trust this seat isn't taken,' Anya asked.

Drake glanced at his companion, ready to admonish her for sneaking up on him. But before he could get a word out, he stopped abruptly, startled by the change that had come over her.

She had discarded her old clothes, donning a black pencil skirt cut above the knee, revealing her long shapely legs, the elegance of which were further enhanced by a pair of high-heeled shoes. She had made up her face as well, applying lipstick, foundation and mascara in a subtle, understated way that highlighted her already attractive features. This combined with a suit jacket and a white shirt open enough to reveal a glimpse of her cleavage, created an outfit that was both sophisticated and subtly inviting.

The impression certainly wasn't lost on him.

'You look . . . different,' he managed.

She flashed a wry smile. 'If that is how you compliment a woman, I'm not surprised you're single.'

'I usually rely on my break-dancing skills,' he returned. 'Seriously though, what's with the get-up? I hope you're not planning a night out on the town.'

This prompted a raised eyebrow. 'Hardly. I came to get you your passport,' she explained. 'And judging by the way you were glancing around the bar, you had a similar idea to mine, I think.'

'Great minds, and all that . . .'

'I suggest you forget what you were thinking and leave this to me.' Her tone told him it wasn't a suggestion.

'Bad idea,' he whispered. 'Last time you had dealings with a man who wasn't me, it didn't exactly go well.'

He saw a momentary flicker of anger in those cool eyes. 'I said I wouldn't lose control again. I meant it. Anyway, I have done this before. You haven't, and now is no time to learn.'

Her gaze shifted from Drake to the other inhabitants of the bar.

Drake's intended target showed no signs of leaving the bar until it ran dry, and would likely be too difficult to separate from his drinking buddies in any case. Anya ignored him, instead searching for a more accessible victim. It didn't take her long.

'There,' she said, nodding towards the bar with its mirrored backdrop and seemingly endless rows of spirits. 'Third seat from the end.'

Craning his neck around for a quick look, Drake spotted a man in a dark suit sitting alone, nursing a vodka with ice. He was facing away from them, but the mirrored bar allowed them a decent look.

Average build, early forties, with short dark hair, glasses and a face that was neither handsome nor ugly, he looked thoroughly nondescript. He also looked as if he'd put away a few of those vodkas judging by his unfocused eyes.

Still, he seemed a rough physical match for Drake.

'Perfect,' Anya decided. 'He's the right age, he's wealthy, he's alone and approachable. And he is British.'

Drake frowned. 'And how can you tell all that?'

'His suit comes from Savile Row, and he is making no effort to talk to anyone. British men are no good at small talk,' she added with a significant look at Drake. 'He has been drinking spirits for a while, so he isn't planning to meet anyone, especially not a woman. And I see the mark of a wedding ring on his hand. Either he is divorced, or he took it off tonight. Either way, he is the one. Once he invites me back to his room, I'll take his passport and meet you back at our suite.'

Drake regarded her with a raised eyebrow. 'What if he blows you off?'

She gave him a wry smile. 'For a man, you have very little understanding of the male mind. Not many men would refuse to sleep with a beautiful woman with no strings attached.'

'Your modesty continues to impress me.'

'I saw the way you looked at me earlier,' she whispered in his ear, her breath warm against his cheek as she stood up. 'Go back to the room and wait for me there.'

Saying nothing more, she turned and sauntered over to the bar, finding a seat close to the target. Straight away she caught his eye, though the man tried to be unobtrusive about it. He kept his gaze averted, as if worried he would scare her off.

Drake watched Anya order a drink. Vodka on the rocks – clever girl. She looked relaxed, elegant, composed as she sipped her drink. She was an attractive woman in a bar filled with men. It was too easy.

Five minutes or so went by, during which a waitress came over to ask if Drake wanted a drink. He ordered a whisky and soda.

The man had kept to himself, minding his own business, but casting the occasional furtive glance Anya's way to check if anyone had joined her. He was attracted to her. Good.

She played it cool, ignoring his first tentative attempts. To turn and look at him too soon might frighten him off, or worse, give the impression that she was a hooker trawling for a rich businessman.

When the target finally plucked up the courage to look at her properly, she smiled at him, her pale blue eyes smouldering in the dim light. Drake saw him smile back, tentative at first. He wasn't used to approaching women, flirting with them, showing interest in subtle ways.

She was speaking now, holding up her drink, using it to start a conversation. Drake couldn't hear what was being said over the general hubbub, but he could tell from the man's body language that he was receptive.

Five minutes later, and she had switched chairs to sit beside him, and the trap was sprung. He was all over her, laughing and joking, his confidence riding high now that her interest was firmly established.

He'd seen enough. Draining the last of his drink, he stood up and quietly left the bar.

Chapter 47

As the elevator made its unhurried ascent to the third floor, Lewis Henderson smiled at the woman beside him, hardly believing his luck. She was beautiful: tall, blonde, slender, with a sultry, intimate voice and an enticingly exotic accent that he could listen to all night long.

He'd bumped into her down at the bar, found they shared a preference for the same brand of vodka, and the conversation had blossomed from there. She'd explained she was in Miami for some financial conference, and that her flight had been delayed until tomorrow. So here she was, alone and bored.

It was he who had suggested they return to his room for a nightcap. Normally he never would have been so brazen, but the vodka was thick in his blood and his confidence was soaring.

He felt her hand, soft and warm, gently stroking his own. The barest touch was maddeningly arousing, and already he could feel his heart hammering against his chest.

'I hope it's not far,' she whispered, her voice deep and purring. 'I'm looking forward to seeing your room, and your bed.'

The elevator pinged and the doors opened. Taking her hand, he turned left and strode down the corridor, eager to be alone with her. He wanted to see that glorious body naked, wanted to run his fingers through that thick blonde hair, wanted to hear that seductive voice moaning in his ear.

Reaching room 312, he fished out his keycard and fumbled to swipe it through the reader, silently cursing himself for being so clumsy.

At last the door beeped and unlocked. He pushed it open and hurried in, with his new companion just behind.

No sooner had the door clicked shut than he felt her mouth on his, her body pressed up against him, hard and insistent. The kiss was so strong it left him breathless.

His hands encircled her narrow waist, then moved up until he felt the soft warmth of her breasts. He was more aroused than he'd ever thought possible. He felt like a teenager again, eager but apprehensive.

She kissed him again, slowly pushing him towards the bed. A playful shove to the chest sent him falling backwards onto the soft mattress.

'Don't move,' she whispered, reaching into her handbag.

'What have you got there?' he asked, wondering if this was some sort of sex game; handcuffs or a blindfold or something like that.

He hadn't dabbled much in that sort of thing. Not that he hadn't wanted to, but his previous partners had always been so conventional, so ordinary, so unwilling to try anything new or creative that he'd never felt comfortable suggesting it. After a while he'd given up thinking about it.

But this woman was something else. She was special, adventurous, exciting and unafraid to exert her authority. She was everything he'd ever looked for, and she had awoken something in him: a desire to break free of the safe, dull monotony of his life, to seek adventure and excitement.

She smiled seductively. 'Something just for you.'

Then, in a flash, everything changed. Suddenly she pulled a weapon out of the bag and aimed it at him. He saw the dull black gun metal gleaming in the wan light.

For a moment he laughed. This had to be some kind of game, surely?

'Shut up,' she hissed, all trace of her former attraction and desire gone. 'Roll over on your stomach. Do it now!'

The look in her eyes erased any doubts he might have entertained. There was a cold, calculating, menacing look in them now. She was like a predator poised to strike.

In an instant, all the life drained out of him. He felt sick, terrified.

You stupid fool! his mind screamed at him. How could you be taken in so easily? She brought you up here to rob you! Then she's going to kill you!

'P-please, don't kill me,' he stammered, trembling visibly now. He didn't care that she saw it. He was terrified. With every ounce of his being, he wished to return to the safe, comfortable life he'd spurned only moments before. 'Please. I made a mistake. Just take what you want. Don't kill me.'

'Are you married, Lewis?' she asked.

His eyes went blank for a moment. 'What?'

'It's a simple question. Are you married?' she repeated. 'I see the mark of a ring on your hand. Do you have a wife at home? Don't lie to me.'

He could feel tears threatening. Sniffing and unwilling to meet her gaze, he nodded.

'Does she love you?'

He nodded again, fighting hard not to break down.

'You think she'd be upset if she found out you'd been murdered in a hotel room by a Russian hooker?'

His lower lip was trembling and tears were running down his cheeks as he spoke. 'I d-don't want t-to die.'

'I didn't ask if you wanted to die, Lewis. I asked if you thought your wife would be upset to know you'd been murdered in your hotel room by a Russian hooker? Well, would she?'

'Y-yes!' he hissed, hating her for making him say it, and hating himself even more for being so weak. 'Yes, she'd be upset!'

She sighed. 'Then you won't invite women back to your room in future, will you?'

Wild, frantic hope surged through him. 'No. No, I won't! I promise!'

'Good.' The look in her eyes hadn't changed, but he did detect something in her voice. A slight softening, a brief moment of understanding. 'Lie face down on the bed and put your hands behind your back. I'm going to tie you up, then I'm going to leave. You'll never see me again. You can go back to your life and pretend none of this ever happened. Understand?'

He nodded.

Three minutes later, she had him gagged and secured on the floor beside the toilet, bound securely with a roll of heavy duty duct tape she'd brought along for the task. Available in any hardware store in the country, it was as good as a pair of handcuffs and far more versatile. No human was strong enough to break it; she knew that much.

Anya was no stranger to securing prisoners, and had made sure Henderson couldn't go anywhere or make enough noise to arouse suspicion, practically mummi-fying him in the stuff.

He was in for a long night, and probably a long day tomorrow before the hotel staff found him, but he would live. His pride and dignity were another matter, though she had no concern for either.

She had already helped herself to his glasses, wallet and the valuable credit cards and identity documents within, but a quick search of his room failed to yield his passport. She did however find an electronic safe, similar to the one in their own room.

It required a four-digit PIN to open. Checking his driver's licence, she found his date of birth was 10/07/68.

She tried 1968. The safe's indicator light flashed green, and there was an electronic hum as the bolt was withdrawn. She shook her head, dismayed at how naive and predictable people could be.

Tucking his passport into her jacket pocket, she paused in front of the mirror to check her appearance, then glanced into the bathroom.

'Thanks for the help. Goodbye, Lewis,' she said, then opened the door and placed the *Do Not Disturb* sign on it.

A moment later, she was gone.

Chapter 48

Anya was feeling good about herself as she strode down the corridor to their suite. Her plan had unfolded perfectly, leaving her with a valid passport that just might get Drake through Immigration.

Perhaps they would make use of that champagne after all. She'd never had much fondness for alcohol, but it would be a shame to waste it.

She would certainly make use of room service, she decided. She was often hungry now, which she took as a good sign. Her body was recovering from the deprivations of Khatyrgan, a hint of her former strength and vigour returning.

But her first order of business would be to change out of her skirt and high heels. How could women wear things like this all day long? She'd never enjoyed such impractical clothing, and resented having to wear it when men were able to walk around in relative comfort.

Still, like many things, it had its uses.

She smiled as she swiped her card through the reader and pushed the door open.

'Drake, I have good news for once.'

He was standing by the window, staring out across the city. Rain was still pattering against the glass.

'You got it, then?' He took a drink of something. Whisky. She could smell it.

'Mr Henderson was most cooperative.' Crossing the room, she handed him the man's passport. 'It may take a little work, but you should pass for him.'

Drake surveyed the picture for a few moments, then glanced back up at her. 'You didn't . . . ?'

'What? Sleep with him?' She kicked off her high heels, sat down on the bed and rubbed her aching feet. Assassinations she could handle. Women's fashion was another matter.

'I was going to say, kill him.'

'I know what you were going to say. But don't worry, I didn't shoot him or sleep with him.' Anya flashed a playful grin. 'Tell me, Drake, which would you have preferred?'

It wasn't in her nature to be flirtatious, but the vodkas she had shared with Henderson had gone to her head a little. She was flushed with success, with optimism, and with something else she hadn't felt for a very long time – attraction. Attraction towards the man who had been her only companion for the past couple of days.

She hadn't thought much about it, hadn't allowed such feelings out, but looking at him now with his jacket off, his shirt open at the collar, and the faint outlines of hard muscle visible beneath, she realised how much her perception of him had changed since that moment he kicked in the door of her cell in Khatyrgan.

'I'm not sure which would be more dangerous,' Drake smiled, seeming to see her comment for what it was. She saw something in his eyes then, a glimpse of something he'd kept hidden all this time, a part of himself he'd been careful to keep under control.

Her body responded in kind, and she felt a sudden blush rise to her face as a tingling warmth spread to other parts.

335

She rose from the bed, suddenly feeling uncomfortable and self-conscious. Crossing the room, she reached into her bag and removed the Glock automatic he'd hidden in the cistern on arrival.

'Very useful,' she said, handing it back to him. 'We will need to dispose of it before we leave tomorrow, though.'

She saw a moment of confusion in his eyes as he took the weapon. She had started down a path, only to turn away without explanation.

'What are you doing?' he asked as she reached for the phone by the bed.

'Ordering dinner. Even I need to eat sometimes,' she replied, careful to avoid eye contact. She didn't want to encourage him any further. 'Then I'm going to bed. You should try to rest too. We have a long day ahead of us tomorrow.'

Chapter 49

The customs official stared at the passport for a few seconds before looking up at Drake. She was a black woman in her fifties, short and rounded, with a severe look in her eyes that suggested she was just waiting for an excuse to haul him off for a full body search.

'And what's the purpose of your trip to Saudi Arabia, sir?'

'Business. I work for a consultancy firm. We're there to advise on a construction project,' Drake replied, reeling off the cover story they'd both memorised over breakfast earlier. If pressed on the matter, he even had business cards courtesy of Anya's contingency fund.

He had done what he could to transform himself into Lewis Henderson, donning a business suit, styling his hair in a severe side parting just like in the man's passport photo, and 'borrowing' his glasses. The man must have suffered from severe myopia, because anything more than 20 feet away was visible only as a painful blur.

He swallowed hard, trying to fight back the tide of nausea that seemed to be rising from the pit of his stomach. Just before leaving their room, Anya had thrust a glass of water into his hands and urged him to drink. When he tasted the tang of salt water, he knew what she'd planned.

Their facial features might have been a broad match, but their physiques were not. Drake was leaner and fitter than Henderson, his skin tanned by years of operations in equatorial countries. Both issues had to be addressed, and for Anya, it was the perfect solution.

After being violently sick, Drake had glimpsed himself in the bathroom mirror, shocked by how pale and ill he now looked. It was as if all the blood had drained from his face.

He'd been sick again in the restrooms after arriving at the departures terminal, and had thought that was the last of it. Maybe he'd been wrong.

'Are you okay, sir?' She looked suspicious.

'Yes, thanks. Well, more or less. Been a bit ill lately,' he added with an apologetic smile. 'Ever since I ate at that Mexican place last week. Spicy food doesn't seem to agree with me, I'm afraid. Or tequila.'

Her expression softened a little. No doubt she thought he was a stupid asshole, but a harmless one, and that was just fine with him. He'd learned a long time ago that if in doubt, always play the hapless, bumbling Brit abroad.

'Maybe that'll teach you to go easy in future,' she remarked.

A moment later, she had swiped his passport through the magnetic scanner and handed it back to him, along with his boarding pass.

He couldn't get out of there fast enough.

Anya was waiting for him beyond the security checkpoint, holding the laptop bag she'd purchased from one of the countless electrical retailers in the main terminal to further her cover as a businesswoman.

'Glad you made it,' she said, offering a tentative smile.

He said nothing as he brushed past her, heading for the nearest restroom.

Part Three

Confrontation

Know thy self, know thy enemy. A thousand battles, a thousand victories.

Sun Tzu's *The Art of War*

Chapter 50

'His name's Lewis Henderson,' the police sergeant explained as he, Frost and Dietrich hurried down the corridor, their shoes squeaking on the cheap linoleum flooring. 'Works for a British investment bank. Last night he was approached at the hotel bar by a blonde woman speaking with a Russian accent. They went back up to his room, then she pulled a gun on him and left him tied up in the bathroom.'

'How did he get the word out?' Frost asked as she struggled to keep up with Dietrich. Despite his limp, he moved at a formidable pace.

He didn't. He was due to check out today but he didn't show at the desk. Security found him when they opened his room, duct taped from head to toe. We brought him in to take his statement.

'How long ago?' Dietrich asked without breaking stride.

The sergeant checked his watch. 'About four hours.'

'Goddamn it,' Dietrich raged. 'Four hours. Four fucking hours.'

If the attack happened last night, Drake and Anya might have an eighteen-hour head start on them. Perhaps more. Why had it taken so long?

He jerked a finger at the door leading to the interview room. 'Buzz us in now.'

Henderson was a bedraggled, pale-faced mess of a man, hunched over in his chair with a blanket draped over his shoulders and an untouched cup of coffee in front of him.

His head jerked around when the door opened and the two agents entered the room. He eyed Dietrich with a look of blank fear, as if he expected the man to pistol whip him at any moment.

'Good afternoon, Mr Henderson. My name's Jonas, this is Kiera,' he began, indicating his female companion. No way was he about to start telling civilians that they were CIA operatives. 'We'd like to ask you a few questions about what happened last night.'

'I've already told them everything I know,' Henderson said, his voice almost a pleading wail. 'I haven't committed a crime – I'm the victim here. I just want to go home.'

Beside him, Frost tutted under her breath. She despised weakness and displays of vulnerability in others, especially men.

'And you will, Mr Henderson,' Dietrich promised him. 'But first we need you to answer our questions. Can you do that?'

Henderson bit his lip, but finally nodded.

'Good. Now, according to your testimony you were approached by the suspect at your hotel bar. Can you describe her?'

'She was . . . tall, slim. She had blonde hair, blue eyes. Pale skin, but she was beautiful.'

'How old was she?' Frost asked.

'I . . . I don't know. It was hard to say. She wasn't young, but she wasn't old either. Maybe late thirties or early forties.'

'Did she speak with an accent?' Dietrich went on.

He nodded. 'Russian, or Eastern European. I'm not exactly an expert, but it was definitely foreign.'

'So once you met up, what happened?'

'We had a few drinks, and after a while we went upstairs to my room.' He shuddered at the memory. 'Then she pulled a gun on me. She made me lie down, then tied me up in the bathroom.'

It all sounded very neat and academic.

'Did she take anything?' Frost asked.

'My wallet – and my glasses,' he added as an afterthought.

Dietrich frowned. She wouldn't have gone to all this trouble just to snatch a few dollars. There had to be more to it.

'Was there nothing else?'

The man thought about it for a few moments. 'I couldn't see what she was doing, but I heard her searching the room. She was looking for something.' Then his eyes lit up as a memory resurfaced. 'The safe!'

'What about it?'

'I heard her entering the pass code. I heard the beeping. I don't know how she knew it, but it must have worked because I heard her open the door.'

Dietrich leaned forward. 'What was in the safe?'

'My passport.'

That was all he needed to hear. He was up and out of the room within moments. Frost followed in his wake.

'Son of a bitch,' Dietrich hissed, angry with himself for not making the connection sooner. Bedraggled and pathetic as he was, Henderson bore enough of a physical resemblance to Drake to stir a sense of familiarity in him. Enough of a resemblance to get the man through Immigration.

'She's planning to leave the country with Drake,' Frost remarked.

'If she hasn't done it already,' the man growled. 'Stupid asshole! I should have seen this.'

He snatched his phone out of his pocket and dialled Franklin's number. It rang only once before it was answered.

'Talk to me, Jonas.'

'She was here. Miami International. She stole a passport from a British businessman – Lewis Henderson. His details are on the police report. I want his name and passport details red-flagged immediately. And contact Homeland Security, find out if his passport's been used in the last twenty-four hours.'

Franklin knew better than to argue, and wasn't about to chew the man out for his brisk tone. 'We're on it. I'll have someone call you as soon as we know something.'

'Hurry, Dan. This might be our last chance.'

Shutting the phone down, he closed his eyes, leaned against the wall and ran a hand through his hair. He felt as though his mind was still working at half speed. Physically he was starting to feel better as the withdrawal effects receded, but his brain was letting him down. He was missing things that should have been obvious.

What else was he missing?

'What's on your mind?' Frost asked.

'A lot.'

She made a face. 'Specifically?'

He sighed and opened his eyes. 'Anya knew Henderson would be found sooner or later. She could have killed him to stop him talking, but she didn't. She let him live.'

She shrugged. 'It was a busy hotel.'

'Have you forgotten what happened on the flight back from Russia?' he asked. 'She's perfectly capable of killing with her bare hands.'

The younger woman's expression darkened. Yes, she

344

knew all too well what Anya was capable of. She didn't care to be reminded of that moment when she'd found herself with a broken shard of glass at her throat.

'Where the fuck are you going with this, Dietrich?'

That was the question, and one for which he had no answer. But something about this whole situation just didn't add up. What were she and Drake trying to achieve? Where were they trying to go? And what were they going to do when they got there?

His confused and rambling thoughts were interrupted when his cellphone started buzzing. Damn, that was fast.

'Dietrich.'

'Sir, we've done the passport trace you requested.' It was the young analyst he remembered as Sinclair.

'Let's hear it, Sinclair.'

'The passport was last used this morning at 09.00 hours for an international flight.'

His heart sank. 'What was the destination?'

'Riyadh, Saudi Arabia.'

Chapter 51

The heat in downtown Riyadh was unbelievable. Every breath of scorching, dusty, smoke-filled air seared Drake's throat as their jeep ground its way forward in heavy traffic, jostling for position with overloaded trucks and vans, sleek saloons and dilapidated old hatchbacks. Scooters and mopeds zipped in and out of the heavy traffic, taking ridiculous chances and leaving angry horn blasts in their wake. It was chaos.

Anya, for once acting as driver at her own insistence, navigated the chaos with a coolness that amazed him. By now he would have been leaning on the horn as hard as their fellow travellers.

Her presence also drew more than a few curious and sometimes hostile glances from their fellow drivers. Saudi Arabia was a staunchly Islamic country with harsh restrictions on women. The notion of female drivers was almost unheard of in this part of the world, not to mention ones with pale skin, icy blue eyes and long blonde hair kept unashamedly uncovered.

'I don't think they approve of you,' Drake remarked as another driver leaned on his horn, shooting Anya a look of pure disgust.

It wasn't that Drake feared for their safety. On the contrary, he was more concerned for any poor bastard who pushed her too far.

'I am not looking for their approval,' she remarked without concern.

'Fair enough.'

She gave him a sly sidelong glance. 'Does it make you nervous?'

'What?'

'Not being in control.'

'Should it?' he challenged her.

'You did not answer my question.'

He offered a faint smile. 'And you didn't answer mine. Nasty habit we have here.'

They were making their way north, albeit slowly, on King Fahd Road, one of the major arteries that ran through the city. Off to their left, gleaming and indomitable in the evening sun, stood the immense Burj Al Mamlaka tower, a 1,000-foot-tall monument to Saudi Arabia's booming oil economy.

Everywhere he looked, he saw symbols of wealth and prosperity. New buildings were sprouting everywhere; shining glass, steel and concrete had replaced the mud brick and sandstone of earlier eras, with the old largely demolished and forgotten to make way for the new.

He took a gulp of water, wiping his sweating brow with his forearm. It was as if the water was leaking out of him as fast as he could replace it, and he was sure Anya felt the same way.

Spotting a gap in the traffic, Anya gunned the accelerator, ignoring the horn blasts and the hostile stares. She wanted to put some miles in, and she intended to do it.

It had been a fifteen-hour flight from Miami to Riyadh, and neither of them was feeling their best when they finally cleared Immigration and spilled out into the burning afternoon sun. Still, they had made it, and that was miracle enough to silence any such gripes. They had been at their most vulnerable while locked aboard that tin can in the sky. If the Agency had found Henderson and learned of their plan, it would have been easy to have a snatch team waiting for them at Customs.

But it hadn't happened. Somehow, through some miracle, they had made it to Saudi Arabia. Now they were barely a day's drive from Anya's contact.

With this in mind, their first port of call had been the nearest used-car dealership, where Anya had parted with 5,000 of her US dollars in return for a ten-year-old Land Rover formerly used by a British survey company.

The vehicle was a little rough looking after being used to haul rock and soil samples across the country, its paintwork scored, dented and weathered by years of sandstorms and hard driving, but a quick check of the engine bay and underside revealed that it had been well maintained. Drake could find no fault with the rugged vehicle.

It was just as well, because they were sure to need it. Their plan was to head north-west on Highway 65, before turning north on Highway 50 to a town called Al Majma'ah near the border. Anya claimed to know a man there who could show them the best place to slip across the border into Iraq.

But however they did it, it wouldn't be by road. They were going to have to hightail it across the open desert, far from any checkpoints or border control stations.

They had also treated themselves to a Magellan satellite navigation system before leaving the airport. Navigating the featureless desert was a nightmare at the best of times, and they didn't have time to waste plotting their position on a map. As long as they had the Magellan, they simply couldn't get lost.

Their stylish Armani business wear was long gone now, discarded in favour of khaki trousers, hiking boots, loose white shirts, vests and sunglasses. Aside from the necessity of having more durable clothing for off-road travel, it was far too hot for anything else.

Drake glanced over at his companion. She was leaning back in her seat, one hand on the wheel, her eyes obscured by aviator sunglasses and her hair tied at the nape of her neck. She looked more comfortable and natural in such clothes than she ever had in a skirt or suit, and he thought he even saw a hint of a smile as she stamped on the gas, the engine roared and the breeze whipped at her hair.

Sensing his eyes on her, she turned to look, and her smile broadened.

'I've wanted to do that for a long time.'

Despite his misgivings, he couldn't help but return the gesture. There was something infectious about her smile, made all the more so because it was so rare. Already an attractive woman, a smile transformed her features in a way he couldn't explain, rendering her truly, radiantly beautiful.

For a moment he found himself wondering at the soul lurking behind her icy exterior. He had caught glimpses of it at times, or thought he had, but she remained an enigma. A fascinating enigma.

'Is everything all right?'

'Yeah,' he replied, glancing away. 'Everything's fine.'

For perhaps the first time, he actually felt good about their situation. They were almost at the end of their long journey now, their early problems and difficulties behind them. Soon they would find Typhoon, contact Munro, and he would see Jessica again.

He was quiet for a time, just watching the road ahead.

'You know, when I passed my driving test I couldn't wait to do stuff like this,' he said, recalling her sudden burst of speed. 'I wanted to be out there tearing up the road. Then one evening my dad takes me aside, drives me out to a stretch of road in the middle of nowhere and tells me to floor it – just drive as hard and fast as I can. I actually thought he was joking. He'd never done anything like that before. But he leans in close and looks me in the eye, dead serious – the kind of look that used to scare the shit out of me when I was little, and he says, "I'm not kidding. Do it now."'

He chuckled a little at the memory. 'I wasn't about to argue. So off I went, pedal to the metal. I lasted about twenty seconds before I bottled it and slowed down, but God, those were the best twenty seconds of my life. My heart was pumping so hard I could hear it in my ears.

'Then my dad turns to me with that same look and says, "Right, you got it out of your bloody system. Don't ever let me catch you doing it again." He was acting pissed off and serious, but I saw the look in his eyes. He'd never admit it, but I think he was proud he'd shared it with me.'

But instead of laughing, smiling or even dismissing the anecdote altogether, the woman looked strangely moved by his words. For a moment, an expression of such sadness and longing touched her that he wondered if he had said something wrong or offended her somehow.

'Your father. He is . . . a good man?'

Drake shrugged. 'He was like everyone, I suppose. He had his good days and his bad days. He was no saint, put it that way, and we didn't often see eye to eye. But . . . he was my dad.'

He and his father had enjoyed a strained and often tumultuous relationship, especially as Drake grew older.

His father had been a complex, demanding man; quick to anger, quick to criticise, quick to make him feel unworthy, often cold and distant, yet at the same time capable of quite surprising and spontaneous gestures of love and affection.

He'd spent a great deal of his childhood trying to win the man's approval and respect, often without success. Then as a teenager he'd grown resentful, moody and rebellious, finding new and innovative ways to get in trouble and piss him off. Their rows had been so blazing during that time that they would go days without speaking to each other.

Only when he became an adult had their relationship stabilised a little, and the two men had at last developed a certain tolerance and respect for each other. For a time, at least.

She hadn't missed his choice of words. 'Was?'

He nodded slowly. 'He died, three years ago. He had a heart attack one Sunday afternoon . . . died right there and then in his bedroom. The doctor said he didn't suffer, it was like a light being switched off or something. I suppose they always tell people stuff like that.' He blinked, pushing the memory away, then turned to look at his companion. 'What about you? What are your parents like?'

She still had that distant, sad look about her.

'Come on, even you must have had a mother and father.'

She avoided his gaze, keeping her eyes glued to the road. By now he'd recognised it as her standard way of killing a conversation.

Taking the hint, he leaned back in his seat and watched the suburbs of the Al Aqiq district flitting past. Ahead of them lay an endless expanse of shimmering desert.

* * *

351

'Explain to me why we couldn't intercept them at Immigration,' Dietrich ground out, clutching his cellphone tight as he strode through the international arrivals terminal at Riyadh International. 'We had Henderson's passport number. Why the fuck wasn't it red-flagged when he tried to enter the country?'

Passers-by gave him curious and disapproving glances, but he ignored them. He was seething with anger that they had missed such a perfect opportunity to intercept Drake, and he wanted to know who had fucked up.

'It took time for the orders to filter through. Plus the Saudis weren't being very cooperative,' Franklin said from half a world away, sounding as tired and strung out as Dietrich felt. 'You should consider it a miracle they even let a Shepherd team into the country. You don't want to know the kind of favours I had to call in to make this happen.'

If Franklin was looking for gratitude, he was talking to the wrong man. Something wasn't right about this. As contentious as their relationship might have been with the Saudis, the Agency wasn't without resources in this part of the world. They should have had their own team on standby when Drake and Anya touched down, ready to lift them when the time was right.

'Seven hours, Dan. They've got seven fucking hours' head start on us.'

'Then I suggest you don't waste time bitching to me,' Franklin snapped. 'Don't give me problems, Jonas. I've got enough of them here in DC. Do your goddamn job and find Drake.'

'That went well,' Keegan remarked as Dietrich ended the call. After their long flight, he looked even more crumpled and careworn than usual.

Dietrich gave him a sharp look but said nothing.

According to the briefing they had received just before leaving the United States, a representative of the Saudi government would be there to meet them in the arrivals area. That was all they had been told – no name, no description, nothing.

Dietrich scanned the sea of faces that confronted him, all eagerly awaiting the arrival of friends, loved ones and business colleagues. He had no idea who or what he was looking for.

Typical government operation. Then again, these were the same people who had once sent him a FedEx with nothing in it, and a cheque for zero dollars.

Just then, a tall, slender man in a grey suit emerged from the crowd and approached him. He was in his mid-fifties, with short greying hair swept straight back, and a neatly trimmed beard.

With dark unsmiling eyes and a hard, severe-looking face, it was obvious this guy wasn't from the country's tourism board.

'You are the team I was briefed about?' he asked without preamble, speaking in a hard staccato-like fashion that reminded Dietrich of a typewriter. His dark gaze took in all three operatives, resting a moment longer on Frost.

For her own part, Frost returned his unwelcoming gaze with a hard glare of her own. She was on the wrong end of a fifteen-hour flight, and looked it.

'We are,' Dietrich replied.

'My name is Tariq. I represent the Mabahith.'

Dietrich's brows rose. He had expected state police or some other security force, but this man was from the General Investigation Directorate. It was an innocuous enough name, but it represented a very murky and dangerous agency tasked with rooting out political

353

dissidents and enemies of the kingdom, by any means. The Mabahith had been targeted by numerous human rights groups over the years for sanctioned torture, imprisonment without trial and summary executions based on flimsy or falsified evidence.

'You will come with me now,' he said, gesturing towards the terminal's distant exit. It wasn't a request. 'We have a car waiting.'

As Tariq led the way, forcing his way through the crowds like an ice-breaker, Keegan leaned in closer to Frost. 'Not real big on conversation, is he?'

'Let's hope he's better at cooperation.'

Chapter 52

Anya didn't speak much unless she had something to say, and seemed to have a general dislike of small talk in others. Thus, their journey north-west on Highway 65 was often interspersed with long spells of silence.

With nothing but the drone of the engine and featureless desert for company, Drake's thoughts returned, as they often did, to his sister. Again and again he replayed their brief phone conversations, analysing every word, every nuance of tone and inflection, trying to discern some hidden meaning, gain some insight that might help him find her.

Again and again, he came up with nothing.

It was maddening being kept in the dark like this. She could be dead already. This whole journey might be for nothing, and he had no way of knowing.

Stop this, he said to himself. This line of thinking would achieve nothing. She was alive; he knew it, because he refused to accept any other possibility.

His thoughts were interrupted when a sudden bang reverberated through the vehicle. Straight away the Land Rover slewed sideways as if it had a mind of its own, and only Anya's frantic counter-steering prevented them from rolling over.

Stamping on the brakes, she brought them skidding to a halt by the side of the road, kicking up a cloud of dust and sand.

Drake was out first, already bracing himself for the worst, with Anya close behind. One look at the driver's side front wheel was enough to confirm the cause of their problems.

'You're fucking kidding me.'

Reaching down, Drake gripped the long, jagged, twisted piece of metal still lodged in the tyre wall and yanked it out. It was aluminium judging by the weight, maybe 18 inches long. If he didn't know better, he would have said it was part of an aircraft fuselage. In any case, it had shredded the tyre like a razor, buckling the wall and tearing half of it away.

There was shit all along the side of the highway, he realised now. Loose stones, bits of metal, bolts, nails, rusted old exhausts and countless other bits and pieces that had sheared off passing cars over the years. Negotiating such roads seemed to be a case of knowing which path to take through the debris.

Sighing, he tossed the offending piece of scrap aside. 'I'll get the jack.'

'I'll get the spare wheel.'

Drake shook his head. 'Forget it. You're better off in the cab.'

The woman eyed him suspiciously. 'I hope this is not some misguided attempt at chivalry.'

'Not my style,' he assured her. 'You haven't been outside in years, now you're in the middle of the desert. You'll fry like a vampire in this sun.'

Her skin was already reddened from her limited exposure. She glanced up at the fiery orb beating down on them, and seemed to see the logic of his argument.

'Fine,' she conceded, looking unhappy about it. He had come to know her expression of reluctant acceptance quite well.

'By the way, did you actually use any of that suncream I bought you?'

'No.'

He stared at her. 'Why not?'

She shrugged, looking uncomfortable. 'Because I hate creams and lotions. I hate the feel of them. I would rather burn.'

Drake shook his head. 'You know what? I give up.'

Ten minutes later, he had the Land Rover jacked up and was busy undoing the bolts holding the wheel in place. It was a physically demanding task at the best of times, but with the temperature soaring in the late-afternoon sun, it soon turned into a grim test of endurance.

The last bolt was a tough one. God only knew what kind of tool they had used to fix it in place, but it must have been a lot more powerful than the foot-long metal wrench he had at his disposal. Even setting it horizontal and jumping on it had failed to dislodge the bolt.

Sweat was pouring down his back, soaking his thin T-shirt, but hard effort was just no substitute for a high-powered pneumatic wrench. Other cars and trucks roared past on the highway, showing not the slightest interest in their plight.

'Come on, you bastard. Move!' Drake grunted, heaving once more. The bolt groaned under the strain but held firm.

'Yelling at it will not help,' Anya reminded him.

He looked up at her. Sitting in the shade and relative cool of the vehicle's cab, she looked annoyingly comfortable as she sipped a bottle of mineral water. She was watching him with a mixture of sympathy and, much to his chagrin, playful amusement.

'Are you enjoying this?'

She shrugged, though the hint of a smile remained as

she surveyed his sweating torso. 'Well, there are worse ways to spend the day.'

Shaking his head, Drake went back to work. 'This could qualify as sexual harassment, you know.'

'Wishful thinking.' Growing more serious for a moment, she asked, 'Is there anything I can do to help?'

'Well, you could talk to me,' Drake said, muscles straining as he tried again.

'What would you like me to say?'

'I don't know. Surprise me. Tell me about yourself, where you grew up. Give me a funny anecdote. I'm quite easy to please, really.'

'I don't remember much from Before.' She sounded almost apologetic.

'Before what?'

'It doesn't matter.' She sighed, took another sip of water and looked out across the desert. It was a while before she spoke again, but when she did, her voice was different. Softer, quieter. 'You asked me before what my parents were like. I did not tell you because, the truth is, I can barely remember them. My life was different then, I was different. All I see is . . . flashes, like a camera. Little moments printed on my memory.'

He couldn't help himself. 'What happened to them?'

'They died. In a car crash. They were driving home when another man cut across the road and hit them. They went straight into a tree . . . and they died. As with your father, it was like a light going out. Or so I was told.'

She closed her eyes, fighting back the feeling of wrenching, aching helplessness that such memories still evoked. 'I was waiting for them to come home, but they never did,' she said once she trusted herself to speak again. 'After that, I was surrounded by police, social workers, men in suits who I did not understand. I seemed to spend my life in offices and interview rooms. Everyone kept asking me questions and telling me everything would be all right, that they would look after me.'

Anya sat with her head tilted down, hands in her lap, saying nothing as Leonid Cherevin, the director of Atsigrezk State Orphanage, surveyed the folder that represented the sum total of her life. Fifteen years compressed into a few dozen pages of thin, yellowed paper.

She could hear the scratch of his pen. It was almost out of ink, forcing him to press down harder. Sometimes he'd have to go back and rewrite a word that hadn't printed right.

'Anya, Anya . . . What are we going to do with you?' he chided, finishing up his notes and closing the folder. 'You broke a young man's nose, bit his face so hard he'll be scarred for life. This is a serious incident. Very serious.'

Anya said nothing, didn't move a muscle. She had nothing to say. There was no point.

He leaned back in his chair, watching her. Cherevin was in his mid-fifties, with jet black hair that she was certain he dyed. But there was no disguising his expanding midsection, or the lines around his mouth and eyes. He smoked too much, ate too much, probably drank too much as well.

She saw a brief glint of something metallic in his hands. The silver letter opener he always kept on his desk, no doubt an antique; a throwback to the days when men of power and status would use them to open vital documents and communiqués.

Like the letter opener, his office was ornate, over-decorated, pretentious. Everything about him spoke of ambition that outstripped ability.

'Don't you have anything to say?' he prompted.

She sighed and closed her eyes. He wasn't going to stop

until she said something, offered some kind of explanation, even if he chose to ignore it.

'He tried to attack me.'

'He beat you?'

'No. He . . .' She swallowed hard, a blush rising to her face.

She had been a child when she arrived here, a skinny slip of a girl, tall for her age, gangly and awkward. But not now. Her body had filled out, her breasts and hips swelling as she assumed the curves of womanhood. The older boys had begun to notice the changes too, and today one had cornered her in the girls' washroom.

She had fought him off the only way she knew how. She hadn't wanted to. She had abhorred violence when she was younger, but the alternative was unthinkable.

'I see.' She couldn't be sure, but she thought she saw a smile flick across his face.

She had never liked Cherevin, and the feeling had grown stronger over time. There was something about his accommodating smile, his half-handsome face, his outward veneer of charm that frightened her.

Rising up from behind his desk, he paced slowly across the room. She didn't move, but she could hear the soft thump of his footsteps on the carpet behind her.

'The board of directors want to send you to a young offenders' institution. They feel you're too dangerous to remain here.' She heard him sigh wearily. 'I don't want that to happen, but I must be able to assure them that you can be trusted.'

She felt his hand on her shoulder, the gesture almost like that of a father showing love and reassurance toward a wayward daughter.

'Can I trust you, Anya?' he asked.

His hand moved lower, cupping her right breast. She froze, a shiver of revulsion and fear running through her. Her eyes opened wide and her heart started beating wildly.

When the young man had accosted her in the washroom, her reaction had been instinctive. But now her instincts had deserted her. From the earliest age she had been conditioned to respect authority, to obey the rules and abide by what her elders told her.

But now she was torn. Cherevin was abusing his authority – of that she had no doubt – but it was still his authority. He ran this place. There was nobody higher than him within her reach.

'Stand up, Anya,' he commanded.

Unwilling or unable to protest, she rose to her feet and turned to face him. She was shaking. She couldn't stop it. She wanted to be sick.

He was standing close. She could smell the cigarette smoke on his breath. He smiled at her gently, almost tenderly, reached up and brushed a lock of blonde hair away from her face. His finger grazed her cheek, tracing the line of her jaw down to her chin.

'I can make your time here as easy as you want,' he whispered. 'But you must give me something in return. Will you give me what I ask, Anya?'

She felt his hands on her breasts again, fondling them, squeezing them harder until she let out an involuntary gasp.

She backed away a step, trembling, tears in her eyes.

'No. I . . . I can't,' she stammered. 'Please, I don't want—'

She was cut short when he swung his arm around and backhanded her across the face. The blow caught her completely unawares, and she fell back, her momentum carrying her around so that she landed face down on his desk. Papers, folders, pens and other paraphernalia clattered to the floor.

Still dazed by the strike, she felt him pulling and yanking

361

at her trousers, trying to tear them away. With his other hand, he grabbed a handful of her long hair and pulled hard, jerking her head back.

'It's not your place to refuse me, Anya,' he hissed in her ear as her trousers at last came away, exposing her. 'I own you now. You do what I say, when I say it. It's time you learned that.'

Tears were streaming down her face, blurring her vision. She could taste blood in her mouth, her ears rang from the blow.

She knew what was coming. She didn't know what it would feel like, but already she felt the growing disgust, the horror, the hatred of knowing what he was about to do, and being powerless to stop it.

She heard the clinking sound of his belt being undone, and tensed up, trying somehow to prepare herself for what he was about to do. Just get it over with, she thought. It won't take him long. Once it's over, I can leave.

Then, through her blurred, tear-streaked eyes, she saw something glinting on the table in front of her. Something metallic.

The letter opener.

She didn't think, didn't pause even for an instant to consider the implications. The moment she felt him, hard and insistent against her, she snatched up the crude weapon, swung it around and plunged it into his kneecap.

'He was right about one thing,' Anya conceded grimly. 'The board did want me transferred to a young offenders' institution. Only he could have stopped them, but he would never do that. Not after I left him walking with a stick for the rest of his life.

'They spent a good hour telling me all the reasons I was a bad person, why I couldn't stay at the orphanage, why I needed "a higher standard of care". I wasn't listening, not really. I knew what they were going to do the moment I picked up that letter opener. I didn't see

how they could send me anywhere worse than Atsigrezk.'
She sighed. 'I was wrong.'

A crowd had gathered in the canteen to watch the spectacle, cheering and hollering every time the new girl took a hit.

Anya grunted as her back slammed into the unyielding wall, knocking the breath from her lungs. She looked up just as the bigger girl, Ludmilla, drew back her clenched fist and slammed it into her face.

Pain exploded through her head and her vision blurred as she fell to her knees, blood dripping onto the scuffed linoleum floor. Once more the other young women cheered and laughed, glad it wasn't happening to them.

It was a pack mentality, and Ludmilla was the alpha female. Anya knew they weren't going to interfere in this. She was on her own. She had been on her own since the night the police arrived at her house.

Taking a step forward, Ludmilla snatched a clump of Anya's hair, brought her arm back and struck her with a brutal right hook.

This time there would be no absorbing the hit. She went down, limp like a rag doll, her head striking the hard floor. Blood flowed from her burst lip, pooling around her, staining her hair and face. Stars and strange blobs of light swam across her eyes.

'Had enough now?' Ludmilla yelled right in front of her, specks of spit flying in her face. 'Stay down you stupid little bitch, or you won't get up next time!'

'I should have listened to her,' Anya said, looking back on the scene with a sad, reflective expression. 'All she wanted was respect. She would leave me alone if I stayed down. Just stay down.'

No.

You did everything they told you to. You accepted every

decision they made, every humiliation, every piece of you they took away. And what did it get you?

She could endure no more, could sacrifice nothing else.

Get up.

A sudden fire of defiance leapt up inside her, burning away fear, pain, grief, weakness. Her vision clearing, she spat bloody phlegm on the floor, managed to get her arms beneath her and slowly pushed herself upright.

The laughter and roars of approval were fading now, replaced by the pounding of her heartbeat, strong and vibrant.

Ludmilla stared at her, her expression a mixture of shock, disbelief and growing anger. The other girls weren't cheering for her now. Many of them were glancing at each other, exchanging nervous looks. Some were even looking at Anya with grudging respect.

Ludmilla's scarred, ugly face twisted in rage as she rushed at her.

And then something happened. Anya saw the tightening in her right shoulder, the muscles bunching and contracting, signalling that she was about to swing another wild hook. She couldn't explain it, but instinctively she understood. It was as clear to her as if the young woman had told her what she intended to do.

She will swing now. Now!

This time the crushing blow hit nothing but air. Ducking aside, Anya lashed out with her right hand.

The blow caught her opponent on the bridge of her nose. She felt a crunch, and when she saw the first spray of blood, she knew she'd broken it.

A startled gasp rose from the crowd as the bigger girl staggered back, clutching at her face, blood flowing down her shirt. Nobody had ever stood up to her like this. Nobody had hurt her like this.

For the first time in her young life, Anya felt an odd thrill, a sense of mastery, of dominance that she'd never experienced before. She had stood her ground when others might have wavered, and she had won.

She had won!

The others sensed it too, and suddenly she realised they were shouting and cheering again. Only this time, it was for her.

There was no holding it back. Letting out a raw, almost primal scream of triumph, she turned to look at them. Battered, bloodied, bruised, but unbowed, she had stood when others would have fallen. She had not hesitated, she had not shown weakness or fear. And she had won.

Her first impression was of being struck in the back with something, like another punch, but different. An instant of coldness was followed by a spreading sticky warmth. Her own blood.

'I told you to stay down, you fucking bitch,' Ludmilla hissed in her ear, yanking the sharpened piece of wood out of her back. A shiv.

Her new-found strength vanished, her legs gave way beneath her and she fell to the ground. Blood pooled around her.

She was in her own world now. She felt no pain, only cold slowly creeping into her limbs. Her heart still beat in her ears, but slower now, laboured, trying to pump blood that was no longer there.

Vaguely she was aware of Ludmilla screaming and cursing, then there was more shouting from other places – male voices, rough and angry. The wardens had at last intervened.

Then her consciousness faded and the world went dark.

'I finally stayed down, just like she said,' Anya finished, looking down at her hands. She still bore the scars of that fight, and the many that came afterwards. 'Only when they saw the knife and the blood did the guards step in. They took me to the infirmary. I suppose they saved my life, though at the time I wished they hadn't.'

She slowly tensed her hands into fists. 'I was tired, Drake. So tired. I just wanted it to be over.' The muscles in her throat tightened as she swallowed. 'I prayed for death that night in the hospital bed. I even thought to tear the stitches open and let the wound bleed out. But I didn't do it. I kept remembering the fight, the moment I broke her nose. I saw the looks in the eyes of all those girls. Someone had done what they never could, someone had upset their world. And for a moment, they believed in me. I was more than just another prisoner.'

He saw a faint smile then, and a flash of old pride in her eyes. 'If I could do all that with one clumsy punch, imagine what I could do with an entire lifetime.'

Kaunas had been the most brutal but effective learning experience of her life, until that point at least. She had learned to stand up for herself, defend herself, take back the life that had been stolen from her. It was an outlet, a means of reasserting control.

She learned to work within the system while simultaneously planning to escape from it. Whenever she was called up for hearings or behavioural reviews, her conduct was exemplary, her manners impeccable. She was respectful and cooperative to the people whom the State entrusted to make decisions for her.

But for any girl who tried to hurt or intimidate her, she showed no mercy. She had learned to leave such emotions behind, knowing they were weaknesses she could ill afford in Kaunas.

Life in a State-run prison, even for minors, was a brutal struggle for survival. Only the strong prevailed, and she was determined to prevail.

It wasn't just her outlook that changed. Gradually her soft and weak body was transformed, developing hard, firm musculature that she learned to use to great effect.

Always fast and agile, she now commanded real physical strength. She developed a tolerance for pain that she never would have thought possible, easily able to shrug off the cuts and bruises that inevitably came from fighting. She cut her hair short so her opponents couldn't grab at it; another luxury she could no longer afford in that place.

She began to apply herself intellectually as well, knowing she would need every skill and scrap of knowledge at her disposal when she was released. Naturally bright and intelligent at school, she had fallen far behind during her time at the orphanage as she lapsed into depression and indolence. But at Kaunas she threw herself back into learning. She spent long hours in the seldom-used library, absorbing everything from history to geography, mathematics, physics and philosophy.

She became enamoured with Sun Tzu's *The Art of War*, eagerly devouring the volume again and again, memorising those lessons she considered most useful to her. And from this, she began to develop her own philosophy on how to live her life; a life free of compromise, free of weakness and doubt. Life for her became a series of absolutes.

'My time there changed me. It made me fight back, made me take control again.' She nodded slowly, as if to herself. 'It wasn't until I had given up all hope that I found a reason to live. By the time I was released, I was . . . different. I think I had learned to leave my old life behind.'

Drake had long since stopped what he was doing, listening spellbound to every word she said.

She managed a faint smile. 'Thank you.'

'For what?' he asked, confused.

'For listening.'

Drake glanced away, saying nothing. He looked down at the wrench again, and the wheel that had thus far defeated him. Kneeling down beside it, he picked up the tool once more, fitted it onto the bolt and, with every ounce of strength he could command, strained against it until his muscles trembled.

There was an aching groan of protesting metal, and suddenly the bolt turned, released from its grip at last.

It took another five minutes to lever the damaged wheel free, manoeuvre the spare into place and bolt it on. Sweating, breathing hard and shaking from his efforts, Drake almost collapsed into the passenger's seat as Anya gunned the engine and threw it into gear.

They were on their way again.

Chapter 53

'As I said before, we have good reason to believe that two wanted terrorists are operating in your country,' Dietrich said, explaining their mission for the third time with mounting impatience. 'We were sent in to find and arrest them. I'm sorry, but I can't tell you any more beyond that.'

They had been ferried from the airport to the Mabahith's headquarters building – a big square structure that reminded him more of a fortress or prison than an administrative centre – and escorted to Tariq's personal office to brief him on the situation.

Tariq for his part did not look impressed with Dietrich's explanation. Seated behind his desk with a cup of strong black tea – he hadn't offered them any – in front of him, he seemed quite content to keep them here all day.

Behind him was a younger man in an olive green uniform, standing ramrod straight and with his hands clasped behind his back. He hadn't introduced himself, but Dietrich presumed he was some kind of aide or subordinate.

'Mr Dietrich, you will understand that the internal security of Saudi Arabia is the responsibility of *my* agency. If there is a threat, I need to know the exact nature of it. Otherwise you may as well board the next flight home.'

They were wasting time here. They should have tried to slip into the country covertly, just like he'd suggested. At least then they wouldn't have to deal with assholes like this.

Clenching his fists, Dietrich struggled to hold in check his growing anger. 'We were promised cooperation from your government.'

Tariq spread his arms to encompass his office, and the distant skyscrapers of Riyadh visible from his window. 'You are here, are you not?'

'Indeed we are. And if we stay here in your office much longer, two high-value suspects will escape.' He fixed Tariq with what he hoped was a piercing gaze. At least, it was the best he could manage after fifteen hours in the air. 'And when I report back to Langley, I'll be sure to mention your name.'

Tariq's expression didn't change, but Dietrich thought he saw the man pale just a little.

Sensing a confrontation brewing, the young man leaned forward and spoke quietly in Arabic so the three operatives couldn't understand. Tariq immediately cut in with a burst of angry words, silencing him. The younger man waited until he had finished before speaking again.

At last, whatever argument he was making seemed to cut through the older man's anger, and he nodded reluctantly, turning his attention back to Dietrich and the others.

'We will allow you to conduct your investigation,' he decided, as if the entire thing had been his idea. He gestured to the young officer behind him. 'My aide, Lieutenant al Ameen, will be your liaison. He will take responsibility for you.'

Dietrich got the message. Tariq was pawning them off onto a subordinate. If they caused trouble, the blame would fall on the younger man. If they were successful, Tariq would be sure to take all the credit.

'Thank you,' he said.

'This operation is still under Saudi jurisdiction,' Tariq was quick to remind him. 'All intelligence gathered will be shared with us. Do we understand each other?'

Go fuck yourself, Dietrich thought. 'We do.'

Al Majma'ah, Ar Riyad Province

It was almost dark by the time they pulled into the outskirts of the small desert town, with the sun just touching the horizon and long shadows stretching across the dusty ground.

They had covered a good 100 miles or so since leaving Riyadh, putting them within range of the Iraqi border if they left early tomorrow.

Tired, sweaty and with dust stinging his eyes, Drake stepped out and looked around.

There wasn't much to see. The houses around them were two-storey affairs, mostly weathered sandstone but with a few bare brick dwellings scattered around. There were few people out and about at that time of day; almost everyone was attending Maghrib, the Islamic prayer offered at sunset. A scooter chugged past at the far end of the road, exhaust billowing grey smoke. The place was a stark contrast to the frantic activity of Riyadh.

Drake watched a pack of mangy-looking dogs nosing at an upturned bin nearby, searching for food amongst the garbage.

'What exactly are we supposed to find here?'

371

'Help,' was Anya's simple answer as she slammed her door shut. 'We'll need it to get across the border tomorrow. Stay with me and don't cause trouble.'

'That's *my* line,' he remarked as they approached a nearby house, slightly larger and more elaborate than the others.

Enclosed by a high sandstone wall, and with a single wrought-iron gate leading to a small courtyard beyond, it had obviously been an impressive property once. Now, however, the gate was rusting, the small fountain in the centre had long since dried up, and straggling weeds grew between the flagstones. The windows on the ground floor were shuttered, the heavy wooden front door locked. Its paint was peeling, its boards worn, but it still looked solid.

'It's quiet,' Drake remarked as they approached the front door.

'He's here,' Anya assured him. 'And he knows we are too.'

She pounded on the door.

Nothing happened.

The seconds stretched out, a dog barked in the distance, the desert wind stirred up sand and dust around their feet, and the door did not move.

Drake was starting to wonder if she'd made a mistake. Anya had been away for four years, after all. There was a good chance that whatever contact she'd once had here had since moved on.

'Maybe we should—'

He was cut short by the rasp of a bolt being withdrawn, and the click of a lock disengaging. A moment later, the door swung open.

Oh, shit.

The giant standing before them filled almost the entire

doorway, easily weighing 300 pounds and standing a good 6 inches taller than Drake. The impression of sheer mass was enhanced by his ankle-length shirt of spun wool, which seemed to flow down from his broad shoulders like a tent.

In that moment, Drake became acutely conscious of their lack of weaponry. They had been forced to leave the Glock behind in Miami, and there hadn't been time to find another weapon after their arrival in Riyadh.

If this guy turned out to be hostile, they were in trouble. Even Anya would have her hands full trying to subdue a man twice her size.

His dark gaze took in both visitors, giving the woman a particularly hostile look. She wasn't wearing the traditional *abaya* required of women in public. He mumbled something in Arabic, concentrating his attention on Drake.

Fortunately Anya was able to step in, speaking quickly and, it seemed, fluently, in the man's own language. Much to Drake's surprise, her attitude had changed in an instant, becoming almost deferential and submissive. Her head was lowered demurely, her eyes cast downward.

But despite her sudden display of gentle femininity, he could see she was holding her body in preparation, muscles taut and ready to react in an instant if he tried to attack her.

Drake couldn't tell what she was saying, but he did pick up on the word Hussam being used several times. The name of her contact, he assumed.

The big man listened as she spoke, his expression changing from one of outright anger that a woman dared to speak out of turn, to surprise, confusion and growing comprehension as her words sank in.

When she finished speaking, he stood silently in the

doorway, mulling over everything she had said. Then at last he grunted something and stepped aside, beckoning for them to come in.

Giving Drake an encouraging look, Anya stepped inside. With little choice if he didn't fancy keeping the stray dogs company, Drake followed her, giving the giant as wide a berth as possible.

They were standing in a wide tiled hallway with doors leading off on either side. The walls were bare stone painted over white, though they were largely covered by several big tapestries set at intervals along the corridor.

They could smell food, tea and tobacco smoke. Voices echoed from further down the corridor.

With the giant keeping a wary eye on them, they were led onward and conducted into the second room on the left.

The air was thick with tobacco smoke, blurring details and stinging Drake's eyes. Still, even he could tell that the place was busy. Half a dozen men of various ages sat scattered around the room on padded cushions, smoking, drinking tea and talking together.

The talk abruptly ceased when Drake and Anya entered the room, an uneasy silence descending on the gathering as half a dozen pairs of eyes fastened on the two strangers.

Drake said and did nothing. Not knowing a word of Arabic, there wasn't much he could say in any case. Better to wait and see what happened.

One man rose from his seat, which was no easy task considering how overweight he was. He was dressed in a crumpled grey business suit, but even this couldn't conceal the voluminous gut hanging over his belt.

He looked to be in his late fifties or early sixties, with a thick greying beard, wide fleshy face and eyes like coals.

His wavy hair, probably once thick and dark, was now grey and thinning on top.

His eyes never left the woman as he barked a sharp command. Straight away the other men in the room started to pack up their belongings, finishing off their tea or stubbing out cigarettes.

One by one they filed out in silence, each giving both Drake and Anya a hostile glare, until only the fat man and the giant remained.

The first took a step towards her, his fists clenched, his eyes piercing the smoky gloom. Drake felt the irrational need to interject himself between them, though he rejected the notion as soon as it entered his head. Anya had neither need nor desire for his protection.

Stopping in front of her, the fat man looked her up and down slowly, as if comparing the woman before him with some mental picture stored away in his mind.

'You've gotten old,' he said at last, speaking in gruff, accented English.

Anya stared right back at him, her icy blue eyes boring into his. 'And you've gotten fat.'

Drake held his breath, sure she had just signed their death warrants.

But to his surprise, the fat man's face broke out into a wide grin.

'Ameera!' he laughed, throwing his arms around the woman and embracing her in a crushing bear hug. 'Praise Allah! I had never thought to see you again! Come, let me look at you properly.'

He pulled back and looked her over again, beaming with joy like a father reunited with a long-lost daughter.

'You grow more beautiful with each passing year,' he decided, all trace of his former hostility gone now. 'How long has it been?'

'Too long,' the woman replied, sadness in her eyes.

The man was perceptive enough to realise that was a conversation for later. 'And who is your young companion?' he asked, turning his attention to Drake.

'His name is Ryan Drake. We're travelling together. Ryan, this is Hussam. He's an old friend.'

Hussam thrust a hand out to him. '*Salaam alaikum*,' he said as Drake shook it. 'You travel in good company, my friend.'

'It's certainly never dull around her,' he remarked with a pointed glance at his female companion.

Hussam laughed again. 'This much is true.'

'I apologise for our sudden arrival, Hussam,' Anya began. 'I would not have come here if there was another way, but you are the only man in the country I trust.'

'Of course. You are always welcome here, Ameera.' He looked at both of them, then gestured to the seating pads laid out around the room. 'Come, sit and we'll talk. I believe you've already met my nephew Haifaa,' he added with a nod to the giant by the door. 'He is good for frightening small children, but he is harmless. Mostly.'

Drake was inclined to take that one with a pinch of salt. No man who looked as though he could crush boulders with his bare hands was harmless.

They sat down on the stuffed cushions, and within moments a woman came in to serve them tea and bowls of dates. Drake assumed she was Hussam's wife, though she looked many years younger than him.

As he'd expected, her body was hidden under a shapeless black robe called an *abaya*, though her face was uncovered. He guessed her to be in her mid-thirties, neither beautiful nor ugly, but rather plump and with an oval face, a prominent nose and a weak jawline.

She avoided eye contact with him, and he didn't spend

long looking at her. In this neck of the woods, it was impolite to show a man's wife anything beyond casual disinterest. The last thing he wanted was to put Haifaa's peaceful nature to the test.

The tea was strong and sweet, served without milk in the traditional Middle Eastern style. It certainly wasn't to Drake's taste, and after a couple of hours spent bouncing along hot desert roads, the thought of a steaming hot beverage was even less appealing. However, a stern look from Anya persuaded him to accept a cup anyway.

He thought he saw a flicker of amusement in Hussam's eyes as this happened. They must have seemed like an old married couple.

'So, Ameera, tell me what brings you here?' the old man asked.

'We must get across the Iraq border tomorrow. I need to know the best place to make the crossing. We also need weapons, preferably assault rifles.'

Hassam surveyed her with heavy-lidded eyes. 'That is much to ask.'

'I know you have the weapons. You always have them. And I know you have men watching the American border patrols. How else could you smuggle petrol into the country?'

For a moment, Drake saw anger and surprise flare in the old man's eyes, though it was soon masked.

'I would not ask if it were not important,' Anya went on, perhaps trying to sooth his wounded pride. 'Across the border in Iraq, there is a man we must find at all costs. He holds secrets that people are willing to kill for. Many lives may depend on this, Hussam.'

She was smart enough not to divulge anything about Munro holding Drake's sister hostage, or the secret arms deal that Anya's contact apparently had evidence of. The less he knew, the less chance there was that he could compromise them if he was ever captured.

'If the wrong people find him first, there's no telling how much damage it could do,' Drake lied, hoping that together their words might sway him.

'Only you can help us,' Anya chimed in.

Hussam reached for a date, chewing it thoughtfully for several moments before coming to a decision. 'Very well. Whatever you need will be yours,' he said, then his expression softened a little. 'You have not eaten tonight, have you?'

Anya gave him a rueful smile that somehow made her seem a lot younger than she was. 'Aside from an apple in Riyadh . . .'

Hussam laughed again. 'Then the two of you will be my guests tonight. I will have a room set aside where you can wash and rest.'

Chapter 54

'Tell me something, Lieutenant,' Dietrich began as they strode away from Tariq's office. 'What did you say to your superior to change his mind?'

Al Ameen was in his early thirties, he guessed, with a good-looking, clean-shaven face and keen eyes that missed nothing. Unlike most of the grim-faced bastards who inhabited this place, he possessed an easy, almost disarming smile. The only reminder of his true age was his receding hairline, though he had cut his hair short to disguise this fact.

'You can call me Rahul,' the lieutenant informed him. 'I told him you were not worthy of his time, and that I would relieve him of the burden of dealing with ignorant foreigners.'

'Very generous of you,' he remarked.

'Why are you so eager to help us?' Keegan asked.

'Men like Tariq are part of the older generation. They see the West as an enemy to be guarded against. I do not.'

'Yeah? So how do *you* see us?' Frost pressed him.

'As partners,' he answered. 'We work together, and we both profit. We work against each other, and we both fail. My country is the wealthiest and most developed in the Persian Gulf because of American money. I would not wish for this to change.'

Fair enough, Dietrich thought. 'Tariq will blame you if we fail here.'

The younger man flashed an almost boyish grin. 'Then we should make sure you do not fail, yes?'

'Yes.'

'Good. Then what do you need?'

'Frost, enlighten the man,' Dietrich said, turning to the young woman.

'I need access to the entire security camera system in central Riyadh. Traffic, surveillance, security – everything,' she said straight away. 'Our best chance is to find them when they left the airport and follow their movements from there.'

Rahul's eyes opened wider and he shook his head vigorously. 'No, no. This is no good.'

'Why not?'

'You are American. And you are a woman,' he explained. 'This is no good for you to be doing such things. It is not allowed. You can instruct our own technicians on what to look for.'

Her eyes flared. 'It'll take twice as long.'

'There is no choice.'

'I thought you said we should work together,' Dietrich challenged him.

'I did. But there are things even I cannot allow. This is not America.'

Dietrich took a deep breath, marshalling his patience before turning his eyes on Rahul again. 'Ms Frost is the best technician we have.' He ignored Frost's look of surprise as he carried on. 'She's also our best chance at finding these two fugitives. If she can't do her job, we can't do ours, and we will fail. And I think you know what happens if we fail.'

Rahul looked at him for a long moment. 'I will see what I can do.'

Drake leaned over the sink to splash a handful of water on his face. It was delightfully cool, and a welcome relief from the stinging dust that had been their constant companion since arriving in the country.

'What's this Ameera business?' he asked. 'Is that your cover name or something?'

They had been lent a room on the building's upper floor, its single window facing westward. Drake had opened the shutter to let some air in, allowing the warm evening breeze to sigh through. Outside it was dusk, the sky in the west turning deep orange now that the sun had dipped below the horizon.

The room itself was a simple affair: just a bed in one corner, a small wardrobe that wobbled slightly on uneven legs, a chipped sink, an old writing desk that looked as if it had seen better days, and a couple of wooden stools scattered around.

Anya, seated on a stool with her feet up on the desk, shook her head. 'No, it is . . . a nickname. Something Hussam gave me a long time ago.'

'What does it mean?'

She looked almost embarrassed when she spoke again. 'It has no direct translation, but I suppose the closest word would be princess.'

Drake, in the middle of drying his face, turned to look at her. 'Princess, eh? Not quite how I pictured you.'

It was quite a contrast from a goddess of war.

She shrugged. 'It was his choice, not mine.'

Turning her attention to more practical matters, she

logged into her Hotmail account using Drake's phone, and from there pinged Typhoon's private chat room.

It took about thirty seconds for him to join her online, and Anya wasted no time getting to the point.

Guest: I AM IN SAUDI. WHERE DO WE MEET?

Host: *LAT − 30.8136, LON − 43.6717. BE THERE TOMORROW BY 18:00 OR I WON'T BE.*

Anya exhaled slowly, mulling over his words. He was getting nervous and agitated now that the witching hour was approaching. The initial euphoria of making contact with her again had faded, and now doubts and insecurities were creeping in. To make himself feel in control, he was exerting authority he didn't have.

She was under no illusions about the man's desires or motivations. This was not some sentinel of truth and virtue out to expose wrongdoing − he was a selfish, greedy man who had seen an opportunity to improve his lot in life. And he needed her to make it happen, otherwise he would have ignored her.

Guest: I WILL BE THERE ON TIME.

Host: *IF I THINK YOU ARE COMPROMISED, THE DEAL IS OFF.*

Guest: NO SUCH THING WILL HAPPEN.

Host: *AS YOU SAY. TOMORROW, THEN.*

Host is now offline.

With relief, she jotted down the latitude and longitude coordinates, terminated the connection and laid the phone aside.

'Well? What's the verdict?'

'He will meet us tomorrow. He gave me coordinates.'

'Let's see them,' Drake prompted, digging the Magellan out of his pack and firing it up. He inputted them as Anya read them out, then waited a few seconds for the unit to lock down the location.

'It's near a small village called Ash Shabakah, about a hundred miles across the border,' he reported. 'Middle of nowhere, basically.'

Anya leaned back in her chair and ran her hands through her hair. Her head and eyes hurt from exposure to the harsh sunlight, and she could already feel the itchy beginnings of sunburn on her arms and face.

'Tomorrow will be a long day. For both of us.'

He gave her a wry smile. 'I'm used to that.'

Chapter 55

'At last! I've got them,' Frost exclaimed.

For the past hour she had been trawling through a backlog of security footage from the dozens of cameras dotted around the airport, looking for just one glimpse of their targets. Now at last she'd found them.

Dietrich and Keegan were beside her in a few seconds, leaning in close to examine the frozen black-and-white image. Sure enough, they saw a man and a woman walking out of the airport terminal together. Anya's blonde hair made her easy to pick out amongst the crowd.

'Where did they go after that?' Dietrich demanded.

'You,' Frost said, pointing at one of the Saudi technicians nearby. 'Give me a wide-angle shot from one of the exterior cameras. One that's facing south-west. Use the same time frame.'

The man shot her an angry look, but a stern glare from Rahul was enough to silence any protests. He had made good on his agreement to get them access to the airport security camera system, either persuading or intimidating his way into the building and resolutely ignoring the protests about foreign intervention. He was Saudi internal police – his word was law.

Within moments, the image on her screen changed to an outside shot of the terminal building. It took them a few seconds to pick out Drake and Anya amongst the throng of passengers, but once they had them, there was no letting go.

They watched as the pair made for the bus terminal and spent a couple of minutes wandering between the stands before selecting one.

Dietrich made a note of the bus number and turned to Rahul. 'Can you pull up the route that bus takes?'

It took a couple of minutes to find the route, forcing them to delay their observation while they searched for available cameras at each of the bus stops. Much to their dismay, fewer than half of the stops were covered.

Dietrich chewed his lip as Frost scanned each of the available stops during the time the bus was meant to arrive there.

On the fifth stop, Keegan piped up. 'I see them. There!'

Damn, the man had good eyes. No wonder he became a sniper.

Sure enough, Drake and Anya disembarked on a fairly unremarkable street in central Riyadh, and were making to cross the busy road.

'What are they looking for?' Dietrich wondered.

Frost was on it. 'Can we get a shot across the street?'

Once again the image changed, this time displaying the output from a camera on the opposite side. Straight away Dietrich understood where they were heading.

'They're buying a car.'

It was surreal watching them browsing the ranks of parked vehicles, knowing it had happened hours ago. Settling on one in particular – a light brown Land Rover – they wasted no time attracting the attention of the dealer.

Frost fast-forwarded the protracted negotiations, missing about half an hour of footage, until at last they had a decent shot of the vehicle pulling out of the forecourt.

'Freeze that shot,' Dietrich ordered.

It was a perfect image of Anya and Drake up front, just before they pulled out onto the main road. They were both wearing sunglasses and had changed into casual clothes, but it was unmistakably them. More important, it gave them an unobstructed view of the licence plate.

A smile crept across Dietrich's face as he noted down the number. 'Follow them every inch of the way. I want to know every move they made.'

'On it.'

As Frost resumed her work, Dietrich pulled out his cellphone to call Franklin's office back at Langley.

Hussam proved to be as generous as he was jovial. Returning downstairs a short time later, Drake and Anya were greeted by a meal of spit-cooked lamb, grilled chicken, rice, dates, fava beans cooked in olive oil, loaves of flat unleavened bread and coffee served Turkish style with the ground beans still in the cup.

They fell upon the food as only starving people can. Drake was amazed that such a feast had been prepared in such a short time, and had thought to pass his compliments on to Hussam's wife, though he suspected it wouldn't be appropriate.

There was little talking during the meal. Anya had explained in advance that conversation was not encouraged during dinner so that guests could enjoy the food. Drake wasn't complaining.

Hussam was putting food away with the best of them. He suspected the man had already eaten tonight, but by the looks of him, he wasn't the sort to refuse a good meal.

'So, my friend, tell me more about yourself,' he said, addressing Drake as the meal wound down. 'How is it you come to know my Ameera?'

At this, Anya cocked an eyebrow, though Drake saw a hint of a smile too. He was quite certain that few other men would get away with referring to her in such a way.

'We both work for the same people, but we only met a few days ago. Things have been . . . eventful so far,' Drake began, not sure how much to tell him, or how much he already knew. He glanced at his female companion, smiling, though his eyes held an accusatory look. 'One thing I'll say about her – she's certainly full of surprises.'

At this, Hussam threw back his head and laughed. 'Of that, I have no doubt! She certainly surprised me when I met her for the first time. What was it, Ameera? Fifteen years ago?'

'Sixteen,' Anya confirmed.

'Ah, yes. The Battle of Khafji.' He leaned back in his seat, his ample stomach protruding before him. 'During the Iraq War, I had the misfortune of leading a platoon into the city to capture an enemy communications centre, but instead we were ambushed by Republican Guard and surrounded. I was ready to meet Allah when chaos erupted outside, and suddenly the Iraqis were fleeing and shouting in fear. A moment later, a young woman with yellow hair came rushing into the building, her face all streaked with dust and dirt, and blood on her bayonet. She looked at me with eyes like two pieces of ice, and then just like that, she straightened up and saluted as if she were a recruit on the parade ground.' He laughed and shook his head at the memory. 'Never in my life have I been more surprised, or more relieved, to see a woman.'

Drake looked over at Anya, noticing a little more colour in her face. Was she actually embarrassed?

Draining her coffee, she laid her cup down and looked

at Hussam. 'Maybe we should go over the plan for tomorrow?'

He nodded agreement, and called out for someone to take away the remains of the meal. While his wife cleared away the empty plates and bowls, he spread a map out on the wooden coffee table, depicting the border region between Iraq and Saudi Arabia.

'I have spoken to a couple of my drivers while you were upstairs,' he began. 'The best place to make the crossing is here, about a hundred miles west of Kuwait. You will have to leave the highway after Hafar Al Batin, and from there it is about a forty-mile drive to the border. The terrain is rough and hard going, so the Americans tend to avoid it with their Humvees. But there is a deep wadi running north–south that should keep you hidden from any patrols in the area.'

Anya was nodding slowly as she studied the map, already visualising the route they would take.

At least we won't have to worry about aerial surveillance, Drake thought. With all Predators grounded after Munro's little stunt, their way should be more or less clear.

'Minefields?' Drake prompted, looking up at Hussam. Iraq had laid hundreds of thousands of mines along their borders to guard against invasion. Even years later they were an ever-present threat, as many civilians and Coalition soldiers had found to their cost.

The old man shook his head. 'No mines there, my friend. My drivers have used that wadi a hundred times.'

Drake said nothing. He was inclined to take assurances like that with a grain of salt.

'What about weapons?' Anya asked.

The old man grinned, pushed himself away from the table and lumbered out of the room, returning a few moments later with two large cloth-wrapped bundles under his arms. Laying them down gently on the table, he undid the cordage that held them together and pulled back the coverings to reveal a pair of AK-47 assault rifles.

Drake nodded in satisfaction. He had no intention of starting a shooting match tomorrow, but if the worst happened, he wanted a weapon he could rely on. In that regard, he couldn't think of anything better.

The design dated back to the Second World War, when Soviet weapons manufacturers began to search for a weapon that combined the range of a conventional rifle with the rate of fire of a sub-machine gun. A couple of years later, an enterprising young designer named Mikhail Kalashnikov produced one of the finest infantry weapons ever made.

The basic design hadn't changed much in the past sixty years. Cheap and easy to produce, reliable and rugged, accurate and long ranged, the AK-47 was everything a soldier could want. Their reliability was legendary. Even when dropped on hard surfaces, clogged up with snow, mud or sand, or exposed to extremes of heat or cold, they almost always kept working. Drake had even seen one fired on full automatic until the wooden barrel guard caught alight from the excess heat.

These were the paratrooper version, with folding metal stocks instead of wooden ones. He picked one up to inspect it. It wasn't a light weapon like the American M4, but there was a certain elegance and economy to its design that told him a great deal of thought had gone into it. He racked back the priming handle to check the working parts, then pulled the trigger. There was a simple, precise click as the firing pin hit an empty chamber.

Anya was doing the same with her own rifle. She had

used AKs many times, and though she appreciated the weapon's undeniable strengths, she had never been a great fan. It was heavier than she liked, suffered from powerful recoil that was almost impossible to control on automatic, and the trigger assembly was too large for her hands. Still, a gun was a gun, and she had what she needed now.

'Excellent,' she decided. 'Thank you, Hussam.'

The old man beamed under her praise. 'For you, anything.'

She laid the assault rifle down on the table again. 'We must leave in a few hours if we're to make our rendezvous tomorrow. I'd like to cover as much ground as we can before sunrise.'

'A sound plan,' he agreed. 'I will make sure your jeep is fuelled.'

She flashed a wry smile. 'I imagine you have plenty to spare.'

The old man spread his hands. 'Life here has its advantages.'

As Anya set about wrapping the two assault rifles again, Hussam moved closer to Drake and touched his arm. 'I am going outside to take some air. Walk with me, my friend.'

Drake glanced at Anya, who he noticed was studiously avoiding his gaze. He was reluctant to leave her, yet Hussam had proven to be a great aid to them so far; he didn't think it wise to refuse the man. He was also intrigued about what he had to say.

Leaving Anya to her own devices, he followed Hussam outside.

Chapter 56

Dietrich's phone was ringing. It was Franklin. 'Yeah?'

'Jonas, we just got an alert in from the NSA.' He was trying to be calm and businesslike, but Dietrich could hear the mixture of excitement and anxiety in his voice. 'They found Drake's vehicle. It's parked up beside a house in a small town called Al Majma'ah, about fifty miles from the Iraqi border. The house is registered in the name of Hussam Khariri, a former major in the Saudi Army.'

Dietrich could barely hide his smile of triumph.

Frost had managed to track their movements as far as Highway 65, heading out of the capital, but after that the camera coverage became sporadic until they were reduced to mere guesswork. Still, it seemed logical to conclude they were heading north, towards Iraq. Dietrich had instructed Franklin to concentrate their satellite assets on that area, and it seemed his assumption had paid off.

'Copy that, Dan. We're gearing up now.'

It was all coming together for him. He could feel it. Already he could imagine the praise and commendations that would be heaped on him for this. His previous transgressions would be forgotten about. He would be redeemed, vindicated.

And as for Drake . . .

'Remember, we need them alive,' Franklin reminded him. 'Don't get trigger happy.'

Dietrich smiled. 'We'll do our best. I promise that.'

Signing off the call, he turned to Rahul. 'Get an assault team together, fully armed and equipped for a house raid. And we need a chopper. Something big and fast. We don't have much time.'

The temperature had fallen with the setting sun, a cool breeze blowing little clouds of dust across the courtyard as Hussam ambled away from the house. High above, the first stars twinkled in the vast darkened sky.

The peaceful scene was interrupted when two young children darted across the open space, yelling and shouting at each other. A boy and a girl, perhaps eight or nine years old. Drake knew nothing of their language, but it seemed there was some disagreement over a little toy sailing ship that the boy was trying to wrestle from the girl.

A stern reproach from Hussam was enough to silence the dispute, for now at least. Both children turned to face him, as if they were young squaddies on a parade ground waiting to get an earful from their drill sergeant.

As Hussam scolded them for misbehaving in front of a guest, the little girl glanced at Drake for a moment, her large brown eyes filled with curiosity and a hint of suspicion.

Drake felt a shiver run through him. For an instant, he saw a different girl staring back at him. A girl in a blue dress, her eyes wide with terror.

He blinked, and the vision was gone.

'Children,' Hussam said, switching back to English as he resumed his walk. His look of gruff discipline was gone now, replaced by an indulgent smile. 'They can drive a man to distraction, but life would be empty without them. Do you have any of your own, Drake?'

He shook his head. Somehow he couldn't see a family fitting in with the kind of life he lived. 'None.'

The old man said nothing further for a while, and Drake didn't press him. Whatever he had to say, he would say it in his own time. There was a certain deliberate confidence about the man that he found almost disarming, as if everything that unfolded around him did so because he allowed it to happen.

'You have the look of a man who does not know where he is going, my friend,' Hussam observed conversationally.

'You're not far wrong,' Drake admitted.

'You travel in good company. Trust in that.'

Drake sighed and looked upward, gazing into the heavens as if his answers lay there. 'A week ago, I'd never even heard of Anya. Even now, I feel like I have more questions than answers.'

At this, the old man stopped walking and turned to face him, looking him over for a long, thoughtful moment. 'She is the most honourable person I have ever met, man or woman. Whatever she speaks, it is the truth. If she is your friend, you could ask for none better. If you stand in her path, you will fall. But if you betray her . . . then God help you, because no one else can.'

Drake glanced away. Once again, he found himself asking the same question that had dogged him since all this began – who was Anya? How did someone like her end up in a world like this?

'In truth, that is why I asked you to join me,' Hussam went on, resuming his walk. 'It is about Ameera. It has been years since I last saw her, and like you say, much has happened. She is different inside, not the same woman I once knew. What has happened to her?'

'She . . . wasn't in a good place when I met her. She had suffered a lot. I don't know how well she's dealing with it.'

The old man nodded sadly. 'I had feared as much.' He sighed. 'Look at me, Drake. I am old and fat and content with life. She would never have it this way. She will not live to see old age.'

His words felt like a punch in the chest. 'It's her choice.'

'This is true,' Hussam said. 'And any man who tried to change that would certainly regret it. Ameera is the bravest soldier I have ever known, but she is headstrong and stubborn. She will not listen to reason, will not back down. I see her standing alone, surrounded by enemies. And when that happens, she will fall.'

'What can I do?' Drake asked, at a loss.

'Be there for her,' was his simple answer. 'Do what you can to protect her, even from herself. I am too old to play that game now, but you are still young. You can still stand by her side. I think there will come a time when you have to choose, either to stand with her or against her. When that time comes, I hope you make the right choice, Ryan Drake.'

His words sent a chill through the younger man. He couldn't imagine having to protect Anya from anyone, or her ever needing or wanting his help. And yet, he saw the worry and sadness in the older man's eyes. She meant a lot to him. He respected her, cared for her, perhaps even loved her.

Drake understood that more than he cared to admit.

'If there's anything I can do for her, I will,' he promised.

His brooding thoughts were interrupted by the buzz of his cellphone. It was Munro.

He looked up at Hussam. 'I'm sorry. I have to take this.'

The old man nodded understanding. 'I have said what I wanted to. Take as long as you wish.' He paused a moment. 'But remember your promise.'

Drake nodded. As Hussam walked away, he hit the receive button. 'I'm here.'

'Good to speak to you again, Drake,' Munro began. 'I hope I'm not calling at a bad time?'

'Would it make any difference?'

'Not really.'

'I want to speak to my sister,' Drake said. 'I need to know she's safe.'

'First you fill me in on what's happening. You've had three days. I hope for your sake you haven't wasted them.'

Drake sighed and chewed his lip. 'We made contact with Anya's source. He's willing to meet us.'

'Where?'

'Iraq. He'll give us more information once we're in the country.'

'I see.'

'Do you? Good, then put my sister on the phone.'

'Say please.'

Drake gritted his teeth, striving to keep his temper under control. 'Please,' he finally managed to say.

The line grew muffled for a few moments before another voice came on the line. 'Ryan.'

She sounded calmer than before, which didn't surprise him. Jessica had never been the hysterical sort. She could handle anything he could. More, perhaps. She didn't run away from problems.

'Jess.' His voice was low, ragged when he spoke. 'Are you all right? Have they . . . hurt you?'

'No. They promised to treat me well if I cooperated. If I tried anything, they . . . said they would find Scott and the kids,' she added, her voice cracking with emotion. Threats to her own life she could deal with, but her family was another matter.

'Christ, Jess, you have to believe me, I had no idea . . .'

'It's all right, Ryan,' she assured him. 'It's all right. This wasn't your fault.'

'No. It's not all right. I let you down,' he said, facing up to the truth at last. 'I lied to you. I didn't tell you what I really did, the world I was part of. The people I dealt with.'

'Ryan, listen to me,' she said, speaking in the same strong, commanding tone he had heard her use on her two children. 'This wasn't your fault. You didn't make this happen. I don't . . . I don't blame you for any of it. You have to believe that.'

He swallowed hard. Her quiet acceptance, her understanding was more than he could bear. He would rather she had raged at him. He wanted her to be angry with him.

But she wasn't. She understood him just as she always had. Despite everything, she accepted him for who he was.

But that didn't assuage his guilt.

'I'll get you out of this. I promise,' he said, speaking low and quiet. 'You never gave up on me. I won't give up on you, ever. I'll find you.'

Before she could reply, the line grew muffled again.

'Touching, Drake. Very touching,' Munro taunted. 'I was almost tempted to let you keep going. I wonder what else you would've admitted to?'

Drake gritted his teeth. 'You piece of shit, Munro.

You'd better pray I never find you without a woman to hide behind.'

The older man chuckled. 'At least you're honest. That's probably why she hasn't killed you yet.'

'What are you talking about?'

'Wake up. You really think Anya's helping you out of the goodness of her heart? You're just a tool to be used and thrown away. Sure, she'll make you think she trusts you, that you mean something to her. She might even make you feel something *for* her. But believe me, sooner or later you'll outlive your usefulness.'

Drake paused, staring out across the dusty desert landscape stretching off to the horizon, where it met the deep azure sky above. He should have shouted Munro down, told him to go fuck himself, but something held him back.

'She's a killer, Drake,' Munro went on. 'No remorse, no hesitation, no regrets. She doesn't feel emotions like that any more. She has no loyalty to anyone or anything but herself.'

'Is that your excuse for trying to murder her?' Drake hit back.

'So she told you, huh? I guessed she would.' He didn't sound concerned at all. 'She'd do anything to blame me for what happened.'

'You tried to murder your commanding officer and stage a mutiny,' Drake reminded him. 'I know the whole story. You're a fucking coward, Munro. That's all you are.'

'What you don't know – what she never would have told you – is that she was planning to turn rogue and take the entire task force with her! *She* was the one planning the mutiny, not me!' His voice was shaking with anger now. 'So I did the only thing I could. I admit it – I tried to have her killed. I tried to stop her while there was still time.'

He sighed, his voice tinged with sadness and regret when he spoke again. 'But I failed. She survived. I don't know how, but the bitch survived, and she executed everyone who tried to stop her. My men, my brothers in arms, and she executed them. No remorse, no hesitation. She's a fucking murderer, Drake.'

Munro's words felt like a knife driven into his stomach. Fervently he tried to tell himself that Munro was lying, that he would say anything to keep Drake off balance, but deep down he couldn't stop thinking about that night in Khatyrgan when he'd watched Anya brutally murder that guard. Never in his life would he forget the look in her eyes.

There was a killer inside her. Sometimes it was hidden deep down, but it was there nonetheless.

'If you're looking for sympathy, you're talking to the wrong man,' he said at last, summoning up what defiance he could.

'You of all people should know how it feels to be condemned for one mistake,' Munro hit back. 'That's why you're working for the Agency, isn't it?'

Drake's heart leapt and his stomach twisted in a sickening knot. 'And what would you know about that?'

'Operation Hydra ring a bell?'

Drake stood there in stunned silence while the desert wind whipped around him.

'I thought that might get your attention.'

'What do you know about Hydra?' Drake rasped.

'I know there's more to your discharge than meets the eye.' He was enjoying every moment of this. 'You have quite a history, Drake. Almost makes me feel better about myself.' He chuckled with amusement. 'I wonder how your new friend would take it if she knew what kind of man you really were?'

Allowing that ominous threat to hang in the air for a moment, he added, 'Time's running out. For you, and your sister. I'll be in touch.'

The line went dead.

Chapter 57

Sighing, Anya leaned back in her chair, relieved to take her eyes off the map she'd been poring over for the past twenty minutes. She was worried about crossing the border tomorrow, not just because of what lay beyond, but because she had no current knowledge of the area. Four years ago she could have hand-drawn every Iraqi observation post and patrol route, but now she was little better than a lost tourist.

A commotion outside drew her thoughts back to the present. Walking over to the window, she found herself overlooking the small courtyard at the rear of Hussam's house. His two small children were playing a game of some sort which, typical of such games, involved a lot of running and a lot of shouting.

The boy was yelling that his sister was cheating. He was short and heavyset, much like his father, and obviously not well suited to games like this. In response, the little girl stuck out her tongue mockingly and took off on nimble feet as he chased her again.

Despite her worries, Anya couldn't help but smile at their antics. They were young yet, neither having seen ten years, and still ignorant of the roles their society would one day require of them.

Anya had never had children of her own; something for which she was usually grateful. She had never considered herself maternal. Even as a girl, her head had been filled with thoughts of excitement and adventure, not babies and motherhood.

Anyway, the choice had eventually been taken out of her hands. After what happened to her in Afghanistan, children were no longer an option. A lot of things had changed for her after that horrific ordeal.

Perhaps it was fitting. She was a soldier, not a mother. She existed only to take life, not to create it.

And yet there were times, very rare times, when she felt something. Something as inexplicable as it was unsettling. Not a specific emotion or thought, but almost a physical sensation – a sense of emptiness, of longing, as if her body somehow remembered the purpose for which it had been created and tried to remind her.

Absently she reached down and touched her abdomen, hard and flat from long years of physical exercise, and wondered what it would feel like to be full and rounded, to feel the kick of a tiny limb, to sense a new life growing within her . . .

She turned around abruptly as the door opened and Drake entered.

'You and Hussam were gone a while,' she remarked, studying his reactions carefully.

Drake avoided her questioning gaze. 'He likes to talk.'

She laughed with amusement. 'I'm not here to interrogate you, Drake. If Hussam chose to have words with you, they were for you alone.'

'That's very trusting. What if he told me to kill you?'

She regarded him with a raised eyebrow. 'You could try.'

And yet, studying his reactions, she sensed there was more to it than a mere conversation with Hussam.

'Did something else happen out there?' she asked.

401

Drake looked at her sharply, but before he could reply he felt the phone vibrate in his pocket. He fished it out and checked the number. It was Munro.

'What now?'

'Get out of there, Drake!' Munro yelled, his voice hard and urgent.

'What—'

'Your location's been compromised. I don't know how, but you've got a Shepherd inbound on your position. If you don't want them to catch you, get out of that building now. Move!'

Anya had stopped what she was doing to listen in on the conversation. Straight away she saw the change in Drake's posture, the sudden tension in his muscles. Something was wrong.

Drake wasted no time on explanations as he shoved the phone back in his pocket. 'We have to bail.'

She was moving in an instant, throwing her gear into the pack she'd brought with her.

Even as Drake reached for the weapons stashed beneath the bed, they both became aware of a noise outside. Hard and heavy, a rhythmic thudding. Rotor blades.

'That's it!' Dietrich called, staring at the building below through his night-vision scope as their Black Hawk helicopter, on loan from the Saudi army, thundered in on approach. 'Alpha Team is good to go!'

Sure enough, he could see the Land Rover parked nearby. The rest of the town stretched out like a model below, all small buildings and narrow alleyways.

He turned to the other members of his assault team, all dressed in black body armour. 'Both suspects are armed and should be considered extremely dangerous, so don't take any chances. Understood?'

He was met by a chorus of affirmative responses. But one member of the team remained silent.

'Frost! Are you hearing me?'

'Yeah, goddamn it!' she snapped.

Leaning out, he clipped his fast-descent harness into the pylon mounted on the side of the aircraft.

Tearing out of the bedroom and into the hallway beyond, Drake and Anya almost collided with Hussam. The old man's eyes were wide with fear. Outside, a hurricane of wind from the aircraft's downwash rattled the window shutters, the roar of the engines making the floorboards tremble.

'They've found us,' Anya said, yelling to be heard over the din. She was clutching her AK-47, a rucksack stuffed with whatever items she'd been able to gather slung over her shoulder. 'We must leave now.'

Hussam knew better than to waste time on questions. 'Come!' he said, beckoning them as he turned and rushed for the stairs.

He moved with a speed that belied his size and age, leaping down the stairs two at a time. Even they were hard pressed to keep up.

Turning left at the bottom, he grasped one of the wooden panels beneath the staircase and wrenched it open, revealing a doorway that neither of them knew existed. Beyond lay another, much older, set of stone steps that descended to a basement or cellar of some kind.

A flashlight was fixed to the inside of the secret door. Taking it, he switched it on and descended the stairs, moving slower and more carefully this time. The steps were narrow and worn. Drake and Anya followed behind.

The stairs brought them to a small stone-walled room,

perhaps 10 feet wide and twice as long. The air was cold and dry, smelling of dust and great age. Packing boxes sat along one wall, painted dark green and with Cyrillic writing emblazoned across them. Drake recognised weapons crates straight away. He wondered how many more AKs resided down here.

'Over there,' he said, shining his flashlight at the far end of the room. Another door stood there, closed and bolted from their side. 'My last gift to you. It will take you into the old sewer system. Follow the tunnel for three hundred paces, then look for my mark. Go!'

Anya glanced at the door, then back at the old man. 'Come with us.'

He gave her a bitter-sweet smile. 'I'm too old to play these games, child. I will delay them as long as I can. If Allah wills it, we will see each other again.'

Rushing forward, Drake unbolted the door. It swung open on old, rusted hinges to reveal a dank passageway, perhaps 5 feet high. There was no smell of human waste, these tunnels having long since been abandoned, but mould and damp were prevalent.

'Anya! We have to go.'

Anya looked at the old man again, and he saw true gratitude in her eyes. 'I'm in your debt.'

'My Ameera,' he said, reaching up and gently stroking her cheek. 'The debt was always mine. Good luck to you, child.'

In a rare display of affection, she reached out and grabbed him, pulling him close in a fierce embrace. A moment later, she let go, took the flashlight and hurried towards the door without looking back.

The front door was locked and barred, but two rounds from a Mossberg breaching shotgun soon changed that.

Kicking aside the shattered remains of the door, Dietrich rushed inside, with Keegan, Rahul and Frost spreading out to take flanking positions. Four more operatives in full armour were with them, weapons out and ready as they fanned out through the house.

Everywhere there was noise. The thump of the circling Black Hawk's rotors, the crash of doors being kicked open, yells from his fellow team members, the crackle of radio transmissions in his ear, panicked screams as women and children found themselves confronted by masked men with guns.

Suddenly the door beside him flew open and he found himself confronted by a giant of a man who seemed to occupy the entire breadth and height of the frame. He saw the glint of something metal scything through the air towards him, and ducked instinctively as the man swung what looked like a meat cleaver.

Using an MP5 sub-machine gun as a makeshift club, he parried the next vicious blow and slammed the weapon's stock into the man's face. He stumbled back, stunned by the impact, but remained on his feet.

Frost wasn't about to let him get back in the fight. Dietrich watched the young woman calmly level a bulky plastic pistol at the giant and fire two metal prongs into the centre of his chest. The harsh clicking as the taser discharged thousands of volts into his body was soon drowned out by his howl of pain. Size didn't matter when it came to weapons like that. He went down like a ton of bricks, his massive body hitting the ground with enough force to make the floorboards shake.

'Tango down!' she called.

Their eyes met, and he gave her a fleeting look of gratitude, but said nothing. There was no need.

In under a minute, it was over. All of the rooms had been secured and the house's inhabitants rounded up in the living room – two females, probably mother and daughter; the giant, now awake and groaning in pain; a young boy who could count perhaps eight years; and an old man with a greying beard.

No sign of Drake or Anya.

'We swept the house. They ain't here,' Keegan reported.

'They *were* here.' Dietrich was convinced of that.

He looked at the old man again. He was standing with his arms held protectively around the sobbing woman – his wife, no doubt. He was glaring at Dietrich, his dark eyes burning like coals.

'Where are they?' he demanded.

The man said nothing, just stood there glaring at him.

'I know you speak English, you fat fuck! Your Army personnel file says so.'

Still no response.

'Rahul. Translate for me.'

The young Saudi officer repeated his demand, speaking fast and urgent. The man took his time replying, as if having to think the matter over.

'He says he doesn't know what you're talking about.'

'Bullshit,' Keegan cut in. 'The son of a bitch is stalling.'

Dietrich looked him up and down. He was an old man, fat and grey, wearing a crumpled business suit and shoes that looked as if they'd seen better days.

He frowned, looking closer at the shoes. What he had thought were scuff marks were actually some kind of dust or powder. He had left footprints on the otherwise pristine floorboards when they'd marched him in here. Where had he been?

Struck by an idea, Dietrich snatched a flashlight from

one of the assault operatives and retraced the footprints out into the hallway.

They seemed to be leading towards the staircase, but they weren't heading up it. They simply stopped. It was as if he had emerged from the wall itself, just where one of the polished wood panels jutted out a little . . .

Reaching out, he grabbed the panel and yanked it hard. It came away easily, revealing a doorway with a set of steps leading down.

Dietrich's eyes lit up. 'Keegan! Frost! On me.'

The old sewer tunnel curved north in a wide arc as Drake and Anya rushed down it, having to duck to avoid the low ceiling. Along the way, they passed various side tunnels which emptied into their own, all long since dried up. They were far too small for a human to crawl through.

With only the bouncing light of their torch to illuminate the way, it was impossible to tell where they were. The only thing that mattered was that they were putting some distance between themselves and the house.

By Drake's reckoning they had covered a good 100 yards or more, which was probably enough to put them outside whatever perimeter the tactical teams had established for the assault.

Anya was behind him, covering their backs. 'I don't understand how they found us,' she hissed, hurrying to catch up.

'They must have traced Harrison's passport,' he reasoned, though he had no idea how they had tracked them to Hussam's house. 'Or maybe your mate Hussam was playing for the other team?'

'Never!' she hit back. 'I know him. I trust him.'

'You trusted Munro once, and look where that got you.'

Anya said nothing to that, but her eyes flashed with anger.

'All teams, be advised, targets are in the sewer system,' Dietrich barked into his radio as he strode back down the corridor. 'I want teams on every manhole cover within a half-mile radius. Move!'

He had already sent four men down the tunnel in pursuit, though considering the head start their targets had, it was unlikely they'd catch up.

'That's a pretty big search area,' Keegan reminded him. They could call on perhaps a dozen operatives in total; a scratch force thrown together at the last minute. There was no way they could cover every access point.

'I know,' Dietrich growled. They were slipping from his grasp just when he was about to close his hand around them.

Come on, you're smarter than this. Think, goddamn it! Think!

'Rahul, can we get a plan of the sewer layout?'

The younger man shook his head. 'That tunnel is part of the old system, no longer used. It could be hundreds of years old.'

'Shit.'

He threw the front door open and strode outside. The street was a chaotic scene of police vehicles, armed operatives and local civilians desperate to get a look at the action. Already the tactical teams were dispersing, moving off in a desperate effort to cover as many sewer outlets as possible.

'It's his escape route. He designed it for himself, so it would have to be somewhere close,' Dietrich mused. 'He's old, and fat as shit. There's no way he could travel far.'

'And he wouldn't want to pop up in the middle of a crowded street,' Keegan added. 'He'd want to know his exit was secure.'

Frost was starting to see his reasoning. 'And he'd want a vehicle of some kind. Something to get him out of the area.'

Dietrich stopped in his tracks and turned to Rahul. 'Does he have any garages leased in his name?'

Chapter 58

'There!' Anya called, pointing to a section of wall that looked no different from the rest.

Drake skidded to a halt, turned and looked at her. 'How do you know?'

She brushed past him and gestured to a mark cut into the stone. 'That is Hussam's mark.'

To Drake's eyes, it seemed like nothing but a random set of lines and curves carved into the wall, perhaps a builder's note or something similar.

'I don't get it.'

'It is his name in Vedic Sanskrit. Almost no one can read it today,' she explained. 'Shine your light on me.'

Gently touching the ancient stones beneath the carved symbol, she found one in particular that had a different feel from the others, and pressed it hard. There was a click, and suddenly the innocuous section of wall she'd been standing next to moved just a little.

It was a door, he realised. A hidden door.

Pushing it open, Anya exposed a smaller chamber beyond. Perhaps 4 feet square, its only feature was a metal ladder leading up.

'I'll go first,' Drake said, shouldering his AK.

Anya nodded, turning to pull the door shut behind them as he clambered up with the flashlight gripped in his teeth.

A metal manhole cover blocked his way. Taking a deep breath, he leaned into it with his shoulder and heaved upward, feeling the cover rise up with a grating rasp. As soon as it was clear of the rim, he shoved it aside and hoisted himself up. Unshouldering the AK in one hand and taking the flashlight in the other, he allowed the beam to play over his surroundings.

He was in a room; a big one, maybe 30 feet long and twice as wide. Judging by the concrete floor, toolboxes and bare brick walls, this was no house or living space. It was a workshop.

He listened, straining to hear any shuffling or clicks that might indicate the presence of people with weapons, but detected nothing. In the distance he could make out the rhythmic thumping of helicopter blades. The chopper was still circling the area.

There was a light switch mounted on the wall beside him. Backing up beside it, he flicked it on. A single fluorescent strip light mounted in the ceiling pinged into life, revealing a grey Toyota Hilux 4x4 in the centre of the room. The vehicle looked as though it had come straight from the showroom.

The main doors stood opposite; big reinforced steel shutters linked up to an electric motor. Beside them was a smaller conventional door for day-to-day use.

'Clever boy,' he said, impressed by Hussam's foresight.

Anya was up beside him a moment later. Glancing around, she focused on the Hilux and nodded in satisfaction.

'Find out if it'll start,' Drake instructed. I'll get the shutters open.' He was already moving towards the motor control box, having no doubt that Hussam kept the vehicle well maintained.

But no sooner had he started moving than the door exploded inwards, a fist-sized hole blasted in the lock. Men in dark assault gear rushed in, weapons raised, yelling at him not to move.

Drake didn't stop to wonder how they had found Hussam's supposedly secret escape route, or whether they had seen Anya.

He was in survival mode now. There were three of them that he could see, with the possibility of more outside. They were in full assault gear, with face masks, armoured combat vests and Kevlar plates covering their arms and legs. All three were armed; one with a breaching shotgun that was no doubt responsible for punching a hole in the door; one with an MP5 sub-machine gun, and one with a Heckler & Koch USP pistol.

The shotgun was a nasty weapon at close range, but the MP5 was the biggest threat. Unprotected as he was, one burst would put him down. Reacting on instinct, Drake brought the AK to bear on the nearest target.

'Forget it, Ryan!' a voice hissed.

Drake's heart leapt. He knew that voice all too well.

'Put the gun down,' Dietrich ordered, covering Drake with the MP5. 'It's over.'

All three of them had the drop on him.

'Jonas, listen to me—'

'Put the gun down. I won't tell you again.' As far as Dietrich was concerned, Drake was just a target to be taken down. And he wouldn't hesitate to pull the trigger.

Cursing, Drake lowered the AK and placed it on the ground at his feet.

'Kick it away.' The MP5 didn't leave Drake's centre mass for a second.

Placing his foot beneath the weapon, he slid it forwards. The assault rifle gave off a harsh screech as the metal parts scraped the concrete floor, but by the time it came to a halt it was well out of his reach.

Drake raised his hands to show he was unarmed.

'Where is she?' Dietrich demanded.

'She's gone.'

The older man wasn't buying it for a second. 'You're lying. That's a bad play for a man in your situation.'

'For fuck sake, Jonas, I'm not your enemy. Neither is Anya.'

'Bullshit,' Frost retorted. He had suspected it was her based on her height and build, and the voice confirmed it. 'Why the fuck are you protecting someone like her?'

'Because she's the only one who can help me.'

Dietrich's brows drew together in a frown. 'What do you mean?'

Drake opened his mouth to reply, but at that moment the light blinked out, plunging the room into darkness.

An instant later, he heard a crunch followed by a low groan of pain, and then the dull thud of a body hitting the floor.

'Contact!' Frost cried out in warning.

'Rahul's down!'

It could only have been Anya. Drake had no idea where she was, especially in pitch darkness, but she was in there somewhere with them. He felt the hairs prickle on the back of his neck, and a creeping sense of dread rising up from the pit of his stomach. She was a predator stalking her prey; silent, remorseless, deadly.

Maras – a goddess of war.

Without hesitation, he made a dash to the right, reached down and felt his fingers close around the stock of the AK-47. Snatching the weapon up, he thumbed the safety catch off and backed up against the Hilux.

413

Suddenly the room blazed with red light as Dietrich triggered a signal flare, dropping the device at his feet.

For a brief moment, Drake saw the man silhouetted against the crimson glow, his weapon up and ready. Then there was a blur of motion on his left. A figure leapt from the shadows, grasped the weapon in a vice-like grip and yanked it from his hand.

Dietrich lashed out with his fist, meeting nothing but air. She was a ghost, no more substantial than the grotesque shadows cast by the flare. Before he could recover, Anya moved around to his other side, grabbed him and drove her knee into his stomach. A hard strike to the back of his neck sent him sprawling on the concrete floor.

She wasted no time contemplating her victory. Frost was mere yards away, searching the flickering shadows for a target. Hearing the commotion, she turned towards the source of the noise, bringing her USP to bear.

Anya was on her in a heartbeat. Staring in horrified fascination, Drake watched as her hand shot out, gripped the weapon's slide and shoved it backward just as Frost pulled the trigger.

Nothing happened. With the slide in its rear position, the hammer was blocked, preventing it from striking the round in the chamber.

Twisting the weapon away, Anya drew back her left arm and drilled Frost across the jaw, snapping her head to the side. Stunned, the young woman slackened her grip on the weapon.

Anya pulled it out of her grasp before she could recover. With casual ease, she ejected the magazine, pulled back the slide and pressed the release pin on the right side of the frame. With the locking assembly disengaged, the weapon literally fell apart in her hands, its components clattering to the floor.

414

But Frost wasn't finished. The blow had enflamed her already wounded pride, and the older woman's brief pause to disarm the weapon had bought her a vital second or two to regain her wits. Unsheathing a combat knife from her webbing, she spun back to face her adversary, lashing out with the blade in a vicious backhanded swipe.

Anya stepped back a pace, allowing the blade to sail past her throat by mere inches. From her perspective it was a clumsy swing, lacking speed or finesse, and easily evaded.

For a fleeting moment, Frost glared at her enemy in the flickering red light. Anya made no move either to advance or retreat. She was just standing there, waiting for Frost to attack. Only her eyes glimmered in the light of the flare, cold and blue and utterly without mercy.

Maras – a goddess of war.

'You fucking bitch,' Frost hissed, tightening her grip on the weapon. 'I should have killed you on the plane.'

With aggression born from simmering resentment and anger, she came at Anya, thrusting and swiping the blade, aiming for any vulnerable spot she could find.

But her target proved as elusive as she was intimidating. Twice Frost swung, and twice Anya dodged aside with infuriating ease, the blade slicing nothing but air. When a third unsuccessful attack left her overextended and vulnerable, Anya at last went on the offensive, catching Frost's arm and twisting it behind her back.

The young woman cried out in pain and fear, bucking and kicking with desperate strength to try to free herself, but Anya's grip was unrelenting. The pressure increased, stretching sinews and tendons. The knife fell from her grip, her fingers numb and tingling.

Nearby, Drake caught movement out of the corner of

his eye. It was Dietrich, struggling to rise after being knocked down by Anya. The sight of the two women locked in combat was enough to revive him, and he snatched up the MP5 that the woman had taken from him.

Rushing forward, Drake grabbed the long silencer protruding from the end of the barrel. Dietrich's instinctive reaction was to squeeze the trigger. Drake jerked the weapon upward as a burst of automatic fire scythed the air, pattering into the roof overhead.

But the superheated gases inside the weapon caused the barrel to heat up almost immediately. Drake winced as the hot metal seared his skin, and wrenched the weapon aside. He was stronger than his adversary and he had surprise on his side.

For an instant, their eyes met. Dietrich's held a mixture of shock and anger. A hard cross to the jaw sent him down for good.

Wasting no time, Drake threw the red hot weapon aside. Adrenalin was masking the pain for now, but he would feel it later, he knew.

Anya almost felt sorry for her adversary. Young, proud and arrogant, she possessed both speed and aggression, but little skill. Her actions were predictable, her movements easy to read. Anya could have disarmed her at any time, but she had waited for the right moment, wanting to minimise the risk of injury to herself. Even an amateur could sometimes get lucky, and she couldn't afford to get injured tonight.

Now she had Frost at her mercy. The young woman who would have sliced her throat without a second thought, who would have put a bullet through her skull without hesitation. She could kill her in a heartbeat.

Anya felt the familiar thrill of victory, of having pitted

herself against an enemy and prevailed. She should kill her now and get it over with.

'Anya!'

She glanced up, and saw Drake standing before her, the barrel of his AK levelled at her head.

'Let her go.'

In an instant, she weighed up the odds and made her decision.

Leaning in close, she whispered in the woman's ear. 'Remember this moment. Remember what I could have done.'

Exerting downward pressure, she forced Frost to her knees, raised her arm up and brought an elbow down on her shoulder. She heard the telltale pop as the joint gave way and felt the arm go slack, followed immediately by an agonised scream. Frost was out of the fight. Grabbing her by her webbing straps, Anya hurled her aside, out of the path of the Hilux.

'Jesus Christ!' Drake yelled, appalled.

Anya looked at him, exasperated. 'She'll live. Get the shutters open.'

Turning away, she pulled open the driver's door of the Hilux and clambered in. As she'd expected, the keys were laid beneath the seat.

Drake by contrast stood rooted to the spot, staring at the injured woman who was now curled into a ball and moaning in pain.

'Drake! Come on,' she yelled, turning the engine over. It spluttered once then roared into life. 'Get the shutters.'

Shooting her a vicious glare, Drake hurried over to the shutter control and pressed the button to retract them.

He was visibly shaking with anger when he returned to the vehicle. 'This didn't have to happen. They would have listened to me.'

'Were you willing to bet your life on that? And your sister's?' Anya shot back. As the shutters ground upward, she turned to look at him, her eyes shining with baleful fire in the glow of the dashboard light. 'And unless you plan to pull the trigger, don't ever point a weapon at me again.'

With that, she turned her attention back to the road ahead and gunned the accelerator. The big vehicle lurched forward out of the garage and took off down the street in a spray of dust.

Chapter 59

'Goddamn it! This was supposed to be a clean take-down,' Franklin raged down the phone. 'What the fuck happened?'

Dietrich winced, holding the phone with one hand and an ice pack against his head with the other. The medics had told him he might have a minor concussion, which did little to improve his mood.

'They had help. They bailed out of the house before we could secure it. We tracked them to a garage nearby, but Maras ambushed us.' He clenched his jaw. 'She blew through us like we weren't even there. I've never seen anything like her.'

'So people keep telling me,' Franklin observed sourly. 'What's your status now?'

'I'm hanging in there. Frost is hurt, though.'

That changed his attitude. 'How bad?'

The young woman was being attended by a pair of medics. With one man holding her steady, another gripped her dislocated arm and pushed upward to reset her shoulder, eliciting an angry cry of pain.

'Ow, goddamn it! Son of a bitch!' she yelled, pushing the first man away. He stared at her open mouthed, too surprised to respond.

Defiant to the end. Dietrich couldn't help but smile. 'She'll live.'

'Good. Now what are we doing to find them?'

'It seems logical to assume they're heading for Iraq. We've alerted all border guards and put out an APB on the vehicle, but we've got six hundred miles of largely unpatrolled desert to cover. That's a big search area.'

'Just do what you can, Jonas.'

Great advice. Dietrich was about to hang up, but thought better of it. 'There's something else . . .'

'Well, spit it out, for Christ sake,' Franklin snapped.

It took a great deal of self-control not to voice the first thought that came to mind. 'Before the lights went out, Drake said something about Anya being the only one who could help him.'

Silence greeted him for several seconds. 'What are you getting at?'

'Something else is going on here, Dan.'

'Like what?'

'I don't know,' he admitted.

'Damn it, Jonas. I need more than vague theories and cryptic hints. Don't you have anything useful to tell me?'

Dietrich bit his lip. 'I'll get back to you.'

Closing down the phone, he walked over to talk with Frost, doing his best to hide his limp.

'How are you feeling?'

The young woman's shoulder was heavily strapped up, the right side of her face discoloured by dark bruising along her jawline.

'Like I just lost a fucking fight,' she spat. 'How do you think?'

The physical injuries would heal, but there was no tonic for wounded pride. 'We'll get you on a flight home soon.'

She looked up at him, her grey eyes blazing. 'The hell

you will. If you try to take me off this op, I swear to God I'll kill you, Dietrich.'

'You're injured.'

'So are you,' she reminded him, then lowered her voice. 'And not forgetting your . . . "condition". Wouldn't want anyone to find out about that, would we?'

Dietrich glared at her, torn between anger, frustration and a certain grudging respect for her determination. 'If you slow us down . . .'

'I won't,' she assured him.

He shook his head in dismay. 'Fine. Have it your way.'

If she was determined to get herself killed, he wasn't about to stop her.

Leaving her to it, he walked away in search of Rahul. The man was on the other side of the street outside the garage, a couple of plastic sutures holding together the cut on his forehead. Anya had struck him with a wrench; checking her force so as not to deal him a fatal injury.

Another man she could have killed, but hadn't.

'Are you going to survive?'

The Saudi lieutenant offered him a pained smile. 'I'm beginning to wish I had not volunteered for this job.'

'You're not the only one,' Dietrich assured him before turning to more practical matters. 'Where are we on leads?'

'We have found nothing so far, though with such a big search area, it will be almost impossible to box them in. We are trying to tie in with local Army commanders to help with the search, but they are not being cooperative.' He offered a lopsided grimace. 'Apparently their units are tasked to "other operations".'

He had expected as much. 'What about Khariri?'

'We have him at an interrogation centre not far from

421

here. He continues to deny any involvement with or knowledge of the woman.'

'He gave them food and shelter, and helped them escape,' Dietrich reminded him. 'He must know something.'

'No doubt, but I do not think he will break easily. He is former Saudi Army, trained to resist interrogation.'

Everyone could be broken. Dietrich knew that much from experience. All you had to do was find the right buttons, and push them.

'We have his family in custody, don't we?'

He had an idea. It wasn't an idea he would have contemplated under normal circumstances, but at that moment he could think of nothing else.

'Yes.'

He looked at the younger man, his expression hardening. 'Better bring them in.'

Chapter 60

With the powerful engine rumbling away, they raced northward on Highway 50, their speed never dropping below 70 miles per hour. There was little to stand in their way at such a late hour.

Drake said nothing, but Anya could feel his silent, brooding anger as he worked to bandage his burned hand. He had injured himself to save her life, she realised. She could have used Frost as a human shield, but she was glad it hadn't come to that.

Still, he was angry with her. She understood why, yet what else could she have done? If she hadn't fought to defend herself, they would both be in custody now, or dead.

She had seen the look in Dietrich's eyes just before Drake intervened. He would have happily killed Frost to get to her.

'How is your hand?' she asked, hoping to concentrate on something practical, something she could deal with.

Drake said nothing.

'Look, I know those people were your friends.' She was groping for a way to express herself. 'You would not want to see them hurt, but—'

'Spare me the lecture, all right?' he bit back. 'I'm not in the mood.'

She fell silent, feeling oddly contrite.

There should have been something she could say, some way to reach out to him and rebuild the trust he had shown in her, but she didn't know how. She wasn't used to dealing with people in this way.

So she kept her eyes on the road and drove, watching the miles slowly creep by. Relationship problems would have to wait for now. Survival was their priority.

That at least was something she was good at.

Their first goal was to put as much distance between themselves and Hussam's house as possible. The assault force would be confused and off balanced by their escape, but that wouldn't last. Soon they would regroup and resume the hunt.

She hoped the old man was all right. He had put himself in great danger by helping her. The Saudi police didn't have much of a reputation for respecting human rights.

You can't think about this now, she scolded herself. You have to concentrate on yourself and your mission. That's all that matters now.

The silence was broken by the buzz of Drake's cell-phone, though he made no move to answer it.

'It must be Munro. Aren't you going to take it?'

He shrugged. 'Fuck him. Let him wait.'

The seconds passed and the phone kept buzzing. Anya was on the verge of reaching for it herself when Drake at last fished it out of his pocket.

'What do you want?'

'So you made it,' Munro concluded. 'Well done.'

Drake was in no mood for congratulations. 'How did you know they were coming for us?'

The older man chuckled. 'Drake, really. A good spy never reveals his sources. You should know that.'

'I'm not a spy.'

'That's a pity. You play the game pretty well,' Munro cut in. 'Speaking of which, is your partner in crime there with you?'

Drake glanced at the older woman. 'She is.'

'Put her on speaker.'

'He wants a word with you,' Drake said, switching the phone to speaker mode.

'Hello, Anya. I'd ask how you've been, but I have a pretty good idea . . .'

'What do you want, Dominic?'

'Now, is that any way to talk to your old friend?' Munro chided her.

Her grip on the wheel tightened. 'We haven't been friends for a long time. Not since you tried to kill me.'

'I did what I had to do, Anya. It was never personal.'

'It was always personal,' she hit back. 'You were jealous, Dominic. You wanted what I had, and you didn't care what you had to do to get it.'

'Fuck you,' he snarled. 'I was trying to save our unit, not destroy it. You were hell bent on fighting the whole fucking Agency yourself . . . You would have got us all killed. I had to stop you.'

The woman smiled a little, knowing she had found a chink in his armour. 'But you couldn't stop me, could you? All your scheming and planning came to nothing. You failed, Dominic. I could have killed you that day. I should have killed you, but I let you live. I took pity on you. That was my mistake.'

Munro was silent for several seconds, though they could both hear his breathing on the line. He was struggling to hold years of rage and anger in check.

'Well, it seems we're both in the habit of sparing each other's lives,' he remarked at last.

'What do you mean?'

'I broke you out of that Russian shithole you were rotting in, Anya. You owe your freedom and your life to me,' he reminded her. 'If it wasn't for me, you'd still be pacing that tiny cell, feeling the walls slowly close in, waiting for the next group of guards to come. Waiting for the next beating, the next interrogation, the next rape.'

Drake watched Anya intently as Munro's words sank in, watched the tiny changes in her facial muscles, the clenched jaw, the gritted teeth, the tightening in her arms and shoulders.

'Or was it really rape?' he taunted. 'Didn't you tell me once that you can learn to accept anything in time? Was that just another thing you learned to accept? Or did you learn to enjoy it?'

'Go fuck yourself,' Drake snapped.

'Stay out of this, Drake. This is none of your fucking business.'

Anya's voice was icy cold, devoid of emotion when she spoke again. 'I did not enjoy it, Dominic. I was wrong. There are some things you can never learn to accept.'

'Then we agree on something at last,' he remarked with grim amusement. 'You have until tomorrow to deliver your source. Don't disappoint me.'

The line went dead.

Anya said nothing, though her eyes burned with cold fire as she stared off into the night.

Hussam sat with his eyes closed, breathing slow and heavy as he waited for what was coming. His hands were bound behind him, the ropes cutting into his flesh. He paid it no heed. He was no stranger to pain.

Blood flowed from his cut lip, and his left eye had swollen almost shut. He'd been roughed up by the Saudi interrogator already, but had said nothing. Beatings he could endure. The more serious stuff would come sooner or later.

Anya must have escaped, otherwise they wouldn't be working on him like this. He smiled a little. They would never catch her. She was too good.

His smile faded as the door swung open and a man walked into the room. He was no Saudi police interrogator. This was a white man, tall and lean, with dark hair and a stern face. Remorseless grey eyes looked him up and down.

Behind him, another man was busy setting up a laptop computer on the metal table opposite. Hussam frowned, wondering what they were planning.

'Mr Khariri, I know you can speak English, so don't insult me by pleading ignorance,' the white man said. 'I want to know where the two fugitives you were harbouring tonight were planning to go. If you give me the information I want, I'll make sure you're treated fairly.'

'I don't know what you are talking about,' Hussam replied.

The man looked unperturbed. 'I had a feeling you'd say that.'

Moving aside, he allowed Hussam to see the laptop that was now up and running. It was displaying a video feed.

His eyes opened wide in shock and horror at what he saw. 'No!' he screamed, straining and twisting against his bonds.

His wife, his daughter and his son were lined up on chairs one after the other, gagged and bound. They were surrounded by several armed men in black masks. He could see abject terror in their eyes.

'You get the picture,' the white man said. 'Tell me what

427

I want to know or watch them die one after the other. Your son will be first.'

'I . . . I don't know anything!'

'Bullshit!' he snarled. 'Tell me what I want to know or your son dies!'

In the observation room opposite, Frost was watching the scene unfold with growing dread. Dietrich was threatening to execute innocent civilians.

He hadn't briefed her on what he was planning, saying only that he was going to play hardball with Khariri, and that they weren't to interfere under any circumstances. Now she knew why.

They had their own laptop, allowing them to see the same video as the one in the interrogation room. She could barely bring herself to look at it.

'Jesus Christ, this is going too far.'

'He knows what he is doing,' Rahul assured her.

That was what she was afraid of. 'Fuck you! I didn't sign up to watch women and children get executed!'

'Are you seriously gonna let this happen, man?' Keegan demanded.

'Be patient,' the Saudi officer urged. 'He will break.'

'Yeah? What if he doesn't?'

He said nothing, just stared at the screen.

'This is your last chance!' Dietrich yelled right in Hussam's face. 'Tell me now. Don't make me do this.'

The old man had tears in his eyes. 'I told you, I know nothing!'

'Fine.' He'd had his chance. Dietrich reached for his radio and without hesitation, barked a single order. 'Kill the boy.'

'No!' Hussam screamed, staring in horror at the screen. The camera was now focused in on his son Amir, his eyes wide with terror as one of the armed men kicked his chair over, drew a pistol with casual ease and fired three rounds into him.

In the observation room, all conversation abruptly stopped. Frost was staring at the image on the laptop, of the small form lying limp and unmoving on the ground. There were tears in her eyes.

'Oh, Christ . . .'

She wanted to throw up.

He had done it. He had really done it.

And she had allowed it to happen.

Hussam's head was down, tears rolling down his cheeks.

Dietrich leaned in close. 'Your son is dead, Mr Khariri,' he said quietly. 'You can't do anything about that now, but you can still save your wife and daughter. I *will* make you watch them both die. Believe that.'

The old man raised his head, eyes blazing with absolute hatred. 'You killed my boy! You will die for this!'

Dietrich's expression didn't change. 'But your wife and daughter will die first. Tell me where they went. Tell me now and put an end to this.'

Hussam said nothing.

'You could save them, but you choose to let them die,' Dietrich said, reaching for his radio again. 'The girl next.'

'All right!' the old man cried. 'All right! Make them stop!'

He lowered the radio, but kept it to hand. 'Talk to me.'

Hussam was broken, defeated when he spoke again. 'I don't know their destination. That is the truth – I swear it! They told me only that they intended to cross the border into Iraq.'

'Give me something useful,' Dietrich implored him.

The old man looked down, tears still in his eyes. 'They had a . . . satellite navigation unit with them. They must be using it to find their destination.'

Dietrich's eyes lit up. 'What kind was it?'

'A Magellan.'

Wasting no time, he turned and strode away, hammering on the door to be let out of the room.

He was back in the observation room alongside Frost, Keegan and Rahul within moments.

'They're using a GPS to navigate,' he said, reaching into his pocket for his pack of cigarettes. His hand was trembling. 'Chances are they bought it after they arrived here. Frost, go back over that security camera footage and find out if they went into any electrical stores.'

'Fuck you,' she replied. 'You murdered an innocent kid, you fucking bastard. You really think I'm going to help you now? I'm done with this shit.'

Saying nothing in reply, Dietrich turned to Rahul. 'Bring up the feeds from the holding area. The real ones this time.'

A few mouse clicks later, and the image on the screen changed to show all three members of Hussam's family being untied from their chairs. They looked pale and shaken, and the daughter was sobbing uncontrollably, but they were alive.

Frost stared at Dietrich in disbelief, the realisation dawning on her at last. 'You faked it.'

All it took was a gun loaded with blanks, and a freeze-frame shot of the boy after his chair had been tipped over, creating the impression that he was lying dead and unmoving. The rest had been accomplished through intimidation and fear.

'I wasn't sure if he'd go for it,' Dietrich admitted. 'It was lucky he didn't look too close.' Lighting up, he took a long draw on the cigarette. 'Now, I need that footage.'

The young woman stared back at him for several seconds, then turned and left the room, saying nothing.

'Gutsy move, man,' Keegan remarked, still shaken by what he'd seen.

'A gamble,' he said simply. 'It paid off.'

Turning away, he closed his eyes and let out a ragged, shuddering breath. He wanted to be sick, but he couldn't stand to see his reflection.

Hate yourself later. Just do your job.

Chapter 61

Turning off the main highway about 50 miles short of Hafar Al Batin, they took a smaller single-track road heading west across the desert, making for a town called Al Jumaymah just short of the border. The Hilux was more than capable of driving off-road, but negotiating a desert at night was a slow and wearying process.

Stopping to switch places, they carried on with Drake at the wheel. Their route took them through a procession of small towns and villages, some developed enough to have shops and basic infrastructure, but most little more than clusters of sandstone buildings surrounded by mud walls, all huddled together like life rafts in an endless sea of sand.

Chancing their luck, they stopped at an isolated gas station just outside a town called Limah. The Hilux had been full when they departed, but its 2-litre engine was thirsty on fuel, and they had covered a lot of miles.

However, by 3.00 in the morning, they were both exhausted and could go no further. The adrenalin rush of their earlier escape had long since faded, leaving them drained and weary.

They would attempt the border crossing just before dawn, giving them a few precious hours to rest up.

Pulling off the road about 20 miles south of Al Jumaymah, Drake drove several hundred yards across rough ground, manoeuvred the jeep down a rocky slope into a wadi and killed the engine.

It was an ideal hiding place. The wadi was deep enough to obscure them from passing vehicles, as well as shield them from the prevailing winds.

Snatching up his AK from the footwell and checking that a round was chambered, Drake pushed open his door and stepped out into the night. It was cool and crisp, the stars glimmering in an almost cloudless sky with only the barest sliver of moon visible in the east. A light breeze stirred up little wisps of sand around them.

The temperature had dropped to about 10 degrees above freezing, which was fine as far as he was concerned. He'd only been in the country for a day and was sick of the burning heat already.

The river that had carved this channel across the landscape had run dry long ago, but withered scrub and straggling bushes still eked out an existence in the old river bed. Gathering up this kindling, they soon had a small fire going.

Exhausted they might have been, but neither was ready to fall asleep.

Leaning against one of the jeep's massive front tyres, Anya busied herself field stripping her AK-47, laying out the working parts on a mat in front of her. She'd known the weapon was in good order from her brief inspection earlier, but cleaning it was one of those little things that made her feel more secure. And it kept her occupied, giving her an excuse not to talk to Drake.

She was wearing just a white vest top, having removed her shirt so she could work more easily. Her hands and arms were soon smeared with gun oil. A loose tendril of blonde hair escaped the tie at the nape of her neck, and she tossed her head back to get it out of the way.

'You should get some sleep while you can,' she suggested. 'We will leave in a few hours.'

Drake didn't reply. He sat hunched over the fire with his rifle cradled in his lap, staring into the flames without seeing anything.

He was still angry with her. She supposed he had a right to be. But she didn't regret what she'd done.

She looked up, staring into the vast darkness of space and the thousands of tiny points of light. 'I am sorry things have turned out as they have, Drake. I am sorry you find yourself stuck out here, with me. And I am sorry you have been forced to fight against your own friends. You do not deserve any of these things.'

Her gaze rested on him again. 'But I am not sorry for what I did back there. I only did what I had to do to survive. I am not proud of it, but I am not ashamed either.'

He was avoiding her eyes, staring instead into the flames.

'You saved my life when you snatched that weapon away. He would have fired on us both. I saw the look in his eyes.' She looked down at her hands, smeared with oil and grease. 'I have not had reason to thank anyone in a long time, Drake, but I thank you now. Twice you have saved my life. Whatever else happens, I won't forget it.'

She sighed and turned her attention back to the weapon. 'That's all I have to say.'

As she carried on working, Drake watched the dancing shadows cast by the fire, the occasional spark drifting upward into the darkness like fireflies.

It was mesmerising, hypnotic. Even as he sat there watching, he could feel the creeping sense of disorientation as his exhausted mind lost its grip on the world.

Images of Anya, of Dietrich and Frost and Jessica and Munro whirled around in his head, blurred together and separated; a confusing kaleidoscope of thoughts and memories and emotions.

He was so tired, it was an effort just to keep his eyes open. If only he could rest just for a moment.

Just for a moment.

With blood painting the inside of the windshield, the ruined car slewed sideways off a road, trailing smoke and steam from its shattered engine. Coming to rest in a shallow ditch, it pitched forward, the passenger door swinging open on broken hinges.

Drake awoke with a start, heart pounding, primal fear surging through his veins, sweat coating his brow. Instinctively he gripped the AK and brought it to bear, frantically searching the darkness for a target.

'Drake!'

He turned, bringing the weapon around. Anya was standing before him, but not as the woman who had returned to the room last night. She appeared as she had that night in Khatyrgan, dressed in filthy ragged clothes, her face and hair stained crimson with blood, her cold blue eyes focused on him, shimmering with that same inhuman lust for murder.

She was horrific, nightmarish. She was a demon made real, and she was coming for him.

His finger tightened on the trigger.

In a sudden blur of movement, he felt something close around his hand. An instant later the weapon was torn from his grip, gone before he could pull the trigger, and his head was jerked around by a hard slap across the face. White light exploded through his brain, blobs of colour like camera flashes imprinted on his eyes.

Hurling the weapon aside, Anya rushed at him, knocked him to the ground and pressed an elbow against his throat.

'I warned you not to point a weapon at me unless you were ready to pull the trigger,' she hissed, her face only inches from his. Do you think you have what it takes to kill me, Drake?'

His answer was to wedge his knee against her chest and drive it upward with all the power he could summon, dislodging her grip and throwing her off. She landed with graceful ease, rolled once to lessen her momentum and sprang back up, ready to finish what he had just started.

'Stop,' he said, holding up his bandaged hand.

His heartbeat was returning to normal, the adrenalin thinning in his blood as the nightmare receded. Like a deadly predator, it had withdrawn to the shadowy recesses of his mind. For now.

She relaxed a little and unclenched her fists, some of the tension leaving her muscles, though she remained on her feet. Her gaze held lingering suspicion, and something else. Sadness.

'What is wrong with you, Drake?'

Wiping a hand across his sweat-soaked brow, he reached for his water bottle and gulped down several mouthfuls, splashing some on his face for good measure.

'I asked you a question.'

He shot her an angry look. 'It's my problem, Anya. Not yours. I don't need you.'

She stared at him intently, watching the tiny changes in expression, the movement of his eyes, the set of his jaw, the tension in his muscles. All of them told her one thing.

'This isn't going to work if we can't rely on each other,' she said at last. 'Do you remember those words? You spoke them to me not so long ago.' Letting out a breath, she lowered herself to her knees, still staring at him. 'If I can't rely on you, if I can't trust you, then we can go no further together. It's that simple.'

'Trust,' he repeated, as if the word were a cruel joke. 'Would you trust me if you knew the things I'd done?'

'Try me.'

He glanced up to the sky, as if seeking answers there. There were none. Only the distant glimmer of the stars, hard and cold and remote.

He swallowed hard and looked her in the eye, steeling himself for what was coming next. He had come down to it at last. There could be no more evasion, no more excuses or reprieves.

All he had left was the truth.

'I shot a kid,' he said at last. 'A little girl. She was twelve years old.'

Anya said nothing. Watching him in the flickering light of the fire, she waited for him to go on. She knew as well as he did that it had to come out.

'It was my first tour in Afghanistan. We'd been in the country a couple of months, running patrols along the highway west of Kandahar. They were worried about the Taliban regrouping in the area to try for an assault on the city, so we were sent in to help secure the western approaches.'

He inhaled deeply, taking a moment to collect himself before he went on. 'We'd bedded down one night in a forward operating base, and we were just passing through the main checkpoint to start our next patrol. Then suddenly we spotted a car coming the opposite way. An old beaten-up thing that looked as old as I was,

437

going full speed straight for the main gate. We tried to wave it down, get the driver to stop so we could inspect it, but he ignored us. He was just staring straight ahead, oblivious. Then I saw his passenger.

'It was a girl. Young, skinny, terrified. I can still see her so clearly. She was wearing a blue dress, her hair was braided. The bastard was using her as a human shield, gambling we wouldn't fire on them. I could see the look in her eyes. She knew she was going to die.'

He trailed off, having to fight just to keep his composure. Anya could see the battle raging within him; the guilt and self-hatred and anger all striving to break through whatever barriers of self-control remained.

She knew what was coming, but she also knew he had to say it for himself. 'Go on,' she said gently.

'The . . . others, the men on my patrol were yelling at me for orders. They knew what was about to happen as well as I did, but they needed me to make the decision. It had to come from me.'

He sniffed and raised his chin. A condemned man facing up to his crime. 'So I gave the order.'

He closed his eyes, seeing for a moment a windshield shattering under a volley of automatic fire, little blossoms of red painting it from the inside. He saw a car slew sideways off a road, trailing smoke and steam from its shattered engine. He saw a door swing open on broken hinges. And like a knife driven into his stomach, he saw a blue dress, tattered and stained crimson. When he opened his eyes again, they were wet with tears.

'I did it. I killed her,' he said quietly. 'Whatever she was, whatever she could have been . . . I took it all away in an instant.' A smile touched his lips then, bitter and filled with disgust. 'And you know the best part? I was *rewarded* for it. I was given a commendation for stopping

438

a suicide bomber. That was how they dealt with it – give them a medal and send them on their way.'

The horrible irony was that the entire incident had earned him a reputation for making difficult decisions under pressure, and brought him to the attention of other, more secretive military units where men with such abilities were in high demand.

Eager to escape the constant reminders of what had happened, he had leapt at the chance, and barely six months later was back in Afghanistan as part of a covert UK–US task force – 14th Special Operations Group. But any hopes of making a fresh start had been utterly dashed by events later that year.

That, however, was a whole other chapter of history. Another series of mistakes and missed opportunities in a life filled with them.

He turned his eyes back towards the fire. 'So you wanted to know the truth about me, Anya. There it is.' He swallowed hard. 'I'm a killer – a murderer.'

He didn't look at her again. He didn't want to see the look in her eyes. The disgust, the embarrassment, the hatred for what he had done. He felt all of those things towards himself, and more.

He heard movement, the slight rustle of footsteps in the sand, and felt the woman sit down beside him. He felt her hand on his arm. He didn't take his eyes off the fire.

'Drake.' Her voice was gentle, but with an undertone of strength and authority that he'd never heard before. 'Drake, look at me.'

His eyes rose to meet hers. She was sitting close. He could smell the faint scent of her, could see the pain and sadness in her eyes.

'Twenty years ago, I killed a man,' she said. 'My first.

He was a Russian sentry, not much more than a boy himself, but he was an enemy with a weapon who could have compromised us. So I took him out like I was trained to do, severed his windpipe with my knife. He didn't even fight back as I cut him, just stared at me like a frightened animal, as if he expected me to stop.' Her throat rose and fell as she swallowed. 'I will never forget the look in his eyes.'

Reaching down, she took his hand and placed it against her chest. He felt the beating of her heart, the strong and steady pulse of life. 'I'm alive now because I killed him. I'm not ashamed of this, and I do not ask for forgiveness. I did what I had to do to survive, just as you did.'

Drake's own heart was pounding as hard as hers. He had never spoken to anyone about what happened, never shared his grief or his guilt, never let it out. But here, at last, he had found someone who understood, who had felt what he did, who knew the same pain.

'We are both soldiers, Drake. No matter what they tried to make us, we are soldiers, and we do what we must to survive. That is the life we chose for ourselves.'

She understood, and she accepted. Without condoning or condemning, she accepted him for who he was and what he'd done.

She understood.

Still clutching his hand, she moved it slowly lower until it was cupping the soft swell of her breast. She was still staring at him in the flickering firelight, her lips slightly parted, breathing a little faster. But there was something else in her eyes now, something primal, something compelling and entrancing.

Always the soldier, she was challenging him, trying to provoke him.

'No,' he rasped, pulling his hand away. 'We're not doing this.'

But she wouldn't let go of his wrist. She had it clamped in a vice-like grip.

'You want me, Drake. I know you do.'

As always, she was right about him. He had wanted her this whole time, even if he'd never consciously acknowledged it. But now there was no denying it. Now he wanted her with such all-consuming ferocity that it left him breathless.

'Not like this,' he said, shaking his head. 'Let go of me.' Trying in vain to pull his hand free, he finally lost patience and shoved her in the chest, knocking her backward.

She rounded on him, her eyes blazing.

'Are you afraid of me?' she taunted. Before he could reply, she had delivered a stinging slap that left his ears ringing and his cheek burning.

'Is that it? Are you a coward, Drake?'

She drew back her arm to slap him again, but this time he caught her by the wrist, and suddenly she was in his arms, her body pressed against him. Her mouth found his, hesitant at first as if the act was unfamiliar to her, then harder and firmer as her need grew more intense.

He could feel the strong beating of her heart, the hot life coursing through her veins. Holding her close, feeling the warmth of her body against his own, he wanted her, needed her with a desperate urgency he'd never known.

He couldn't help what happened next. Sensation and instinct had taken over, driving rational thoughts aside. Exerting her strength, Anya pushed him backward onto the sandy ground and straddled him, her hands tearing at his shirt. His body responded in kind, and he felt his own need rise almost instantly.

441

Grasping the light fabric of her T-shirt, he pulled it quickly off, exposing her full breasts. Anya stifled a gasp as his tongue ran over a nipple contracted by the cold air, and pressed herself against him, running her hands through his hair.

As they kissed again, his hands ran up and down her back, tracing the curve of her spine, her shoulder blades, the firm muscles tightening and releasing. And criss-crossing it all, the faint indentations of scar tissue. He felt no hesitation, no hint of embarrassment or revulsion. They were part of her, testimony to the life she had lived, for good or ill. He accepted them as he accepted everything about her.

Drake was no longer thinking about what he was doing. He perceived what happened next as a series of moments, viewed as if through the eyes of another. He saw himself push her over onto her back, saw the hunger and need in her eyes. He saw himself yank her boots off while she fumbled to undo her belt. Her trousers came away a moment later and he threw them aside, eager, desperate to rejoin her.

In a heartbeat he was on top of her, forceful and unrestrained. There was no hint of fear in her eyes as she lay naked beneath him, her heart racing, blood pumping through her veins. She wanted it as much as he did, and she was ready for him.

We are both soldiers, Drake. No matter what they tried to make us, we are soldiers, and we do what we must to survive. That is the life we chose for ourselves.

Her breath was coming faster with each thrust as she matched his movements with equal force, giving herself as completely as Drake gave himself. Her fingers raked his back, drawing blood, feeling the powerful muscles clench and release with each movement.

He accepted her as she had accepted him, and in the dancing shadows of the fire, they came together the only way they knew. Pleasure and pain, joy and grief, hope and fear mingled together and rose to an unbearable crescendo as their cries mingled together and were lost amidst the endless desert.

Chapter 62

Drake lay by the fire with the woman pressed up against him, her head resting in the hollow of his shoulder, her long blonde hair in tangled disarray. Her body was warm in the cool night air, her breathing slow and regular, but he didn't think she was sleeping.

He wondered if she ever truly slept.

His hand idly traced a path across her shoulder, from the firm deltoid muscle to the hardness of ribs, and finally to the rounded swell of her breast. He noted with a slight feeling of arousal how the skin was thinner and softer there; such a strange contrast of unyielding strength and tender vulnerability combined in one body. He heard an intake of breath as his finger brushed a nipple, feeling it harden under his touch.

She stirred, raised her head to look at him, her normally pale blue eyes shimmering in the firelight. She didn't smile, but there was a sensuous glimmer in her gaze that he had never seen before.

She sighed and looked up at the sky and overhead, at the thousands of tiny points of light glimmering in the darkness.

'It is beautiful here, isn't it?' she said quietly, speaking with the hushed reverence of a pilgrim visiting a holy place. 'When I was a child, my mother once took me outside at night. She pointed up at the sky and told me that the moon and the sun were husband and wife, and the stars were their daughters.' She smiled with faint longing. 'One of the few memories I have of her.

'She still believed in the old ways. The stories of gods and goddesses, demons and spirits of the old world. All the women in her family had learned them, passed down from mother to daughter. She said that one day I would teach them to my own children.' He heard a faint sigh. 'Things did not work out quite the way she expected.'

His hand traced the scars on her back, old wounds from old battles.

'That was where I got my name in the Agency. Maras, the goddess of war and death. I think it was Cain's way of showing respect, paying tribute to my heritage. But . . . it was not a name I would have chosen.'

Letting go of her, Drake sat up and ran a hand through his dishevelled hair, unwilling to meet her questioning stare. 'I'm sorry.'

She frowned. 'For what?'

He gestured at the clothes that lay scattered around them. 'For this. For using you like that. For hurting you. I didn't mean for it to happen.'

It had been rough and fast. Not tender lovemaking, but a sudden, violent act and explosive release. Now that the moment had passed, he was ashamed of his loss of control.

Drake had needs as much as any man, but they had never taken over him as completely as they had tonight. He despised men who couldn't control themselves, who used sexual desire as an excuse for hurting women. Now it had happened to him, and he hated himself for it.

Anya sat up, not bothering to cover herself, and grabbed him by the arms, gripping so hard that it hurt.

'Do you think I'm so weak and fragile that you have

to touch me gently in case I break?' she demanded, visibly angry. 'I can take just as much as you can, and I wasn't afraid of you. I wanted you tonight – all of you, good or bad. Don't you understand that? I didn't want you to hold back.'

'But not like this,' he protested. 'Not after . . . what happened to you.'

'This was nothing like that,' she shot back. 'Believe me, I've lived long enough to know the difference. Do you think I would have *let* you do that to me? It happened because I wanted it, and so did you.'

Drake said nothing to that, because there was nothing to say. She was right, and he knew it.

His expression softened as he looked at her, naked and defiant before him, oblivious to the chill night air. Never in his life had he encountered a woman like Anya. She could endure any hardship, face any danger, over-come any enemy.

She was dangerous and fearless, cold and passionate, beautiful and terrible. She was all of these things, and more.

'All right,' he conceded reluctantly. 'Where do we go from here?'

She smiled and stood up. 'The first thing I'm going to do is put some clothes on. It's cold,' she said, reaching for her T-shirt.

'That's not what I meant.'

'I know what you meant.' She glanced at the sky in the east. It looked the same as any other patch of sky, but she was apparently able to discern some meaning from it. 'It will be dawn in a few hours. You look like you need sleep more than I do. I'll stand watch and wake you when it's time to go.'

She was herself again. The barriers and armour were back up.

446

Pulling her trousers back on, she returned to the other side of the fire and sat down next to the weapon she had dismantled, as if nothing had happened. Drake watched as she reassembled the assault rifle with practised ease, careful to keep her eyes from meeting his.

It would be futile to try to talk to her. Pulling his own clothes back on, Drake crawled into the back seat of the Hilux and closed his eyes. She was right – he was exhausted, but sleep was long in coming.

Chapter 63

He was awoken in the grey half-light of dawn, cold and stiff and uncomfortable. And yet, despite the cold and discomfort, he felt more rested than he had after many a night in a warm bed.

Anya, naturally, was already awake and ready to leave. Breakfast was nothing but a bottle of water that Hussam must have stowed aboard the vehicle, then they were off again, heading north across the desert with the sun just peeking above the eastern horizon.

They crossed the border into Iraq about an hour after sunrise, though the only reason they knew this was because the Magellan said so. There was no signpost, no fence or physical boundary of any kind to mark the transition from Saudi Arabia to Iraq; just endless swathes of desert that seemed to stretch from horizon to horizon.

The terrain was rocky and undulating, forcing them to take a winding route around sand dunes and steep canyons that was both frustrating and time-consuming. Still, after about 5 miles the ground evened out, allowing them to pick up the pace a little.

Buried beneath the drifting sands of Iraq were vast reserves of oil conservatively estimated at more than 140 billion barrels, the second largest in the world, but most of these fields were concentrated in the south and north-east of the country. The western half of Iraq was, by contrast, vast and mostly empty desert, devoid of strategic or commercial value.

As a result, they encountered no other vehicles during this time. No military installations, no checkpoints, no observation posts, nothing.

The only sign of humanity came when they cruised past a small group of men on camels, swathed in robes and headscarves. They were Bedouin, the nomadic tribesmen who lived in the deserts where few others could survive. The invasion and the ongoing war in Iraq probably meant nothing to them – their way of life had carried on unbroken for hundreds of years, and would likely continue to do so for hundreds more.

Sitting in the passenger seat, Drake tensed and relaxed his right hand, wincing as the stiff muscles protested. It had been paining him since he'd woken up, no doubt due to the cold night.

'That hand bothers you,' Anya remarked without turning round. It was her first real attempt at communication all day.

'It's stiff sometimes in the morning,' he explained. 'It's nothing.'

'You injured it?'

He nodded. 'In a fight. A long time ago.'

'What kind of fight?'

For some reason, he felt himself blush. 'A boxing match.'

'*You* were a prizefighter?'

'Is that so hard to believe?' he asked, feeling slighted.

She gave him a dubious look. 'I took you for an intelligent man.'

'Jesus, you sound like my mother,' he couldn't help retorting. 'Anyway, you're hardly in a position to criticise me for fighting.'

She shrugged. 'Killing for duty or ideology is one thing. Beating a man unconscious for money is another.' She looked over at him. 'Anyway, this fight of yours. What happened?'

Drake sighed, thinking back to that night. 'Well, as unlikely as it might seem, I was a pretty decent prospect in my day. I turned professional after a year or so, won my first eight fights by knockout, and soon people started taking notice. Then I got talked into fighting some old piece of shit club fighter. A big old brawler; you know the sort. He would have been a real threat ten years earlier, but by the time I ran into him, he was slow and out of shape. He was only out to make some money before he retired, and I was happy to send him on his way. I knocked him down sixty seconds into the first round. He got up, so I knocked him down in the second. And he got up again.

'No matter what I did, no matter how many times I hit him, the stupid bastard just wouldn't stay down. He was fighting as if his life depended on it.' He shook his head, still struggling to accept it. 'I broke both my hands trying to knock him out.'

He looked down, slowly tensing his hand into a fist. Just for a moment, he felt the power that had once been there, heard the roar of the crowd cheering him on.

'It was six months before I was cleared to fight again.'

'But you did not go back?'

He shook his head. 'I'd moved on. I wasn't making any money sitting on my arse waiting for my licence to get renewed, so I'd had to find a job. I suppose I lost the edge in those six months, and you don't get it back easily.'

'You mean your pride took a beating.'

'I didn't feel like starting all over again, working my

450

way up through shitty club fights for fifty-quid purses,' he replied with more heat than he'd intended. 'Bit of a fucking climb-down when you were on the brink of a title shot.'

She'd pushed his buttons, and she knew it. 'Well, at least you learned something from that fight.'

'Yeah? What's that?'

She offered a wry half-smile that he'd come to know all too well. 'Just because someone is old, doesn't mean they can't hurt you.'

'This is them right here,' Frost said, indicating the slightly fuzzy CCTV image of a woman with blonde hair and a man walking into an electrical retailer. 'They went in at 14.07, and they came out again eight minutes later. You can see the package Drake's carrying.'

The young woman looked drawn and haggard, as well she might. She had been up most of the night trawling through surveillance footage yet again, searching for clues on where Drake and Anya might have stopped to buy a GPS system.

At last her perseverance had paid off, and she'd found them entering a store within the airport terminal itself.

Dietrich exhaled, impressed by her sheer, bloody-minded determination. It was a shame she was such a prickly little bitch. 'Good work, Frost.'

'Stop it, I'm getting all misty eyed.'

He laid a congratulatory hand on her shoulder, forgetting it had been dislocated only hours before. His gesture elicited a sharp gasp of pain, and an angry glare.

'Sorry,' he amended, turning to Rahul. 'We need the manager of that store. I want to know the serial number of the unit he sold them.'

Once they had that, they could contact the manufacturer,

find out the specific frequency that the unit operated on and use it to triangulate a position. It was perfect. The GPS system would be doing exactly what it was designed to do, except it wouldn't just be telling Drake and Anya where they were.

The Saudi man nodded, already reaching for his phone.

Chapter 64

'This is it,' Drake said, checking their latitude and longitude on the Magellan for the third time.

Had the GPS unit not assured him that they were in the right location, he would have had his doubts. They were in a rocky, unremarkable stretch of desert at the base of a low rounded hill. The village of Ash Shabakah lay a mile or so to the north-west, hidden from view by the hill.

Bringing the Hilux to a stop, Anya killed the engine, picked up her AK and stepped out. Drake was by her side a moment later.

It was early evening, with the sun now well past its zenith and drifting lazily down towards the western horizon. It was still brutally hot though, the dry dusty air searing their throats with each breath.

'You're sure this is the place?' Drake asked, scanning the rocky ground around them. He was beginning to wonder if Anya's contact had sent them off on a wild goose chase.

'It is the location he gave me.'

'So where is he?'

Ignoring him, Anya crept forward with her assault rifle at the ready, keeping herself low. She had only gone a dozen paces before she stopped and knelt down to examine the ground ahead.

'Tracks,' she said without looking up. 'Recent. A man, average height, wearing civilian shoes. He walks with a limp.'

'Now you're just showing off.'

She shrugged. 'I am telling you what I see.'

Drake wasn't about to argue. Tracking was a skill he'd learned because his profession had once required it, but he'd never had much aptitude for it. Those who could read the subtle clues to be found in a footprint, the differences in weight distribution, stride length and wear patterns were a breed apart as far as he was concerned.

Together they continued up the slope, following the faint tracks that Anya was able to discern. Both had their weapons up and ready, watching for any movement, any sign that this might be an ambush. Dust and sand swirled around them, stirred up by the hot breeze.

A tangle of large weathered boulders lay up ahead, blocking their advance. Glancing at his companion, Drake pointed right. Anya nodded, indicating that she would go left.

Gripping the AK tight, Drake crept forwards. The weapon was a heavy weight in his hands, the feed mechanism rattling a little with each step he took. Already the working parts were coated in dust, but he knew that didn't matter. The AK could fire in almost any condition.

Backing up against a rock that jutted out of the ground as if some giant had hurled it there with great force, he took a deep breath to compose himself, and rounded the obstacle.

Anya moved at the same moment, and together they met on the far side. To their surprise, they found themselves staring into a small darkened fissure in the side of the hill, perhaps 4 feet high and 3 feet wide. A cave.

'The tracks lead inside,' Anya said, crouching down to examine the faint spoor. She sniffed the air. 'Tea.'

Drake frowned. 'Tea?'

'I will go first. Stay close.' Gripping the weapon one-handed and wielding a flashlight in the other, she crawled inside. Drake was right behind.

The passageway was rough and uneven, twisting and winding its way through the hill, always changing in size and shape. It soon grew tall enough to stand upright, though at times the passage was so tight that Drake had to squeeze between the rocky walls, feeling as if they were pressing in on him.

Anya had been right about the smell. He hadn't noticed it outside, but he detected it now; the faint aroma of tea steeping. Someone was in here with them, but where?

Suddenly light flooded the cave around them as an electric arc light was switched on, pointed straight at them. Their weapons were up in an instant, safety catches off, fingers tight on triggers.

'There is no need for that, my friends,' a voice assured them. It was a man's voice, high-pitched and nasal.

Anya's eyes narrowed. 'Typhoon?'

'Please, lower your weapons.' When they hesitated, he added, 'I trusted you by agreeing to meet today, so trust me now. I would not want to ruin our relationship before we have even been introduced.'

They glanced at each other, seemed to reach some mutual consensus and lowered their assault rifles.

The light was turned aside, revealing a man seated on a low rocky outcrop about 10 yards away on the other side of the cavern. The powerful glow cast his features into sharp relief.

Whatever Drake had been expecting from Anya's mysterious intelligence source, it hadn't been this.

He was a young man, probably a few years younger than Drake, with a thin, almost gaunt face and sharp, bony features. He was balding and slender in build, with narrow sloping shoulders and a thin neck that made his shirt seem far too large. He was wearing a pair of glasses with a crack running through one of the lenses, though his dark eyes spoke of shrewd intelligence.

His attention was focused on Anya, a hesitant smile parting his lips. 'I had given up hope of ever meeting you.' His English was excellent, Drake noted. 'It is very strange to see you standing before me now.'

'I hope you are not disappointed,' she replied.

'Surprised, but not disappointed.' He rose from his makeshift seat and walked towards them, moving with a pronounced limp. 'As your American friends are fond of saying, it is better late than never.'

Halting in front of her, he held out his hand. 'My name is Majid Zebari.'

'Anya,' she replied, taking his hand. 'My companion is Drake.'

Zebari shook hands with him. 'A pleasure to meet you, Mr Drake.'

'And you.'

Zebari's eyes opened wider in surprise. 'You are English. Interesting.' He glanced back at Anya. 'I have brewed tea, if you would like some?'

Without waiting for an answer, he turned and limped back over to what seemed to serve as a makeshift living space. A propane gas stove had been set up, with a blackened mess tin steaming over it.

'Forgive me for dragging you all the way out here, but I wanted a safe location for our meeting.' He indicated the large cavern surrounding them. 'I used to play in these caves as a boy. Believe me, I know them well enough to escape if need be.'

Drake had suspected as much. Any assault team who tried to storm the place would have a tough time securing all the exits. There was no telling how deep or how far the cave network ran.

'And as you can probably tell, I am not so light on my feet these days,' he added with a shy smile that somehow made him seem much younger.

Easing himself down onto his makeshift seat, he stretched his left leg out. Drake caught a glimpse of a metal brace holding his ankle stiff.

'A little memento from the invasion,' he explained, with a glance at Anya. 'A bomb exploded outside my office. I was trapped in the rubble for two days.'

His implication was obvious. He wouldn't be a cripple right now if Anya had met him when they'd first agreed.

'Majid, I was told that you were a highly placed intelligence source inside Hussein's regime . . .' Anya began, ignoring his subtle rebuke.

At this, the young man snorted in amusement. 'Highly placed? Far from it. Still, I should be grateful I wasn't, otherwise I would likely be dead or in prison by now. No, I was an analyst for the Mukhabarat; little more than a filing clerk, really.' He adjusted his cracked glasses, which had begun to slip down his long nose. 'And now here I am, a penniless computer repair man with a false name and a broken pair of glasses.'

Anya's face fell, and Zebari smiled at her reaction.

'But even computer repair men can be useful.'

'At last! We've got them,' Frost exclaimed.

Dietrich was by her side in moments. 'Where are they?'

'We just downloaded the tracking signal from

457

Magellan,' she said, pointing to the latitude and longitude coordinates laid out on the screen. 'According to this, it's a spot out in the southern Iraqi desert, about a mile from a village called Ash Shabakah.'

Fishing out his phone, he dialled Franklin's number at Langley. It only took one ring for the man to answer.

'We've found them.'

'Six years ago I was working for Directorate Eight of the Political Bureau,' Zebari explained. 'We were responsible for logistics and technical support for covert operations. Then, all of a sudden I was transferred to a special project, working under Colonel Mohammed al-Masri. They wanted someone to keep records, log transactions, monitor the flow of money through the Bureau. Our budget was one hundred and fifty million US dollars, with the option for another fifty if needed.'

Anya leaned forward, staring at him intently. 'What was the goal of the project?'

'The purchase of chemical and biological weapons from a foreign supplier. Fifty tonnes of weaponised anthrax spores, five tonnes of VX nerve agent, and five hundred pounds of highly enriched uranium, plus centrifuge technology and design blueprints for primitive tactical nuclear warheads.'

Drake stared at him. 'My God . . .'

'The intention was to use it as a deterrent to invasion,' Zebari explained. 'It was an insane gamble, but those were desperate times. The government knew an invasion would happen sooner or later, and they were looking for any possible way to repel it. The chemical and biological weapons would be useful, but it was the nuclear technology we wanted most of all. With that, we knew the US would have to deal with us diplomatically.'

'Who was the supplier?' Anya asked.

Zebari took a sip of his tea. 'I do not know. I never met the man, but he claimed his name was Yevgeni and that he used to be with Russian military intelligence.'

Jesus, no wonder the Russians were so interested in Anya, Drake mused. If she had exposed the fact that one of their own was selling nuclear secrets to the Iraqis, the repercussions would have been devastating.

'He seemed to be legitimate. He was able to provide us with full technical details, plans for how the delivery would be made, and samples of all the materials he was selling as proof of his commitment. In return we made an initial payment of ten million dollars to secure the rest.'

'So what happened?' Drake asked. 'Where are these weapons now?'

'Nowhere,' he replied flatly. 'The deal never went ahead. When the Americans invaded Afghanistan in 2001, factions in my government knew they would soon turn their attention to Iraq. Your president was eager to fight, and after the attacks in New York he had all the justification he needed. We realised we could never develop nuclear weapons in time to prevent an invasion, so the deal was cancelled, we destroyed our existing stocks of chemical and biological weapons and Yevgeni disappeared.'

Anya leaned back, crushed by the news. She had banked everything on this, on being able to secure the proof of WMD programmes that the Agency so desperately wanted. What she had found was the exact opposite.

'Let me guess – Yevgeni never returned his deposit,' Drake remarked.

Zebari nodded, the movement dislodging his glasses again. 'Indeed. We searched for him, but by that point we had far more pressing concerns. The whole thing was such a fiasco that nobody wanted to be reminded of it, so it was all swept aside.'

'So what the hell do we have here?' Drake said. 'A weapons deal that fell through, a mysterious Russian supplier who disappeared with ten million dollars in Iraqi money, weapons of mass destruction that don't exist . . .' He shook his head. 'We've got fuck all.'

Anya looked away for a moment, deep in thought. Then, after a moment, she turned her gaze on Zebari once more. 'You say you know little about the supplier, except the name he gave you?'

'Correct.'

'And you never saw him in person?'

He shook his head. 'He was careful to preserve his anonymity. But he was a thorough man. He had already drawn up plans for getting the material covertly into the country.'

'How, exactly?'

Zebari sighed, searching his memory. 'Through a private shipping company that he controlled, based out of South Africa, I think. They were called . . . Infinity Exports.'

Drake heard the sharp intake of breath, and turned to look at Anya. She was staring wide-eyed at Zebari, her face frozen in shock and horror. The colour had drained out of her, as if her very blood had stopped in her veins.

'What is it?' he asked.

She ignored him, focusing on Zebari. 'You are sure of this? You are sure it was Infinity Exports?'

He thought it over for a moment, then nodded affirmation.

Anya stood up and turned away, holding a hand against her forehead. 'No . . . It's not possible,' she gasped. 'It's not possible.'

Striding over to her, Drake gripped her arm and spun her around to face him. 'Anya, talk to me. What's going on?'

'Infinity Exports is a front company,' she said. 'They handle illegal arms shipments all over the world. They even helped supply the Mujahideen rebels when I was operating in Afghanistan.' Shrugging out of his grasp, she turned away again, trembling with barely suppressed fury. 'It's the Agency, Drake. They set up the entire thing.'

Chapter 65

'We've got them,' Franklin said, unable to hide his smile. 'They've stopped near a small village in southern Iraq. We have satellite coverage of the entire area. Dietrich and his team are gearing up to intercept them right now. They can be on site in under an hour.'

But to his surprise, Cain's face remained stony and impassive as he surveyed his subordinate across his desk.

'That won't be necessary, Dan.'

Franklin frowned. 'I . . . don't understand, sir. We're ready to roll on this one. We've been chasing them for—'

'I said it won't be necessary,' Cain repeated, his voice cold and hard. 'I can't afford to let them slip through the net again. I've got my own team who will handle the takedown.'

Franklin couldn't believe what he was hearing. They had been on this case since the beginning, and at the final moment Cain has them removed? 'Sir, I—'

'Order your team to stand down. I won't ask you again,' the older man said. 'Do you have a problem with that?'

Franklin opened his mouth to protest, then thought better of it. Cain could relieve him of duty with a snap of his fingers. 'No, sir.'

'Good.' Cain turned his attention back to his work. 'You have your orders, Dan. Now follow them.'

*   *   *

'What is the meaning of all this?' Zebari asked.

'It was a set-up,' Drake explained. The pieces had fallen into place for him almost as fast as they had for Anya. 'The CIA were trying to sell your country illegal weapons because they knew their case for invasion would eventually hinge on it. One of their men poses as a Russian arms dealer, sells you the gear and vanishes, then a couple of months later their tanks roll into Baghdad and they find everything they need to justify the war.' He shook his head, stunned by their audacity. 'Fucking unbelievable.'

Zebari blanched, dumbstruck by what he had just learned. In that moment, the deal he'd gambled his future on had ceased to exist. He was an enemy of the CIA, not a potential ally. He alone possessed the knowledge and evidence to expose what they had done.

Anya stayed out of the conversation. Her mind was in turmoil.

Turning her attention back to Zebari, she strode over and gripped him by his narrow, bony shoulders. 'You can prove all of what you have just said?'

'I kept a digital record of all the email conversations, all the signed agreements, bank account numbers . . . everything.'

The woman's expression hardened as a plan took shape in her mind. 'Then listen to me, and listen well. Forget the CIA, forget the Russians and the Iraqis. *Your life* hangs in the balance now. If you want to stay alive, you will come with us and do exactly as we tell you.'

The young man stared at her wide-eyed. 'You will honour our deal?'

She nodded again. 'It might not happen the way we planned, but I will see to it that you get a new life and all the money you need. But only if you deliver your proof.'

He paled visibly at her threat, but raised his chin and did his best to meet her baleful gaze. 'I will not let you down.'

Drake gripped the woman's arm. 'What are you planning, Anya?'

The look in her eyes reminded him of that moment in Khatyrgan when she had stood over the corpse of the guard she'd killed, drenched in blood and smiling with vicious glee, only it was colder, more controlled now. And somehow, he knew that was far more dangerous.

'Retribution.' She looked at Zebari again. 'Come on. We don't have much time.'

'What do you mean we've been denied?' Dietrich raged. 'We're on the ready line, for Christ sake. We can end this thing right now.'

'This came straight from Cain,' Franklin said, hating every word. 'He's ordered us to stand down.'

'And what do *you* say, Dan?'

Franklin looked down, still clutching the phone to his ear. Dietrich was asking him to disobey direct orders from the director of the entire division.

'It's not my call. I'm sorry.'

'Yeah. Me too.' The derision and scorn in his voice was obvious even on a bad line from the other side of the world.

Saying nothing further, Franklin shut down the call and laid his cellphone on the desk, staring at it for a long moment as the anger and resentment boiled away inside him.

'Fuck!' he snarled, slamming his fist down on the polished surface.

His thoughts were interrupted when his desk phone started ringing. Gritting his teeth, he snatched it up.

'What?' he demanded.

'I-I'm sorry to disturb you, sir,' a voice stammered, unnerved by his harsh tone. 'It's Sinclair in the ops room. We've got a problem here.'

Who doesn't? 'What is it?'

'We just lost the satellite feeds from the target area. We're blind.'

He frowned. 'Are they out of range?'

'No, sir. I called the National Reconnaissance Office and the bird is still overhead. The feeds have been rerouted internally. Someone shut us down.'

In that moment, the truth dawned on him. It was Cain. He didn't want them to see what he was about to do.

'I . . .' He trailed off, his gaze resting on the picture taken of himself and Drake when they were serving together in Afghanistan. Both young, both grinning like idiots, both convinced of their own invincibility.

'Come up to my office right away, Sinclair. Hurry.'

What he was about to say had no place on an internal phone.

Emerging into the blinding light of early evening, they stood blinking for a few moments as their eyes adjusted. The Hilux lay where they had left it, perhaps 50 yards further down the slope.

'We will cross the border back into Saudi Arabia tonight,' Anya decided, starting towards the vehicle. 'Then we will contact as many news agencies as we can find and give them Zebari's evidence.'

'You know this could bring down the entire Agency,' Drake warned her, matching her stride. 'When news of this gets out, it won't stop.'

Already he could envision the chain reaction of scandals, investigations, resignations and disgraces, each compounded by the ones that had come before, each bringing the entire US intelligence machine closer to disaster. Personal grudges would resurface, old wounds would be reopened, mistrust and paranoia would spread like wildfire, until at last the entire thing collapsed like a house of cards.

Her eyes flashed like steel. 'I have no loyalty to them now.'

I will show no mercy. I will never hesitate. I will never surrender.

Drake could see the determined set of her shoulders, the purpose in her stride, the tension in her back. She was committed to this cause; she would see it through to the end, or die trying.

'Haven't you forgotten something?'

She stopped for a moment and turned to face him.

'Munro. He's the reason we're here. He might have the same goal.'

She thought about it for a moment. 'Maybe,' she conceded. 'But I can't trust him. Munro would see me dead long before he moves against the Agency – I have no doubt about that.'

She turned to walk away.

'And what about my sister?'

That stopped her in her tracks.

'She's innocent. She doesn't deserve to be caught up in this. Those were your words. Or have you forgotten?'

She didn't look at him, but he saw her head tilt down, saw the look of grim determination on her face. 'I haven't forgotten.'

'If we don't hand Zebari over, she's dead. He'll execute her.'

Anya said nothing.

'Who is this Munro?' Zebari asked, nervously watching

the confrontation brewing between his two would-be saviours.

'Stay out of this,' Drake hissed, in no mood to explain the situation. 'You know what I said was true, Anya. Can you live with that?'

'I have lived with a lot of things, Drake,' she assured him. 'If I must, I can live with one more.'

She started walking away again, keeping her back to him.

'Well, I can't,' he said, reaching for the AK slung over his shoulder. No way was he letting her walk with the one man who could save his sister's life. If need be, he would take Zebari himself.

She was way ahead of him. Spinning around, she charged, summoning a terrifying burst of speed, her eyes burning with cold fire. Even as he brought the rifle to bear, she closed the distance between them, swept her hand up and seized the barrel, twisting it aside.

Before he could yank the weapon clear, she delivered a stinging right cross that snapped his head back, leaving stars dancing across his vision. His grip slackened, and an instant later he felt the rifle torn from his hand.

'Don't try to stop me, Drake,' she warned, tossing the weapon aside like a toy. 'I don't want to hurt you.'

Focused on each other as they were, neither of them heard the sharp, vicious hiss of an inbound missile travelling at close to the speed of sound. Neither of them thought to look up, to watch for the telltale white streak of exhaust gases.

But what happened next was more than enough to get their attention.

Their first impression was of a blinding white flash, followed almost immediately by a horrific orange glow that lit the ground around them. The next moment, the concussive blast wave hit like a physical blow, knocking them both to the ground. A deafening roar filled the air, tearing through them as if to split them apart from the inside.

Chapter 66

'There's nothing I can do, Frost,' Dietrich said irritably as he lit up another cigarette. 'Franklin says to stand down, we stand down.'

'Fuck Franklin, and fuck his orders! Are you just going to abandon Drake? Is that right?' she demanded. She was bristling with anger, oblivious to the fact that he was almost a foot taller than her. 'You know, for a minute there I was actually starting to think you weren't a complete asshole. Shows how fucking wrong I was.'

Suddenly he rounded on her. 'What do you expect me to do?'

'What's right,' she replied simply.

Dietrich turned away in disgust.

Going against orders would spell the end of whatever career he had left, destroy any future he had a hope of building. She was asking the impossible.

He wasn't going to do that. Not now. Not for Drake.

'Drake could have left you behind in that prison,' Frost reminded him. 'Instead he risked his life to save yours. Doesn't that mean anything to you?'

Dietrich closed his eyes, willing himself not to listen. He was going to lose everything. With one stupid, emotional decision, he would lose everything he'd fought to regain.

'I guess I was right about you all along, Dietrich,' Frost

469

concluded, turning to walk away. 'You're a coward. You always were.'

Dietrich said nothing as he took a deep pull on his cigarette.

It took Sinclair all of three minutes to climb two flights of stairs and sprint down 50 yards of corridor to Franklin's office. He was red faced and out of breath by the time he entered.

Franklin rose from his desk and walked over to join him, keeping his voice low. 'Sinclair, I want you to listen very carefully to what I'm about to say. Whatever else is going on here, Director Cain is pursuing his own agenda.'

'Y-yes, sir,' the young technician replied hesitantly.

'He's the one who shut down our satellite coverage.' Sinclair's eyes lit up.

'Something's about to happen that he doesn't want us to see.' Franklin leaned forward and eyed him hard. 'I want two things from you. First I want you to monitor all incoming and outgoing communications from Cain's office.'

You just crossed the line, a voice in his head told him. There will be no coming back from this.

Sinclair swallowed, daunted at the prospect of hacking the divisional director's computer. 'If I get caught . . .'

'If you get caught, you'll tell them that I specifically ordered you to do it. I'll take full responsibility for everything.' He gripped the man by the shoulders. 'Now, can it be done?'

Sinclair thought it over for several seconds, his mind racing. 'There's a back door in the firewall I can exploit,' he finally admitted. 'Nobody else knows about it. It won't be pretty, but it should work.'

'Good. Get on it.'

'And the second thing, sir?' Sinclair prompted.

Franklin chewed his lip. 'I need that satellite link back.'

'Sir, are you sure you want to do this? If Director Cain finds out . . .'

Franklin sighed, took a step back and glanced over at the framed picture again. 'You see that photograph? Five years ago my Humvee hit a roadside bomb in Afghanistan. When I came to, the vehicle was upside down and on fire. I couldn't move my legs, couldn't get out. I knew then I was going to burn to death. But one man came back to pull me out. Only one.' He turned to look at the young man again. 'Drake risked his life to save mine. I owe him.'

Sinclair stared at him, shocked by what he'd heard. But at last he nodded. 'I understand.'

'Good. Then get to work.'

Drake was in a fog. A world without dimension, with only the pounding of his own heartbeat to interrupt the dull ringing in his ears. With great effort he forced his eyes open, finding himself lying face down on hard stony ground. Anya was a few yards away, her face obscured by a tangle of blonde hair.

What the hell had happened?

Groaning in pain, he managed to get an arm beneath himself and sat up, his back cracking as he did so. He could feel blood on his arms and face where sharp rocks and debris had cut him, but he didn't seem to be seriously hurt. Everything still worked.

The Hilux was another story. Almost nothing

remained of the vehicle, save for a few smoking, twisted scraps of metal embedded in the 5-metre-wide crater where it had sat. It had been obliterated by high explosives, but from where? And by whom?

Hearing movement at his side, he turned to see Anya pulling herself upright, wincing in pain. A growing red patch stained her shirt just above her left hip, perhaps a piece of shrapnel from the destroyed vehicle. He couldn't tell how bad the injury was.

She looked at him, her expression a mixture of uncom-prehending shock and pain.

Then suddenly her eyes flicked over his shoulder, and he saw her tense up. She had seen something. Her hand went for the assault rifle lying beside her.

'Don't move!' a voice cried out. It was male. American.

Twisting around, Drake found himself staring at a man in black fatigues and full combat gear. He was covering them with an M4 carbine, the US military's standard assault rifle.

Another man rose from behind a boulder next to him, armed and dressed in similar fashion. Within moments, they were surrounded by six operatives, all carrying automatic weapons.

Anya remained frozen where she was, her hand poised in the midst of reaching for the AK.

'Lie the fuck down right now!' the man commanded. 'Lie down with your hands behind your heads. Do it, or we open fire.'

To resist would be futile. As fast and dangerous as she was, even Anya couldn't defend herself against six men who had the drop on her.

Withdrawing her arm, she eased herself down onto her stomach and placed her hands behind her head. Drake did likewise, staring into his erstwhile companion's eyes as footsteps crunched on the stony ground towards them.

He saw no fear there.

Nearby, Zebari was whimpering in pain as his hands were bound and he was hauled roughly to his feet.

One of their captors, perhaps the leader, keyed his radio transmitter. 'Targets secure. We're coming in.'

Chapter 67

The operations room was almost empty, save for Franklin and Sinclair. He had ordered all other personnel to leave, explaining that their part in the operation was over, just as Cain had instructed.

'We're in,' Sinclair said, speaking low and urgent as if afraid someone might overhear. His fingers danced across the keyboard, a blur of frantic movement. 'I'm through the firewall. Access server routing grid, redirect incoming feed, and . . .'

The viewing window in his laptop sprang into life, showing an overhead video feed from the site in Iraq where Drake's vehicle had parked up.

'Bingo.'

Franklin leaned in close, ignoring the aching pain in his back as he studied the screen.

'Oh, shit.'

Drake's vehicle was gone, replaced by a smoking, wreckage-strewn crater. It must have been hit by some kind of high-powered explosive ordinance, because almost nothing remained of it.

But there were other vehicles nearby; two of them. 4x4s of some kind, though he couldn't identify them from the air. Black-clad figures were sweeping the area, escorting three prisoners towards the nearest vehicle. Two men and a woman.

It had to be Drake and Anya. He couldn't tell who the third man was.

Bundling them into the truck, the remaining armed men mounted the second vehicle and, in a spray of dust and sand, they took off, heading north.

'Son of a bitch.'

Turning away, he dug his phone out and dialled Dietrich's number.

'Yeah!' the older man answered, yelling to be heard over a muted roar in the background.

'Jonas, I can barely hear. Where the hell are you?'

'I'm outside. It's a sandstorm here. What do you want, Dan?'

Franklin closed his eyes for a moment, straightened his shoulders and raised his chin a little, steeling himself against the recriminations that would one day descend on him.

'Change of plans. You have a green light to go after Drake. I say again, you have a green light.'

He couldn't have sworn to it, but he thought he heard the man laugh. 'I was hoping you'd say that. We're airborne now and en route. It seems we "borrowed" a Saudi Army chopper.'

The son of a bitch had ignored his instructions and launched the operation on his own initiative. Franklin might have been angry were it not for his own blatant insubordination.

'They've been taken prisoner by some kind of Black Ops team. I don't know who they are, but we can assume they're working for Cain. They're currently heading north in a pair of 4x4s. We're downloading the satellite feeds to you now.'

'Got it. What are the rules of engagement on this one?'

'Don't fire unless fired upon. They might be working

for Cain, but we don't know their intentions yet. I won't kill our own men without good reason.'

'And if they do engage us?'

Franklin exhaled. 'Do what you have to.'

'Understood.' Dietrich hesitated a moment. 'Oh, and Dan?'

'Yeah?'

'Thanks.'

He couldn't help but smile. He was staring at the end of his career, and he had never felt more certain that he was doing the right thing.

'Good luck.'

Drake was jolted forward in his seat as the vehicle screeched to a halt amidst a cloud of swirling dust. Gloved hands grabbed him and hauled him outside, giving him his first proper look at his surroundings.

It was an airfield, or had been once. Blackened, bombed-out buildings, ruined vehicles and concrete runways pockmarked with deep craters were everywhere. The place hadn't been in use for years, no doubt bombed into submission prior to the invasion.

An aircraft boneyard stretched away to his right; line after line of ancient MiG-23 and 25 fighters lying abandoned, most of them hacked apart and broken up so that looters could salvage the valuable components inside. All that remained were the empty air frames, rusty and weathered.

Jerking him forward, his armed captor led him towards the nearest building, probably once used as the base's air control tower and operations centre. The steel doors at the main entrance had been blown open, lying twisted and broken on both sides of the corridor beyond.

It was dark inside as they carried on, the electric lights

having long since stopped working. The only illumination came from a couple of glow sticks dropped at regular intervals, investing the passageway with an eerie green light.

Anya was somewhere behind him, shoved from time to time if she didn't move fast enough. She said nothing, and neither did he. These men were here to bring them in, not to answer questions.

They were approaching a room at the far end of the corridor, perhaps once the operations room. He could hear voices within, along with the hum of machinery. The flickering glow of computer monitors played against the wall opposite.

Shoved inside, he stopped only for a moment before a sharp blow between his shoulder blades dropped him to his knees. A grunt of pain to his right told him that Anya had been made to kneel in similar fashion.

He twisted around to look at her. Her hair had escaped the tie at her neck and hung in disarray, she was covered in small cuts and grazes, and her face was tight with pain from the shrapnel wound in her side.

Beyond her, Zebari had also been thrown to his knees, though he was unable to balance on his crippled leg and pitched forward to land in a heap. He was trembling with unconcealed terror.

'Well, well. Ryan Drake,' a familiar voice taunted.

Glancing around, Drake watched as Munro walked into the room from another doorway to the left, smiling with pleasure while his glass eye glittered in the glow of computer screens. Like the others, he was dressed in black combat gear, his heavy boots crunching through the debris that littered the floor. He was a big man, both tall and physically strong judging by his broad chest and the tight corded muscle in his arms and shoulders.

But it was more than that. There was a presence about him, a charisma, a dominating air of command and that went far beyond physical size. Munro had been a leader of men, born to take them into battle, and despite everything, he remembered that.

'It's good to finally meet face to face.'

Drake glared back at him. 'I wish I could say the same. Where's my sister?'

Munro smiled. 'Family loyalty. It's so fucking touching.' Turning towards the doorway he'd just come through, he raised his voice. 'Barnes, bring her in.'

Drake's breath caught in his throat as a woman in dirty, sweat-stained office clothes was pushed roughly into the room. Her captor, a middle-aged man with a shaved head and a long grey goatee, was just a pace or two behind, keeping her covered with a Glock pistol.

Her hands were bound behind her back, just like Drake's. Her shoulder-length brown hair was in disarray, stray locks falling in front of her face, grimy with sweat and dirt. She had clearly been kept in poor living conditions for the past couple of days, yet he could see no obvious signs of abuse. No bruising, cuts or grazes. Her eyes, vivid green like his own, were locked on him.

'Ryan!' she cried, trying to run to him. A hard blow to the back of the neck dropped her to her knees, dazed and moaning in pain.

'You fuck,' Drake spat, glaring at Barnes with absolute hatred. His wrists strained against the cuffs with bruising force.

'I'm a man of my word, Drake,' Munro said, unconcerned with the casual violence. 'I said you'd be reunited with your sister. If you have anything to say, I'd do it now.'

'Jess. Jess, look at me,' Drake implored her, his voice

softer now, gentle and coaxing. It was the same voice he used to use when they were children, and she was angry with him.

Blinking to refocus her vision, the woman looked up at him. Her eyes were wet with tears. 'Ryan . . . I'm sorry,' she managed to say, struggling to hold it together now that they were so close.

It was more than he could bear to see her like this. His voice was thick, his throat tight when he spoke. 'It's going to be all right. I promise. We're here now. They'll let you go.'

Tiring of the game, Munro nodded to Barnes. 'Get her out of here.'

Moving forward, Barnes gripped her beneath her arms and lifted her right off her feet, dragging her back towards the doorway. Jessica bucked and kicked, lashing out with her feet and catching him several times across the shins, but the blows lacked power or purpose.

'Ryan! Ryan!' she screamed, her frightened voice echoing off the bare concrete walls.

'It's going to be all right, Jess!' he shouted after her. It was a futile gesture, but it was all he had. 'I promise! I'll find you.'

Munro stood with his arms folded, watching the drama play out as if it were a soap opera. 'Very touching, Drake.'

'You got what you wanted,' he said through gritted teeth. 'Let her go.'

The older man shook his head. 'You know I can't do that. You knew it from the moment I took her hostage.'

That instant, Drake's last kernel of forlorn hope flickered out. Munro was right; as much as he hated to admit it, he knew the man wouldn't release her. He'd always known. He just hadn't wanted to admit it to himself.

His sister was going to die here today, and so was he.

Munro grinned as the hope died in Drake's eyes, then turned his attention to Anya. She was on her knees, hands cuffed behind her back, keeping her eyes locked straight ahead. She had said and done nothing this whole time.

'And look what we have here.' He moved to stand in front of her, looking down on his former commander with absolute contempt. 'What's the matter, Anya? Don't you have anything to say?'

At last she lifted her eyes to meet his. 'Kill me now, while you still can.'

In response, Munro drew back his arm and struck her hard across the jaw, snapping her head around with the force of the impact.

'You piece of shit!' Drake tried in vain to rise to his feet, but a well-placed strike from a rifle butt at the base of his neck put him firmly down again, leaving stars dancing across his eyes.

Munro nodded to the man who had struck him; the same man who had captured him outside the cave. 'Good work, Cartwright.'

'A pleasure, sir.'

His attention returned to Anya. A trickle of blood was flowing from the corner of her mouth, and another from her cheek where the blow had grazed the skin.

'Do you know how long I've waited to do that? How many mornings I looked in the mirror and saw this –' he pointed to his glass eye – 'and thought about the woman who gave it to me?'

Her expression remained impassive when she spoke again. 'You brought it on yourself, Dominic. You got what you deserved.'

His face darkened in anger. It was quickly masked, but she had seen it all the same. She had provoked him.

Saying nothing, Munro circled around behind her, taking his time, savouring the moment. His gaze rested on the blood staining her shirt, the ragged hole torn in the fabric.

Kneeling down behind her, he closed his eyes and leaned in close, smelling the scent of her hair, her skin, as if she were a lover that he would hold in a tender embrace. He could feel the warmth of her body, could almost imagine he heard the beating of her heart.

A beautiful woman even now.

He had once idolised the beautiful, ruthless and enigmatic leader of his unit, entranced by her strength, captivated by her charisma, willing to follow her to any end. In time that infatuation had turned to love, but it had been a turbulent, temperamental love wracked by conflicting emotions.

He had wanted her above all else, but knew he could never have her unless he earned her respect. Driven by his obsession, he had thrown himself into his training with a determination that none could equal. He took on the most difficult operations, the most dangerous aspect of any plan, always seeking new ways to prove himself.

Seeing his potential, she took him under her wing and became a mentor. But as high as he climbed, always she remained beyond his reach. Even as he rose through the ranks, so she began to move away from them.

His love and adoration gradually turned to resentment and bitterness. He began to see her actions in a new light, perceiving her not as the wise and fearless leader he'd once known, but as a strutting coward who took credit for other people's work. His work.

The tipping point came when Marcus Cain approached him personally and, in a secret conversation amongst the endless graves of Arlington Cemetery, warned him that his former mentor was plotting to leave the Agency and turn mercenary. Worse, she had grown jealous of Munro's influence within the group and intended to remove him.

It had been more than he could take. At that moment, he knew she had to be stopped before she dragged the entire unit into disaster. She would never willingly surrender control, and as long as there was breath in her lungs, she would remain a threat.

There was only one option, as inconceivable as it might have seemed only a few short years earlier. She had to be killed.

'You know something, Anya? I used to look up to you,' he whispered softly in her ear. 'You took me in, taught me everything I know. But there's one lesson I learned by myself.'

Reaching up, he gently brushed aside a long strand of blonde hair, then moved his hand down her neck, across her shoulder, tracing a lazy path down the graceful curve of her spine.

Her face was an emotionless mask, but Drake could see the muscles in her throat tightening as his hand moved lower.

'Sooner or later, we all get what we deserve.'

With a malicious smile, he pressed his thumb into the open wound left by the piece of shrapnel, twisting and turning it without mercy. The woman's body went rigid, muscles trembling, teeth gritted against the agony that tore through her. A low groan escaped her lips, and she squeezed her eyes shut as Munro pressed in deeper.

'It's all right,' he said gently, enjoying every moment. 'You can scream . . . if you want. Scream for me, Anya.'

She was trembling with the effort of staying in control. Tears were in her eyes, but still she didn't cry out. She wouldn't give him the satisfaction.

When he finally withdrew, she collapsed forward in a limp pile, drawing in deep shuddering breaths as fresh blood pooled on the floor.

Munro circled back around in front of her, a massive imposing figure. Anya was small and frail by comparison, hurt and bleeding.

'Tough old bitch,' he remarked, both irritated and impressed by her refusal to yield. His Nomex combat glove dripped with her blood. 'Stubborn to the end. I'd expect no less.'

She pulled herself up, flicking her head back to get a clump of tangled, bloodied hair from her eyes so she could look right at him. The sheer, absolute hatred in her eyes even made Munro pause.

'You're a piece of shit, Munro,' Drake spat, shaking with rage at what he'd just witnessed. 'You're a fucking coward.'

Munro turned to face the man. 'I wouldn't point fingers, Drake. You're the one who brought her here.'

'Because you demanded it.'

At this, Munro shook his head. 'Not me. I was just the messenger.'

'What the fuck are you talking about?'

'You still don't understand, do you?' His triumphant smile returned; an expert hunter about to spring his trap. 'It was Cain. He was the one who made this whole thing happen.'

Chapter 68

'It's confirmed. They've stopped at Hijazi Airbase,' Frost reported, studying the satellite images that were downloading in real time to her laptop. 'It's an abandoned Iraqi Air Force facility about fifty miles south-west of Karbala.'

The thump of the massive rotor blades overhead combined with the rush of air as their Black Hawk streaked along barely 50 feet above ground, forcing them to use the aircraft's internal communications system. Outside, the vast yellow-brown sweep of the Iraqi desert swept past at 150 knots.

'Far from prying eyes. A perfect place for an execution,' Dietrich remarked, glancing at his meagre assault team; Frost, her shoulder still heavily strapped up beneath her body armour; Keegan, clutching the crucifix on his charm necklace as he stared out the open door; and Rahul, busy checking the feed mechanism on his MP5.

Not much of a strike team, but there hadn't been time to gather more operatives. In any case, this one was as unofficial as they came. The fewer people who knew about it, the better.

He switched frequency to talk to the pilot. 'What's our ETA at Hijazi Airbase?'

'Ten minutes.'

'Punch it, will you? We need to be there now.'

'Copy that.'

As the engines roared with increased power and the desert whipped along beneath them, Dietrich closed his eyes and sent a silent prayer to whatever deities might be inclined to hear him. His plea was simple but heartfelt.

Don't let this be for nothing.

In that instant, all the colour drained from Anya's face.

'No . . .' she gasped.

Cain. The one man she had always believed in. The man who had given her a chance when no one else would, who had guided and encouraged her, who had made her who she was. The man she had trusted with absolute conviction . . .

It was him. It was all him.

She was distraught, devastated. Had the situation been different, she might have broken down in tears at what she had just learned.

Munro folded his arms. 'Our friend Cain is a rising star in the Agency. He's going to be promoted to Deputy Director in a couple of months, but you don't get to that kind of level without making enemies. There are plenty of guys who would like to see him take a fall, and his dirty little arms deal in Iraq would have made perfect ammunition. It was a sword hanging over his head that he had to deal with. That's why he cooked this whole thing up.'

Munro turned his eye on Anya again. 'He knew you'd come close to finding out his little secret once before, and that there was a source out there who still had the evidence to bring him down. But he couldn't find him alone. And even if he could, there was always a chance you might tell the Russians what you knew and compromise him again. So he did what he does best – he found a way to kill two birds with one stone.'

'He knew you were being held in Khatyrgan Prison, but he needed justification to break you out. A disgraced former operative holding the Agency to ransom was just perfect, so he arranged for me to be transferred to another prison, and he made sure the guys driving the truck were all on the Agency payroll. As soon as I was free, he brought me in and explained what he needed, said he'd wipe the slate clean if I could deliver for him. He even offered me money, but you know something? When I found out I'd get my hands on *you*, I said I'd do it for nothing.'

He gestured to the computer equipment on the far side of the room. The laptop in the centre of it all was displaying an overhead image of the abandoned airfield. Drake recognised the rows of ruined aircraft and the bombed-out runways. It was a feed from a Predator drone.

'Another little gift,' he explained. 'An encryption unit taken from the Agency's own inventory. With it, we can hack any Predator drone we want. We used it to destroy your car earlier, and launch a strike in Mosul a week ago. That was enough to convince the Agency that the threat was real, so they green-lighted an operation to bring you home.'

He glanced at Drake. 'Cain asked your buddy Franklin to recommend someone for the prison break. He chose you, and Cain knew he would – an old friend, a troubled man desperate to clear his name. You were perfect.' He smiled in amusement. 'Cain made sure you had everything you needed to evade the search operation. He hampered the Shepherd team trying to track you down, he made sure you got through Customs with that stolen passport of yours, and he even warned me when they were closing in on you at that house last night.'

'But why go to all this trouble for me?' Drake demanded. 'Why not use one of your own men?'

'Still don't see it, do you?' Munro gestured to Anya. 'This little firecracker can see through a lie like we see through windows. Putting one of our agents in with her would have been a waste of time. She had to believe the threat was real if she was going to lead us to Zebari. More important, she had to believe there might be a way back into the Agency at the end of it.'

His remaining eye glimmered with malice as he watched Anya's reaction. 'Even then, after everything, after all those years of compromises and betrayals, you were still loyal to Cain. You actually thought this was your ticket back. If you could deliver evidence of Iraqi weapons programmes, you thought it would redeem you, that he'd welcome you back with open arms and everything would be like it was twenty years ago. Jesus, were you really that naive?' He leaned in close. 'Those days are over. You're old, Anya. You're old and broken and obsolete. You should be put down like a fucking animal.'

Drake stared at the woman. The look of utter desolation in her eyes was heartbreaking.

'Speaking of putting people down . . .'

Walking over to Zebari, Munro halted in front of the Iraqi man, drew a Smith & Wesson automatic from the holster on his right thigh and levelled it at his head. Unable to rise on his crippled leg, and with his hands cuffed behind his back, he could do nothing but sit there trembling as Munro flicked the safety catch off.

'No!' Anya cried.

The crack of the gunshot echoed around the small concrete room like thunder, reverberating back and forth for a second or two before dying away.

Zebari slumped back and collapsed, a limp pile of meat and bones now divorced from life. Blood and brain tissue coated the floor in a sticky red carpet around the shattered remains of his skull.

Devastated, Anya sat staring at the dead man. He had been her hope, her lifeline, first her bargaining chip and then her instrument of retribution. Now he was nothing – just another dead body in a country littered with them.

All her hopes of bringing Cain's wrongdoing to light had died with him.

Holstering the weapon, Munro looked at Anya again. 'What was it you used to say to me? *"I will show no mercy. I will never surrender,"* he repeated, his tone mocking and derisive. 'What do you have to say now?'

She remained silent.

Balling up his fist again, he drew his arm back and struck her with a right hook, sending her sprawling on the ground in a daze.

Anya's head was whirling as she lay there, blood flowing from the corner of her mouth and nose. His last blow had been delivered with such savage strength that even she was stunned by it, her vision dim as her consciousness wavered. Desperately she fought at the gathering darkness, clawing her mind back from the brink.

She rolled onto her back, and felt a renewed surge of pain as the piece of shrapnel embedded in her flesh was pushed in further. Munro's little torture session must have dislodged it.

He was going to kill her. She knew that with absolute certainty. He had killed Zebari without hesitation, and he would kill her too, though she doubted her death would come quick or easy.

With her hands cuffed behind her back, she could do nothing to defend herself, much less attack Munro and his cohorts.

She had to get the cuffs off. She had been well trained at escape and evasion over the years, and the locks on most handcuffs were simple to pick. All she needed was a piece of metal.

A piece of metal.

Her eyes lit up as she pictured the shrapnel still lodged in her back.

It might work. It might not. She could only try.

Closing her eyes for a moment and preparing herself for the pain that was about to come, she gently probed around the edge of the wound with her fingers. She could feel something hard beneath the skin, and a tentative movement of it prompted a sudden burst of pain. That had to be it.

Don't think about it. Just get it done.

Gritting her teeth, she pushed two fingertips into the wound, ignoring the burning pain and every instinct in her body which told her to withdraw them. She pushed deeper, felt something sharp and hard, and grasped one edge of it, gripping it tight. The last thing she wanted was to lose her grip at the crucial moment.

'I did everything you asked of me,' Munro said.

There was no anger in his voice. It had drained out of him as he watched the formidable and intimidating woman he'd known lying on the floor with blood pooling around her.

'I risked my life for you again and again, and it meant nothing. You were happy to stay in Washington and take all the credit for our work. We meant nothing to you.'

489

Do it now. Now!

With a sharp, strangled gasp, she yanked the metal sliver free from her body. Her vision swam for a moment and she felt warm blood coating her hands, but she held her prize in a tight grip. A slender piece of car chassis, perhaps an inch long and tapered to a narrow point at one end. It was far from a perfect tool for her needs, but it was all she had.

'You're . . . wrong,' she gasped, adjusting her grip on the metal fragment before going to work on the cuffs. They were secured by a simple lever lock mechanism. Normally it would present no challenge, but having to work while lying on her back in a pool of her own blood without tipping off Munro was rather more difficult. 'I was weak, Dominic. I was weak with you.'

He hesitated. Her words had struck a chord.

Just keep him talking. Keep him occupied.

'You still don't understand, do you? I trusted you. I trusted you to lead the unit without me, because I couldn't be there for you any more. I had to go back to Washington.' She could feel the first lever with the tip of the metal shard, and pressed it down as she moved on to the next one. 'They wanted me to replace Cain as division leader. Men from the board of directors approached me, told me their plan to remove him. That was why I left you. I wasn't trying to destroy him; I was trying to help him.'

For all her field experience and prowess in combat, Anya had virtually no knowledge or understanding of the politics within the higher echelons of the Agency. Almost without realising it, she had found herself thrust into a new world; a frightening and difficult world of clandestine meetings, planning sessions and power plays.

She was neither a desk jockey nor a politician, yet some within the Agency had begun to encourage her down that path, telling her she was too valuable to waste on the front line, encouraging her to take her rightful place as Cain's successor.

Even then, after years of mistrust and growing rifts between them, she had baulked at the notion of destroying Cain's career and ousting him from power. Whatever his flaws, he had remained a brilliant intellect, a force to be reckoned with. There were no limits to what they could achieve together.

But it couldn't be the same as before, with him dictating policy and her acting as the unquestioning instrument of his will. They had both changed too much for that, and on some level she had sensed the passage of time more than before. Deep down, she knew she was getting older.

Time was running out. If she wanted to make a meaningful contribution to the world when her fighting days were over, it would have to be from within the corridors of Langley. If she was to survive, she had to adapt.

But she couldn't do it alone. She had desired instead a partnership with Cain, fair and equal, where each could harness their strengths and experience to their greatest effect. That had been her final vision for her life. It would allow her to finally make real the vague, childish fantasy she'd harboured since that night in the infirmary.

A chance to make a difference.

But as she tried to negotiate the confusing and difficult political landscape of the Agency's top levels, her attention became diverted away from the task force she had once led. She failed to see the growing rifts and discontent amongst her former comrades. It would be a fatal error.

Two levers down. Come on, come on.

She swallowed hard. 'We came so close, Dominic,' she said, eyes filled with aching sadness as she relived that brief moment of hope and optimism. She had come tantalisingly, agonisingly close to making it work. 'Most of the Agency's senior directors supported me. I was ready to take my plan to Cain when you tried to have me killed.'

There were tears in her eyes now as she stared at him. She made no effort to hide them. 'Even then I didn't want to believe it. You were the best I had – my favourite. I told myself there had to be another explanation, so I came after you to find it.'

She felt the tip of the metal shard brush the final lever. With desperate haste she went to work on it.

'Don't you understand what you did? You ruined everything. Everything I spent my life building, you destroyed in a single day. But even when it was over, I still couldn't bring myself to kill you. That was my weakness,' she lamented. 'You had been like a son, and I showed you what mercy I could.'

For a brief moment, Munro stood frozen in shock, his single eye blank and unfocused. Only now did he understand the full magnitude of his mistake, the scale of the misguided destruction he had unleashed. He had been so young then; rash and arrogant and filled with ambition, only to see it stifled by Anya, his commander, his unchallenged leader, the woman he had hated and loved in equal measure.

The moment passed, his gaze hardened, and the weakness was gone. He smiled. 'You know something? When this was all over, Cain wanted you brought back alive. He still has a soft spot for you, even now.'

Reaching for the knife at his belt, he yanked it from its scabbard, the blade rasping against the metal sheath as it came free. For a moment he held it up in front of her, allowing the light to glint off the wickedly sharp blade.

'Me, on the other hand . . . Well, like you said, there are some things you just can't accept. So I'll show you the same mercy you showed me.'

He knelt beside her, fingers clamped around her neck with one hand as he brought the knife down to carve out her right eye. The last thing she would see was his face smiling in triumph.

'An eye for an eye.'

Anya stared back at him. She wouldn't look away. She wouldn't give him that satisfaction.

'Sir, we've got an inbound chopper!' Redfield, the technician manning the Predator terminal, yelled in warning.

Munro's head snapped around. 'What?'

'A Black Hawk. Coming in fast and low. Looks like a strike package.'

'A Shepherd team.' Munro made his decision in an instant. 'Target them with the Predator and take them out.'

It was the opening Anya had been waiting for. With a click, the lock disengaged. Yanking her wrists out of the cuffs, she swung her right hand, still clutching the jagged piece of shrapnel, into Munro's neck.

He cried out in pain as the improvised blade bit into his flesh just above his shoulder, cutting a deep gash through skin and muscle. He pitched sideways, yanked the sliver of metal free and turned on her, his remaining eye burning with fury.

She saw the gleaming flash as he plunged his knife down, and twisted aside to avoid it. The blade bit into the concrete floor, ringing with the impact and jarring his arm.

493

Capitalising on his brief lapse, she reached down, closed her hand around the Smith & Wesson holstered at his thigh and yanked it free. He raised the knife for another strike, but before he could bring the blade down, she managed to plant a foot firmly against his chest and kicked out with all the strength she could summon. The blow caught him off balance and he was thrown backward, landing in a sprawl several feet away.

Even as he hit the deck, she brought the automatic to bear, thumbing the safety off with practised ease. Rising up from the ground, he stared at her, his face frozen in shock and disbelief.

I will show no mercy. I will never hesitate.

She had shown him mercy once. Not this time.

Movement to her left.

The black man called Cartwright, armed with an M4 carbine. In an instant she knew he was the greater threat. Swinging the weapon around, she caught a glimpse of him raising his assault rifle just before she snapped off a round.

His head jerked back as the projectile impacted just above his right eye. She didn't even bother watching what happened next. He was down for good, and that was all she cared about.

The man by the computer terminal was starting to react. Hurling his chair aside, he spun to face her, going for the weapon at his hip.

Two rounds to the chest and another to the head was enough to put him down. He crumpled in a heap, his blood painting the computer equipment behind him.

With the two armed men eliminated, she switched her attention back to Munro, her eyes flicking right even as she brought the weapon around.

But the second or two it had taken her to dispatch his

two comrades had bought him the time to rise to his feet, still clutching the knife. Lips drawn back in a snarl of hatred, he hurled the weapon at her with all the force he could command.

His aim was true, but she twisted aside even as the blade flew through the air, clattering off the wall behind her. She rolled over and adjusted her aim, but the delay had bought her opponent a vital second. Munro was already moving, sprinting for the door.

In the half-second before he vanished, she snapped off a shot. A cloud of blood sprayed from his shoulder, followed by a howl of pain as he vanished from sight.

Chapter 69

Dietrich winced as the first round slammed into the Black Hawk's airframe. The heavy chopper was well protected against small-arms fire, but a well-placed shot to a vital system could still bring them down.

'We're taking fire! We're taking fire!' the pilot yelled.

'No shit,' Frost replied, ducking as a stray round zipped in through the open door and whanged off the roof of the compartment.

'I can't hold us here.'

I guess it's safe to assume these guys aren't on our side, Dietrich thought with a wry smile.

Keegan was crouched in the open doorway, his long-barrelled rifle against his shoulder. 'I see the shooter. Control tower, top floor,' he said, calm and composed. He was in business mode now. 'Just hold us steady.'

The fuselage resounded again with the clang of projectiles ricocheting off the armour belt. Sure enough, Dietrich could just make out the telltale muzzle flare of an automatic weapon snapping off bursts from the upper floor of the ruined control tower.

'I have to break,' the pilot warned.

Keegan didn't take his eyes off his target. 'Fire, fire, fire.'

The sharp crack of the rifle almost drowned out the thumping of the rotors. Dietrich caught a momentary glimpse of red spray within the tower.

'This is it! We go now.'

Latching his fast-descent harness onto the restraining pylon just outside the door, he gripped the friction hitch tight, stepped out and released his hold.

The descent took all of three seconds. Three seconds of sickening helplessness as a storm of wind and dust swirled around him and the rope slipped through his hands.

He landed hard, rolling aside and rising up to his knees as he unclipped himself. Frost came down next, groaning in pain as her injured shoulder took the strain of the descent harness, but made a good landing.

Keegan was making his descent when more fire started pouring in on them, rounds whizzing past their heads and churning up the sand at their feet.

'Cover!' Dietrich yelled, sprinting for a collapsed wall that had once been part of an anti-aircraft battery, his weapon up at his shoulder. The stabbing pain in his injured leg was a concern he had no time for now.

Simple survival was the priority.

'Anya, cuffs!' Drake yelled the moment Munro disappeared.

He had no idea how she'd been able to free herself, and now wasn't the time to ask. He could do nothing with his hands bound.

She glanced at him for a moment, decided she had no time to assist him, then shook her head.

'I'm sorry, Drake.' She was already turning away.

'Anya, wait. Anya!'

But it was no good. She wasn't hearing him, and a moment later she had disappeared through the doorway. She was gone.

'Fuck!'

Allowing himself to fall back on the hard floor, he drew his knees up to his chest and passed his cuffed hands beneath his feet.

Cartwright, the man who had brought him in, still lay where he had fallen, blood pooling around the gory exit wound at the back of his head. Heaving himself up, Drake rushed over and fell to his knees beside the body, frantically searching his pockets and webbing.

He found what he was looking for in one of the side pouches of his body armour, and a few seconds later his unlocked cuffs fell to the floor. Wasting no time, he snatched up the dead man's carbine and checked the action. The weapon was loaded and ready.

Outside, he could hear the crackle of automatic fire, and the distinctive thump of helicopter blades. Munro's men were being engaged by someone, and Drake had a feeling who.

He hesitated, torn about what to do. Anya had gone after Munro herself, and she would show him no mercy if she found him. But with Zebari dead and his evidence gone, Munro was the only one left who could bring Cain down. He was no good to them dead.

His gaze turned toward the corridor his sister had been dragged down. She was in the building somewhere. Munro had ordered Barnes to take her away. She had to be close. He just prayed she was still alive.

It took him less than a second to make his decision.

Rising up with the weapon at his shoulder, he hurried out of the room and into the corridor beyond, eyes and rifle eagerly searching for a target.

There were doors set at intervals along both sides, some hanging ajar and others fastened shut. She could be anywhere. The building was large, possibly with further construction underground.

He ached to call out to her, but couldn't chance it. There was no telling how many of Munro's men were in here with him. She could be anywhere.

Suddenly an image leapt into his mind: a memory of Jessica being dragged out of the room by Barnes, her feet trailing behind her. Trailing along the floor.

The bare concrete floors were covered with debris of all sorts, from broken pieces of glass, plastic and wood, to discarded pieces of paper and a fine coating of sand that had blown in over the years. Looking closer, he could see the distinctive tread patterns of numerous pairs of boots. No doubt Munro and his men had been using this place for several days at least.

But there was another mark on the floor – two parallel lines cut into the sand and dust. Drag marks.

Gripping the carbine in sweating hands, Drake hurried forward, following the tracks which turned right at a T-junction, leading deeper into the building.

Blood pounded through his veins and sweat dripped into his eyes as his body wrestled with fear and adrenalin. Even as he advanced, his boots crunching through the broken glass and the crackle of weapons fire echoing down the ruined corridor, he could imagine Jessica huddled in a tiny cell, terrified, waiting for that bastard to put a bullet in her head.

It could happen at any moment. If her captor suspected the game was up, he might well execute her and make a run for it.

Suddenly one of the doors further down swung open on rusted hinges, and a bald head leaned out, a long grey goatee trailing down from the chin. It was Barnes.

The weapon was already at Drake's shoulder, his finger on the trigger. It was a perfect shot. He tensed up slightly as he adjusted his aim and squeezed off a round.

There was a flash, the weapon kicked back into his shoulder, and an instant later he saw a cloud of blood paint the pale concrete wall. Barnes collapsed to the floor, his body jerking spasmodically as his destroyed brain misfired, sending random signals to his muscles.

A scream of fear and horror echoed from beyond the door.

'Jessica!' Ignoring the man he'd just killed, he leapt over the body and into the room beyond.

She was there, crouched in the corner of what looked like an old storage room, tears in her eyes as she stared at the dead body.

Drake couldn't help himself. Laying the weapon aside, he knelt down beside her and threw his arms around her, pulling her close in a crushing grip as if to confirm she was solid and real and alive.

'Oh, Christ, Jess. I'm sorry . . .' he managed to say, blinking back tears of his own.

She was crying now. He could feel her convulsive sobs. She had held herself under control all this time, stayed strong for the sake of survival, but not now. 'I heard shooting. I thought . . . you were dead. I thought I'd lost you.'

He pulled back to look at her. With her hair in disarray, her clothes torn and grubby, her face streaked with dirt and tears, she was a pathetic sight. But she was alive. 'You can't get rid of me that easily,' he said, managing a reassuring smile. 'I told you I'd find you.'

Her gaze flicked back to the dead body lying sprawled in the doorway, slick blood coating the floor. 'I didn't know, Ryan. I mean, I always knew you did dangerous work, but . . .'

'Jess, look at me. Look at my eyes.' Taking her face in his hands, he turned her towards him again. 'It's going to be all right. I'll tell you everything when this is over, but we have to get you somewhere safe. Can you walk?'

She swallowed and nodded.

'Good. Let's—'

He hesitated, a noise out in the corridor catching his attention. The scrape of a boot on the dirty concrete floor.

In a single fluid motion, he reached out, grabbed his carbine and brought it up to his shoulder just as a body-armoured figure appeared in the doorway.

He'd kill any bastard who tried to touch her. No hesitation, no regrets.

He tensed his shoulder as before, preparing for the recoil of the first shot.

'Hold your fire, Ryan!' Dietrich yelled.

His grip on the trigger slackened as relief surged through him. 'Jonas.'

'You owe me a big fucking explanation.'

Drake had one. 'We found Munro. He's been working for Cain the whole fucking time. This entire thing was Cain's plan to destroy evidence of an illegal arms deal he tried to broker. He allowed Munro to hack the Predator drone that killed all those civilians, and Munro threatened to kill my sister if I didn't cooperate.'

For a moment, Dietrich simply stared at him, dumb-struck. His gaze turned to the woman still handcuffed on the floor, then back up to Drake.

'You can prove this?'

'The control station is right in there,' Drake said, pointing back down the corridor. 'So is Anya's source. Munro shot him dead.'

Dietrich's eyes were wide in amazement.

'You've got to believe me, Jonas. Anya's innocent in this.'

501

'I believe you,' he said at last. 'But I should fucking shoot you for all the trouble you've caused.'

Drake couldn't help but smile just a little. 'You can shoot me later. First we have to find Munro. He's the only one left who can bring Cain down.'

Chapter 70

Hurrying forward with his weapon at the ready, Rahul scanned the rusting hulks of derelict aircraft for targets. Most of Munro's men were clustered around the terminal building, holding Frost and Keegan at bay with sustained automatic fire. But there was so much noise and confusion that it was hard to tell who was firing at who.

He had to hurry. He was circling around to outflank them, but the longer he waited, the more chance there was that they might escape.

He almost didn't notice the sudden flurry of movement to his right. Whirling around, he brought his MP5 to bear on this new target, only to find the barrel caught in a ferocious grip.

In a heartbeat Rahul found himself face to face with a man: big and tall and powerful. Two eyes stared back at him, one glassy and unfocused, the other filled with rage and murder.

Rahul saw something glinting in the sun as the man brought his arm back, and realised an instant too late that it was an aluminium reinforcing strut from one of the broken airframes, one end bent and jagged.

Without remorse or hesitation, Munro plunged the makeshift dagger into his adversary's throat, forcing it through the man's windpipe.

Rahul's eyes went wide, his mouth gaped open as if

to scream, but all he managed was a sickening gurgle. With blood pumping from severed arteries in his throat, he fell to his knees, desperately trying to draw breath that wouldn't come.

Tearing the MP5 from his limp grasp, Munro kicked the dying man to the ground and turned away, quickly assessing the situation. His men were under attack by God knew how many Shepherd team operatives, and with at least two of them dead at Anya's hands, they were up against it.

He had little confidence in the men supplied by Cain. They were Private Military Contractors, mercenaries who fought and killed for the highest bidder. They were nothing compared to the elite, battle-hardened troops he had once commanded in Task Force Black.

Pain burned outward from his left arm. The round had passed straight through, leaving blood seeping down to his fingers in crimson tracks. It wasn't a critical injury, but the pain was another reminder of his failure.

'Goddamn you, Anya,' he hissed, reaching for his cell-phone as he started moving. He had a Ford Explorer parked on the other side of the aircraft boneyard. That was his ticket out of this goddamned mess.

Dialling a familiar number, he waited a couple of seconds while the line connected. It rang only once before it was answered.

'Talk to me.' Even from half a world away, he could hear the tension in Marcus Cain's voice.

'We're fucked,' Munro said, wasting no time. 'A Shepherd team just showed up. They're securing the place as we speak.'

'What?'

'Anya's still alive. She knows everything, Marcus.'

'You stupid son of a bitch!' Cain hissed. Realising he

had no time to waste on petty recriminations, he forced calm into his voice. 'What about her source?'

'He's dead. I made sure of that.'

Cain was silent for all of two seconds. 'Get out of there. I'm going to handle this.'

'Copy that,' Munro said, tossing the phone away. He was under no illusions about his prospects when this was all over. Cain showed no mercy to those who failed him.

He was going to have to disappear when this was all over.

On the other side of the world in his expansive office at Langley, Cain slammed his fist down on the desk. Everything he'd planned so carefully was falling apart at the last moment. Only now did he realise on how slender a thread his entire career, even his very life, now hung.

Reaching for his phone, he dialled the number for the CIA reconnaissance centre in Baghdad. He had a direct line to the chief of operations there.

'Kaminsky,' a deep voice announced a moment later.

'This is Director of Special Activities Division Marcus Cain, Mr Kaminsky. You are to commence with Case Orange immediately. Authorisation Charlie, Delta, Victor, Victor, Kilo. I repeat, commence Case Orange immediately. Do you understand?'

'Yes, sir. We have a Predator standing by. We're vectoring in now.'

Cain replaced the phone, closed his eyes and exhaled slowly, willing himself to stay calm and rational.

There was a danger, no doubt about that, but he could still prevent disaster if he acted quickly. The whole reason he'd insisted on having the Predator standing by was in case something like this happened. It was his fallback, his final line of defence.

He had learned a long time ago never to underestimate Anya, but even he hadn't expected this. God, the things they could have achieved if only she'd learned to work with him instead of against him.

He hadn't wanted it to play out this way, but she had forced his hand. If need be, he would flatten that entire airfield and everyone in it to stop her.

'He what?' Franklin gasped, incredulous.

'The order just went out,' Sinclair confirmed, staring at his computer screen. 'Director Cain ordered an air strike on Hijazi. They're vectoring in a Predator right now.'

'Jesus Christ.' He was already reaching for his cellphone.

Taking a deep breath, Frost leapt from cover and charged across the open windswept ground between two crumpled fuel bowsers, nimble as a gazelle trying to evade a lion. A fresh burst of fire erupted from the nearby building, rounds whizzing past her head to bury themselves in the ground around her.

Switching direction, she threw herself behind the twisted remains of the vehicle's cab. More projectiles slammed into it, some tearing right through the metal skin to leave gaping holes as big as her fist. Mercifully none of them found their mark.

With her heart pounding, she peered through one of the bullet holes, trying to get a fix on her would-be killer. Sure enough, she caught movement at one of the windows of an office block about 50 yards away. She couldn't tell what he was armed with, but judging by the volume of fire, she suspected some kind of belt-fed support weapon, probably an M60.

As if to prove the point, he opened up again in a long, sustained burst, sacrificing accuracy for weight of firepower.

Ducking as more holes were torn in her scant cover, she keyed her radio. 'Keegan, I'm pinned down. Need support.'

'I got your back.' His voice was calm and composed. 'You got a fix on the shooter?'

'Office block, north-west side. First-floor window.'

It only took him a moment to spot the target. 'I see him.'

Frost jumped as another hole was punched right through the wing only inches from her face. 'Nail that son of a bitch!'

Nearby, Keegan slowly let out a breath, his face a picture of calm.

The rifle kicked back into his shoulder as he squeezed the trigger, the gas discharge from the expended round causing a slight ripple to pass through his clothing.

An instant later, his target toppled back and disappeared from sight. A perfect head shot.

Chapter 71

Heart pounding, lungs burning, sweat running down his face in the hot sun, Munro sprinted through the ranks of ruined aircraft and ancient vehicles. The air around him was stifling, his T-shirt already soaked with perspiration as dry gritty sand swirled around him.

He was almost there. He could see his jeep parked behind the stripped-down remains of a refuelling truck. Ignoring the pain in his arm, he rushed for it with a final burst of speed.

'Dominic,' a cold, ghostly voice whispered.

Oh, no.

Reacting on instinct, he whirled around, weapon up and ready, finger already tightening on the trigger.

Nothing. Just sand and derelict aircraft.

He could have sworn she had been behind him. She had to be. She couldn't possibly have circled around in front.

He exhaled, his finger easing off the trigger.

The jeep was mere yards away.

But he didn't go for it. His instincts told him he was being watched. He could feel it. She was here.

He spun, twisting the MP5 around to fire.

'Don't,' Anya warned before he could bring the weapon to bear. She was standing a dozen yards away with the Smith & Wesson handgun levelled at his head.

His own weapon was trained on him.

'Put down the gun,' she ordered.

It would be futile to try anything. She could snap off three or four shots before he could draw down on her, and he knew she wouldn't miss.

Glancing down at the MP5, he hesitated a moment, then threw it aside in disgust. She'd been right – he should have killed her when he had the chance.

Now unarmed, he turned slowly to face her.

'If you expect me to beg, you're wasting your time,' he spat, glaring at her with every ounce of malice that years of hatred and bitterness commanded. 'I'm not afraid to die.'

Her eyes glimmered; cold and hard and remorseless. She said nothing, just kept the weapon levelled at him.

'Go on, do it,' he taunted, deciding to try one last desperate gamble. 'Shoot me, like the fucking coward I always knew you were. Prove me right, Anya.' Her eyes flashed, and just for a moment he saw her mask of control slip aside. He saw the long-buried anger and betrayal that still lurked deep within her.

Saying nothing, she turned the weapon aside and hit the magazine eject button. The clip fell free from its housing, clattering to the ground. Racking back the slide to eject the round still in the chamber, she tossed the useless weapon away.

'This is between us, Dominic,' she said as she brought her hands up, readying her tired and injured body for one more fight. 'It was always between us.'

Munro smiled, hardly believing she had allowed herself to be so easily provoked. The stupid bitch actually thought she could beat him in a fair fight, hand to hand. Even now, she still clung to some obsolete notion that there was honour to be found in battle.

It was the last mistake she would ever make. He would make sure of it.

With Jessica now freed from her cuffs, Drake and Dietrich hurried back into the building's former operations room, still bathed in the soft glow of computer screens.

Dietrich's phone started ringing.

'What is it, Dan?'

'Jonas, you've got to get out of there!' Franklin's voice was loud and urgent. 'Cain's bringing down an air strike on your position.'

'What?'

'The order just went out. They're vectoring in a Predator to flatten the fucking place.'

In that moment, any lingering doubts he might have had about Drake's story vanished. 'I don't believe it. He's trying to cover it all up.'

'Cover what up?'

'Cain's been behind this whole thing. Munro was working for him. He even launched the first Predator attack to make it seem legit. He tried to sell nuclear secrets to the Iraqis before the invasion, and when the deal went bad he took the money and ran. Drake just told me the whole story.'

'You found him?'

'He's with me. So is his sister. Munro took her hostage, used her as leverage to get Drake to cooperate.' Further explanations would have to wait. 'How much time do we have?'

'Not much. I suggest you find a hole and hide in it.'

Like that would do any good. Hellfire missiles were designed to penetrate strike-hardened bunkers. There could be no refuge from them here, and the Black Hawk chopper had peeled away to avoid ground fire.

His eyes swept the room, coming to rest on the control station opposite.

'I've got a better idea,' he said, a hasty plan forming. Killing the phone, he turned to Drake. 'We've got problems.'

'So I heard.'

'Cain's bringing in an air strike to flatten this place. He's going to kill everyone who knows the truth.'

Drake glanced down the corridor leading outside. The corridor Munro had retreated down. Along with Anya.

Dietrich saw the look in his eyes and guessed his thoughts. 'You go,' he decided. 'Find Munro. I'll take care of the Predator.'

Drake's eyes met his for a moment, and he nodded in gratitude.

'Ryan, what are you doing?' Jessica asked.

He turned towards her, wishing he had more time to explain. 'I have to find the woman I came here with. She's in danger.'

Her eyes narrowed. 'Why you?'

'Because there's no one else. And because I owe her.' He was out of time. Reaching out, he pulled her close in a fierce embrace, then released his grip and turned away. 'Dietrich will keep you safe. Stay here until I get back.'

Hefting the carbine, he turned and sprinted through the door.

Dietrich hit his radio pressel. 'Frost, what's your position?'

'North office block. We're securing the first floor now.'

'Forget it. Meet me in the air control tower. And make it fast. We don't have much time.'

Central Intelligence Agency Field Ops Centre,
Baghdad, Iraq

In the operations room, Kaminsky watched the live feed from the Predator drone as it made a wide turn to start its attack run.

'Good roll,' the terminal operator reported. 'Bearing now three-one-five degrees. Time on target, ninety seconds.'

'Go hot,' Kaminsky ordered. He didn't know what the hell was going on at that abandoned base or why it was so vital that they destroyed it, but that was little different from any other day in the pit. Their orders came down from above, and they followed them without question, without hesitation.

And in this case, their orders had come from very high indeed.

'Copy that. Weapons free. Arming Hellfires.'

Chapter 72

Balling up his fist, Munro swung hard for a crushing right hook, but Anya ducked it before he could connect. Quickly shifting his weight to keep himself on balance, he threw a left jab, but she twisted aside with ease, caught his arm and countered with a stiff right that snapped his head back.

She was going to try to lock his arm. He knew it. He had sparred with her enough times to know her fighting style, the moves she tended to employ and the tactics she favoured.

That was his key; the one advantage that none of her other opponents had ever possessed.

Sure enough, she began to twist his arm down and around, exerting all her strength to force it behind his back. She would show no hesitation in breaking it.

In response, he lashed out with his other arm, trying to catch her with his elbow. She saw it coming and ducked to avoid it, but the reprieve bought him the opportunity he needed to wrench his arm free.

Rounding on her once more, he lashed out with a round-house kick to her left side, aiming for the vulnerable injury that he knew still caused her great pain. But she was ready for him, jumping back to avoid the crippling blow.

She was standing a few paces away, fists up and ready, eyes locked on him. She was a daunting figure, and still a deadly opponent, but Munro noticed she was breathing harder from her exertions. Tiring fast. Her time in prison had weakened her, and loss of blood from the shrapnel wound had further sapped her stamina.

He sensed she was thinking the same thing. She would have to finish this quickly, before her strength deserted her. And in that instant, he knew it would be her undoing.

Munro had come to know Anya well in the years they had served together; well enough to realise she was by nature a defensive fighter, preferring to block and evade her opponents until they made a mistake and left themselves vulnerable. She disliked taking the initiative, because it negated her ability to read body language and anticipate her opponent's actions.

He could hardly believe it. The solution that had eluded him seven years ago was shockingly obvious now. To beat her, one simply had to let her attack.

Allowing his breathing to come louder and faster than it needed to be, he dropped his arms a little as if struggling to hold them up. Then, muscles clenched in eager anticipation, he waited for the inevitable attack.

It happened fast. Trying to capitalise on what she saw as weakness and fatigue, she rushed him, fists clenched, moving with the sinewy grace of a predator born to end lives.

Munro saw her punch coming and, reacting with speed and strength that caught her unawares, grabbed her outstretched arm and twisted it with savage force.

He had her. She couldn't escape now.

His next blow, aimed at the bloody wound on her left side, was delivered with all the strength, all the malice, all the hatred that welled up inside him like an unstoppable tide.

There was no thought of staying silent this time, of taking the pain and maintaining her composure. Her back arched, her face twisted as her scream of agony echoed off the derelict aircraft hulks around them.

It was like music to his ears. Elation and sheer, unfettered hatred surged through him. At last, he had her at his mercy.

Mercy. She had shown him her tender mercy when she took his eye, when she murdered the men who had followed him in his bid for power.

He would show her none today.

'I always hoped it would come down to this, Anya,' he hissed in her ear. 'Just the two of us, like it should be.' Bringing his arm back, he delivered another savage punch to the bleeding wound.

She went limp in his arms, her consciousness fading as pain and darkness threatened to overwhelm her. She was done; broken and defeated at his hands. Munro hurled her to the ground like a rag doll and turned away in search of a weapon to finish her.

It didn't take him long to spot a hydraulic pipe hanging from the landing gear of a wrecked MiG-25. A hard yank was enough to snap it free of its restraining brackets, leaving him with a 4-foot length of metal ending in a jagged, wicked point.

Perfect, Munro thought, gripping it tight as he turned on his crippled adversary.

Chapter 73

'Dietrich! What the fuck's going on?' Frost demanded as she hurried into the makeshift command centre, sweating and out of breath. Her gaze swept over the three dead bodies littering the floor, and the woman in civilian clothes standing nearby.

Dietrich was at the computer terminal, frantically trying to make sense of the complex system. 'Cain's bringing in an air strike to flatten this place! Munro was working for him, and now he's trying to kill anyone who knows the truth.'

It took her a moment to process everything she'd just heard. 'Then we need to get the fuck out of here.'

'They can target us no matter where we go.' He turned to look at her. 'But I've got an idea. Get over here and help me.'

'Time on target, thirty seconds,' the operator reported, his voice icy calm as he brought the Predator in for its attack run. 'Missiles are hot. Laser designators active. We are weapons free.'

Kaminsky nodded. 'Strike is authorised.'

'Time on target, twenty seconds.'

He could see the ruined airbase on the monitors now. The cluster of control and administrative buildings, the collapsed hangars, and the rows of derelict aircraft destroyed years earlier.

'Time on target, ten seconds. I have tone. Good target lock.'

This was it. In a few moments, fireballs would erupt across the base as the Predator deployed its full load of munitions.

Then, just like that, the screens went blank. All telemetry from the drone ceased as if the thing had just blinked out of existence.

Kaminsky blinked, hardly believing what he was seeing. Not again.

'What the hell?'

Pain.

Pain and intense, burning light all around her.

Lying in a heap, Anya coughed, leaving a trail of blood on the sandy ground. Her mind was a hazy fog of agony threatening to engulf her. Yet somehow, through some supreme effort of will, she held it at bay.

Struggling to focus, she looked up as the man wrenched a length of metal pipework free from a nearby aircraft and turned towards her with murder in his eyes.

She had to get up. She had to defend herself.

Clutching the dusty ground, she tried to push herself up. Pain and weakness assailed her from all sides, blood pounded in her ears and her vision grew dim as she sank back down.

She was finished. She could do no more.

Then, through the fog of pain, she heard a voice, faint and distant, yet at the same time clear and strong. It was her own voice.

You will endure when all others fail.

'It's just like I told you, Anya. Sooner or later, we all get what we deserve,' Munro spat as his boots crunched through the sand towards her. He was taking his time, savouring the final moments of her life before he took it. 'And you've had this coming for a long time.'

You will stand when all others retreat.

A hard kick to the stomach sent her sprawling on her back, pain blossoming outward from the point of impact. He wanted to look into her eyes when he killed her.

Weakness will not be in your heart.

'You know something?' He smiled as he raised the makeshift spear, staring right into those chilling blue eyes without fear. She was no threat to him now. 'I was always better.'

Fear will not be in your creed.

With a sudden, desperate burst of strength, she lashed out with a vicious kick to his right knee. It was a perfectly placed strike, hyper-extending the ligaments and tearing muscle. Pain exploded out from the damaged joint and he sank down, face twisted in shock and disbelief.

You will show no mercy.

Adrenalin surged through her veins, blotting out the pain, burning away fatigue and exhaustion. None of that mattered now. All that mattered was her enemy.

You will never hesitate.

Forcing herself up from the bloodstained ground, she turned towards Munro, ready to finish him before he recovered.

You will never surrender.

An instant later, she froze.

Munro smiled with vicious hatred, clutching the MP5 he had been forced to drop earlier. Her sudden retaliation had crippled his knee, but it had bought him a few moments to snatch up the weapon lying half buried by the drifting sand.

His eyes gleamed as his finger tightened on the trigger.

At last, this was where it ended.

Anya winced at the loud crack as the weapon discharged, already bracing herself for the searing pain as a projectile tore through her flesh.

It never happened. To her amazement, Munro staggered back as a round slammed into his combat vest, quickly followed by a second. Turning the MP5 on his unknown attacker, he loosed a burst on full automatic, spraying fire indiscriminately, then turned and ducked behind a ruined aircraft fuselage.

'Anya!'

In disbelief, she watched Drake advancing towards her with an assault rifle up at his shoulder, still covering the gap Munro had disappeared through. Smoke trailed from the barrel, carried off by the fitful breeze.

She felt his hand on her arm, the touch sending a shiver through her.

'Are you all right?' he asked, his vivid green eyes

shining with fear, worry, relief, and something else. Something she had never expected to see.

He had saved her life. Just as he had the night he burst into her cell in Khatyrgan, he had saved her.

'Anya. Are you all right?' he repeated.

'I—' Her reply was cut short by the roar of a vehicle engine firing up.

In that instant, her mind snapped back into focus.

'Munro! We have to stop him.'

Ignoring the stabbing pain in her side, she reached down and snatched up the Smith & Wesson she had discarded, slapped the magazine back into the port and racked back the slide to chamber the first round.

Together they sprinted between the ruined aircraft, emerging onto the ruined tarmac runway just in time to watch a Ford Explorer roar past, exhaust spewing fumes, tyres churning the arid sand. Munro was at the wheel.

Kicking up clouds of dust, the powerful 4x4 ploughed straight through the chain-link fence at the edge of the airfield as if it didn't exist. They could do nothing but watch in helpless silence as the vehicle receded into the distance.

They had failed.

Half blinded by sweat, dust and sand, neither of them saw the tiny trail of white smoke that arced in towards the vehicle.

Their first impression was of a bright flash that erupted next to the speeding jeep, replaced an instant later by an expanding blossom of smoke and flame. The blast lifted the Explorer clean off the ground and hurled it aside as if it were a toy. Staring in amazement, they watched as the ruined vehicle rolled across the desert floor, trailing smoke and hurling wreckage in all directions before finally coming to rest on its side.

Glancing up, Drake could just make out the tiny but ominous shape of a Predator drone orbiting overhead.

In the ruined ops room, Dietrich let out an uncharacteristic shout of elation as the broken remains of the vehicle came to rest. It was so surreal to view it on a computer screen, it was almost possible to believe it wasn't real.

But it was real. That same Predator had been poised to kill them and flatten the building they were in.

'Damn it, Frost. That was some good shooting.'

The young woman glanced up from the terminal. And for the first time, she grinned at him with genuine warmth. 'Easy. It's just like *Call of Duty*.'

Chapter 74

Gasping for breath, Drake and Anya slowed as they approached the wrecked vehicle, keeping their weapons up and ready.

The blast and subsequent crash had reduced the 4x4 to a broken, twisted mass of metal. Smoke and steam drifted from the ruined engine bay. Shattered glass lay everywhere.

Suddenly the cracked and partially destroyed front windscreen resounded with a crash from inside, bending outward. The blow was repeated with greater force, causing the damaged screen to shear off.

Standing in silence, they watched as Munro, bleeding from countless gashes and with one arm hanging slack by his side, tumbled out through the gap to land on the sandy, rock-strewn ground. He was badly hurt, but he was still clutching the MP5 with his good arm.

Drake and Anya had him covered in a heartbeat.

'Put it down, Munro,' Drake ordered. 'It's over.'

His cut and bloodied face twisted into what could have been called a smile. He glanced up at the sky, as if he could see the Predator that had thwarted his escape.

Anya took a step forward, keeping him covered with the Smith & Wesson. 'Put the gun down, Dominic.'

He turned to look at her with his single remaining eye. There was no trace of hatred or revenge in him now. He knew what was coming, and he wasn't afraid.

'I was wrong about you, Anya,' he said. 'I was wrong, and . . . I'm sorry. Cain lied to me. He lied to all of us.'

Anya swallowed. 'Then help me stop him. Together we can—'

Munro smiled a bitter-sweet smile and shook his head. 'We can't stop him. Men like him can never be stopped.'

He glanced down at the weapon in his hand, weighing up what he was about to do.

'Don't even think about it,' Anya warned, thumbing back the hammer on her Smith & Wesson.

'I was a soldier once, Anya. At least let me die like one.'

'It doesn't have to end this way,' she pleaded, knowing he wouldn't listen.

'Not everything ends the way you think it should.' He closed his eyes and took a long, slow breath. His last. 'I'm ready.'

With a fast, practised motion, he brought the MP5 to bear on her.

He never got the chance to pull the trigger. Jerking as a flurry of rounds from Drake and Anya's weapons tore through his body, he collapsed backward with an exhausted, agonised groan.

Shoving her weapon down the back of her trousers, Anya ran over and dropped to the ground beside her fallen comrade.

His fading eyes met hers, and just for a moment a look of understanding passed between them. With a final effort, he reached up and clasped her hand.

'Don't . . . end up like me . . . Anya.'

He could hold on no longer. His grip slackened and his hand fell away.

Anya bowed her head, reached out and closed his unseeing eye as tears ran from her own.

'Too late,' she whispered.

There was nothing more for her here. Rallying what reserves of strength remained, she rose to her feet with difficulty, turned and walked slowly away, her footsteps kicking up small wisps of dusty sand. Battered and bruised, injured and bleeding, she remained defiantly on her feet.

'Anya!' Drake called out.

She halted and turned to look at him. The barriers were back up again.

'What are you doing?'

She glanced at Munro's body. 'There is nothing left for me here, Drake. It's over.'

'You have to come back with me.'

'I have played that game long enough.' She shook her head slowly. 'Not this time.'

'What about Cain? He has to answer for this.'

'And he will,' she promised him. 'But I must do it alone, my way. This isn't your fight.'

Not his fight. It had been his fight from the first moment he saw her photograph in that briefing room at Langley. He just hadn't realised it.

'It is now.'

Cain had threatened his family, manipulated him, destroyed his career, sacrificed innocent lives and risked many more in order to cover up his own mistakes. Drake was involved now, part of Anya's story, whether he wanted it or not.

And in that moment, he couldn't help but remember the brief conversation with Hussam the previous night.

I think there will come a time when you have to choose, either to stand with her or against her. When that time comes, I hope you make the right choice, Ryan Drake.

'I promised Hussam I'd protect you, Anya. Whether

or not you think you need it, I'll be there for you, and I won't give up on you.'

He saw a change in her eyes then, a lowering of her defences. She looked as she had last night, when they had at last opened up to each other, bared their souls in the flickering light of the campfire.

Hesitating a moment, she walked towards him and held out her hand, saying nothing, waiting for him to take it.

He did so without reservation, without regrets or deception. He accepted her as she had accepted him.

Gripping his hand tight, Anya smiled. But it was a bitter-sweet smile, tinged with sadness and regret.

'You know your problem, Ryan? You're a good man.'

Moving with frightening speed, she reached for the weapon tucked into her belt, levelled it at his stomach and fired.

The impact of the bullet felt like a sledgehammer driven into his guts. In an instant, the hot searing pain of the impact was replaced by a cold numbness that crept outward from the injury. Gasping in shock and disbelief, Drake fell to his knees, staring at the woman with wide, unfocused eyes.

With the ease born from long years of experience, Anya yanked the carbine from his grasp before he could bring it up against her, then ejected the magazine and tossed the weapon away.

'It's all right,' she whispered, easing him down onto the ground. 'Don't fight me. It's all right.'

Vaguely, through the fog of shock and pain, he felt warm sand against his back as she laid him down with gentle care.

'Why?' he gasped, staring up into her eyes.

'Remember what I told you once, Drake? We are both soldiers. No matter what they tried to make us,

525

we are soldiers, and we do what we must to survive,' she said, looking at him with genuine pity. 'This is what I must do for both our sakes. Because where I'm going, you can't follow.'

He felt Anya take his right hand and press it against the bullet wound. 'Hold here, press down hard,' she instructed. 'The pressure should slow the bleeding. When they ask what happened, you tell them you tried to bring me in, but I shot you. I betrayed you. Do you understand?'

Drake's pain-filled eyes opened wider as her words sank in. 'No! I won't . . .'

'You do it, or they will blame you for everything!' she said through clenched teeth. Only her eyes betrayed her true feelings. 'I told you I have learned to live with a lot of things, Drake. But that is something I couldn't live with.'

She rose to her feet again. She was hurt and tired and in pain, yet she stood tall and unbowed, her dishevelled and bloodied hair fluttering in the breeze.

Maras – a goddess of war.

'Too many men have followed me to their deaths. I won't let it happen again. You still have a life, a future.' She shook her head. 'I can't give you any of those things. But . . . if it means anything, I am grateful to you, Ryan Drake.'

She sighed and looked up at the sky, blazing orange and gold now as the sun dipped below the horizon.

'For both our sakes, I hope we don't meet again.'

With that, she turned and walked away.

She had hardened herself to emotions like love and compassion a long time ago, but today her armour had slipped. Just a little, but enough.

Bleeding and weakened, Drake could do nothing but watch as she faded into the distance, her blonde hair whipped up by the breeze.

Part Four

Resurrection

The supreme art of war is to subdue the enemy without fighting.

Sun Tzu's *The Art of War*

Chapter 75

Iraq, 13 May 2007

This is how it ends.

Lying there with one hand loosely pressed against the bullet wound in his stomach, he was alone. His strength was exhausted, his reserves gone, his blood staining the dusty ground. A trail of it led a short distance away, mute testimony to the desperate, feeble crawl he had managed before his vision swam and he collapsed.

He could go no further. There was nothing left to do but lie here and wait for the end.

A faint breeze sighed past him, stirring the warm evening air and depositing tiny particles of wind-blown sand across his arms and chest. How long would it take to cover his body when he died? Would he ever be found?

Staring at the vast azure sky stretching out into infinity above him, he found his eyes drawn to the contrail of some high-flying aircraft, straight as an arrow. Around him, the sun's last light reflected off the desert dunes, setting them ablaze with colour.

It was a good place to die.

Men like him were destined never to see old age, or to die peacefully in their sleep surrounded by family. They had chosen a different life, and there would be no reward for them.

You know your problem, Ryan? You're a good man.

Had she been right?

Could he look back on his life honestly and say he'd been a good man? He had made mistakes, done things he wished he could undo, and yet his final act had been one of trust and compassion.

That was the reason he was lying here, bleeding to death. That was his final reward.

A low, rhythmic thumping was drowning out the sigh of the wind. The pounding of his heartbeat in his ears, slowly fading as his lifeblood flowed out between his fingers. He might have slowed the bleeding, but he couldn't stop it. Nothing could.

He was dying.

You know your problem, Ryan? You're a good man.

However he had lived, he knew in that moment that he would die as a good man. And that had to count for something.

A faint smiled touched his face as the thudding grew louder. He closed his eyes, surrendering to the growing darkness that filled the world around him.

Then, to his amazement, something loomed over him. A shape, vast and dark. And loud. A high-pitched whine filled the air, mixing with the hammering thump that he had mistaken for his own heartbeat.

The peaceful scene around him was engulfed in chaos as a storm of dust and small stones erupted. Vicious winds whipped at his clothes, blasting his face and exposed skin.

In an instant, his consciousness returned, and he stared up in awe at the vast underbelly of the Black Hawk helicopter.

Shapes appeared in the doorway, and then suddenly they were descending on him, falling as if they had just thrown themselves out of the door.

There was a thud, and a few seconds later Frost had detached herself from the fast-descent harness and knelt down beside him.

'Ryan, can you hear me?' she asked, having to yell to be heard over the whine of the engines and the thumping of the rotors. 'Ryan! Look at me, goddamn it!'

With some effort, he focused his attention on her.

'Can you hear me?' she repeated.

'Yeah,' Drake replied, squinting against the dust that was being kicked up into his eyes.

'You've got a gunshot wound to the abdomen. I'm going to stabilise you, then we'll get you airborne. I want you to keep talking to me. Okay?'

'My . . . sister?' he asked, his eyes suddenly wide with concern.

The young woman smiled and nodded. 'She's okay. She's in the chopper right now. It was all we could do to stop her roping down!' Her smile faded as she went back to work. 'I'm gonna give you something for the pain.'

Just as the syringe went into his arm, Drake looked up as another man in uniform rushed over and knelt down beside him.

'It's all right, Ryan,' Dietrich assured him, his face etched with worry. 'You're safe now.'

'So people . . . keep telling me.'

'Where's Anya?'

Anya. He had some faint recollection of her looking down on him with sadness in her eyes, then turning to walk away.

'Anya?' he repeated.

'Yes, Anya! Come on, Ryan. Focus on me. Where did she go?'

His vision was growing hazy as the drugs took hold, and it was an effort just to form the words.

'She left. I couldn't follow her. Where she was going, I couldn't follow,' he managed to say before the darkness swallowed him.

Sir! Sir, you can't go in there,' Cain's private secretary protested, rising from behind her desk as if to stop him.

'Fuck you!' Franklin snarled, striding past without so much as glancing at her. He didn't give a shit who tried to get in his way. He was past that now.

Throwing open the door, he practically burst into Cain's office, scanning the room for the older man.

He found him over by the window, staring out across the dark waters of the Potomac.

'I figured you'd show up, Dan,' he said without turning around.

'What the hell have you done?' Franklin demanded. His shoes rustled on the expensive carpet as he took a step toward the director.

'What have *I* done?' Suddenly Cain rounded on the younger man, blazing with anger. 'Do you have any idea of the damage you've done today? Disobeying direct orders, interfering with an active operation, launching an unsanctioned mission against a foreign country . . . You just destroyed your own career, you stupid fuck.'

A week ago, Franklin might have been intimidated by such a threat, but they were playing a different game now. Cain was backed into a corner and he knew it.

'If I go down, you go with me,' he promised. 'I know what you did, and nothing you say can change that.'

Cain smiled in amusement. 'Tell me, what do you think you know?'

'You tried to broker an illegal arms deal with a dictatorship, you tried to plant weapons of mass destruction in their country to justify an invasion, and when it went south you kept the money for yourself. You launched an attack against a civilian target, you authorised a strike against a Russian government facility, you hijacked intelligence assets and you tried to kill everyone who knew about it. Well, you failed, you son of a bitch.'

'And you have proof of this, I assume?' Cain challenged him. 'There's nothing to connect me to this "arms deal" you keep talking about. I don't remember trying to kill anyone, and I certainly don't recall hijacking intelligence assets. The raid on Khatyrgan was authorised by the Agency's board of directors. Everyone signed it off, and the record will show that.'

Franklin hesitated, daunted for a moment by his calm, reasoned argument. Why wasn't he sweating? Why wasn't he begging or trying to explain himself? It was as if Franklin's threat carried no weight, as if he were nothing more than an irritating fly to be swatted away.

'What the record *will* show is that you worked behind *my* back, interfered with *my* operation, and tried to subvert *my* authority. It will show that Drake turned renegade and helped a known criminal escape, assaulted government personnel and put innocent civilians at risk. It will also show that Dietrich and his Shepherd team took part in an illegal operation without orders.' Cain eyed him with disdain. 'So tell me, Dan, who do you think will really take the fall for this?'

The colour drained from Franklin's face. He had been so sure when he came storming in here, so certain that Cain would crumble in the face of his wrath, that he could bring him down with a snap of his fingers.

But the director was made of different stuff than that. He hadn't risen to his current level by backing down in the face of ill-judged threats. He wouldn't crumble, because he had faced dangers far worse than this.

Cain could fucking destroy him.

Then, in an instant, he realised he didn't care. He had done the things he'd done to save Drake's life, and the lives of the team he'd sent in to bring him home. He didn't regret it for one moment, and he never would.

Franklin was no longer a soldier, but he hadn't stopped thinking like one. Loyalty to one's brothers in arms came above all else. That was one thing a man like Cain would never understand.

'I don't have to give them all the answers,' he said. 'If I blow the whistle on you, it won't matter whether I can prove it or not. There will be investigations, hearings, accusations . . . People will be going over every decision you've made in the past twenty years, and sooner or later, you know they'll find something. Nobody can hide the truth that well, not even professional bullshit artists like you.'

His heart was pounding as he spoke, and it took a great deal of self-control to stop himself trembling. He was attempting a desperate final gamble in a very dangerous game, with his career and perhaps his very life at stake.

Cain said nothing, though Franklin noticed his smile had faded a little. And just like that, with that one glimpse of weakness, the game changed.

I've got you, you son of a bitch. You're not going to slip out of this one. I can destroy you, destroy everything you built. All your plans, all your little schemes, all your lies and betrayals . . . All of it will come tumbling down like a house of cards.

I've got you.

Walking away from the window, Cain settled down behind his desk and surveyed the younger man for a long moment.

'And what exactly do you intend to do?'

Franklin didn't flinch. 'You have to answer for what you did.'

'Bullshit,' Cain retorted. 'If that was true, you would have come in here with a dozen security agents and had me arrested.' He leaned forward. 'You're smarter than that.'

'Am I?'

'This is your get-out-of-jail-free card, Dan. You're going to save it for a time when *you're* in deep shit, when *you* need a favour to call in. And when that happens, I'll be there for you.'

Franklin said nothing.

'Let me tell you a little secret,' he went on. 'I'm about to be promoted to Deputy Director of the Agency. It's been on the cards for a while, and the announcement will be made in a couple of weeks. That means I'll need someone to take over as Divisional Leader.' He regarded Franklin with a raised eyebrow. 'I can't think of anybody better for the job.'

Franklin couldn't believe what he was hearing. First the man threatened to destroy him, now he was offering him a promotion? 'You're serious, aren't you?'

'Perfectly,' Cain assured him.

'And why the hell would I accept an offer like that?'

'This is a tough business we work in, son. You don't rise through the ranks by baking cookies and hosting cocktail parties. You broker deals, you take risks, and you make compromises. How do you think I got this job?' Cain gave him a knowing smile. 'You might find this hard to believe, but I was like you once. Young, filled with fire and bullshit, convinced I was going to change the world. It took me a long time to realise the truth.'

Franklin's eyes narrowed. 'I'm nothing like you.'

'No? Then maybe you can do a better job than I did,' Cain suggested. 'Special Activities Division is all yours if you want it, Dan. All you have to do is reach out and take it. Maybe the Agency needs a man like you; a man with honour and principles.'

Franklin didn't buy that for a second. Cain despised him. He would destroy his career in a heartbeat if he thought he could get away with it.

And yet, he couldn't. Not now. They both knew that. As much as Cain might hate the offer he was making, it was real all the same.

'And what about you?' he asked. 'Does it need you?'

Cain smiled. 'Men like me will always be needed. Believe that.'

Sensing his opponent wavering, he leaned back in his chair and locked eyes with Franklin. 'This is an opportunity you won't get again, Dan. Leadership of an entire division, the chance to make your mark. It's all there, just waiting for you. All you have to do is say yes. But you have to do it now.'

Franklin hesitated, his earlier fire and indignation fading in the face of such calm, persuasive temptation. As much as he hated himself for even acknowledging it, there was no denying the merits of Cain's offer, and his threat.

If he went public with this, he might well end Cain's career, but at the cost of his own. Not only that, but he would be sure to take Drake and others down with him.

'If I was to consider this even for a moment, I'd need your word that Drake and the others won't be touched.'

Cain spread his arms in a conciliatory gesture. 'As long as they don't start digging in things that don't concern them.'

'And as far as the Agency is concerned, this conversation never happened.'

'Now you're speaking my language.' Cain smiled, firmly in control of the situation again. 'So . . . we have a deal?'

Franklin glanced out the window, at the dark clouds reflected in the distant waters of the Potomac.

Honourable suicide, or a dishonourable compromise.

Hell of a choice.

Chapter 76

Langley, Virginia, two weeks later

'So that's all you can tell us? She shot you in the stomach without warning and left you to die?' Franklin asked.

Drake's full written report was spread out on his desk. It was his desk, but not his office.

Several days earlier the official announcement had been made that Franklin was being promoted to Divisional Leader, taking over Cain's old job, and his expansive office. Packing boxes lay everywhere, most still waiting to be opened.

The place was starting to remind Drake of his own house.

'That's right.' It was a lie, but a necessary one. He knew that now.

After some basic but life-saving medical attention by Frost, he had been flown to a military hospital in Baghdad for further treatment. The doctors had later confirmed that the round had passed straight through him, missing the major organs. He was lucky to be alive, or so they said.

His condition was much improved by two weeks of rest and recuperation, and he was expected to make a full recovery, though he would carry the scar for the rest of his life. A permanent reminder of the woman who had given it to him.

'And she said nothing about where she was going or what she was planning to do?'

Drake hesitated, remembering her final words. Like the scar, he felt sure he would carry them with him for the rest of his life.

No trace of Anya had ever been found. She was still on several Most Wanted lists worldwide, but he knew they would never find her. She would be found only when she wanted to be.

'Nothing,' he said at last.

Franklin eyed him dubiously for a long moment, then closed the folder with an audible thump.

'What are you going to do with that now?'

Franklin's hand rested on the folder. 'There are a lot of very serious accusations in here, Ryan.'

'Cain brokered a deal to sell weapons of mass destruction to the Iraqi government and justify an illegal war. He sacrificed innocent lives to kill the only man who could prove it. He took advantage of a woman who'd already been through so much shit, it was a miracle she was still sane. He put the lives of myself and my team at risk, and he did it all to save his own arse. Is that serious enough for you?'

Franklin avoided his gaze. 'The matter's being dealt with, Ryan.'

'If we let him get away with this, we might as well have done it ourselves . . .'

'I said it's being dealt with!' his friend snapped. 'For both our sakes, I suggest you let it go.'

'Let it go. Just forget that it happened. Is that how things are done around here?' Drake glanced around the big office, packing boxes lying everywhere. 'By the way, congratulations on your promotion. It's good to know someone did well out of this.'

Franklin's eyes burned with anger. 'Ryan, I'm about the only thing standing between you and a one-way trip to Guantanamo Bay,' he warned. 'You should keep that in mind.'

'I haven't forgotten.'

Calming himself, Franklin gestured around his new office with a sweep of his arm. 'Special Activities Division is my ship. Whatever mistakes Cain might have made, they're in the past. Things will be different now.'

Drake almost felt sorry for him. Maybe he actually believed what he was saying. Maybe he thought he was going to change things, clean up the entire Agency, put the world to rights.

But the problem with making a deal with the Devil was that sooner or later, he always came to collect.

'Speaking of which, we haven't talked about *your* future, Ryan.'

Drake tensed, saying nothing.

His friend leaned back in his chair. 'For a while, the Agency couldn't decide whether to give you a medal or put you in front of a firing squad. You went rogue, freed a dangerous suspect and put your fellow team members in danger.' Franklin surveyed him for several seconds. 'But . . . it seems you're more useful alive than dead, for now at least. Pending rehabilitation you'll return to active duty, reporting to me. Questions?'

He only had one. 'They're sweeping this under the carpet, aren't they?'

Franklin met his gaze evenly. 'I don't know what you're talking about.' He tucked Drake's report into one of his drawers, which he then closed and locked. 'Now, if there's nothing else, we both have a lot of work to do.'

It would do no good to argue. Rising from his chair

with some difficulty, he turned to leave. Only when his hand was on the door handle did he pause for a moment.

'Dan?'

'What?'

Drake's green eyes glimmered in the afternoon sun. 'The day before we crossed the border into Iraq, an old man told me something about Anya – something I think you should keep in mind.

'If you stand with her, you could never ask for a better ally. If you stand against her, you'll fall. And if you betray her, then God help you because nobody else can.'

Whatever history lay between those two, Drake knew with absolute certainty that Anya wasn't finished with Cain. Her vengeance, when it came at last, would be swift, merciless and brutal.

And for anyone who stood by Cain's side . . .

Franklin sat in silence, a chill running through him at Drake's grim warning. He glanced away for a moment, and Drake saw the muscles in his throat tightening as he swallowed.

'I'll see you around, Dan,' he said, closing the door behind him, and leaving the young divisional director alone to ponder what lay ahead.

In his new office on the top floor of the vast intelligence complex, Marcus Cain sat behind his expansive desk, staring at the magnificent view beyond his window and seeing nothing.

He should have felt elation that his long-awaited promotion had finally come to pass, should have felt relief that he had saved his career from the brink of disaster, should have felt optimism about the great things he could achieve, and yet he felt nothing.

Anya was alive. Despite everything, she had survived. She was out there somewhere at this very moment.

And she was coming for him.

He had been wrong about her. She couldn't be controlled, couldn't be manipulated or coerced. She would never compromise, would never bend her will or make concessions, would never sacrifice her morals or her honour.

All of those things which he had once seen as failings and weaknesses, he now saw for what they truly were.

He had once believed her too weak to make the hard decisions their job required, too naive to accept the harsh reality of the world in which they lived, but now he knew the truth.

She understood, she perceived the world as it was, but she chose never to give in. Even if it meant great sacrifice and hardship, even if it cost her life, she was the only one of them who had remained whole, who had preserved that vital part of herself which he had lost.

She was the best of them. She always had been.

Her life served only to highlight his own failings, her endurance brought home his own weaknesses and shortcomings. He had sacrificed too much, had compromised too many times.

At last he understood.

He was the weak one. He was the one who had chosen the easier path, who had compromised and conceded when he could have stood firm. He was the one who had lost himself.

And he was the one she would hold to account.

Sooner or later, she would come for him. She couldn't be stopped, couldn't be reasoned with or persuaded or manipulated as Franklin had. She didn't conform to anyone's plans, didn't fit into any scheme, didn't adhere to any vision except her own.

She was a soldier, and he was her enemy.

The battle lines had been drawn, they had chosen their sides, and this would end only when one of them was dead.

Cain leaned back in his big leather chair, staring at his office and seeing nothing. All around him lay luxury, power, influence. All the things he had fought for.

And none of it mattered.

Chapter 77

'Looks like you're not getting rid of me just yet,' Drake remarked with a wry smile as he, Dietrich, Frost and Keegan walked slowly along the Reflecting Pool towards the Lincoln Memorial. 'Dan's decided to keep me around, for now at least.'

In stark contrast to the last time Drake had been this way, it was a beautiful warm day, light from the evening sun glistening on the pool's undulating surface and casting long shadows across the nearby parkland.

'Shit, man. And I was hoping for a quiet life,' Keegan groaned.

'I don't believe that for a second.' Drake grinned at him.

'So they're not laying any charges on us at all?' Frost asked.

'Dan made a deal. He saved our arses, and his own.'

It didn't take her long to make the connection. 'Cain's going to get away with this, isn't he? After everything he did, the bastard gets to just walk away.'

'Don't bet on it. Anya has unfinished business with him.'

'I hope she leaves us out of it,' Dietrich remarked. 'I wouldn't want to go up against her again.'

Drake glanced at his former nemesis.

Dietrich's reputation had been much revived by his

conduct over the past few weeks, other Shepherd team leaders regarding him with new-found respect for the risks he'd taken. His past transgressions hadn't been forgotten, and likely never would be, but Drake was of the opinion that everyone deserved a second chance. Perhaps Dietrich would get his.

'With any luck, we won't have to.'

They still weren't exactly friends, and he doubted they would see much of each other after today, but the man was all right in his book.

'Who is she, Ryan?' the older man asked in an uncharacteristic display of curiosity. 'I spent a week hunting her, and I don't know a thing about her.'

Drake sighed and stared out across the Reflecting Pool to the Washington Monument.

'I don't know who she is,' he admitted. 'Because she didn't want me to know. The only thing she wanted me to know is that she lived her life without compromise. She never gave in, she never surrendered. I understand that now. And you know what? I would have followed her.'

'She shot you and left you to die, Ryan,' Frost reminded him.

'She gave me a second chance,' he replied, still staring out across the pool. 'The only chance she could.'

The young woman said nothing.

His gaze rested on another woman standing at the far end of the pool, near the base of the Lincoln Memorial. Tall, slender, dressed now in jeans and a light jacket, her long brown hair tied back in a bun. It was Jessica.

He turned to the small group. His team, his comrades, his friends. 'Look, I never got a chance to say this properly until now, but . . . I know what you did to get me,' he said, looking at each of them in turn. 'I know the risks you took – each of you. I promise you I'll never forget it.'

Frost said nothing, but appeared strangely moved by his words. The normally fiery and strong-willed young woman glanced away for a moment, and he saw the muscles in her throat tightening.

Keegan grinned. 'You gettin' soppy in your old age, Ryan?'

Drake couldn't help but smile. 'I'm working on it.'

He glanced over at Jessica again. She was waiting for him, and he was eager to speak with her.

'I'll see you all soon,' he promised.

He was just walking away when Dietrich spoke up. 'Hey, Ryan.'

Drake stopped and turned around. To his surprise, Dietrich held out his hand. 'I was wrong about you,' he said, no trace of hesitation or deception in his eyes now. 'You're a better man than I thought.'

Drake said nothing as they shook hands. There was no need. The look in his eyes said it all.

'That being said, I'm not eager to work with you again,' Dietrich added with a wry smile. 'You're a dangerous man to be around.'

Drake couldn't hide a grin of his own. 'I'm working on that, too.' He released his grip. 'I'll see you around, Jonas.'

Excusing himself, he skirted the edge of the pool to join his sister.

He got to within about 20 feet before she rushed forward and threw her arms around him in a fierce display of affection. He returned the gesture in equal measure, almost as if to assure himself that she really was whole and safe.

'You're looking well,' she began, looking him up and

down. 'Much better than the last time I saw you, at least.'

In truth, they had seen little of each other since their evacuation from Iraq. After being debriefed by an Agency team, Jessica had flown back to the UK to be reunited with her husband and two children. She had been there for the past ten days, only arriving in Washington a few hours earlier to meet with him.

Typical of the intelligence community, her sudden disappearance had been covered up with an outright lie about her being taken into protective custody after hoax threats were made against her brother.

Later, in private and well away from their two children, she had told her husband the truth about what had happened.

Drake had heard little of the reaction from him or the rest of the family, but he gathered he wasn't exactly flavour of the month back home. Some things never changed.

'Rest and relaxation seems to agree with me,' he replied, grinning. One advantage of his enforced leisure time was that he'd finally gotten round to unpacking all those boxes scattered around his house. Better late than never, he supposed.

'So how did it go with Dan?' she asked.

'Well, they're not planning to send me to Guantanamo Bay.'

She smiled. 'That's a relief. Orange really isn't your colour.'

However, her smile faded when she saw the look in his eyes.

'You're not coming home, are you?'

He sighed and looked away, saying nothing. She knew already.

Jessica too was silent for a time, searching for a way to express herself. 'Ryan, I know there were always . . . things about your work that you didn't talk about. I knew you were trying to protect me, but I've seen it for myself now. I've seen what you do, the things you have to live with.'

'You never should have been put in that position,' he said. 'I tried to keep all that away from you.'

He felt her hand on his, soft and warm and reassuring. 'You don't have to apologise. I know why you do the things you do, and I know why you're staying behind. I wish you weren't, but I understand why you are. You have a job to do.'

She hadn't said it out loud, but he sensed a change in her then. A gulf, a divergence in their two lives. He ached to return with her to the UK, but they belonged to different worlds now. He could visit hers, at least for a while, but he could never truly be a part of it. Not any more.

And as for his own world, inhabited by people like Anya and Cain, their conflicts and struggles for power, the future remained undecided.

He couldn't help but remember Munro's words to him that night before they crossed the border; how he knew about Operation Hydra, and how there was more to Drake's court martial and discharge than he'd ever been told. Had the man really known something he didn't, or had he merely been trying to provoke him? As with many things that had happened over the past few weeks, Drake felt as though he had more questions than answers.

All he could say for certain was that he was alive, he had survived, and he intended to do what he could to make things right.

'But I'm afraid for you. I'm afraid you might end up

548

like all those others.' She swallowed and looked down for a moment, composing herself. 'I love you, and I don't want to lose you.'

For a moment, he caught himself wondering if Anya had ever found herself in this position, caught at a crossroads in life with no clear way forward. He wondered if she had ever thought about leaving it all behind, if she had made that conscious choice to keep going, or whether there had even been a choice to make. Perhaps there was no escaping who and what she was.

She might not have had that choice, but he did. Right here and now.

And he knew right here and now what his choice would be. Maybe he'd always known.

'You won't,' he said quietly. 'I was given a second chance, Jess. I'm not going to waste it.'

He heard her faint sigh, her sad acceptance of what she'd known all along. 'So what will you do with this second chance?'

He thought once more about Anya. She had lived her life without fear, without hesitation, and without compromise. No matter what the cost.

'My job,' he answered at last. 'Maybe that's enough.'

You know your problem, Ryan? You're a good man.

He smiled as he stared out across the city.

We'll see.

Acknowledgements

There was a time when I, rather naively, believed novel writing to be a solitary business. However, my experiences with this book have taught me that taking a story from a vague idea to the finished product involves the work and creative energies of countless individuals, many of whom receive little recognition.

In particular are three people I wish greatly to thank. First and foremost, my agent Diane Banks for representing me, for believing in me, and in turn helping me believe in myself. Second, my editor Kate Burke, who took a chance on an unpublished author (an increasingly rare thing these days), and whose advice has been greatly appreciated. And last, but by no means least, my wife Susan, who endured many nights of me locking myself in the office to write, and whose support meant more than I ever admitted.

To each of you, my thanks and my gratitude.

COMING IN SUMMER 2013...
THE NEXT HEART-STOPPING THRILLER
IN THE RYAN DRAKE SERIES:

SACRIFICE

Afghanistan, 2008.

A helicopter carrying a senior CIA operative
is shot down and its lone passenger is taken
hostage by a fanatical new insurgent group.
Brought in to find and rescue the lost operative,
Ryan Drake and his elite Shepherd team are
confident about their mission but, within hours of
arriving in the war-torn country, they find
themselves caught up in a deadly conflict.

And lurking in the shadows is a
woman from Drake's past who would sacrifice
everything to get what she wants...

CENTURY